MATERIAL GIRL

Also by Julia London

Historicals

The Devil's Love
Wicked Angel

The Rogues of Regent Street

The Dangerous Gentleman
The Ruthless Charmer
The Beautiful Stranger
The Secret Lover

Highland Lockhart Family

Highlander Unbound
Highlander in Disguise
Highlander in Love

The Desperate Debutantes

The Hazards of Hunting a Duke
The Perils of Pursuing a Prince
The Dangers of Deceiving a Viscount
The School for Heiresses, Anthology. "The Merchant's Gift," Sabrina
Jeffries, Liz Carlyle, Julia London, Renee Bernard

The Scandalous Series

The Book of Scandal
Highland Scandal
A Courtesan's Scandal
Snowy Night With a Stranger, Anthology. "Snowy Night with a High-
lander," Jane Feather, Sabrina Jeffries, Julia London

The Secrets of Hadley Green

The Year of Living Scandalously
The Christmas Secret, novella

The Revenge of Lord Eberlin
The Seduction of Lady X
The Last Debutante

Contemporary Romance and Women's Fiction

The Fancy Lives of the Lear Sisters

Material Girl
Beauty Queen
Miss Fortune

Over the Edge (previously available as Thrillseekers Anonymous)

All I Need Is You (previously available as *Wedding Survivor*)
One More Night (previously available as *Extreme Bachelor*)
Fall into Me (previously available as *American Diva*)

Cedar Springs

Summer of Two Wishes
One Season of Sunshine
A Light at Winter's End

Special Projects

Guiding Light: Jonathan's Story, tie-in to *Guiding Light*

Anthologies

Talk of The Ton, "The Vicar's Daughter," Eloisa James, Julia London, Rebecca Hagan Lee, Jacqueline Navin
Hot Ticket, "Lucky Charm," Julia London, Dierdre Martin, Annette Blair, Geri Buckley
The School for Heiresses, "The Merchant's Gift," Sabrina Jeffries, Liz Carlyle, Julia London, Renee Bernard
Snowy Night with a Stranger, "Snowy Night with a Highlander," Jane Feather, Sabrina Jeffries, Julia London

MATERIAL GIRL

THE FANCY LIVES OF THE LEAR SISTERS

Julia London

Copyright © 2003 Julia London
Previously published in 2003, 2011
Montlake Edition published in 2013

Published by Montlake Romance

PO Box 400818
Las Vegas, NV 89140

ISBN-13: 9781477805770
ISBN-10: 147780577X

Dear Reader:

I am so happy that the Fancy Lives of the Lear Sisters trilogy is available to readers once again! I had so much fun creating these sisters. They are three privileged daughters of a wealthy magnate who learns he is dying. He realizes he has pampered his girls, and he worries that when he is gone, they will not be able to stand on their own feet. Did he underestimate them?

His oldest, Robin, loves the trappings of wealth, but it takes Jake, a man who has had to bring himself up by his bootstraps, to show her that there is more to life than things. Rebecca has it all: a beauty queen title, a baby, and a wealthy husband to keep her in the style to which she is accustomed. But when her husband betrays her, Rebecca realizes she has nothing but her looks to fall back on. Enter Matt, a guy who calls them as he sees them, who makes her see that looks are only skin-deep—it's what's inside that counts. Last but not least is the youngest, Rachel, who is still in school, still trying to decide what she wants to be when she grows up, and still making bad choices. When Daddy cuts her off, Rachel has to learn how to negotiate life and to get rid of the consequences of her choices. Fortunately, Flynn is there to pick up the pieces of her messy attempts…even if he does have an ulterior motive.

I so enjoyed writing these books! As the third of three sisters, with a baby brother to boot, I could relate to how the women are alike, yet different. DNA can only do so much when it comes to the affairs of the heart. But in the end, all three sisters find their unique ways to love and happiness. I hope you enjoy these books a second time around.

Happy Reading,
Julia

PROLOGUE

NEW YORK

The news that he was going to die arrived like a distant rumble of thunder, a disturbing sound so far on the reaches of his consciousness that he lifted his head and wondered what he had heard. Aaron Lear looked to the windows of his office on the forty-third floor in lower Manhattan and noticed that the afternoon light was beginning to fade. Was it that late already?

He was still sitting where the call had left him—on his haunches, against the polished oak wall down which he had slid as his mind tried to grasp the words *cancer* and *aggressive.* His office was suddenly sweltering; the light was fading rapidly now, gray and black shadows draped his office. Aaron tried to breathe—he was not prepared for this, had not considered the possibility of his mortality. Even when he had first begun to have trouble—a strange bit of discomfort was all, really—he never thought it was something so...so foul. So goddamned final.

We don't know much of anything yet. Just hold on to that for now, his doctor had advised. How could he hold on to something so vague? Aaron pulled himself to his feet, but his limbs felt as if weights had been tied to them and he leaned heavily against the desk. The room was now almost dark;

he wondered how much time had really passed since he'd picked up the phone. A lifetime.

Of course he had suspected something was terribly wrong for weeks now, from the moment he had felt the hostile invasion of his body, had sensed the vague but undeniable state of war being waged within him when he had, by some internal monitor, felt the cancerous cells advancing like an army of ants through his stomach, into the winding turns of his colon, throwing their incendiary bombs down the chute.

He was only fifty-five!

It was impossible to even contemplate that he might be brought down. There was so much left to do, to see, to *be!* What about the dynasty he had built and still operated from his position as president and CEO? This vast shipping empire was all his doing, his creation, one he had started after he escaped West Texas and the life of a cotton farmer when he was nineteen. He had built this company truck by truck, plane by plane. He had begun by driving line-haul between Dallas and San Antonio, scrimping and saving until he could buy his own truck. Then there were two. Then four, then a fleet, expanding and growing under his guardianship until he was shipping freight around the world. Lear Transport Industries, better known as LTI, was like another child to him, the proud mark of a man and his life and accomplishments.

He was not ready to let go!

Bonnie. He had to talk to Bonnie, still his wife in spite of their fifteen-year estrangement, still his one and only true love. Bonnie Lou Stanton, his high school sweetheart, the homecoming queen with the laughing blue eyes, the only one to believe in him when the relationship with his father had soured. It was Bonnie who had come with him to Dallas when he had left the family cotton farm behind, Bonnie who had stuck by him those lean years when everything looked bleak and had encouraged him when he thought he was failing. And later, with a baby on her hip, smiling cheerfully as she made one can of ranch-style beans last two days. They had been closest then, drawing on one another's strengths. Exactly when they had begun to drift apart, Aaron couldn't really remember anymore, but he knew that he still loved her, would always love her.

His gaze fell to the picture of his daughters on his desk, and he felt the smile spread across his lips. They were the best thing he had ever done. There was Robin, his oldest, her curly black hair indicative of her spunk, her blue eyes steely with determination. And Rebecca, sitting gracefully in the middle, as pretty now as she had been the day she was crowned Miss Houston. Then Rachel, the baby, laughing when she should have been smiling, her blue eyes sparkling with the gaiety that was always with her. Three beautiful women whom he had a hand in producing. Biologically perhaps, but he couldn't claim much credit beyond that, could he?

He had been an absent father for the most part—one of the more egregious things about him, according to Bonnie. God, how many times had they argued about it? He insisting that his work was what enabled them to live a life of privilege, Bonnie arguing just as strongly that wealth and privilege were not as valuable as a father to the girls.

A thousand tiny spears of bitter disappointment jabbed Aaron; there was no denying the truth, not for a man being consumed alive by cancer. He had been a mean lover, a sorrier husband, and a pathetic excuse for a father while creating his empire. He had let Bonnie down in the worst way, his girls even more, and the pain of that realization was almost as lethal as the cancer in him.

The worst of it was that the cancer scared him to death, left him practically trembling in the dark at the prospect of what lay ahead. The coward in him needed Bonnie like he had never needed her before.

In the dim light, Aaron found the phone he'd thrown aside and dialed her cell. It rang three times before she answered it. "Hello?" The sound of crystal clinking in the background pierced his consciousness—Bonnie had her own life now. She wasn't waiting for his call anymore. Hadn't she made that abundantly clear?

"Aaron, I know it's you, I have your number on caller ID."

"Bonnie." His voice sounded empty, hollow. "Bonnie, how are you?"

She covered the phone; Aaron heard her whisper to someone. "Ah, fine."

"Good...good." How exactly did one go about telling his wife he was dying? "How's the weather in LA?"

Her sigh was full of tedium. "Aaron, I'm in the middle of something. What did you need?"

He cleared his throat, tried to force the ugly words out. "Actually, there is something I need to tell you—"

"Is it one of the girls?" she asked quickly.

"No, no, not the girls. I...I don't know how to say this..."

"Say what?"

He closed his eyes, squeezed them tightly shut against the burn of tears. "I've had some bad news...I had a little thing happen this summer, and I went...well, I guess I don't have to give you the blow-by-blow, but it's..." He paused, pressed his knuckles into his eyes again, unable to say the words that would commend him to death.

He could hear Bonnie moving, the click-click-click of her heels on pavement. "Aaron," she said low, her voice softer now, the way he remembered it. "What is it? What's wrong?"

The burn of tears burst through his knuckles, slid hot down his cheeks. "I'm sick," he whispered coarsely. "*Really* sick. And...and I know I don't have any right to ask this, but...but I need you, Bonnie. I need you bad."

There was no immediate response from her; Aaron caught his breath, felt the wet burn of his tears etch their grooves in his cheeks. He waited. Waited through the long pause in which he could hear the shortness of her breath, and when he thought he could not hold his own any longer, she said simply, "I will be there as soon as I can."

CHAPTER ONE

HOUSTON

Everyone would always remember where they were the day they learned Aaron Lear was dying. For Robin, his oldest daughter, that day started off as usual—with a frantic search of her spacious, empty, and covered-with-dust Tudor mansion for a stupid shoe.

She was in something of a hurry, seeing as how she had a stack of reports six feet high on her desk, the result of having spent the entire month of January in London. And there was the business of the deal with Atlantic, an idea that had come to her at a cocktail party after the Atlantic rep had bought her several drinks. She had been working on landing them for four or five weeks now and needed the deal sooner rather than later because Dad didn't like her region's sales figures. Or anything else, for that matter.

Which was why she was a little worried about yesterday's call from Mr. Herrera, the owner of one of LTI's oldest accounts, Valley Produce. He had given her assistant, Lucy, quite an earful, complaining heatedly that an unacceptably large percentage of his produce LTI transported was arriving wilted and spoiled at the grocer's destinations, and none of the LTI account reps seemed to want to do anything about it. Therefore, he had felt obliged to call the vice president of

Southwest Operations (that would be her, Robin) demanding satisfaction. If he couldn't rely on LTI to get his produce to the customer in the time or condition he required, he was very certain he could find a freight company that would.

What startled Robin about his call was not that he was unhappy, but how in the hell his unhappiness had escaped her. Valley Produce was one of the first companies to sign on with her father when he had begun his business some thirty-odd years ago, and she was very certain Dad would not be very happy to hear from Mr. Herrera right now. Especially since the last time they had talked, he had been very displeased with her handling of a similar situation in Austin.

Yeah, well, Dad was easily displeased; that went with the territory.

Where the hell was her *shoe?* Dressed in a sleek, black (all her sleek outfits were black) Donna Karan short skirt and jacket, Robin searched the wreckage of her bedroom for the left of a pair of Stuart Weitzman black leather pumps. This chaotic state of living, while not entirely foreign to her, was still highly undesirable, and she was, she realized, desperate to finalize the deal with Jacob Manning to do the renovations she had started and abandoned.

Okay, so her friends were right—the purchase of this house *had* been something of a lark. She had stumbled on it one Sunday afternoon as she drove, lost, through the Village, looking for the barbecue her friends Linda and Kirk were hosting. The house was nestled on a wide boulevard with giant live oaks and huge mansions. It was perfect, of course—not too big, not too small. So she had phoned her attorney, told her to buy it. When she'd moved in, she'd stored her belongings, shoved her clothes into one room, set up the dining room table with the leather chairs, and let the rest of it sit empty in anticipation of the renovations she would do herself.

At least she had every intention of doing them herself. But she had succeeded only in knocking a couple of huge gaping holes in the walls before she was off to Madrid, and then London, and New York, and then…whatever. How could she have known so many things would come up? Needless to say, she was hiring out the work before she went stark raving mad, and it was, come hell or high water, the *one* thing she would accomplish today.

When the wayward shoe was at last located, Robin emerged from her house looking completely cool and sophisticated. The only accessory that did not reek of chic was the black leather headband she had stuck on her head as a last resort for keeping her short, wildly curly hair in some sense of order.

Robin marched out onto the drive, passing Raymond, her yardman, with a jaunty wave, and proceeded to her Mercedes 500 E-Class. She fired up that sweet ride and sped out onto North Boulevard.

As she turned off the boulevard, a man on a Harley pulled into her drive. He parked the bike, waved at Raymond. "You doing okay?" he asked as the yardman walked up to the door to unlock it for him.

"Can't complain, can't complain," Raymond said. "You gonna be long, Mr. Manning?"

"Nah. Just need to look at a couple of things. I'll put the key out."

"That'll do," Raymond said.

Jake Manning walked inside the empty mansion, pausing in the foyer to peer into the dining room, where Ms. Lear had obviously set up shop. His nose wrinkled as he surveyed the wreckage—empty yogurt containers, papers strewn about, a bra curiously draped over one chair, the obligatory computer, one running shoe, an empty wine bottle.

Jake moved on, up the great curving staircase to the upper floors.

Now here was the odd part, he thought as he reached the second-floor landing and surveyed the gaping hole in the wall directly ahead. That hole made no sense. She had freely admitted to it, had told him on the phone that she "had started the renovations." It made no sense because first, that hole served no conceivable purpose, and second, while he'd never actually *met* Robin Lear (she preferred to have Raymond let him in), her house had all the markings of a society bitch. He should know—he did enough of their houses, could spot them a mile off. But this hole thing had given him pause. No dainty, cosmetically enhanced woman was going to make a hole *that* big.

With a shrug, he continued on to the master bath to double-check the dimensions.

In the meantime, Robin was cursing traffic, which was, as usual, moving at a snail's pace. She punched a number into her cell phone and used the morning crawl to reschedule a dinner date, return two business calls, and track down Darren Fogerty's assistant—Darren being her contact at Atlantic—to set up a meeting for the next morning. When she clicked off that call, she was at the elevator, headed for the tenth-floor suite of offices that housed the LTI Southwest corporate offices. All four of them. Oh, and a conference room.

She marched through the glass doors emblazoned with Lear Transport Industries, Inc., her briefcase swinging carelessly from her shoulder, and said hello to the receptionist as she stopped to pick up her phone messages. There were several new ones—from Bill (*Flying in. Drinks tonight?*), Darren from Atlantic, a sales manager of a cable manufacturer, and three that really caught her attention. Mr. Herrera (she needed a cup of coffee for that one), Dad (an elephant tranquilizer), and Jacob Manning, who would, if she was lucky, commence the renovation of her house today.

Pink slips firmly in hand, Robin marched on, right past Evan Iverson's door—at which point her heart did a little start when she saw him seated at his desk—and stuck her hand in Lucy's cubicle to signal that she had, indeed, arrived, before disappearing into her own office. Tossing her briefcase aside, Robin went immediately to her wet bar and the pot of coffee Lucy had put on. French roast. Pedestrian, but potable.

In the midst of pouring a cup, Lucy came in with a "*Yo.*" Robin glanced over her shoulder at Lucy, who stood in the doorway of her office wearing a lime-green sweater and black pants. Her long red hair was piled on top of her head with a pencil stuck through to hold it. Robin paused to sip the nectar of gods before asking, "Hey, did you take Dad's call?"

Lucy came farther into the room, adjusted her black-rimmed matchbox glasses. "I took the first one. He said he assumed you would manage to drag yourself in before noon, and if you did, you should call him immediately. At the ranch."

The *ranch*? Oh great. When or why Aaron had made the trek to Texas, Robin couldn't imagine, and frankly, didn't even want to think about it.

"Mr. Herrera has called twice. Are you going to call him? You need to call him."

Well, hello, she *knew* that. Robin took another sip of coffee. "Was that Evan I saw?" she asked, trying very hard to be nonchalant.

"Yep."

"What's he doing here?"

"Don't know," Lucy said with a shrug, and plopped down in one of two leather armchairs in front of Robin's desk. "But he needs to talk to you before he goes back to Dallas. He asked if you had lunch plans."

Oh frabjous day, her father *and* a former lover all in one Monday. "Ah...I don't think so."

Lucy looked suspiciously at Robin. "Why are you making that face?"

"What face?"

"*That* face."

"There is no *face*."

It was obvious Lucy believed there was a face. There were a lot of things the old girl knew about Robin, but her affair with Evan was not one of them. In his position as chief operating officer, Evan was her father's most trusted man—his loyalty to the company was unquestionable, and he was very good at what he did. His was a classic rags-to-riches story— he graduated from the University of Texas in Austin and started by selling freight carriers to businesses. That's how he met Dad and came to LTI. From there, he worked his way up, making LTI extremely profitable and himself rich in the process—Robin had heard the golden boy's story enough times from Dad to know.

It happened that Evan was also a very handsome man in addition to being smart, and Robin could not help the attraction she had developed during her four-year stint with her father in New York.

But it wasn't until she had talked Dad into opening the Houston offices and had moved back to Texas that the affair had begun. At a corporate meeting in Dallas, she had flirted, Evan had taken the bait, and the rest was the ancient history of inconspicuous dating, which had gone on until Robin began to realize that good looks did not necessarily mean interesting.

When he began to hint around about their relationship taking a more serious and permanent bent, Robin had balked outright and had bowed out under the pretense of work. There probably could have been a little more finesse on her part, but still, it did not end too terribly badly, she supposed, given that Evan promised her—"for the sake of the company" —that he would not make it uncomfortable for her.

Unfortunately, she clearly made it uncomfortable for him without even trying. She didn't mean to do it, but every time she saw him, he looked at her with cow eyes and would ask, in that quiet, we-have-a-secret voice, "How *are* you?"

That was exactly the reason why, in the midst of another failed relationship in London, Robin had promised herself to never, ever, dip her pen in the company ink again.

"HUL-LO-OH!" Lucy all but shouted.

"What?" Robin exclaimed, startled.

"You drifted into Robin-land," Lucy said with a snort and popped up out of her chair. "I've got some stuff for you to sign. I'll be back." As Lucy went out, Robin picked up her phone and phoned Guillermo, the sales rep at the Rio Grande Valley freight yard.

"Hey, Miss Lear, how are you?" he asked cheerfully when she got him on the phone.

"Good. Listen, I had a call from Mr. Herrera yesterday from Valley Produce? He's a little agitated. He says we are delivering spoiled product."

"Yes ma'am, we are," Guillermo said matter-of-factly. "It's those refrigeration units we got on the trucks. They don't work for crap, pardon my French, and it seems like every time one goes out, it's his freight we got on there."

"*What* refrigeration units?"

"The refrigeration units! With all due respect, Miss Lear, I told you about this before Christmas. See, the coils, they're not working like they should. It's a short in the—"

"Guillermo, I don't remember anything about coils," Robin said sternly.

"Sure, don't you remember? When we had that holiday party in Padre, I was telling you about the coils."

Robin was suddenly struck with the memory of Guillermo holding a longneck in one hand, a half-eaten monster turkey leg in the other, which he used to emphasize his monologue about coils and refrigeration units…and something in there about the average lifespan of a head of lettuce. Robin groaned. "Yes, I remember that, but I didn't realize at the time you were telling me there was a problem—it was a *holiday party*, for Chrissakes!"

"Well, sure, Miss Lear. That's why I called you the next week."

Oh.

Right.

She had been on her way to London and had stacked Guillermo's message to call along with all the others she'd decided could wait. Of course, she'd expected to return in two weeks' time, but then again, she hadn't counted on meeting Nigel. That idiot savant had cost her two extra weeks—

"...so I told him, it's all at corporate, but sure, go ahead and call. And he did."

"What? Did what?" she demanded.

"Called. Mr. Iverson. He ordered all new units. We should get them in today, have 'em installed by the end of next week."

Fabulous. All she needed was to have Evan cleaning up this little mess for her. She punched a key on her computer—the e-mail screen popped right up. "Okay, thanks, Guillermo," she said, and winced at the e-mail from Evan, *Valley Produce refrigeration units*. Her head was beginning to hurt.

Robin glanced again at the stack of pink phone messages. Jacob Manning's number was a cell phone; he picked it up on the third ring. "Manning here."

Having exchanged no less than fifteen phone tags with him, the sound of his voice actually startled Robin. "Oh! Uh...Mr. Manning, this is Robin Lear."

"Hey, good to hear from you."

Speaking of hearing, he certainly had a nice, silky voice, Robin thought absently. "Listen, thanks for sending your estimate so quickly for the work on my house. I like all that you suggested."

"Great. You've got a nice place."

"Thanks. I just have a few questions if you don't mind."

"Sure. Fire away."

Yes, a *very* nice voice. "I calculate this work to be about forty dollars a square foot, is that right?"

"Sounds about right—"

"I had other bids for the same work that came in *much* lower than that." That was really a teeny-tiny lie—she'd actually had only one other bid.

Mr. Manning said nothing at first, then chuckled softly, a sound that sent a quick and curious shiver down Robin's spine. "I'll just bet you did, Ms. Lear. But if you want a quality job, you're going to have to pay for it."

Well, wasn't that just a typical male response? "Really?" Robin asked in her shy, I'm-just-a-woman voice. "And do you think I should have to pay as much as ten dollars more per square foot than any other expert in renovations? Perhaps you didn't notice, but it's just a house, Mr. Manning, not the Galleria."

"Well, now, Robin, even *I* can see that it's not the Galleria," he said, the amusement irritatingly evident in his deep voice. "In fact, I'd bet I've seen more of that house than you have in the last few days, and I can assure you, it is just a house. Now, if you don't want to pay for the work I propose to do, I understand. Not everyone does. Won't hurt my feelings one bit if you decide to go with someone ten dollars a square foot cheaper—it's your call."

His remark took her aback, but not nearly as much as the casual slip of her first name, which sounded, much to her surprise, incredibly sexy from his lips. With a shake of her head to clear it, Robin demanded, "What about materials? How can I be assured the materials are the quality I'm paying a premium for?"

"You can inspect everything I bring into your house."

"Receipts?"

"I'll copy you on everything I do."

"And consult me if there is any change to your proposal?"

"I don't know," he sighed. "Are you going to want to pick the colors, too?"

The question was so ludicrous that Robin was left momentarily speechless.

"It's a joke," he said in that voice.

"I knew that!" she lied. "I need this work to be done right away and finished quickly. I suppose I could see my way to your cost if I could have your guarantee that you can start this week. How long will it take you to complete?"

Mr. Manning laughed. "Do you always bounce from one extreme to the other like that? There for a minute I thought you were going to fire me before you even hired me."

Robin rolled her eyes heavenward. "Did you say how long?"

"You need to understand that this sort of work takes time. And once I get under that old paint, if there is any sort of abatement that needs to be done, you can count on two extra weeks at a minimum. That's an old house you're in there, Robin. It's not going to be a six-week job, I can tell you that, not with what you want done to the bathrooms and kitchen. Not to mention the other work I've got going on, too. Let's see..." Robin could hear a tapping sound. "We're looking at two months, easy. Maybe three."

"Three months!" she exclaimed. "But I can't live like that for three months. Is there anything you can do to readjust your schedule?"

His laughter was full and very rich—Robin could just picture him, probably an older gentleman, gray at the temples, wearing a crisp white shirt and sitting in his luxury sedan—

"I'll see what I can do, but I'm being honest with you— this is not going to go quick. You want a start of *this* week?" The tapping again. "I can rearrange a couple of things, I guess, but Thursday is the soonest I can get started. I sent a contract with the bid to your attorney. Let me know if there's anything you want to change. Once that's signed, we've got us a deal. Appreciate the business and we'll talk soon."

The connection was suddenly dead.

Surprised, Robin held the receiver out from her head and looked at it. Well, at least his reputation was excellent— she had called four references and they had all raved about the quality of his work. She supposed she ought to be happy that she had managed to get him at all, much less get him to agree to start this week—

"Robin."

She started at the sound of Evan's voice; she hadn't even heard the door open. But there he was, half in, half out. Robin put the receiver down, suddenly embarrassed that she had avoided him so completely since her return from London.

"Hello, Evan," she said, motioning him forward, and watched him walk in without actually looking at him. He was still as handsome as ever, his blond hair perfectly trimmed, his jaw clean shaven. And as usual, his style impeccable— from the crisp knot of his silk tie to the perfect pleats of his gray suit pants.

"I'm sorry to interrupt, but I need to talk to you before I leave for Dallas."

"Not a problem," she lied and stood, gesturing for him to sit. "Want some coffee?"

He shook his head, sat uneasily in the chair she had indicated. Robin made herself come around to sit next to him. "Sorry I didn't stop in earlier. Lots of calls," she said, motioning vaguely at her desk.

"You look great," he said.

Her self-conscious smile burned. "Uh, thanks...so what's up?"

"I was hoping we could do lunch—"

"Well, I—"

"But you look buried," Evan quickly interjected with a shrug. His perfectly manicured hands fidgeted unconsciously with the bottom of his tie. Robin folded her hands in her lap.

"I just needed to talk with you before I talk to Aaron."

"Aaron?"

Evan looked at her fully then, a slight frown on his face. "We lost the Valley Produce account. Herrera has gone to American Motorfreight. He told me this morning."

The news stunned her. How could they lose the account? She hadn't even spoken to Herrera yet! "You're kidding."

"No, I'm not kidding, Robin. Herrera was our biggest Texas account. And one of our oldest. He's been with your dad since he started up."

Yes, yes, she was aware of that, and nodded in complete agreement, but Evan's frown just deepened. "Robin, *you* lost that account."

"Me?" she exclaimed in surprise, but the twinge of guilt had already started to pierce her conscience.

"You've spent too much time looking for a big fish—"

"What's that supposed to mean? I thought the object was to strive for the new and very big accounts, Evan, the ones that ship *tons* of freight—"

"The object is to take care of your customers."

Ouch. "I hope you are not lecturing me," she said defensively. "And you don't need to talk to Dad for me. I am perfectly capable of telling him that we lost the account."

"I know you are capable, but let's not forget that I run this pop stand. I let you handle the valley accounts, just like you asked before you took off for London—"

"I did not *take off*—"

"Whatever. I'm just saying that Aaron is going to want an answer from me, too."

Robin fought the urge to squirm in her chair. "All right, it's my fault," she admitted reluctantly. "I didn't realize what it was Guillermo was telling me, and then I was gone for a month—"

"Five weeks, but who's counting? Anyway, what's done is done," Evan said, then stood abruptly, shoved his hands into his pocket as he walked to the windows. "I'm going to fly to Harlingen tomorrow and talk to Herrera, but I don't think it will do any good. Now listen, Aaron will know immediately that this was something that should have been easily handled. Don't bullshit him."

As if she needed to be reminded. "I'll call Dad right now." She stood, swiped her coffee cup off her desk, and marched to the wet bar to pour another.

"Still drinking too much coffee?" he asked, his voice noticeably lighter.

"I guess," she said and dumped three sugars into her cup. She stirred her coffee slowly, aware of the silence filling the space between them. After what seemed an eternity, she heard Evan move behind her.

"I'm going back to Dallas this afternoon," he said, standing directly behind her. There was that thing in his voice, that uncomfortable sound of longing. Robin did not turn around, but simply nodded, waiting. Evan sighed. "I'll talk to you soon, all right?"

When Robin turned around, he had gone.

She stood at the wet bar for several long moments, staring at the door before finally, slowly, returning to her desk.

The phone message, on which the receptionist had written CALL YOUR FATHER AT THE RANCH IMMEDIATELY, was staring up at her. Damn.

Dad picked up the phone on the first ring. "Hello?" he said anxiously.

"Hey, Dad, it's me."

"Robbie! Good God, does the word *immediately* mean anything to you? I've been trying to get hold of you for two days now!"

"I was out yesterday with Mia. You remember her—"

"I asked that you call me when you came in. Did you just come in?"

Robin suppressed a groan. "Dad, I had some other calls to return. Listen, I know why you're calling, and—"

"No, Robin Elaine, you don't. I need you to come to the ranch."

"Uh...to the ranch?" That was most definitely not in her plans. "Gee, Dad, I don't think I can make it right now."

"Rebecca and Rachel are coming, too," he continued, as if he hadn't heard her. "Bec is going to pick up Rachel in Dallas this morning and then they are driving down. You can get here tonight if you leave before rush hour—"

"Dad!" Robin exclaimed, laughing nervously at his sudden determination to see his daughters. "I can't just up and come to the ranch—"

"Why the hell not?" he barked, then made a strange sound. "Robbie, listen," he said, his voice hoarse and soft, "there is something I need to tell you, but I can't do it over the phone. I need you to come here."

That sobered her—her father was demanding, but not the sort to make anxious demands, unless...unless something was awfully wrong. "Has something happened?" she asked quickly.

"Yes. No. Well, *is* happening."

"What?" she asked, unconsciously curling her hand into a fist, steeling herself. "Is it Mom? Did something happen to Mom?"

"Oh baby, no, your mom is fine," he said softly and sighed wearily. "God, Robbie, I don't believe it myself, but... it's *me*."

CHAPTER TWO

The entrance to the Lear family ranch—massive limestone pillars framing iron gates, an overarching frieze of cattle and crosses with the name Blue Cross Ranch scripted in the middle—had stood open since Aaron and Bonnie arrived two weeks ago.

The event was remarked by the locals in and around the town of Comfort, Texas, and every so often, one of them would be curious enough to drive through the gates for a friendly look around. The caliche road, marked by cattle guards, wended through mesquite trees and old live oaks with branches so long and low that they formed a canopy for long stretches. To the right and left of the road, 1,500 head of cattle and about 500 sheep grazed on the green, hilly landscape. In the spring, bluebonnets, buttercups, and Indian paintbrush grew so thick that it looked as if the cattle slept on a bed of flowers.

Eventually, the road widened and a dozen gaslights lined the last hundred yards or so to the ranch house, which was nestled in the shadows of the long, twisting limbs of the live oaks along the banks of the Guadalupe River. Slung long and wide, the house was a two-story limestone, marked with an abundance of windows so that no vista was left unframed. A wide veranda stretched endlessly around the structure, dotted with wicker furniture, green ferns, and whitewashed porch swings. In the small front yard stood an old iron kettle, filled with antique roses that matched those planted along the railing of the porch. A century-old boot scrape and horse tether stood next to the path leading to the flagstone skirt spread around the entrance to the porch.

Robin had seen this house a million times, but today, as she coasted into the circular drive at dusk, she thought it looked strangely hollow—the setting sun reflected on the second-floor windows, giving the house orange eyes and a gaping black mouth where the front door stood open.

As she climbed out of her car and gathered her things, she could see the familiar shapes of her sisters rise from two wicker chairs and move across the porch, Rachel distinguished from Rebecca by the wild curl of her long hair and the glowing tip of her cigarette. Rebecca, sleek and slender, had her hair pulled back—she was the first one to come off the porch, walking gracefully but purposefully.

It was the determination in her stride that unnerved Robin. She felt a small panic in the pit of her belly—she wasn't ready to do this, or to hear it, or to *feel* it, and realized with surprise that her hands were shaking. *God, this was so unlike her.* She was always the one who was so put together, so sure of herself. Everyone said that of all of them, she most resembled Dad.

"Hey," Robin said lamely as Rebecca came around the side of the car.

Rebecca responded by taking Robin into her arms and hugging her tight. "I'm so glad you're here."

She let go, grabbed a bag from Robin's hand, and stepped aside.

Rachel dropped her smoke and ground it out with the heel of her boot. "Hey, Robbie," she said.

Robin picked up her purse and put her arm around Rachel's shoulders, giving her a gentle squeeze as they followed Rebecca up the flagstone path to the house. "Rach, you're still smoking?" she asked, as the house loomed larger and larger before her.

"Sometimes," Rachel answered sheepishly.

"Oh yeah?" Robin stopped, looked up at the windows of the master suite. "Then give me one."

Rachel obediently fished a smoke from her pocket and handed it to her, then offered up a light. Robin grimaced at the taste but welcomed the soothing race of smoke through her blood. In front of them, Rebecca dropped Robin's bag at her feet, looked up at the master suite, too, and shook her head. "I can't believe this," she said, gesturing for Rachel to give her a cigarette, too. "This just all seems so unreal."

Robin glanced at Rebecca, who shrugged as she inhaled, then daintily let the smoke escape her lips. It was a fact that Rebecca could, just by breathing, be the most elegant woman on the planet. She had that special air about her, as if she walked on spun gold—unlike Robin, who marched through life in army boots, kicking her way to clear a path, and Rachel, who pretty much floated along, barefoot and picking flowers.

"So how are Mom and Dad? I mean...is everything okay?" Robin asked.

Rebecca settled her pale blue gaze on her. "They are doing *remarkably* well. It's weird. It's like the last fifteen years didn't happen."

"That is so weird," Rachel murmured.

Robin's sentiments exactly. She took another drag from her smoke. "So has he told you anything? Like what his doctors are saying? H-how...long?" she forced herself to ask.

The question silenced them all; Rachel looked nervously at the ground. Rebecca, the rock, calmly shook her head. "He wanted to wait for you. He hasn't said any more than what he told us on the phone—just that it's bad."

"Maybe he's exaggerating. You know how some people are—they think things are a lot worse than they really are?" Rachel said, her hopeful expression dissolving with Rebecca's and Robin's pointed looks. "I mean, how bad can it be?" she asked no one in particular, tossing the cigarette aside. "God, is there any liquor out here? A beer at least?"

The three women looked up at the second-story windows of the master suite, none of them having the guts to take the next step forward.

From the sitting room of the master suit, Aaron watched as his three beautiful daughters gathered on the drive below him. "Since when do my children smoke?" he demanded gruffly as Rachel handed Robin a cigarette.

Seated in a comfortable armchair, Bonnie lowered the book she was quietly reading. "They don't. At least not usually. Rachel can't seem to kick the habit completely. When she feels stressed, she smokes."

"I didn't know Rachel smoked."

Bonnie shot him a sidelong glance. Aaron knew that look; it was the *there's-a-*lot-*you-don't-know* look she had perfected in the last couple of weeks. He sighed, sat in a chair next to Bonnie, and closed his eyes, unable to shake the ill effects of the aggressive drug therapy.

"Why don't you rest a bit? I'll go see about the girls, then bring you some tea in a while."

Bonnie, ah, Bonnie. How I've let you down. Aaron felt her hand on his forehead, opened his eyes, and took her hand, pressing his lips to her palm. "Thanks, but I'm good."

Bonnie smiled; it was the same sweetly beatific smile that had captivated him more than thirty years ago on that dirt football field in West Texas. No matter what had gone on between them—and the Lord God knew there had been a lot—he still loved her, and in moments like these, desperately so. It was just like her, Aaron thought, as he watched her put her book away, that in spite of their estrangement, she had come when he'd called. Her life in California had taken her down a new and different path, but they had never lost touch, neither of them able to completely let go, the bond between them amazingly resilient. She had, instinctively, felt his horror when he'd made that pathetic call to her, and had come to New York immediately to be with him through the surgery and first rounds of radiation and chemotherapy. She'd put the many years of discord and strife aside and had stepped into the old role of partner and soul mate. She had consulted with his doctors, had gotten up in the night to make sure he was okay, had filled him with comfort foods that he could not keep down, and memories and kindness that he could.

He would never have made it this far without her.

When the shock and trauma of aggressive treatment to his body had begun to wear him thin, it had been Aaron's request that they come to the ranch to recuperate. Both of them had wanted some detachment from the world at large to put their minds and arms and hearts around the devastation of a sentence of six months to two years, and while they had not been at the ranch together for many years, it seemed the place to be. Aaron in particular needed to be in a place where he could be silent, in solitude, where he could think of all things that could *not* be left undone before he was gone.

And Bonnie, resolute, had come with him, her mouth set in determination as she gripped his hand on that interminably long flight from New York where he had, for the first time in his life, made use of the barf bag. Twice.

Fortunately, at the ranch, he had begun to improve, regaining some strength. They began every day as if it were his last. They did not call for the usual staff members to join them, preferring to spend the days alone. They took walks in the morning as far as Aaron could go, looked through old family albums and letters in the afternoon, drank from his cellar of very fine wines, and spent their evenings on the porch swing looking at the stars.

More importantly, they talked like they hadn't talked in years. About all of it, their lives, their daughters. About all the things that they had seen grow and blossom between them, then wilt and die, and how exactly it had all happened, beginning with a clear and calm night on the Texas caprock. That was the night of the spring dance of their junior year at Ralls High, when Bonnie had willingly given herself to his wandering hands and neither of them had ever been the same again.

In fact, that night, and all its discoveries, had sparked the struggle within Aaron to be a man—he could still remember how fiercely he wanted to take Bonnie and all that she was, run away with her, find some place where the world did not exist except for the two of them.

Aaron's father, however, saw a different vision for him. There was no one else to leave the family farm to, save Aaron's sister and whomever she might eventually marry. The more Aaron struggled with that plan, the less anyone in his family seemed to understand why or how he could leave generations of farming behind. Only Bonnie had understood his need to see the world, to make his way by himself and escape the drudgery of cotton farming.

So in the weeks that followed their graduation from high school, when Bonnie had impulsively packed a bag and run off with him to Dallas to help him make their fortune, they had sealed their bond and their fate for the rest of their lives.

His father had died a bitter man, and his sister's husband, a no-account dirt farmer from Crosby, had reaped the reward of Aaron's decision. It was, nevertheless, a decision Aaron never regretted.

At first, it had been very hard. Yet at the same time, it had been very good between him and Bonnie—they had been held together by young love and poverty. It was by chance that a foreman at Grantham Engines had taken a look at Aaron's application, saw that he knew how to operate a cotton gin, and put him behind the wheel of a semi, driving line-haul between Dallas and San Antonio. With a little money, Aaron and Bonnie had found a tiny one-bedroom clapboard house on the east side of Dallas, and they were happy.

When Robin came along, Aaron immediately fell in love with her dark blue eyes and dark curls. He had worshipped that baby doll, had taken her everywhere he could, doting on her. Two years later, the same year Aaron bought his first truck, Rebecca had joined them, another beautiful baby girl with crystalline blue eyes. By the time Rachel was born three years after that, laughing and gurgling beneath a head full of black fuzz, he had a dozen of his own trucks running between Dallas and San Antonio.

Lear Transport had been born along with his daughters, but grew much faster. Aaron intuitively understood the fundamentals of success in the business, and he quickly earned a reputation for delivering freight fast and cheap. As the business grew, so did his ambition. He moved the family to Houston to take advantage of the transatlantic shipping lanes that ended there, successfully bidding on several over-the-road contracts to move a substantial amount of ocean cargo that did not end up on the rails. By the time he moved to New York and added air transport to LTI, Bonnie had long gone.

At what point, exactly, the arguments had started, he could no longer remember, but it seemed that was all there was in those last few years together. According to Bonnie, he was never home, never interested in them, had left the raising of their daughters to her. She never understood that building an empire for those three girls took all his energy. Bonnie was right about one thing, however—*both* of them had left the girls flailing about, throwing wealth and more wealth at them as they tried to sort out the mess of their marriage. The result? In spite of all outward appearances to the contrary, they had managed to raise three daughters who each carried the burden of their parents' failure in her own way.

For Robin, as Bonnie had so brilliantly pointed out, it was the need for his acceptance and approval. She'd flailed about until Aaron took her on at LTI. Except that he didn't really take her on. He didn't teach her the business like he should have, but had given her a cushy position that had nothing to do with the running of company. She was a pretty woman, eye candy with a powerful name, and she made a great asset for entertaining his bigger accounts around the world. But in the last couple of years, as Robin had sought more influence and responsibility at LTI, he had found her business decisions to lack the maturity that solid experience would have given her. She was, in a word, a management disaster.

Rebecca, on the other hand, had, for reasons Aaron would never understand, latched on to the first loser to pay her compliments. It was mind-boggling to him, for Rebecca was the most beautiful and refined of his daughters. She could have had any man with the mere crook of a finger, but she had chosen Bud Reynolds. Bud wasn't *all* bad—he was perhaps one of the best high school wide receivers Houston had ever seen—but he was a sorry excuse for a man. When Aaron had left Bonnie, Rebecca had latched on to him and held tight all the way to college, foregoing what had all the markings of a promising career in the arts to be the bastard's doormat. Now, Bonnie said, Rebecca drifted from one social event to the next, miserable in a marriage to a man who would fuck his neighbor's wife in the garage while she was inside, nursing their son.

And of course there was Rachel, sweet Rachel, the most hapless child a man might hope to have. She was *still* in some nebulous graduate program at Brown University, the *same* graduate program in which she had been enrolled four years now. The subject of her study? Ancient British languages. He had to shake his head in wonder every time he thought of it. The one time he had asked her what she intended to do with her graduate degree in languages—ancient British languages at that, the poor girl had blinked and looked very bewildered. "Well...research," she'd said. She seemed to have no direction, no ambition, other than to poke around musty old manuscripts.

Yet Aaron continued to bankroll her.

It astounded him in an odd way, because his three daughters had grown up in the lap of luxury, had never wanted for a damn thing. But each of them was as forlorn in her own private way as if he had abandoned them at birth. If the goddamned doctors were right, he had precious little time left to right that wrong.

That knowledge had created in him a desperate sense of urgency like he had never felt in his life. If there was one thing he had to do before he left this earth, it was to make them face the voids in their lives, make them understand what was truly precious. Teach them to stand up to life and meet it head-on.

Aaron could hear the girls downstairs now, a wisp of nervous laughter floating up to him. He stood, pausing a moment to make sure nothing in him was going to object, his gaze falling to a picture of a younger Bonnie hanging on the wall of the bedroom study. It might be too late for them, but it wasn't too late for his girls.

Determined, Aaron gritted his teeth and walked slowly out of the room to tell his daughters that he didn't have long to live.

Telling his daughters he was dying was the hardest thing Aaron had ever had to do. Judging by Bonnie's drawn expression, it hadn't been any easier for her. The girls had each received the news in characteristic form—Rachel disbelieving, waiting for a punch line that would never come; Rebecca, unobtrusive, off to one side, softly crying; and Robin, defiant, angrily insisting that he seek another opinion, hire the best doctors—*fight it, Dad!*

If only they knew. If only he could impart to them how hard he fought the battle being waged within him, how he begged for his life from a God whom he had not addressed in years. And then one night, the enormity of his fate had descended upon him and he had, miraculously and calmly, accepted what he must. Not that he intended to go down without a fight, no sir, and in fact, he and Bonnie were looking into alternative treatments. But something was different now. His thoughts had turned from himself to those around him.

"I am worried about them," he said to Bonnie. They were sitting in silence in the dining room, both of them lost in thought.

Bonnie smiled sadly. "Me, too. Especially Robbie. She's so headstrong. I worry how she'll do...you know, after."

Aaron paled.

"It's just that she is so angry, so full of frustration. And I don't know how to help her, I have never really known how, because I'm just not...you."

"What's that supposed to mean?"

"Just that—ever since she was a little girl, Robbie has wanted to be just like you. And then Rebecca and Rachel..." Bonnie sighed, looked away.

Aaron could almost hear what she was thinking—how would she manage after he was gone? Frankly, he had wondered the same thing. Not that Bonnie wasn't a good mother, but there was so much those three women had to learn, so much from which they had been sheltered. Not one of them seemed to be in control of her own life but why should he expect them to be? After all, he had controlled it for them from the moment of their birth.

And over the course of the next two days, Aaron became increasingly convinced that he had to do something drastic, had to break the pattern of their dependence on him. They were spoiled, unrealistic about life in some ways, self-indulgent in their own ways, and at times, self-centered.

Robbie was definitely the ringleader of their little band, and Aaron couldn't help but think of the old adage, the blind leading the blind. When she wasn't glued to her cell phone, she was stomping about, insisting to Bonnie that she couldn't leave the office unattended for a few days, because they wouldn't know what to do. What she obviously did not realize was that her office, the little four-member team he had allowed her to set up in Houston, was, in the greater scheme of things, so inconsequential to LTI that it was almost laughable. Her operation was window dressing, nothing more. Evan Iverson ran the Texas operation in addition to the corporate company. Robbie hardly knew how the company operated, no thanks to Aaron. It was something

Evan had pointed out to him on more than one occasion, and something he had patently ignored...until now. Wasn't Robbie the logical one to carry on in his stead? Had he thought himself so invincible that he would never need a successor? Worse, what sort of disservice had he done his own daughter?

And there was Rebecca, so like her mother, who called home every hour, or so it seemed, to check on her son, Grayson, and to see if Bud the Bastard had left a message for her. Of course he hadn't. Yet she continued to call, continued to hope for the affection of a man so far beneath her that it made Aaron cringe every time she picked up the phone.

And his baby, Rachel. She had gained a few pounds since he'd last seen her. He pictured her in some stuffy library room, a package of Oreos on her lap as she leafed through some ancient manuscript. Rachel had always been the dreamer, and while he loved that about her, the girl was her own worst enemy. Yet she was quick to point to her boyfriend when she felt challenged—another winner, Aaron thought disgustedly. Myron was a professor at Brown, who encouraged her study of ancient British literature with an absurd enthusiasm.

Aaron listened to his daughters over those two days, observed them, felt their attention returning to their own lives, away from his fleeting mortality. The more he glimpsed their lives, devoid of any meaningful relationships, the less he could bear it. As sick and tired as he was, his patience had worn very thin. By the time dinner was served on Wednesday night, Aaron was feeling a sort of panic that only a dying man can feel. Something had to be done. The chicks needed to be pushed from their feathered nests and taught to fly, or be eaten by stronger predators.

His idea was drastic and perhaps cold, but desperate times called for desperate measures.

CHAPTER THREE

It was Wednesday evening when all hell broke loose, beginning when Robin came back from a late-afternoon run. She was standing in the entry, speaking through short breaths to Darren Fogerty on her cell phone when Dad made his way downstairs, taking the steps very carefully, as if his whole body hurt.

"I'll be straight with you, Robin," Darren was saying. "I've got some other options on the table. Now, you have guaranteed your transport times, but the rate is a little higher than I was hoping."

Robin cringed; the rate she had quoted him for ground transport was cheaper than any contract LTI had. To go any lower would mean approval from Evan and Dad. "Let me check on a couple of things, will you?" She glanced up as Dad came to a halt directly in front of her.

"When? I really need to wrap this up."

"Umm, by the end of the week for sure," she said, and nodded hopefully at Dad for confirmation, but Dad responded by angrily mimicking a fork to the mouth to remind her that it was time for dinner.

Robin covered the mouthpiece of her cell phone. "Jeez, Dad, this isn't Luby's," she whispered. "I'll be there in a minute."

Dad looked a little taken aback as she said to Darren, "Count on Friday at the very latest. Can you wait 'til then?"

"Sure. Maybe I can take you out to dinner to celebrate."

Robin smiled as if Darren were in the same room with her—she could feel this deal gelling very nicely. "I'd really like that, Darren. I'll give you a call tomorrow."

With that, she flipped the little phone shut and looked at Dad. His eyes narrowed. "Who is Darren?"

Robin flushed, dropped her phone in her purse. "No one you know," she said, and put her hands on her hips. "So, Dad, what is this dinner thing, anyway?"

His scowl deepened. "This dinner thing is to help me keep a shitload of medicine down. I'm sorry if that interferes with your dining schedule—"

Robin instantly threw a hand up. "Sorry. I was just asking." She brushed past him, bounding up the stairs to the shower.

"Sorry to be keeping you from your date," he snapped after her.

God, what was the matter with him? "He's not a date, Dad!" she called as she disappeared into the corridor above. It was obvious Dad was miserable; Mom said the medicine was making him sick and moody—he was almost tearful at times, or too angry, or too stoic. And more than once she'd caught him staring at her like he was seeing her for the first time.

God forbid anything should come up about LTI, she thought as she grabbed some panties and a camisole and headed for the shower. Everything she said was wrong. Like when he asked her about the regional sales figures. She told him that they were improving over the last quarter, but that only seemed to agitate him. *"They aren't improving! They're abysmal! Don't you know anything?"* And when she tried to explain, he had almost twisted off into an epileptic fit.

It wasn't just her, either. He was constantly on Rebecca about her calls home, dogged Rachel about her eating habits, and generally seemed to despise everyone except Mom. Which, Robin thought, seemed especially bizarro, seeing as how they had been separated all these years.

The abysmal mood had not improved when Robin entered the dining room dressed in a white cotton T-shirt and faded Levi's. Rebecca caught her eye, and with her hand, made a slashing motion across her neck. Dad didn't see Rebecca; he was trying to drink the herbal cocktail Mom made for him every night. But when Rachel came in behind Robin, she missed Rebecca's warning.

"Is there something I can get you, Dad? Some medicine or something?"

He shook his head, swallowed the last of the stuff with a groan.

"Are you feeling all right?"

"Would everyone stop asking me if I am all right?" he snapped. "Jesus Christ, I feel like I am surrounded by a bunch of Nurse Betties!"

Rebecca rolled her eyes and went through the swinging door to the kitchen; Rachel was close on her heels, head down. Dad didn't seem to notice; he was rubbing his eyes and looked to be in pain. Reluctantly, Robin took her seat. Fortunately, the door swung open again, and it was Mom, carrying a steaming dish of beef Stroganoff.

She set the dish down and looked at Dad. "I hear you are feeling a little out of sorts."

"I have to eat at six," he grumbled. "You know that."

"Fifteen minutes one way or another is not going to make a great difference. I know you are not feeling well, Aaron, and I know you are worried about any number of things, but you might try and remember that this very is hard on everyone."

"You'd never know it was hard on anyone around here but me."

"Oh please. The girls are walking on eggshells around you," Mom countered, just as Rachel came through the swinging door, a bottle of wine in one hand, wineglasses in the other, and a pretzel clamped between her teeth.

"What's that, an appetizer?" Dad muttered.

Oh man. Robin immediately grabbed a glass and made an attempt to change the heavy atmosphere. "I love Stroganoff, Mom," she said and turned a beaming smile to Aaron. "Remember that little restaurant on Fifty-Third? They had the best Stroganoff!"

"I remember. And I remember how you would send everything back because it never met your exacting standards. I used to think it was funny." His expression clearly relayed that he no longer thought so.

"I don't remember that," Robin said, almost meaning it, as Rachel took her seat and a glum Rebecca slipped in the room and into a chair next to Robin.

"Well? Let's dig in," Mom sighed, and Robin passed the wine to Rebecca, who looked as if she could use a good belt. "Honey?" Mom said to Rebecca as she passed the salad bowl to Rachel. "Did you speak with Grayson?"

"*Nooo.* I guess Bud's got something going on—they aren't around much."

Rachel leaned over to spoon salad onto Dad's plate; he angrily snatched the utensil from her hand. "I can do it." Rachel dropped the bowl like a hot dish.

Dad helped himself to salad, shifted his glare to Rebecca. "What's this about Mr. Bud? Isn't he crying for you to come and take his son off his hands?"

The question seemed to rattle Rebecca; unsteadily, she reached for the wine she had poured. "I didn't talk to him."

"Didn't talk with him yesterday, either," Dad said and impatiently motioned for the Stroganoff.

Rebecca responded with a long sip of wine. She grimaced, put the glass down, and looked at her hands. "Mom, Dad, there is something I need to tell you." Mom immediately put her fork down and looked at Rebecca. Dad accepted his plate from Rachel and stabbed at the noodles. "I didn't want to tell you this week, what with…well, everything," Rebecca said, looking at Dad from the corner of her eye. "But…but I can't—I need to get back to Dallas."

"Why?" Dad demanded through a mouthful of noodles.

"Because B-Bud has left me for another woman."

Her stunning announcement was met with a gasp of shock from Mom, deadly silence from Robin and Rachel. Dad looked relieved. "Thank God!" he said, and shoved a forkful of noodles into his mouth.

Rebecca gaped at him.

"*Aaron!*" Mom cried, horrified.

With a shrug, Dad pushed more noodles into his mouth, swallowing them whole. "He's a fucking loser, Bec. You should never have married him in the first place."

"*Dad!*" Robin exclaimed.

"Bud Reynolds is a bigger bastard than his old man, and trust me, that is quite an accomplishment. Good riddance, I say. It's about damn time you found your own way in this world, Rebecca, instead of relying on men to make it for you."

"Oh. My. *God!*" Rebecca whispered hoarsely and buried her face in her hands.

Shocked to the core by Rebecca's announcement, and perhaps more so by her father's coldhearted response, Robin stared at Dad, speechless. The old man had never been short on opinions, but this…this was cruel, cancer or no cancer.

"That's inexcusable, Dad," Rachel said indignantly, voicing Robin's thoughts. "You have no right—"

"I have *every* right," he snapped, turning on her. "I have every right to say that Rebecca married a loser, that you are wasting your life with your books and that creep you call a boyfriend!" he said, stabbing his fork in the air for emphasis.

"Aaron, stop it!" Mom cried. "Stop it right now!"

Dad suddenly winced like he'd been hit in the gut. He dropped his fork, pressed a hand to his forehead.

"Dad!" Rachel exclaimed, putting her hand on his arm. "Are you all right?"

"No, I'm not all right," he said, in obvious pain. "I am all wrong." He lifted his head and looked at an ashen Rebecca. "I just meant to say that I never thought much of him, baby. You're beautiful and gifted, and you could have the whole world at your feet if you'd only reach out for it. Get rid of that bastard. Go find someone who will cherish every damn moment they have with you, and settle for nothing less. *Nothing* less! You deserve that and more!"

They all gaped at him. Except Rebecca, who stared at her plate. Dad winced again, quickly shoved more noodles into his mouth as if he were afraid they might disappear. The room fell silent as the meal was resumed, save the occasional clink of silver on china. Rebecca had passed on the food in favor of the wine; Robin could hardly eat, either, appalled more than usual by her father.

Only Rachel seemed to have an appetite, and it was she who broke first, unable to endure the awkward silence that had surrounded them. "I...I learned something sort of interesting a couple of weeks ago," she said uncertainly. Mom and Robin gratefully gave Rachel their full attention.

"Did you know that according to Nordic legend, a troll has four fingers on each hand, and four toes on each foot, and can have as many as nine heads?"

Rebecca lifted her head at that and looked at Rachel as if she had lost her mind. Which, Robin thought, she most certainly had. What was it with her and make-believe?

Rachel nodded. "I was reading about them in an old Breton manuscript—"

"Do you mean to tell me I am paying a goddamn fortune for you to read about *trolls*?" Dad rudely interrupted.

"Well, I...it was just something I found interesting and I thought—"

"Here's something interesting—just what exactly are you going to do with a degree full of useless nonsense? I swear to God, Rachel, you are wasting your life!"

"It's not useless, Dad. The evolution of language tells us how the human race has—"

"Like hell it isn't. What do you think you can do with something like that?"

"Teach!" Rachel exclaimed. But she was shrinking in her chair.

"Yeah, teach, teach about trolls, for Chrissakes," he said, shaking his head. "If you ever finish. At the rate you are going, you'll gain fifty pounds before you do anything remotely close to finishing school. But I suppose I am to blame—if I wasn't so ready to bankroll your perpetual schooling, you might have made something of yourself."

"Oh, Dad," Rebecca said wearily.

"Wh-what does that mean?" Rachel demanded. "I *am* something! I teach graduate classes!"

Dad gave a shout of incredulous laughter. "You wanna try living on that? Maybe you think Brian is going to help out? Wake up, Rachel! That's *life* out there, not trolls and fairies and castles!"

Rachel colored. "His name is Myron," she muttered, dipping her gaze away from him, and dropped her fork onto her plate, her appetite apparently gone.

It was more than Robin could bear. "Jesus, Dad, you are in fine form tonight, aren't you?"

Dad shifted his gaze to Robin, braced himself against the table, and leaned forward. "Just calling them like I see them, Robbie."

"Look, we all know you are feeling terrible, but—"

With a snort of laughter, Dad cut her off. "You have no idea what you are talking about, baby girl."

God, how condescending—she hated when he spoke to her like that. "Don't I? You've been snapping at us for two days now, disapproving of everything we do."

"Well, forgive me if I am a little testy, but I am dying of cancer."

"Dad, you are feeling so bad that you think you can say anything—"

"I *can* say anything!" he roared, slapping his palm against the tabletop so hard that the silver clattered loudly against the china. "I can say whatever I want to say in the short time I have left. I can tell my children that I have ruined them! You're all too weak and self-indulgent to make it without me!"

"Aaron—"

"Don't, Bonnie," he warned her. "I've had enough of her arrogance!" he shouted, gesturing wildly at Robin.

So now suddenly *she* was arrogant? "Oh, that's rich!" Robin said indignantly.

"You don't believe me? It was your damn arrogance that cost us the Herrera account!"

Robin felt the blood drain from her face. She hadn't told him—*Evan*. Dammit! She suddenly came forward, her elbows hitting the cherrywood table. "That is so unfair! Whatever Evan told you, it was a mistake—"

"Your mistake! You were the one playing in London while one of my oldest accounts was trying to get something very basic and very fundamental fixed!"

"I wasn't playing in London, I had gone there to check on two accounts—"

"No, to run away from Evan Iverson, just like you run from all of them—"

Robin gasped. "That is really none of your business, Dad!"

"Well in this case, it is my business, or are you so arrogant you have forgotten even that?"

Robin fell back against her chair, disbelieving. "Dad, when are you going to let me live my life?"

"Right now!" he exclaimed heatedly. "Don't you see? I want you to live, Robbie! I want you to stop running away and take a risk, but I am afraid you are too goddamn full of yourself—"

"*Stop it!*" Mom cried.

"No, Mom, let him go," Robin said, her voice suddenly shaking. "Let him tell me what a rotten daughter I've been, how I've done nothing for the company, how I've failed to give it my all and marry his golden star Evan. Come on, Dad, tell me what a failure I am! And while you are telling me, let me tell you that I have been working around the clock to bring you a new client, one bigger and better than any you have! I've been working like a dog to bring you Atlantic Cargo and Shipping!" she cried, almost shouting in her triumph.

Her announcement stopped Dad cold. He stared at her, inhaled sharply. "Atlantic?" he finally managed in a hoarse whisper. "Oh God, what have you done? Are you insane? Do you even know who Atlantic is?"

"Only the biggest shipping company between here and the Far East," she said smartly, in spite of the terribly cold and sudden feeling of uncertainty. "And they are looking for a new partner in ground transport."

"They are also Canada Shipping and Ocean Transport's biggest competitor. God, Robbie, do you have any idea who pays your salary? Who pays *mine?* Did you ever stop to think who Atlantic's chief competitor might be?"

"What?" she asked weakly, feeling the ground shift beneath her. Beside her, Rebecca muttered something unintelligible; Rachel guzzled her wine. "What do you mean?"

"What I mean," Dad said, suddenly sounding weary, "is the reason we don't have the Atlantic account already is because we have CSOT. When those two ships dock, it just won't do to transport the biggest competitor to our chief client, will it? Why? Because we are a large part of the reason CSOT is so successful, Robin. When they dock, we get their freight to the distributors FASTER AND CHEAPER THAN ATLANTIC!" he roared.

"Oh God," she whispered, stunned that she could have missed something so basic.

Dad pressed his hand to his forehead, seemed to be in pain—physical or emotional, Robin wasn't sure. "I should have taught you," he said miserably. "But I stuck you in a vice presidency and sent you off to Europe to run around and look pretty."

Whoa. Had she heard that that right? He'd sent her to Europe to *look pretty*? "What did you say?"

"Well, surely no harm has been done," Mom said quickly. "I mean, Robbie, you didn't sign anything, did you?"

Stunned, hurt, and whacked right off her pedestal, Robin could hardly think. "No, Mom," she responded impatiently. "I didn't sign anything, but I made certain assurances…oh, never mind, you wouldn't understand—"

"That's exactly what I am talking about!" Dad snapped again. "Arrogant!"

Robin jerked her head up, glared at her father. "If I'm arrogant," she said between clenched teeth, "I learned it from the master." She suddenly shoved to her feet, tossed her napkin aside. "I am so out of here."

"Robin!" Mom exclaimed, coming to her feet, prepared to follow. But Robin was too quick, out the door before

Mom could stop her, spurred on by the pain of her father's disdain.

Behind her, Bonnie bestowed a very heated gaze on Aaron. "You just never seem to get it, do you? You will reap what you sow!" she snapped, and went after Robin.

There was no amount of appeal from her mother that would change Robin's mind to leave Blue Cross Ranch. Robin was sick to death of tiptoeing around him, of watching him wallow in self-pity. She packed quickly, tossed her things into the back of her car, and said a quick good-bye to her sisters, promising to call soon.

She hugged her mom and reluctantly bowed to her pressure to at least say good-bye to Dad. Robin poked her head into the library to tell her sulking father she was leaving, but naturally, he wasn't about to let her go without one last dig, and even that was delivered under the pretense of an apology.

He was sitting in a big leather chair, hunched over. "I shouldn't have yelled," he said instantly. "I know you were trying to help."

"Yeah, well," she muttered, shrugging, uncertain what to say, because she had, apparently, been very wrong. She felt like a monumental fool, a silly little girl playing grown-up games. She could just see Evan's little smirk in her mind's eye, hear him say in that way of his, *I tried to tell you...*

"But I just wish you weren't so arrogant, Robbie," her father continued, shaking Robin loose from any remorse she might have had. "That arrogance costs you too much— just look at your life and tell me it isn't so."

For a moment she could only stare at him, reeling from the pain of his inexplicably complete disapproval, a stinging criticism that had, as far as she was concerned, come out of nowhere. A million things went through her mind, things she should say, things she should definitely not say, but in the end, all she could manage was, "Bye, Dad." And she walked blindly out of the library without looking back, out of his ranch house and to her car, uncertain when—or whether—she might ever see her dad again.

She drove nonstop to Houston, testing the upper bounds of her Mercedes, uncaring about anything except to get as far away from Comfort and Aaron Lear as possible.

She reached Houston after midnight, but she was too keyed up to return to her empty house, especially now, when she was so desperately in need of someone to say she was not a horrible person, that her dad *did* love her, that she meant something to him. And as there was no one at her home to do that, she went instead to her office and made a pot of decaf.

She toyed briefly with the idea of calling Evan, but dismissed the notion quickly. (And what exactly did Dad mean, *running* from Evan? Had Evan said that?) Robin flipped on her computer—there were a dozen new messages since this morning, all of which she bypassed, and went directly to the company's database. As painful as it was, she looked to see how much the rate she had quoted Darren would have undercut CSOT. The two companies, Atlantic and CSOT, had the same distribution lanes, the same class freight, almost the same ports. Yep, she was quoting a couple of cents cheaper per pound to Atlantic. She'd calculated it down to the bare bones trying to land the big fish and had never once thought of CSOT.

Dad was right. She was arrogant. And stupid.

Robin turned off the computer. The ache in her heart had spread to her head, and now, everything hurt. She loved her father, there was no question of that, and she desperately wanted to please him, she never wanted to lose him, but God, she couldn't seem to do *anything* right. The more she thought of the things he had said, the more confused and indignant she became until she could no longer think straight. At two in the morning, with a blinding headache that had turned her mind to mush, she decided to go home and try to sleep.

Robin reached for her bag, plunged her hand inside, rooted around for her keys. When she did not immediately find them, she dumped the contents of her purse onto the desk. She proceeded to sort through lipsticks, change purse, business card holder, passport, cell phone, allergy pills, an old condom (*very* old), until she found them. Keys firmly in hand, she slung the bag over her shoulder and marched out of the office.

The night was warm and muggy, and she rolled down her windows, letting the moist air sweep over her as she made her way toward Loop 610. With the rhythm of rock and roll pounding out over the stereo, she picked up speed, floating around big rigs and old pickups as she went from lane to lane, her car almost driving for her.

The blue-and-red lights behind her startled her; with a gasp, Robin sat up, looked at the speedometer, and groaned. She was only doing seventy-five, give or take— what, was this one of those end-of-month quota things to generate a little extra revenue for the police ball? She coasted onto the shoulder, put her car in park, and watched her side-view mirror as the police officer cautiously approached her, one hand on his gun, staying close to the side of her car.

He paused just outside her peripheral vision and leaned over, peered inside. "Good evening, ma'am. Late night?"

"Seeing as how it is two-fifteen a.m., I guess so," she said irritably and abruptly sat up.

The officer stepped back and grasped the butt of his gun. "I clocked you doing eighty-three in a sixty-five. Is there an emergency?"

Apparently, it was a slow night in Houston. "Look at everyone else out there!" she said sharply, gesturing wildly to the traffic on the loop that was speeding by them in case he hadn't noticed. "Like I am the only one going a little over the speed limit?"

"You were also weaving in and out of traffic. Have you been drinking tonight?"

Oh, if only! Robin gripped the steering wheel and tried to keep check on the explosion she felt building. "No, I have not been drinking. I have been at work."

The officer peered at her. "You haven't had anything to drink?" he asked skeptically.

"No! So if you are through interrogating me, I would like to go home. It's late, I'm tired."

"I need to see some ID."

"So, what, you're going to check me out against your most-wanted files now? Well, be careful, because I am definitely an ax murderer," she snapped and jerked her purse up, reached inside for her wallet...but could not find it. With a sigh of exasperation, she turned the purse upside down and let the contents fall onto the passenger seat.

It wasn't there.

In a moment of sheer panic, she realized she had left her wallet on her desk. "*Oh shit,*" she muttered beneath her breath, felt her pulse jump a notch or two, and turned to look into the blinding light of the officer's flashlight. "You're not going to believe this—"

"You wanna step out of the car?"

The panic filled her throat. "I don't need to get out of the car. This is really ridiculous, sir. I left my wallet in my office, and it had my license and registration—"

The officer opened her door. "Step out of the car. Now."

"*Now* what are we doing?" Robin whined as she reluctantly did as she was told. "Are you allowed to waste my time like this? Isn't this against the law? Okay, so I was going a little fast, so what? Everyone speeds on this loop. Is this the reason the city raises taxes each year? So they can put more cops on the street to keep Houston safe from riffraff like me—"

"Lady, you are about to talk your way into a trip to central booking. Now why don't you put a lid on it and walk around to the back of your car with me?"

Robin followed him, but somewhere between the driver's door and the back bumper of her car, all good sense and reason escaped her, fell right out onto Loop 610 and was flattened beyond recognition by a passing eighteen-wheeler. "This is police harassment!" she said sternly. "You have no right to detain me. If you want to write me a ticket for the dangerous speed of eighty-three, go ahead and do it, but you can't just march me around like this."

"What is your name?"

"If I told you, you'd be sorry. My family is very prominent in Houston, and believe me, they won't be happy that you were harassing me like this—"

"You are trying my patience, miss. Now tell me your name."

"Ha! I won't!" Robin said, knowing, somewhere within the confines of her deadened instinct that it was exactly the wrong answer.

To confirm that it was, the officer smiled, stuffed his ticket book in the back of his pants, and reached for the cuffs dangling from his belt. "Got some bad news for you, Ms. Smart-Ass. You're going to jail—"

"*What?*" Robin cried, jumping away as he reached for her. "You can't arrest me!"

"Oh really? Well try this on for size. I am arresting you for failure to identify and driving without a license or proof of insurance. Take my advice and don't be a complete fool and add a charge of evading arrest to it," he said and grabbed her wrist, slapping a cuff on it.

Robin gaped at the cuff, then at him, disbelieving, as he told her that she had the right to remain silent.

CHAPTER FOUR

Thursday morning, Jake was on the job site at eight a.m. sharp, surprised that he was there before Zaney, the guy he used on most of these jobs. Thinking he was probably stuck in traffic, Jake waited outside for about ten minutes, wanting to make sure Zaney found the place okay. When he got bored with standing on the sidewalk, he decided to stretch his legs and wandered around to the back of the Lear house.

Raymond was already hard at work in the garden he had planted behind the guesthouse and waved Jake over to show him tomatoes as big as softballs. Suitably impressed, Jake had a look around at the rest of the produce, and when Raymond offered to sack some up, he said, very cool. Particularly since Jake didn't really have any food in his house at the moment. After paying taxes and insurance this month, he'd come up a little short.

He put the sack Raymond filled in a saddlebag on his bike and checked the time. Nine o'clock and still no Zaney. Okay, now he was officially worried. His old pal had suffered a head injury a few years ago working on an oil rig, and since then, he could be pretty dumb at times. But he was as steady as the day was long, and when he was *this* late, well...Jake dug out his cell phone and started to make some calls.

So this was what the proverbial rock bottom looked like, and Robin had splattered herself all over it.

It was humiliating enough to have been brought in at all, much less wearing handcuffs. But then they took all of her belongings, including her belt, made her spread her legs so a female guard could pat her down, and when she was completely traumatized, they took her picture, fingerprinted her, and told her to quit whining; she was not going to see the sheriff, she was going to see a judge. Okay, she had said then, fully contrite for her folly, I give, let me out.

They said they would—if and when a judge said so.

And then they showed her the holding cell into which they had managed to defy physics and force at least a dozen women. Robin's bathroom was bigger than that cell. It was a nightmare, a bona fide, unmistakable nightmare, complete with bodies under the benches and scary monster-type-looking humans, and she had no one to blame but herself. And damn it, Robin could not stop shivering—they had turned the air-conditioning on to a full-metal-jacket high, undoubtedly to keep the stench down. How long she sat there, she had no idea, and wouldn't have been the least surprised if days had passed, maybe even weeks, until the door was at last pushed open and a guard came waddling in. "All right, ladies—time to go. You know the drill, everyone on their feet!"

Well, no, she didn't know the drill, but Robin surged to her feet nonetheless, crowding with the others to get out of that stuffy little room.

They were led to an open area with chairs and a bank of phones along one wall and told to make their calls. Robin went to a phone, picked up the receiver, grimaced at the greasy feel of it, and debated whom to call. *Oh, hi, this is Robin,* *and I'm in jail...*Her attorney? Seemed logical, but no—she was also Evan's attorney. Mia? Right—she didn't answer the phone before noon. Lucy? Well, sure, if she wanted it spread all over Houston. Kelly, Mariah, Linda, Susan—God, no! Her CPA? He'd probably have a heart attack.

That left only one viable option.

Grimacing, Robin dialed her grandparents' number, praying to high heaven they hadn't gone off on some trailer trip. Grandma answered the phone on the first ring. "Hel-*lo*-oh!" she sang.

"Grandma, it's me," she said low.

"Oh, hi, honey!" Grandma said cheerfully. "What are you up to?"

"Grandma, now don't freak out, okay? I need you to come pick me up. Or get a lawyer—not *my* lawyer, but...oh hell, I'm not really sure *what* I need you to do—"

"A lawyer!" Grandma gasped. "Why on earth would you need a lawyer? And what is all that racket?"

"It's a really long and stupid story Grandma, but...okay, listen, I'm sort of in a bind. You shouldn't panic or anything, because like I said, it's reallyreally stupid—"

"Where *are* you, Robbie?" Grandma asked, her voice going shrill.

There was no good way to say it. Robin forced a laugh. "You won't believe this, Grandma! Ha haaaa, I'm...I'm...in jail.

They probably heard her grandmother's shriek throughout the entire retirement community. "*Jail!*" she cried out. "*Jail?* Oh no, not *jail!* Elmer! Robbie is in *jaaaail!*"

Robin heard the receiver on her grandmother's end bounce on the phone table. "Grandma!" she cried into the phone.

"Robbie, is that you?"

Thank God, Grandpa! "Yes, yes, it's me, Grandpa! Is Grandma all right?"

"Are you really in jail?"

"Yes, I—"

"Oh yeah? What'd you do?"

"I didn't really *do*—"

"Drugs?"

"*Grandpa!* Of course it wasn't drugs!"

"Well then, what? Murder?" He chuckled appreciatively at his own jest. Robin stared at the phone cradle in front of her. Why hadn't she realized before this crucial moment that her grandparents were insane? "Oh dear, it wasn't *murder,* was it?" he asked, his voice suddenly anxious.

"Of course not!" she cried. "It's too long to explain now, but Grandpa, *please* come get me. This place is horrible! Everyone smells, and who knows *why* they are here, and the guards are just...just *mean,* and I have no idea how long they will hold me or anything, but please, please come get me," she said, feeling suddenly and dangerously close to tears.

"Well, of course we'll come get you, Robbie-girl! You just hold tight. We're gonna come get you."

"Thanks, Grandpa," she whispered tearfully, and heard him shout at Grandma to hurry up as the phone clicked off.

Feeling a little better having called in the cavalry, Robin endured another interminable wait until they were led, single file, into another long room where a judge's bench was elevated above the rows of wooden benches. They formed two groups, men and women on opposite sides of the room. Now Robin was feeling particularly slimy. The last seventy-two hours had been a personal trip through hell, and all she wanted was out—she had never felt so alone or so vulnerable or so insane in her life. What sort of moron picked a fight with a cop?

She shivered. They waited. She wondered what time it was, had that slow and thick feeling of having flown through too many time zones on a long transatlantic flight. When at last the judge did arrive, Robin was surprised; the diminutive African American probably didn't reach five feet.

The bailiff announced Judge Vaneta Jobe and told them all to rise. Judge Jobe climbed up onto her big black highback leather chair, and with her head barely visible, and her feet probably swinging a foot above ground, let her gaze travel the crowd. "All right then," she said, slipping on a pair of round, silver-framed glasses. "Listen up, everyone. Y'all have some rights you'll need to know about..." She proceeded to inform them, in a booming voice that belied her size, of their rights and the different types of bonds available to them. Then she announced she would bring them forward to hear the charges being made against them, and when she had finished her speech, she asked, "Is that just clear as mud? Let's begin, Mr. Peeples."

The bailiff picked up a sheet and squinted at it. "Rodney Trace."

A man from the third row of benches stood and came forward, his head hung low. When he approached the bench, Judge Jobe glared down at him. "Seems like you gone and done a stupid thing, Mr. Trace. How many times are you gonna be stupid? Until you kill someone? Or until they send you down to the farm?"

Rodney Trace shrugged.

Judge Jobe sighed. "Bail set at twenty-five thousand dollars. Who's next on our hit parade, Mr. Peeples?"

Horrified, Robin watched as Judge Jobe and a long string of people who alternately tried to argue their charge or took whatever bond she set with a shrug. She was beginning to feel less and less optimistic about what would happen to her, and started like a jumping bean when the bailiff finally called her name. She hurried forward, clasped her hands tightly in front of her, and tried very hard not to shiver.

The judge leaned over the bench to have a better look at her, shaking her head. "Urn, um, um...don't know *what's* got into you, girlfriend," she said, and picked up a manila folder. "Do you think this town belongs to you?"

Was she supposed to answer that? Robin glanced uneasily at the bailiff. "Uh...no," she stammered. "No, of course not."

"Then why were you so nasty to Officer Denton?"

"I, uh...I d-didn't know that I was."

The judge peered over the tops of her round glasses at Robin. "You trying to tell me that you didn't know you were mouthing off to him? Or that you were being nasty? Or that by refusing to give him your name, or provide your license, or proof of insurance, that you were being disrespectful? Is that the way you do people, Ms. Lear?"

"No..."

"*No?*"

"Uh, yes...well, no," Robin stuttered.

The judge snorted, looked at the bailiff. "Ms. Lear got herself an attitude problem, Mr. Peeples. That superior attitude got her into a little bit of trouble, didn't it?"

"It sure did, Your Honor."

"I'm surprised Ms. Lear managed to make it this long before someone knocked her down a notch or two." The judge tossed the file down and bestowed a fierce frown on Robin that sent another shiver down her spine. "You need to wake up and smell the coffee! How many of your fine and fancy friends get themselves thrown in jail for talking trash?"

"I...I don't know any," Robin answered truthfully.

"Maybe that's 'cause they don't go around thinking they're better than everyone else. If you're gonna walk around thinking you are, you're gonna keep making trouble for yourself, do you understand me?"

"I don't think I'm better—"

"I said, do you understand me?" Judge Jobe demanded.

"Yes, ma'am," Robin answered softly.

"I'm gonna accept your plea of guilty for driving without a license or insurance and fine you seven hundred fifty dollars for wasting my time."

Robin blinked. When exactly, had she pled guilty?

"Now follow the deputy here, and try not to be annoying," the judge said and handed the deputy a piece of paper. He pointed toward the door; Robin walked, head down.

And found herself waiting in another large room after she had received her personal property, which consisted of a belt, a Cartier watch, an emerald ring, and a half-empty purse, in which, fortunately, there had been a lone credit card in the side pocket. The very helpful deputies also gave her a paper with the location of her car and pointed to the window where she would pay her fine along with everyone else in Houston.

Robin made the mistake of asking the clerk when she could pay, which earned her a reprimand to be seated while the clerk and her friend chatted away as if they had nothing else to do. Dejected, exhausted, and feeling terribly low, Robin sat, wondering if it were possible to get a bazooka in here to break up their little coffee klatch. Her head ached, her back ached, even her butt ached from sitting for so many hours on rock-hard benches like the one on which she was sitting now. She felt grimy, her mouth tasted rank, and her stomach was in knots. All she wanted to do was go home and burrow under the covers of her bed for the next five months.

She waited.

Until someone sat hard next to her, jostling her almost off the bench, that she realized she must have been drifting on the edge of sleep. With a jump, Robin blinked, looked to her left. A man with impossibly broad shoulders had fallen onto the bench next to her. He was wearing a weathered leather jacket and faded jeans, had a crop of thick, dark brown hair, and when he turned to look at Robin, he smiled and said with a wink, "Hey."

"Get real," she muttered, and scooched over.

"Oh come on, it can't be *that* bad," he remarked, as if they were sitting in a park somewhere.

"What would you know?"

"Okay, so I'm sorry. I didn't mean to bump into you. Truce?"

She really was not in the mood to make friends just now. With her hand, she gestured for him to move. "Just...please go away."

"Believe me, lady, I'd love to oblige you," he said, his voice less friendly, "but in case you haven't noticed, it's pretty crowded in here."

"You can find another seat."

"Maybe *you'd* like to find another seat. I've been waiting two hours."

Only two hours? How did he get out so fast? That infuriated Robin—she had to wait all night, and this dude was out in two hours? "I was here first," she pointed out.

"Ah," he said, nodding. "Clearly, I misunderstood." But instead of moving, he just settled in.

Robin glared at him. "What do you think you are doing?"

"Like I said, the room is full, so unless you can produce a deed or something that proves you own this bench, I'm not going anywhere."

"Great," Robin snapped, and abruptly stood up.

"Nice talking to you, Miss Congeniality," he said as she started to push her way down the row.

Three or four seats down, she glared at two Hispanic men who, after exchanging a wary glance with one another, moved to make a seat for her.

She squished in between them like a sardine, then glanced down the row just as the jailbird got up and sauntered off. Bastard! But Lord…what a saunter that bastard had! Even in her dejected, repulsed, and generally miserable state, Robin could not help noticing how fine he was in his ancient denim jeans and briefly wondered what he might have done to land himself in hell.

He suddenly turned and caught her staring at his backside and flashed her a lopsided *knew-it* smile. Robin frowned deeply, turned her attention forward, and did not look again. Except once. Maybe twice. By the time they finally called her name, she had definitely lost sight of him and was in such a hurry to get out of that stinking hellhole that she almost collided with him when she turned from the window, clutching her freedom on a receipt marked PAID.

"Oh *man*. Well, hello again, Sunshine," he drawled.

"Jesus!" she exclaimed, holding the hand with the receipt over her flailing heart as she glared up at him. "Can't you take a hint?"

"Hey, Queenie, I'm just waiting in line like everyone else."

"Uh-huh, right," Robin responded irritably and wondered for a split second why men thought women were so ignorant of their motives.

The man all but choked. He stared down at her, his copperbrown eyes wide with surprise. And then he laughed. *Laughed.* Laughed so roundly, as if that was so hilariously preposterous, that several heads turned in their direction. But he didn't seem to care—he leaned forward, bent his head until his mouth was just an inch or two from her cheek, and said, "Sunshine, you're cute"—he paused, lingered there for a tiny moment, his breath warm on her face, so close that she could smell his cheap (but not altogether unpleasant) cologne—"but no way are you *that* cute. And you're *mean*." He straightened up and calmly stepped around her to the payment window.

Okay. Well. She was now officially in hell. Some...*jail guy*...had just dissed her, and it was so unbearably humiliating that Robin beat a hasty retreat out the double glass doors, into the lobby of the processing center, clutching her purse and her receipts like a mad escapee, frantically searching the milling crowd for her grandparents.

Fortunately, her mother's parents were easy to spot. There was her grandfather, who had the distinct misfortune to have been named Elmer, and the even greater misfortune, in his declining years, of actually resembling Elmer. He was round and squat with hugely enormous feet typically encased in white Easy Spirits, which heralded his arrival a good city block before him. And in fact, it was Mr. Fudd's shoes Robin saw in the lobby before she saw him.

Her grandmother, Lil, was the physical opposite of Elmer. She was tall and reed thin, and wore big pink-rimmed octagonal glasses that covered her cheeks and eyebrows and made her eyes look like big blue stop signs. She also wore Easy Spirits. The taupe ones.

Grandma spotted Robin and came hurrying like a squirrel across the lobby, darting in and around people in her haste to get to her granddaughter. "Robbie!" she exclaimed, and grabbed her in a bear hold, nearly squeezing the breath from her. "Oh my *God*, sweet pea! What has *happened*!"

"Robbie-girl, you all right?" Grandpa asked, rescuing her from Grandma's grip.

"I'm fine," Robin insisted. "It's really so stupid. I'll tell you all about it in the car, but please, let's just get out of here," she urged, ushering them in the direction of the door.

Grandpa had scored a prime parking spot into which he had maneuvered his Ford Excursion, an SUV the size of a small condo. Robin gratefully crawled into the cavernous backseat.

"Buckle in, hon. Now, are we going to hear what you did?" Grandma insisted, fastening her seat belt.

Best to get it over. "I got stopped for speeding—"

"Speeding! Where?" Grandpa insisted.

"On six-ten—"

"Well now, six-ten, that's just a death trap."

"—And I guess I sort of mouthed off a little. I mean, I wasn't doing any faster than anyone else, and I told the cop so."

"That's my girl!" Grandpa said proudly as he coasted out of the parking lot.

"So he asked me for my license and registration, but the thing is, I had left them on my desk at work—by the way, Grandpa, I need to go by my office and get my wallet, okay? Anyway, I didn't have my license or registration, and suddenly I'm a criminal! So the cop told me to step out of the car, and...well, I just thought...I just thought that he was overreacting and I shouldn't have to step out of the car."

"Well, he should have taken your word for it!" Grandma said with an indignant nod of her head. "Surely when you told him your name he ran some sort of check or whatever they do in their cars to make sure you weren't lying!"

Robin squirmed.

Grandma swiveled sharply to look at her. "Well?" demanded Grandma. "Didn't he?"

Robin sighed, leaned her head against a headrest covered with a pink baby T-shirt. "I was really tired and really cranky, and I didn't exactly tell him who I was. I just sort of thought it wasn't his business. So he arrested me."

Grandpa gave a shout of laughter, but Grandma threw a hand over her mouth and stared at Robin in horror for a moment. "Can they *do* that?"

"Apparently," she answered dryly. "He arrested me for failure to identify myself, driving without a license, and driving without insurance."

"Oh my goodness, what does this *mean?*" Grandma asked.

Robin grimaced at her grandmother's look of shock and turned away, to the window, where cars were swerving from behind Grandpa and whizzing past as he pushed the SUV up to sixty. "It means they slapped me with a Class C misdemeanor, took seven hundred fifty dollars for their trouble, and told me to go home."

"Did you see any murderers in there?" Grandpa asked.

"*Elmer!* This is no joking matter!"

"I didn't think that was joking!"

"Grandpa, don't forget to go by my office, okay?"

Grandpa acknowledged her request by putting his blinker on a good two or three miles before their exit.

"Well, you can't work today," Grandma said in a huff. "You don't want everyone knowing why you were late— Aaron wouldn't like that at all."

Honestly, Robin didn't know anymore. Maybe Dad would think she deserved to be publicly humiliated. "I just need to get my things and a couple of files, that's all. Maybe Grandpa can go in for me," Robin said absently.

"I just can't believe you have been *arrested*," Grandma said and shook her head again.

Too exhausted to think, Robin stared out the window, felt her eyelids growing heavy. The next thing she heard was Grandpa, saying, "Uh-oh. Looks like a fire."

Robin opened her eyes and glanced out the front windshield. As her mind began to grasp that they were on the street of her office, she suddenly grabbed the back of Grandpa's seat. "*Oh my God!*" she cried. It couldn't be. *Couldn't be!* Robin quickly counted the floors of her office building and felt her heart sink to her toes. Oh yes, it could be, and it was. The LTI offices were on fire. *Her* office was on fire.

In front of her, Grandpa shook his head. "Some fool probably left a cigarette burning or a computer on or something like that," he opined, disgusted.

Left something on... the suggestion was suddenly clawing at Robin's throat, choking her. *The coffeepot.*

She had left the coffeepot on.

CHAPTER FIVE

Grandma found Lucy in the growing crowd on the street and ascertained that everyone was accounted for and all right, and further, that the fire was contained to the LTI offices. Relieved that at least she hadn't killed anyone, Robin begged Grandpa to take her home before anyone started nosing around.

Exactly how her world had suddenly disintegrated into so many little pieces was so far beyond her ability to comprehend that by the time Grandpa eased into the circular drive in front of her house, she was seriously contemplating a trip to the roof of some downtown building and a swan dive off the side. Her father, her job, her arrest, her *office*—God, she was living in a soap opera! She would not be surprised if Maury Povich leapt out from behind the bushes to inform her she was pregnant with her lover's cousin's nephew.

As it was, she practically had to arm wrestle Grandma to keep her from coming in.

"You need to call your mom and let her know you're all right," Grandma said. "We'll come in with you—"

"I'll call, I promise!" Robin said, and dove out the door, slammed it shut, and popped in front of Grandma's window before anyone could take one Easy-Spirited step toward her house. "Right now, I just want to take a bath and crawl into bed and sleep until the next century. Okay?"

Grandma sighed with exasperation; Grandpa waved. "Okeydokey!" he said cheerfully. "We'll check on you later."

"Thanks," Robin murmured and stepped away from the tank as Grandpa checked his side-view mirror before carefully nudging into gear. He turned his attention to navigating the rather wide drive as Grandma hung out the window. "Take an aspirin!" she shouted. "It will help you—"

Who knows what else she might have said—Grandpa suddenly swerved, knocking Grandma back inside the tank.

When Robin was sure they were gone, she headed for the back of the house. Her car was still impounded (another helpful clerk had informed her that for a mere one hundred fifty dollars, she could get her car on Monday), and she had no keys. But at one point, she'd had the presence of mind to hide a key for an event such as this. Only she'd figured such an event would involve fabulous shoes, a man, and a smashing good evening. Now all she had to do was remember under which brick she had hid the damn thing.

As she was attempting to dislodge a brick, she heard a motorcycle roar into her drive and looked up.

Her heart climbed right into her throat; she was momentarily paralyzed by her astonishment. But once she got over her distraction of the thick, dark brown hair he revealed as he removed his do-rag, and the tight fit of his jeans, and the vague feeling that she knew him, she suddenly gave a small shriek of surprised indignation that this...this *sexual pervert predator* had followed her all the way from the jail to her house!

The man stuffed his do-rag into his back pocket, reached into a leather saddlebag, and turned his head. His eyes locked with hers—"Oh *Gawwwd*," he groaned heavenward.

It was the degenerate jailbird all right, and if *this* just wasn't the topping on her cake, Robin didn't know what was. "Un-be-*leeev*-able!"

"Looks like we find ourselves nose to nose again, Sunshine," he said as Robin found the lose brick and yanked it clean of its slot, then grabbed the key. "You remember me, right? The guy you harassed this morning?"

"Ha!" she shouted, clutching the key. "*You* were harassing *me*!"

"Funny, I remember that you were the one who copped a negative attitude."

"Look, I don't know what ridiculous, drug-induced little world you are living in, but I am not interested." She fumbled with the key and the lock while the degenerate opened a saddlebag and rummaged inside. "Let me spell it out for you," she continued. "Ain't gonna happen! So get on your dirtbike and run along before I call the cops!"

His face clouded; he frowned at her like she was the one doing the annoying here. "That is not a dirtbike. You know what?" he demanded as Robin managed to unlock the door, push it open, jump through, and pivot to block his entrance. "You are so full of yourself it's a wonder you don't pop! Trust me, I don't like this any more than you do—"

"Don't *like*—you have nerve! You are following me!"

"*Following?* Oh Jesus—" he moaned, rolled his eyes, and started walking toward her. "You *are* delusional! Believe me, darlin', you are the very last person I would follow!"

Robin was about to respond with equal vigor, but the sack of Krispy Kremes under his arm momentarily distracted her. *Krispy Kremes?* She blinked, disbelieving. So he thought he'd just casually follow her to her house and do whatever perverts did? With doughnuts? "What the hell? So you, the pervert, were in jail for God knows what, and you saw me there, and you decided to follow me—"

"Have you escaped from your nurse?"

"Me? You're the jailbird—"

"If there is a jailbird here, it would be you—"

"I was there by mistake! Are you trying to deny that you were not just in a room with every other lowlife in Houston being released from county jail?" she demanded, infuriated.

"Well now, you might be a lowlife, but not everyone in that room was a criminal. I was there to bail out a friend who happened to have had a little too much to drink last night. His name is Zaney—perhaps you met him during your stay in cell block C?"

Robin opened her mouth, then closed it, confused by the sack of doughnuts. "Wait a minute. Then what..." Something suddenly clicked, and Robin felt her self-assurance begin to crumble like sand. "*Oh no,*" she murmured to herself.

"You really need to get over yourself, you know that?" he added.

"Oh my God—*oh my God!* You *can't* be!"

"Believe me, I wish I weren't. Look, I gotta get to work. Know what work is, or do you spend most of your time in the pokey?" he grumbled as he pushed past her, into the house.

The tears started to build behind Robin's eyes as she gaped at Jacob Manning's back, the man she had hired to renovate her house.

The amount of time Jake Manning spent renovating the houses of strangers exposed him to some of the more colorful characters Houston had to offer, but at that moment, he had to believe Robin Lear had cornered the market on lunatics. How a woman could take an accidental jostling and accelerate that all the way up to pervert was beyond him. And to discover that she was the barracuda who had hired him to practically take down her house and put it up again was just not what he needed to hear right at the moment. The day had started badly enough what with having to bail Zaney out of jail. Now this. Jesus H. Christ.

"What are the odds?" the barracuda blurted behind him. "I can't believe this!"

Well, believe it, baby, Jake thought as he walked in and slapped the doughnuts down on the dining room table. He damn sure didn't like it any more than she did. He grabbed his tool belt, was putting it on as he turned and brushed past her again on his way to the kitchen.

"This is just too much," she continued, following him into the kitchen. "I am being punished for something." She stalked to a cabinet, yanked it open, and studied the insides for a moment. "Well, whatever. I can't deal with this right now. You can't work here today."

"Whoa, wait—are you talking to me?" he asked, incredulous.

She turned abruptly to look at him. "You're going to have to go."

"Ooh no." She might be a lunatic, but she'd signed a damn contract. "No way," he said, shaking his head. "*You* were the one who insisted on a start date of this week. I juggled three jobs to accommodate you, and I'm already behind. I can't afford to lose a whole day."

"But I need to sleep."

"Well, sleep away, sleep until the next century for all I care. I won't bother you." He meant that sincerely. In fact, he'd lock her in the bedroom to make them both feel better.

She shifted her gaze to the cabinet again. "Am I in hell? Is this hell?" she asked the cabinet, her voice noticeably smaller.

Jake was about to suggest that perhaps he was the one in hell, but was startled by the realization that her chin was suddenly trembling. Trembling like she was about to cry. Before he could react, before he could bolt for the door and run screaming into the street, she turned big, wet blue eyes to him, blinking rapidly as she tried to keep tears from spilling. "I don't have any coffee."

That was definitely not what he expected her to say. Jake blinked, confused, "What?"

"I don't have any coffee!" she shouted at him and began to cry. *Cry.* As in a river. Torrents of tears were suddenly washing down her face, and she collapsed, cross-legged, like a rag doll onto the kitchen floor and buried her face in her hands, sobbing. The woman he had pegged as potentially the biggest ballbuster this side of New York was suddenly blubbering all over the place.

"Yo, hey," he said, laughing nervously to hide his sudden and intense discomfort. Women and tears—nothing could undo him faster than that, and he felt it coming at him like a bullet train. "Hey...hey there...uh...*hey.*" He waved his hand at her, only she didn't see it, as her face was buried in her hands.

"Is it too much to ask?" she sobbed. "A lousy cup of coffee? This has been the *worst* day of my life! No wait, the worst *night*! No, oh no, why stop there? The worst *weeeeek*!"

Good God. "Might not be so bad if you'd just ratchet that throne of yours down a notch or two," he offered helpfully.

She groaned. "I know, I know. Sorry," she muttered grudgingly into her hands, and damn it if she didn't almost sound sorry. But she kept crying.

"You know, I could go get you some coffee," Jake offered reluctantly, mentally kicking himself the moment the words were out of his mouth.

The sobbing suddenly stopped on a strangled snort. She sniffed loudly, lifted her head, and rubbed her hand vigorously under her nose. "You would?" she asked with a soft hiccup. "You would do that for me after I was so…so…"

"So rude and obnoxious?"

"Yeah."

He sighed wearily. Truthfully, he'd be doing Greater Houston a favor if he brought her something to help wash down her meds, because he was certain there was a boatload of them somewhere with her name written all over them. "Yeah. Yeah, I'll go."

She considered him with big blue eyes. "But there's nothing on this street."

"No problem." Well, not huge, anyway. "I'll find something. Won't take a minute." Assuming there was a convenience store nearby. Which there wasn't. *Damn.*

But then Robin Lear surprised him by smiling. Not just any smile, but one of those sweet female smiles. Up until that moment, he would have sworn she was incapable. "That would be *sooo* nice, you don't even know!"

Jake took an unconscious step backward, uncertain if her fragile hold on this sudden happiness would take. "Well...okay, then. I'll be back in a few."

She startled him by suddenly coming to her feet and moving toward him. "I lost my wallet. I don't have any cash—"

"Hey, it's on me," he said, quickening his step so that he might reach the door before she reached him, flinging his tool belt onto the counter without breaking stride.

"Thank you," she said sweetly. "You're a lifesaver."

God, he hoped it wouldn't come to that. He stepped through the door and walked briskly down the path to his bike.

"Mr. Manning?"

Jake risked a look over his shoulder.

She was standing in the doorway, her head poked out around the jamb to look at him. "Colombian, instead of Sumatran. I mean, if they have it. If they ask you, you could just say, Columbian."

"Ah...sure."

"And maybe a double mocha?"

Was that a 7-Eleven brand? Seeing as how his drink of choice was Mountain Dew, he rarely paid attention to the coffee bar in those stores, but he nodded all the same.

Robin Lear took a step outside.

Jake frantically shoved his hand into his pocket and tried to grab his keys at the same time he straddled his bike.

"Honestly? A skinny decaffeinated Colombian double mocha latte steamed and with nutmeg instead of chocolate would be *great*." She smiled.

Was this chick for *real*? "Just one question," Jake said. "Want me to handpick the beans, or can we just leave that to Juan Valdez and the donkey?" Before she could answer, Jake quickly revved his bike loud and long and took off so he couldn't hear even a single word from that woman's lips.

Double mocha was not a 7-Eleven coffee. When he paid for his soda, the clerk looked at him like he was an idiot and pointed him toward Java the Hut, "a couple of blocks" down.

Only a couple of blocks turned out to be several. By the time Jake found Java the Hut, he had forgotten the coffee instructions. "Colombian double chocolate," he said.

"*Dude!*" the guy at the register exclaimed as he scratched around the earring in his nose. "Colombian double chocolate what?"

"Whatever you got. With nutmeg," he said, proud that he'd remembered that, anyway. When he emerged at least a quarter of an hour later (the double chocolates had to wait behind everyone else, apparently) with his extra-wide whatever wrapped securely in a heat-containing cardboard sleeve, he was acutely conscious of how much additional time he'd lost in the course of being a good guy. He arrived in something of a huff at the house on North Boulevard a full forty minutes after he had walked out the door, no thanks to Miss Double Trouble Mocha, and paused now to listen for any signs of out-and-out insanity. Hearing none, he rapped lightly on the door.

No answer.

Jake knocked again for good measure, and when she didn't answer, opened the door and cautiously peeked inside. It appeared empty.

Very carefully, he stepped inside, looked around. Maybe she'd left. Well, hell, she might have at least left a note since he'd gone to so much trouble to get her a hot chocolate thing. With a sigh of exasperation, he walked through the kitchen to the dining table and set the coffee down.

That was when he noticed his doughnuts were missing. Not missing, as in disappeared, but missing as in eaten. There was only one of the five plain glazed doughnuts he had brought for his midmorning snack and a few glazed crumbs.

He was still trying to absorb how a woman as svelte as Robin Lear could consume so many doughnuts—without even asking, for Pete's sake—when he heard a noise that sounded remarkably like a snore. Jake looked down the hall, toward the bedroom, the only other furnished room in the house.

There it was again.

He walked quietly down the corridor, cautiously approaching the open bedroom door, and as he neared it, he could hear the sound of someone in the throes of a very deep sleep. He paused at one side of the open door, his back to the wall (just in case), then leaned over slowly and peeked inside.

Robin Lear was lying, facedown, atop the brocade coverlet on her bed, her arms flung wide. Her feet hung off the end and her hair was a mess of wet curls. But even more startling, she wore—and Jake had to look carefully to make sure he wasn't seeing things—red pajamas covered in dozens of Curious George heads. Yep, that was Curious George, all right. But just his head(s).

Robin didn't hear him, and in fact, he rather doubted she would have heard a nuclear blast in the adjoining bathroom. The barracuda was dead to the world, and he couldn't help worry for a moment that she might suffocate, facedown as she was, but then she moved and turned her head to rest on one cheek instead of her face. It struck him then that in sleep, with her mouth shut, the ballbuster was actually a very pretty woman.

Satisfied that she would live to call him a pervert again, Jake quietly pulled the door to. Figuring he had some time before the monster awoke, Jake returned to the entry, where he proceeded to lay tarps, silently cursing Chuck Zaney's name. Zaney had been his best friend since high school—they had played baseball together until Jake had gone on to the minors and Zaney had gone to the oil fields. When a torn Achilles tendon ended any hope he had of playing professional ball, Jake had gotten a job in construction.

He'd landed in the restoration and renovation business by accident, but one job led to another, and before long, he had enough to occupy himself full-time. It was a little lean now and again (now), but he was steadily building a business.

Then Zaney fell off a rig one day and landed on his head. No lie, the dude had landed on his head and had lived to tell about it. The only problem was, his brain was stuck somewhere between 1975 and 1996, and no one wanted to hear about the Clinton years. Jake had taken him on to help out a friend. It had been tough going at first, but he'd eventually discovered that once Zaney knew a task, he could do it well. He just wasn't your go-to guy on something new.

Last night, Zaney had gone out for a few beers after work. He ended up, he'd told Jake at the detention facility this morning, at one of their old haunts on the east side of Houston, and had managed to get himself into a fight over a game of pool. In addition to a charge for public intoxication (for which Jake had bailed him out) and a mean hangover (for which Jake had given him two aspirin), Zaney had severely sprained his right arm (for which Jake had dropped him at the clinic).

Jake could not bear to think how far behind he was going to fall without Zaney. He tried to concentrate on the work in front of him. He was carefully removing years and layers of paint from these old brick walls, a tedious process that allowed him to save any gems of paper or paint he might find beneath the surface. Today, the work was made all the more tedious by the shrill beep of the answering machine picking up calls for Robin Lear.

The first call came from a guy named Evan who sounded totally gay to Jake. "Robin, it's Evan. Pick up if you are there."

"Robin won't be picking up anything for a while, pal," Jake muttered.

"Robbie, are you all right?" the guy asked breathlessly into the answering machine. "I heard about the fire, and I'm worried sick about you. Look, just call me, okay? I need to know you're okay. Call me."

Fire? That piqued Jake's interest. Maybe she was arrested because she started a fire. That was an intriguing thought. A sexy arsonist...

The next call came from a woman who sounded like she soaked her Wheaties in Tabasco sauce every morning. "Where the hell are you, Robin? *Jesus*, you would not believe the calls the yard is getting about the fire!"

Must have been some fire.

"Everyone wants to know where you are, including me, thank you! Your grandma said you looked like hell—were you out drinking last night? Evan has called three times now and says he's coming down tomorrow, so I booked him in at the Four Seasons, but they're having a wedding or something and he can't get his usual room, so he was all upset about that. Oh yeah, and Darren somebody from Atlantic? He's called twice and wants you to call him as soon as possible. I told him about the fire, and he acted like I was bothering him. Man, where *are* you? I'm at the yard, and you know that guy, Albert? He—"

The answering machine clicked off, stayed silent for a while. Jake became engrossed in his work, digging through four layers of paint to old brick that was good quality, antique vintage.

The phone rang again. "Umm, hey, Robin…Bill Platthaus here. I'm back in New York. Long flight." There was a pregnant pause; Jake picked up the Code Red he'd bought at 7-Eleven to wash down his doughnuts, waiting for the Platypus guy to ask about the fire. "Uh, listen, Robin, I have been trying to get hold of you for over a week now…" He paused again, laughed nervously. "You know, I'm starting to wonder if maybe you don't want to talk to me? I'm probably just imagining things, huh?"

Jake rolled his eyes, downed half the Code Red, and put it down. "You're not imagining things, pal," Jake said. "Consider yourself extremely lucky, because you have dodged a bullet."

"Listen, I'd really appreciate it if you would give me a call. I'll be home tonight. Let me make sure you have that number. 212-555-9249—"

"Don't wait up," Jake added, and wondered, as the guy repeated the number again, why he was not surprised that double-trouble mocha mama had a bunch of guys on a string.

The Platypus guy had hardly hung up the phone when it was ringing again. "Robbie, it's your grandpa. You're not in jail again, are you?" Grandpa laughed roundly at his own joke. "Well, I talked to the police, and they say it looks like the fire was probably an accident, so I guess no one was trying to kill you. Okay. Bye now."

Big surprise there. But at least it explained the fire.

It was almost a half hour before the next call came. "Robin, it's Bec. Hey, Mom said your office burned down and you were arrested for hitting an officer! God, what are you *doing*? Listen, I know you are having a bad day, but I really need to talk to you. Bud is already gone! That asshole didn't have the decency to wait until I got home, just left Grayson with his mom—"

The sound of a large object crashing onto the floor in the bedroom covered up whatever else sister Bec might have said, as well as a string of very colorful profanities. Another crash, then Robin's muffled shout. "Rebecca, are you there? Hey, I did not *hit* an officer! God, is that what Grandma is telling everyone?"

The shouting was suddenly crystal clear as the door to the bedroom was flung open, and Robin Lear emerged in her pajamas, her hair a riot of dark walnut–colored corkscrew curls spinning off in every direction. Oblivious to Jake, Robin and dozens of Curious Georges marched blindly down the corridor to the dining table, ear to the phone. "God, *no*, of course not!" she cried, falling into a chair. "I just sort of mouthed off to him, and—I was not drinking! Why does everyone keep asking me that?" She vigorously scratched her head.

Jake lowered his brush, aware that he was unable to keep from looking at her as she exclaimed at the fine of seven hundred fifty dollars for driving without a license or insurance. She was, admittedly, a very attractive woman in a wild, Curious George sort of way. She had slender feet, bright red toenails, and elegant hands. Her hair, while a little on the enormously untamed side, was actually very becoming on her, framing her ivory skin in dark brown curls. And her eyes were electric blue, which also seemed fitting, the lashes dark and thick, and her lips...well now, *those* were a pair of lips.

He watched her as she talked on the phone, still oblivious to him, her free hand slicing and dicing savagely into space as she expounded on her night in jail. Somehow, the conversation shifted to Bec's woes with someone named Bud. Robin listened intently, squinting at the wall in front of her, exclaiming over and over again, without hesitation, that Bud was a huge prick. And then her voice changed again, to a soft, almost vulnerable voice, and she asked nervously, "How's Dad?" Whatever she heard seemed to sadden her. Her shoulders slumped; she nodded, finally said, "I know. Yeah, I know."

But Jake had the strong feeling that she really *didn't* know, and against his better judgment, he felt a little sorry for her.

When Robin finally said good-bye, she carefully placed the phone down, rubbed her fists in her eyes, and looked up. That was when she saw him standing there, and she blinked, surprised. "What are you doing?"

"Working."

She blinked again, nodded as that registered somewhere in her brain. After a moment, she asked, "Where's
my coffee?"

"Where are my doughnuts?"

She gave him a sheepish smile. "Okay, sorry about that.
But I only had a couple. I was starving! Anyway, that was
hours ago."

Like the coffee wasn't? "You ate more than a couple. You
ate four."

"*Four?*" she exclaimed, shocked. "Ohmigod, how many
calories is that? Wait! What time *is* it?"

Confused, Jake glanced at his watch. "Quarter to five."

"Oh *jeeeez.*" She sighed and ran her hands through her
curls, making them look even bigger. "Shouldn't you be
wrapping it up for the day?" she asked, impatiently gesturing in a "wrap-it-up" way.

"Sorry, but I lost a little time going for coffee this morning,"
he said, looking pointedly at the cup full of the cold mocha crap
still on the table, "and I'm not to a place I can quit just yet."

The phone rang; Robin started, glanced at the phone,
then at Jake. It continued to ring, but she made no move to
answer it, and shrugged. "I'm not in the mood to talk," she
said by way of explanation and let the phone ring until the
answering machine picked up.

"Robin Elaine, this is your father! I know you are there,
I just got off the phone with Rebecca! Now pick up the goddamn phone!"

Robin Elaine moved so fast that Jake unconsciously
jumped back a step. She lunged at the phone, and in the
process, sent the coffee sailing from the table across the
tiled floor.

CHAPTER SIX

Robin scarcely noticed the coffee or anything else other than her father's voice blaring out of the answering machine. This was the call she had dreaded, the inevitability of it haunting her exhausted sleep. She grabbed the phone before Jake Manning heard Dad go off like a madman. "Dad?"

"What in the hell is going on?" he demanded the moment he heard her voice. "I heard the goddamn office burned down and that you spent a night in jail for hitting a policeman!"

"I did *not* hit a policeman! I was arrested for driving without a license and—"

"*How in the hell does someone get arrested for driving without a license!?*"

Wincing at the sheer decibel level, Robin jerked the phone away from her ear for a split second, then cautiously put it back. "It's a long story, Dad, and just a really stupid mistake. I sort of talked back to him—"

"Goddammit, Robin, that is *exactly* what I am talking about! You are too arrogant for your own good! You think you know better than everyone else!"

"I do not think—"

"I've had enough of your bullshit—"

"You don't even know what happened!" she cried angrily. Her blood was boiling; she could feel it inflaming her face. She glanced at Mr. Fix-It, who was staring at her like she was starring in some made-for-TV movie. Mortified, she turned and hurried to her bedroom for a little privacy.

"I don't need to know what happened!" Dad was yelling at her. "I already know that you got arrested and your goddamn office—"

"Stop yelling, Dad," she said, and shut her bedroom door behind her.

"Ah to hell with it! I didn't do you right, Robin. I didn't teach you the ropes; I didn't show you how to run a business. I just let you prance around—"

"Oh God, not this again," she moaned, sinking onto her bed.

"I know you try hard, but you just don't know a damn thing. Now, I've given this a lot of thought. I gave you too much too fast. I think the best thing to do right now is send you to school."

"School?" She snorted. "What school?"

"The school of life. The school of the business world, of working your way up the ropes. You have no business being in a vice presidency, not with your lack of experience—"

"I've been with the company four years, Dad."

"And in four years you haven't learned enough to keep one freight yard afloat. I've talked this over with your mother and my mind is made up."

Panic set in; Robin gripped the phone tightly. "Talked what over with Mom?"

"I've decided to put you in a position where you can learn a little about the freight industry. Iverson and I've been thinking of acquiring a subsidiary company—packing materials. It's something you can do from home."

She did not like the direction this was going. "What do you mean, 'do from home'? Do what from home?"

"Put together a proposal for acquiring one of the two companies we've been considering. They teach you that in business school, don't they? Cost-benefit analysis? Acquisition strategies? I hope so, or else I paid a fortune for nothing."

Stunned, Robin collapsed back on the bed, blinked up at her ten-foot ceilings. This could not be happening. She was stuck smack in the middle of one horrendously long nightmare.

"One of the companies we've been looking at is in Minot, North Dakota," Dad blithely continued. "They make bubble wrap, foam packing products, et cetera. The other is in Burdette, Louisiana, just this side of Baton Rouge. It's the same sort of operation, only a little bigger. You need to get out to see them."

Minot, North Dakota? *Louisiana?* Robin used to New York and Paris and Stockholm—not Burdette. "Dad!" she exclaimed in horror, "you aren't making any sense! You don't mean I am going to Burdette! What would I do there?"

"Well, for one, you would meet with the folks and learn about packing materials—"

"Dad! You want me to learn about the stuff that goes into boxes and crates?"

"Well…and boxes and crates, too. You know, how they make them, what it takes to operate an outfit like that, sales volume, revenues, the whole nine yards. And while you're at it, you are going to try and sell yourself and LTI and convince them that letting LTI buy them out is the best thing they could do for the long-term health of their company and their employees. Then you are going to study which one you think we ought to acquire and work out a deal."

"A deal for Styrofoam peanuts and bubble wrap?" she asked helplessly, teetering on the verge of torrential tears for the umpteenth time that day. "Are you trying to punish me? If you want to punish me, choose something a little more urbane, would you? I can't go to Burdette!"

"Oh yes, you can," he growled, "and if you think that is beneath you, or that, for some reason, you are entitled to your salary and perks just because of who you are instead of what you know, then I guess I have no choice."

The meds were making him crazy. Robin suddenly rolled over, propped herself on her elbows to try a different tack. "Dad," she said calmly, "let's talk about what's really bothering you. I know you are mad at me, but—"

"The good thing is that you can work from home and it won't be as time-consuming as what you were doing, although God knows what that was. Don't you see what I am doing here? I want you to slow down, get you to take the time to understand what's important in life. I'm doing this because I love you and I want to do the right thing by you, Robbie. I don't want to leave behind a spoiled kid with no idea how to succeed me, much less run my company."

Myriad emotions—anger, hurt, sadness—filled her throat, and Robin closed her eyes. "You make it sound as if I offer no value to LTI."

"You'll be a whole lot more valuable when you know what you are doing."

A tear slipped from the corner of her eye and raced down her cheek. "And if I don't want to go to Minot or Burdette?"

Dad sighed heavily. "If you don't want to go, then I guess you better find yourself another job, baby."

Stabbed through the heart.

"Now listen! You're going to learn a lot! I'm making you an acquisitions specialist, working directly for Evan. He's going to guide you every step of the way."

Robin caught her breath and abruptly sat up. "So basically, you are demoting me to bubble wrap."

"Think of it as training. Evan is the best in the business and he's been telling me for a long time you need this and he's more than happy to do it."

Well hell, thanks a lot, Evan. And now, of all the people in the universe, he was going to be her mentor. Robin's fragile ego was in a a death spiral.

"Now. What about this arrest? What do I need to do?"

He had already humiliated her enough; she didn't need any more of his help. "It's taken care of."

"What about the office? The operations manager at the freight yard says it is gone."

"Dad, I'm really tired, okay? I don't want to talk about it right now."

He paused, said reluctantly, "Okay, baby. You get some rest. We'll talk again on Monday."

Oh boy, she could hardly wait. "Bye," she said tightly, clicked off, and tossed the phone onto a pillow. So this was what an alternate universe looked like. Robin Through the Looking Glass, where she was not the VP of the Southwest Region any longer, but Queen of Peanuts and Bubble

Wrap. With a groan, Robin pushed herself up off the bed, went to her closet, and pulled, from the maybe pile, a pair of old jeans ripped at the knees and a cutoff Houston Astros T-shirt. Her mind was numb, devoid of everything but two very basic facts: She was hungry. And she needed a drink.

But when she emerged from her bedroom, Robin was startled for the thousandth time by the presence of Jacob Manning. Hadn't he gone home yet? She frowned at his back as she padded into the dining room. Well, if she was going to have to get used to him being around, at least he wasn't hard to look at. Now that she knew he wasn't a total weirdo. She casually took in the breadth of his shoulders, his lean waist, and his very nice butt. He was scraping something; she walked toward him, saw the hint of a tattoo under the sleeve of his T-shirt.

She moved closer.

Handydude glanced at her from the corner of his eye.

Her face burned. He must have heard quite a lot of her exchange with Dad. "Why are you still here?" she demanded, acutely conscious of her flush.

"Ah. I see Godzilla is up and at 'em again. You hired me, remember? Signed a contract?"

"Damn that contract," she muttered.

Fix-it Guy grinned and pointed with his blade to the brick. "See this?"

Robin peered closely.

"Antique brick. People pay a fortune for it now." He paused, stepped back to admire it. "No telling how much of it there is. We'll know when we strip away these hard layers of paint. I'm going to test different areas so we'll know how best to remove it. Then I'll get my crews started." He looked at Robin then, his gaze drifting up to her hair.

Self-conscious, Robin ran a hand over the top of her head, wincing at the wild feel of it. Embarrassed again, she glanced down and remembered she was wearing dirty, torn jeans and an ancient T-shirt cut off at the midriff. Well, looky here, she was already dressing the part of Bubble Wrap Queen. The only thing missing was the double-wide.

Not that Handy Andy seemed to notice. As he continued to brush away years of paint, Robin noticed that he had a very muscular arm. An Atlas arm, one of those you see in commercials holding up the world and babies in tires. An Atlas arm that was connected to an Atlas torso, and—

She abruptly turned away, appalled that, in spite of her total misery, she was ogling a workman in her house. Not good. Actually, pretty bad.

She stalked to the dining room, remembered the spilled coffee. A roll of paper towels later, she reminded herself she was starving, and marched to her kitchen and flung open the fridge. Like she was going to find anything there, other than a pack of AA batteries, two containers of yogurt, and a jar of crushed garlic. *Ugh.* She slammed that door, opened the pantry door. A box of spaghetti she figured dated to World War II, some oil, and one can of stewed tomatoes.

As the food supply wasn't looking too good, she moved to the next cabinet with the pullout wine rack, which usually held several bottles of wine. Except there were none, and Robin vaguely remembered polishing off the last couple of bottles a couple of weeks ago when Mia was fighting with Michael. There was, however, a bottle of vodka, which of course she didn't remember acquiring. Nonetheless, she took the bottle out of the cabinet and returned to the fridge hoping she had overlooked some cranberry juice. Naturally, she had not. "*Damn*," she exclaimed with great irritation, her voice echoing off the bare walls and floor.

"What's that?" El Contractordodo said from the dining room.

Robin took two steps back, looked at him through the arched doorway. He was wiping his hands on a dirty towel, looking pretty damn virile. "Oh, don't mind me. I'm just expiring over here with no food, one lousy bottle of vodka, and nothing to mix it with."

He actually laughed at that, the same warm laugh she had heard on the phone when they had discussed her renovations, which, upon sudden reflection, seemed like fifteen centuries ago. "You expire? I think you're too ornery," he said, still smiling.

Robin sighed. "I know you must think I am a grade-A fruitcake, but I'm not usually so...so..."

"So much trouble?" he finished for her.

Her eyes narrowed.

Hammerman brandished a charmingly lopsided, infectious smile, and Robin could feel a smile of her own spreading across her lips for the first time that day. "Aha—you *do* think I am a complete nutcase!"

"No, I do not think you are a complete nutcase. No more than three-quarters."

Robin couldn't help it—she laughed in spite of herself. "Well, I'm sure you've heard enough by now to know why, Mr. Manning."

"Hey, call me Jake," he said affably, dropped the towel, and put his hands on his hips to better consider her. "And for what it is worth, I figure there's a good explanation for everything."

"Really?" she asked hopefully.

Jake Manning frowned and shook his head. "No. Not really." With a chuckle, he went down on his (very fine) haunches, opened up his backpack, and extracted a soda.

Robin realized she was checking him out yet again and quickly looked at the bottle of vodka she held. Yeah well, he really *was* a very handsome man in a worker-guy sort of way. She looked up as he took a big swig of his soda.

"Code Red Mountain Dew," he said. "Good for what ails you and a perfect complement to any meal."

"You actually drink that stuff?" she asked, coming out of the kitchen.

"Sure. It's pretty good." His cell phone rang; he put the plastic bottle on the table and wrestled the phone off his belt. "Try some with that and you'll appreciate it," he said, nodding at the bottle she held. He answered his phone with a short "Yeah," paused for a moment, then walked out the front door.

Girlfriend, Robin mused, and strolled to the table where he had left his Code Red Mountain Dew. She picked it up, immediately flipped around to the nutrition chart, and frowned. "Look at the sugar!" she muttered to herself, and carried it back into the kitchen and mixed the vodka with his drink.

By the time Jake came back in, looking a little flushed, she thought, Robin lifted the bright red drink on which she had managed to put a frothy pink head. "*Salut*," she said and sipped the concoction, then flopped down on a dining room chair.

Jake looked at her drink, then at the table. "You used all of it?"

Robin nodded. He'd offered it to her, hadn't he?

He frowned. He picked up a putty knife and began to scrape around the window casings with a vengeance, chipping off bigger and bigger pieces of paint. Robin sipped, watching him, wondering what she could say to break the silence. "Seems like that would go a lot quicker if you used one of those chemical peels," she observed, ignoring the fact that all she knew about chemical peels came from facials.

Jake spared her a glance. "I'll do that with the wall. Right now I am trying to see what is underneath."

"You should at least get a bigger knife."

He threw down the knife and picked up the towel. "So," he said casually, wiping his hands, "you hit a police officer, then burned down your office?"

"I didn't hit him!" Robin instantly cried. "I just mouthed off."

"Imagine that."

"The incident has been blown way out of proportion by my grandma."

Jake looked up from his hands, the copper in his eyes shining with...something. Inappropriate glee? "So what'd you say?"

She shrugged sheepishly, examined the ice bobbing in her drink for a moment. "I called him an idiot cop. Which probably wouldn't have been so bad if I could have found my wallet, but my wallet was being burned in the fire at my office at the time, apparently. And then...I refused to give him my name."

Jake nodded thoughtfully, seemed to mull it over. "Why? Was he one of your perverts or something?"

Oh, hardy har. Squirming a bit, she thought about exactly why she had done it, and winced. "Because he was bothering me," she finally muttered, realizing how ridiculous she sounded, especially since it was the God's honest truth. She was such an idiot.

To confirm it, Jake shook his head in disbelief. "So what did he say?"

"He called me a smart-ass and read me my rights."

Jake made a sound as if he were choking, then smiled with far too much satisfaction.

"Is that a smirk?" she asked curiously. "Are you smirking?"

"Damn straight it's a smirk," he cheerfully admitted. "So did you start the fire, too?"

"*No!* I was in jail, remember? There is no possible way I could have started it!"

"So let me see if I have this," he said, drawing to his full height and putting his hands on his hips. "You're just a smart-ass, but not an arsonist, right?" Then he laughed at his lame little joke and started to gather his things. "Probably some wiring gone bad. Happens all the time."

"See? That's exactly what I was thinking." she said, nodding emphatically. "Wiring! Old building, old wires—but a *big* wire, right? I mean, it would be almost impossible for something like, say, an unattended coffeepot to do it... right?"

He paused, gave her a look. "Don't tell me you left the coffeepot on."

Robin was on her feet before she knew it, one hand wildly gesturing, the other gripping her glass tightly. "I don't know!" she cried helplessly. "I think I unplugged it, but I don't know for sure! Oh man, could one little coffee-pot do that? It was an accident! I had just come back from the ranch, and my dad told me he was dying, and then told me I was pretty useless to him, and I couldn't sleep, and I couldn't work, and I made a pot of coffee. But what if it *was* me? Can they arrest me for that?"

Jake shrugged. "Who knows with these idiot cops?

"*Touché.*" Robin groaned.

Jake smiled, nodded at the glass she was holding. "You're sloshing it around," he said, nodding to several large wet splotches on the tiled floor.

Robin sat down.

"That's rough about your dad."

"Yeah," she said wearily. "It was just such a shock. He has always been so...so *strong*," she said.

"What does he do?"

"What does he do? Everything..."

Amazing, Robin later thought, how easily she began to talk about something as complicated as Dad. Jake was a good listener, seemed interested in what she was saying, and really, the whole thing just sort of spilled out of her. For some reason, she didn't stop with her arrest, she even gave him the humiliating news of her demotion and new status as Queen of Bubble Wrap.

By the time she had finished spilling her guts, she was feeling exhausted and a little loopy from the vodka, and was actually laughing about the absurdity of her new job. "*Bubble wrap*, can you imagine? Me?"

"Why not?" he asked.

Robin snorted. "In case you haven't noticed, I'm not exactly a Styrofoam products kind of person."

"I don't see why not," Jake said with a shrug. "Someone's got to make it. They could call you Bubbles?"

"Not funny."

"Okay. How about Peanut?"

He was playing with her. "How about boss?" she said cheekily.

Jake chuckled, folded his arms across his chest. "How about convict?"

"How about fired?"

"Uppity?"

"Unpaid contractor?"

"Maybe," he said, nodding, his gaze drifting to her bare middle.

"You're a nice guy, Jake," she said with a crooked smile. "You didn't have to listen to my wretched life."

"Oh, I bet you do okay most of the time, boss. Doesn't look like you're hurting."

She was about to answer that looks weren't everything when Jake's cell phone rang. He glanced at the number display. "I'd better be going," he said and stuffed the cell down inside his backpack without bothering to answer it.

Robin stood as he hoisted his backpack and pulled the do-rag from his pocket, and followed him to the back door. He paused there, smiled at her with unexpected warmth. "My advice?" he said, pushing the door open. "Don't get out of bed."

"Better safe than sorry, right?"

"No. I just think you should leave the unsuspecting public alone for a while."

She laughed, decided she liked Handy Andy. "Hey... sorry I called you a pervert."

Jake shrugged. "I've been called worse. Have a good weekend," he said, and with a wink, walked out the door, leaving her to stand behind the screen.

Robin stood there for a moment, admiring his form as he mounted the bike. But when he disappeared from her drive, she chastised herself for getting all worked up about his good looks. Okay, so he seemed to be a nice guy (in spite of her earlier, moronic assessments), but...he *was* the contractor renovating her house. She was only thinking of him now in a warm fuzzy way due to a general state of intoxication and hunger.

Right. *Food.*

Robin turned away from the door and headed for the phone book.

At the Blue Cross Ranch, Aaron was lying prone on the king-sized, four-poster bed in the master suite, staring up at the Star of Texas painted on the ceiling and trying to keep his dinner down. At the granite vanity near the master bath, Bonnie mixed a concoction of herbs. "This should help your nausea."

"Nothing is going to help while they've got me on this medicine," Aaron groused and swallowed hard against another swell of nausea.

"I talked to Gordon again today," Bonnie said, and Aaron groaned. "He is sending me a couple of books on biological therapy."

"Gordon is a hack, Bon-bon."

Bonnie frowned at him over her shoulder. "You have nothing to lose by trying his way. Look at him—he's been in remission for eight years now."

"Yeah, well, not because of the crap he keeps pushing on you, I guaran-damn-tee it."

With a snort of exasperation, Bonnie got up from the vanity and glided toward him, carrying the shit she would make him drink in a large Dixie cup. "Drink it."

Aaron made himself sit up, felt the sickening roil in his belly. "I don't think I can," he started, but Bonnie thrust the cup at him.

"You have to do *something*, Aaron. I won't let you just lie there and wallow in self-pity and not do something, do you hear me?"

Her blue eyes were flashing, her hand trembling. Aaron gripped her wrist, stilled the trembling. "Bon-bon, sooner or later you're going to have to accept what is."

"*Shut up*," she snapped and, with a grunt of anger, thrust the cup at him. He reluctantly took it, wrinkled his nose at the pungent smell. Holding his breath, he tossed the stuff down his throat, then handed the cup to Bonnie.

She watched him closely; Aaron waited. And just when he thought the sickness had passed, it surged up on a violent wave. He bolted from the bed to the bathroom, leaning his head over the toilet just as he heard Bonnie lament, "Maybe I didn't mix it right."

CHAPTER SEVEN

Jake almost missed the turn to Zaney's house, no thanks to Robin Lear. His head was filled with the image of her bare belly, her slender knee peeking out of the rips in the denim, her corkscrew mess of curls and that mouth... *God*, that mouth was enough to make a grown man cry.

But it wasn't her near-perfect body that got to him. It was the uncomfortable notion that he was, inexplicably, kind of attracted to a snobby woman with a fat mouth who most definitely had a screw loose, if not a whole series of parts missing. She was nuts! Certifiable! Probably one of those good-looking chicks who thought she was God's gift to mankind. But she also had a smile that could light up all of Houston, a laugh that went all over him like warm spring rain, a definite sense of self, and a refrigerator full of AA batteries.

A man couldn't help but wonder about those batteries.

Attractive or not (definitely attractive), Robin Lear was trouble, the kind of trouble that ought to be broadcast with big neon lights and orange cones so men could steer clear. The only problem was, he couldn't figure out exactly how he was going to steer clear of her, given that the rocket scientist had burned down her office.

He'd think about that later. At the moment, he'd arrived at the house of his most immediate problem, Chuck Zaney. Sometimes it seemed like he had two teenage headaches, as if he didn't already have enough trouble with Cole, the son of his brother Ross, who died two years ago. Then again, Cole was so plainly rudderless that your heart ached for the kid. At twelve, he had lost his father to drunk driving. The very next year, he lost his mother to God knew where—she couldn't handle it, she said, and took off with some guy.

Now Cole was living with Jake's mom, which wasn't exactly a cakewalk, either. Mom was worn out from having raised three boys almost single-handedly, and she did the best she could for Cole, but Cole was just too much for her. When had she called this afternoon to tell Jake that Cole was AWOL, she had sounded exhausted.

Frankly, Cole exhausted *him*, but he was determined to give the boy a sense of direction, a purpose. No one had done that for Ross, himself included—and he didn't want to make the same mistake again. But more times than not, he felt like he was banging his head against a wall. Cole could go along, doing okay, then one of those thugs he called friends would appear, and the kid was lost, running with a crowd that had, somehow, become more familiar to him than his own family.

Tonight he'd run off with Frankie Capellini again, a loser if Jake had ever laid eyes on one. But he had an idea of where they might have gone, and just as soon as he was through with Zaney, he was heading up Old Galveston Road.

Speaking of which, lights were on in every room of Zaney's house; hard rock was blaring out the open door onto the street, and Jake could just make out the off-key strains of Zaney's guitar. Inside, the place looked like a gulf storm had hit it—pizza cartons covered the coffee table, empty beer cans were stacked precariously on one end table. The wide-screen TV was tuned in to a Rockets' game. Jake stepped around an empty McDonald's bag on the floor, headed for the dining room.

Shirtless and bent over his guitar, Zaney grinned the moment he saw Jake. "Dude!" he shouted over the blare of the stereo, grinning wildly as he put his guitar aside.

"*Turn it down!*" Jake shouted back.

With a startled look, Zaney glanced at the stereo as if he had just realized it was on. He hopped up and over to the stereo, and punched a button. The noise was suddenly reduced to the sound of a basketball game on the TV. "Hey! The Rockets are playing!" he happily observed.

Jake grabbed the remote and turned off the TV, then motioned to Zaney's arm. "So, what's the story? Broken?"

Zaney glanced down at his arm. "It's probably all right."

"Probably? What did the doctor say?"

"Ah man, I got tired of waiting for him," Zaney said with a laugh. "There was this screaming baby—I mean, something *fierce* had hold of that little dude."

Jake was momentarily speechless. "You're kidding, right?"

"Nah…he was really wailing."

Great, just great. Jake impatiently thrust a hand through his hair. Zaney smiled sheepishly. Jake clamped his jaw shut before he said something hurtful—Zaney tended to wear his feelings on his sleeve.

"Hey, it's all right!" Zaney insisted, and to prove it, moved his arm from left to right, unabashedly wincing at the pain it caused him.

"Zaney, it's bad enough you got arrested, man. You cost me the whole morning bailing you out and driving you to the clinic. And you skipped out? How in the hell are we supposed to finish all the jobs we've got lined up if you don't go to a doctor?"

Zaney dropped his gaze to the table and shrugged half-heartedly.

"Shit, I've got more work lined up than we can handle. I need you, man!"

"I'll go. Tomorrow, I'll go, I promise, Jake," Zaney said earnestly, and at Jake's dubious look, he insisted, "I promise!"

"You better. I gotta go," Jake said irritably and stalked out of the dining room. "Take care of that arm!" he called over his shoulder, but his words were drowned by the sudden blast of hard rock at his back.

So now he could thank Robin *and* Zaney for his rotten, rotten mood as he roared up Old Galveston Road in search of Cole. He wondered what Robin Lear would do with someone like Zaney. Cut him up and serve him to some garden party. The probability of truth in that only made his mood blacker.

The ride out wasn't helping, either—this stretch of road was littered with graffiti-scarred buildings, pawn shops, thrift stores, and used car lots. He was rarely out here anymore, but was nonetheless desperately familiar with it—when he and his brothers were kids, they'd run these streets like loose mavericks, into the trashed alleys and beyond to the levees, where they would fish for crawdads, make forts out of old tires, and build race cars with boxes. Ross and Todd never left this part of town.

Jake might have ended up here permanently, too, had it not been for his talent to play baseball. By the grace of heaven, a junior high coach had taken a keen interest in him and his abilities. But the coach didn't have to work too hard to convince Jake to turn from the streets—he loved baseball. He was never without his cleats or glove, and in high school, when his father said he'd never amount to anything, and tried to take the glove and make him work, Jake had stood up to the old man for the first time in his life. He had worked hard, spending endless hours throwing the ball against the side of the garage to field grounders. In his senior year, he was scouted by the Astros, then made the roster of their farm team. The day after graduation, he left home to play ball and never looked back.

That had been a magical time. He had seen beautiful, exclusive parts of Houston, awash in palm trees and big white houses behind wrought-iron fences. He had seen the Texas coastal plains and the ranch land that stretched green and lush all the way to the piney woods. He had seen New Orleans and its voodoo magic, then Dallas, where tall glass buildings stretched right up to the relentless sun. He met people far more educated and sophisticated than anyone he had ever known, had sampled exotic food, strong drink, and pretty women.

The more of that world he tasted, the greater his hunger for it grew. And he might have made it, might have gone all the way to the Bigs had he not slid into home plate one sultry Sunday afternoon and torn his right Achilles tendon.

That was a career-ending, dream-obliterating injury that, in the space of a few days, if not hours, had left him drifting. By the time he healed and could walk again, his money was gone. He took the first job he could find, drifted from one construction job to another while he desperately tried to find his bearings and avoid a return to the life he had left behind—to *this* life, on Old Galveston Road.

Jake slowed at a familiar intersection, turned next to a topless dancer joint, where four young thugs stood huddled outside, sharing a smoke. About a mile down, he found the old road he was looking for and turned left again, onto a dirt road that ran out to the levee that wended deep into the bayou. He rode slowly, coming to a stop more than once to peer into the thick foliage for any sign of kids.

Strange how time could fray memories. Sometimes it felt like he had dreamed his years here. His desire to escape the poverty and misery he had known as a child had allowed him to turn his back on this place. When Dad ran off with Mom's friend, Jake had been absent, just as he was when Todd knocked off a liquor store and ended up in the pen for it. He missed Cole's birth, and it really wasn't until Ross was forced into rehab that Jake began to notice his family again. And remember.

By then, Jake was working for A. J. Ackerman. A. J. owned a small construction firm and took a liking to Jake, showed him the tricks of the trade and the business side of things. It was A. J. who told him he had a natural talent for design and had urged him to take a drafting class.

Jake had scoffed at the idea, but A. J. was relentless about it. The upshot of all that badgering was that now, at thirty-eight, Jake was only fifteen hours away from a degree in architecture.

A flicker of light through a stand of brush caught his eye, and he downshifted, brought the bike to a stop. A path cut through the brush, leading down to the levee, where there was, on any given night, a dozen or more teenagers. This, Jake knew from personal experience.

Yep, Jake thought as he kicked his way through the brush, had it not been for Ross's death, he might never have come back. But his brother's death had awakened something sharp and unexpected in him, an instinct that had sliced through his conscience when he'd seen Cole at the funeral. It shocked him to see then how much the boy looked like Ross had when Jake had left home eighteen years before. It was like being transported back in time.

That was a clarifying moment, a moment when Jake suddenly understood that a distance had spread like a cancer between him and a brother he had once loved. That day, he sensed he was being handed a second chance and vowed to himself and to God that he would fight every day to keep Cole from following the same, useless path of alcohol and menial jobs Ross had followed. Just like their father had.

And as Jake stalked through the brush on that old path, he imagined exactly how he'd punish the kid. When he emerged in the clearing on the levee, he spotted Cole right away. Several of the kids saw him at the same moment and scattered, but the bolder ones merely looked at him over their shoulders, lifting their beer bottles in blatant defiance.

"Yo, Manning. Your old man is here," one of them said as Jake marched forward to where Cole was squatting at a makeshift fire, a cigarette dangling from one hand.

The announcement obviously startled Cole; he jerked around and opened his mouth to speak, but Jake grabbed his arm and yanked him up before he could utter a word.

"*Woo-hoo! Manning's going to get a span-king!*" one of them taunted in a singsong voice.

The ridicule passed over Cole's blemished face; his eyes hardened, he thrust his chin out and glared up at Jake. "He ain't my old man!" he responded defiantly.

"Maybe not, but I'm all you've got," Jake said low, and grabbed Cole's smoke, tossed it down, and ground it out with his heel before shoving Cole forward, away from the fire.

"You can't tell me what to do!" Cole snapped, walking backward, still glaring at him, stealing a glimpse of the others.

Jake let him have that one. He understood the kid's pride, and he could strangle him in private just as easily as he could in public. He lowered his head, pointed at the path. "Don't push it. Just walk," he managed through the grit of his teeth.

"Screw you," Cole shot back. But he turned and walked.

Jake looked back at the kids who were left, his gaze instantly falling on Frankie. Frankie's mouth twisted into a sneer, and it burned like acid right through to Jake's heart.

He turned away, striding forward, ignoring the laughter and calls after Cole.

He caught up to his nephew and clamped a hand down on his shoulder, squeezing so hard that Cole's knees buckled. "Shit! Cut it out, Jake!"

"Watch your mouth," Jake snapped. "You and I are going to have us an understanding."

"Whatever," Cole muttered, and Jake squeezed harder. "*All right!*" Cole shouted, and Jake let go. Cole rubbed his shoulder, then walked on as if Jake weren't there.

"First off, you're grounded. And second, if I ever find you with the Capellini kid again, I'll take a piece of hide off both of you."

"You can't touch Frankie," Cole argued.

"Oh yeah? Try me."

Cole rolled his eyes, marched on until they cleared the brush. Then he stopped, gaped at Jake's Harley. "Where's the truck? How am I supposed to ride that? I don't have a helmet!"

The kid had the nerve to complain just now? "Well, hell, Cole, what could I have been thinking? I forgot the limo!" Jake said, and shoved Cole toward the bike. Muttering under his breath, Cole straddled the seat and folded his arms across his chest, refusing to look at his uncle. Jake got in front—hating it more than Cole, he was quite certain—and started the bike.

As he pulled out onto the dirt road, he told Cole that if he ever ran off again, he'd just hunt him down again, personally strangle him with his bare hands, then transport his carcass to juvenile hall. And if Cole was of a mind to upset his grandma again, or disobey her in any way, or cause her another single solitary moment of grief, he would crack his fat head wide open and scramble his brains for breakfast.

But even the threat of serious bodily injury didn't seem to make any difference to the surly teen. It was amazing to Jake that Cole could be such a sweet kid in one moment, a veritable stranger the next. No wonder Mom was so tired all the time. Living with Cole had to be a little like living with Freddy Krueger, never knowing when the nightmare was going to show up again. Which was why Cole needed to come live with him. Jake knew it, but he just couldn't seem to find the time to make that monumental commitment.

Mom was waiting for them on the porch of her modest three-bedroom house, her bony frame bundled in an old, snagged beige sweater she had worn as long as Jake could remember. She stood as Jake pulled into the drive, watched through hard brown eyes as Cole slammed up the steps and brushed past her.

"Get yourself inside to bed," she said as he passed, but Cole didn't bother to look at her—he slammed the screen door behind him.

"*Hey!*" Jake shouted after him.

Cole stopped, dropped his head back in insolent disgust, and slowly turned around. "Good night, Grandma," he said icily, then looked at Jake. "Am I excused now?"

"Yes. I'll be back to pick you up in the morning," Jake said, even though Cole was already pounding up the stairs.

Mom sighed wearily, shaking her head as she stared at the screen door. "Don't know what I'm going to do with him, swear I don't." She paused to fish a pack of smokes from her pocket, tapped it absently against the back of her hand. "Where are you taking him?"

"We're going to throw a baseball around."

Mom sighed again, lit a cigarette, and exhaled loudly. "Baseball ain't the answer for everyone, Jacob."

What is the answer, Mom? "It doesn't hurt anything," he said with a shrug and looked down the street at the line of identical green tract houses. "He likes it."

Mom said nothing, just dragged off her smoke. "Well. I better go up and see about him."

Jake nodded, stepped up, and kissed his mom on the cheek, taking in the familiar scent of stale smoke and soap. "I'll see you tomorrow."

He left; the ride to the Heights seemed to take hours instead of the half hour it actually took. A half hour in which Jake waged a silent war in his head about what to do with Cole. He paused on his porch to pick up his mail, then came inside and tossed his gear onto a chair, mindlessly stepped around the drop cloth and sawhorse in the middle of his living room where he was staging his own private renovation. As he came to the dining room, he looked down at the laptop he had left open, the books stacked neatly to one side, and the pile of papers that marked the class work he had planned to finish tonight. With a sigh, he looked through the mail, tossed the bills aside, then proceeded to his bedroom and a hot shower.

A short time later, he went to the kitchen to make a double-decker sandwich and found himself thinking of Robin Lear again, thinking that she was really pretty…but bossy. And full of herself. He mulled that over, and was reaching for a beer when the phone rang.

With a growl, he put his sandwich aside and picked up the phone. "Yeah," he said unceremoniously.

"Jake?"

"Hey, Lindy, how are you?"

"I'm fine. How are *you*?"

"I had a long day, actually. I'm pretty beat."

"Perfect. I made some brownies for you."

God. That was exactly what had gotten him involved with the girl in the first place. He certainly wasn't in the habit of dating women fifteen years his junior—actually, he wasn't really in the habit of dating—but he'd met Lindy on campus, admired her pert little breasts, and asked her out for coffee after class one night. Lindy came to class the next week with a baggie full of homemade cookies. She was a nice girl, a good girl, the kind of girl who would dote on a man. And although he hadn't really been interested enough to date her, he hadn't been fool enough to turn down homemade cookies. Lindy had taken his acceptance of her cookies as a green light.

"Uh...that was really nice of you," he said uncertainly. "But I don't need any."

"Well, nobody *needs* brownies."

"Umm...well, maybe some other time," he said, not wanting to hurt her feelings. "But I really gotta run. Got a lot to do." *A lot of sandwich.*

"Want help?"

"Not this time, Lindy."

She sighed, and Jake could almost see her twist a strand of hair around her finger. "Okay, well, I guess I'll just have a bath and go to bed," she said listlessly.

At the mention of bath, the thought of a lithe young body flitted across Jake's mind, but strangely, it wasn't Lindy's. "Okay. See you in class." He hung up, turned blindly back to his sandwich, alarmed by the fact that he had just imagined Robin Lear naked. In a bath. And the thought had been strongly arousing.

He took a big bite of sandwich and pondered that. In his work, he encountered a lot of society women who had more money than most governments. They were overly pampered, almost always too pleased with themselves—Robin was definitely all that and change. But then again, she was different, too, and bizarrely interesting. Still...he was not the kind of guy to get his thrills at work. He was way too serious about the business he was trying to build.

Nonetheless, the thought of her was so magnetic that she kept popping into his head the next day. When he took Cole to the park, he thought of her. At the grocery store, buying for his mom, he thought of her. Over his class work, his invoicing, and during the Astros game that Sunday he thought of her, wondered what she was doing. He thought of her in her torn jeans and Curious George pajamas. Worst of all, when he slept Saturday night, he dreamed of making love to a woman who turned out to be Robin Lear, whose blue eyes glazed over in the throes of a powerful, nails-in-the-back climax.

He even thought of her when Zaney called and said he would not be at work on Monday or Tuesday or for that matter, maybe even Wednesday. The news didn't perturb Jake nearly as bad as it ought to have done. The only thing he could think was, he'd be alone with Robin Lear.

But so *what*? She had thought he was a pervert! How he had managed to turn one encounter into a fantasy like this was a little troubling. Yet by the time Monday rolled around, Jake was sort of anxious to go to work and see her again.

He arrived at the house on North Boulevard earlier than he had wanted, but was smiling as he let himself in and put his things in the dining room and noticed the aroma of coffee in the air. And when he heard the bedroom door open, he turned expectantly and looked down the hall... and *whammo*, felt the huge stab of disappointment.

It had never occurred to him, had not once crossed his mind. *What an idiot he was!*

It wasn't Robin who came walking out of the bedroom at all, but a guy, a nice-looking guy at that, wearing nothing but a pair of silk boxers.

CHAPTER EIGHT

When Robin heard the sound of Evan's voice outside her bedroom, all hopes that it was all just a bad dream were effectively obliterated. She lifted her head, winced at the sharp pain right behind her eyes, and dropped, face-down in her pillow, cursing the damned wine Evan had bought. She hadn't intended to drink it, particularly since she'd been so mad at Evan for showing up unannounced last night to begin with. But then Mia had shown up with her Big News. Mia, who had, since their high school days, gone through men like there was some huge race, was getting married.

Her first thought was to call Ripley's Believe It or Not, because Mia was completely incapable of commitment to anything—including a dog she once had. And, she and Michael fought every other week and had ended their affair no less than fifteen hundred times. And now she was getting married. *Married!*

The announcement, made to Robin and Evan when Mia and Michael had arrived for their Saturday night dinner date, had prompted a gushing Evan to run out and buy a few bottles of Pouilly-Vinzelles for a celebration. Robin tried to stop him, told him they already had plans, but Mia, in her near state of euphoria at being given a ring (and it wasn't *that* great of a ring) had proclaimed with great verve, "Oh *noooo*, Evan should stay and help us celebrate!" This, in spite of knowing how Robin felt about Evan, in spite of the very pointed looks Robin gave her, in spite of the universe in general. She just flipped her long blond ponytail over her shoulder and smiled all moon-eyed at Michael.

So Evan had dashed out for the wine, Michael had ordered up Thai, and Robin had drunk heavily as Mia went on and on about her wedding plans, which she had, apparently, given quite a lot of thought.

Actually, Robin might have survived the evening had it not been for the third bottle of Pouilly-Vinzelles and that moment alone with Mia in the kitchen, when in a tipsy moment, Robin had blurted, "Mia, are you insane? You hated Michael two weeks ago and swore you'd never speak to him again. Now you're getting married? This is a *huge* mistake."

To which Mia had smiled in the most condescending way possible and said, "Oh, Robbie, I know how you must be feeling. But you haven't lost me."

"What in the hell are you talking about? I'm talking about this on-again, off-again thing you have with Michael. Who's to say that next week you won't hate him again?"

Mia's smile was so sympathetic that Robin was tempted to try and rub it off her face. "Don't worry. You'll get married too. I mean, you'll chill out in a few years and then, who won't want you?"

Chill out? *Chill out?* Robin had been so stunned that she couldn't even reply. She had stood there, gaping in dumb shock as Mia checked her lipstick in the glass reflection of the cabinet, flipped her hair over her shoulder again, and smiled when Michael called out, "God, Mia, what are you running on about now?" She laughed, walked out of the kitchen to where Michael and Evan were seated around the dining room table, leaving Robin alone in the kitchen in utter confusion.

Chill. *Out.*

By the time Mia and Michael left and Evan opened the fourth and last bottle and asked about her arrest, Robin had—in spite of the annoying little voice warning her to shut up, shut up, *shut up!*—crumbled into despair. She'd lit up like the Texas Commerce building, crying into her Salviati crystal wineglass, and one thing inevitably led to another, and before she knew it, she was wailing about her dad, her demotion, the fire, and even Mia's engagement. And then, somehow, Evan was kissing her, and then...

This was precisely the sort of thing that always got her into trouble.

Robin lifted her head again, groaning beneath a monstrous headache, and peered bleary-eyed at the clock. Eight a.m. Fabulous. Still enough time left in the day to learn all about the many intricacies of Styrofoam peanuts. She could hardly wait.

She heard Evan's voice again, managed to push herself up, and as she groped around for her robe, the door opened and Evan came in, carrying two cups of coffee, wearing little more than a ridiculously broad smile. "Good morning, sweetcakes."

"Uh-huh," Robin muttered, and wrapped the thick terry cloth robe tightly around her while Evan stood there smiling at her. Self-conscious, she pushed her hands through her Amazon hair. "Who were you talking to?" she asked as Evan handed her a cup of coffee.

"Your contractor."

Her contractor…*Oh! Oh Oh Oh!* How could she have forgotten that the delicious hunk of a man would be here this morning? Worse, he'd seen Evan—in his boxers, no less. Robin could feel herself color deeply, and while she was trying to figure that out, Evan reached for her waist, leaned down, and kissed her neck. "Hello, gorgeous."

What a colossal mistake she'd made. Disastrous! "Evan—"

"You were wonderful last night. I'm getting hard just thinking about it."

"Yeah, but I was sort of lit—"

"Baby, you were lit, all right. I'd forgotten how feisty you can get."

Well, someone had to be feisty, although she really did not care for the reminder. "What I'm trying to say is, I really shouldn't have done…that," she said, gesturing to the bed.

Evan laughed deep in his chest. "You can do *that* anytime you want." He nibbled her ear and Robin wriggled out of his embrace, spilling a little coffee on the thick oriental carpet she had bought on one of her shopping whims.

"Please listen to me," she pleaded, and turned to face him. His boxers were tenting. She did not care for the tent. So she abruptly turned away, put her coffee down, and tightened her robe around her. Her temples were pounding, her mouth tasted like dirt. "You know what?" she said, avoiding Evan's gaze—and boxers—"I can't talk about this now. I need to get dressed for my new job. Can't leave the bubble wrap waiting."

"Want me to help?"

"No!" she said quickly, and grabbing her coffee, darted into her bathroom, shut the door behind her, and locked it.

After a moment, Evan said, "Robin?"

His proximity directly on the other side of the door startled Robin, and she reared back, held a hand over her heart for a moment before sinking onto the edge of the spa.

"Okay. I'll use the guest bath."

She heard him move away, and slowly released her breath. So. How did she get into this mess, again? As if her life could get any more ludicrous, as if it were possible that one person could make so many stupid, *stupid* mistakes in the space of a week! A sudden attack of panic assailed her, a strange feeling like she was standing too close to the edge of some deep hole and was in danger of throwing herself off.

Run. Not away, although that sounded pretty appealing at the moment, but down the street, far enough to pound out her frustration. Yes, run.

Robin got up, brushed her teeth, tried to brush her hair, found a bottle of aspirin and took four. No sense beating around the bush. She then peeked out the bathroom door, saw her bed was made, but all other signs of Evan removed. Cautiously, she hurried to her closet, found her running gear, and hoped that he was gone from her house.

No such luck. Evan was seated at her dining table, dressed in slacks and a polo shirt, one leg casually crossed over the other as he read the paper. Worse, Jake Manning was quietly working in the entry, wearing carpenter pants that hugged his very fine butt and a T-shirt that strained across his chest.

Evan looked up from the paper and smiled. "Ah, there she is! Hey, you're going out for a run? You should have told me—I would have gone with," he said cheerfully.

Robin tried very hard not to look at Jake. "Yeah, but you don't have time, do you, Evan? Aren't you headed back to Dallas?"

He casually sipped his coffee. "Actually, I'm going to be around for a few days. We have to get you set up, don't we?"

We? She did not like the sound of that at all, and walked to the kitchen before he could say more. She opened the fridge, studied the empty box, and vowed to make it to the grocery store this calendar year. With a sigh, she went back into the dining room. That was when she spied the box of Krispy Kremes on the edge of the table and instantly looked at Jake.

He was watching her, expressionless. He glanced at the box and turned away. Hey...he'd brought her doughnuts. He had, hadn't he? Jake Manning had brought her dough-nuts! *Cha-cha cha-cha cha-CHA! Cha-cha cha-cha cha-CHA!* Evan could bring all the outrageously expensive wine he wanted, but doughnuts—now here was a man who really knew how to impress a woman.

With two fingers, Robin lifted the lid to the mouth-watering treats, until a T-square came crashing down on the lid, missing her fingernails by a hairbreadth. Robin squeaked, jerked her hand back, and looked up at Jake, who was holding the T-square firmly on top of the dough-nut box, glaring at her. "Those are mine. Remember our little talk?"

"You almost hit me with that thing!"

"Let's review—I am not your local Pac-n-Sac. Keep out of my stuff."

"Goodness," Evan said. He turned the page of the busi-ness section and continued reading.

"They're just doughnuts," Robin groused at Jake's back as he walked back to the foyer.

Evan looked up over the business section, one brow lifted above the other. "Get up on the wrong side of the bed, sweetheart?"

Actually, just the wrong bed, and at the moment, she wished Evan would go far, far away. But he turned his attention back to his paper. "IBM stock is down."

Robin looked at the doughnut box, then at Jake over the top of Evan's head. That was a smirk on his face, she thought. At the very least, a smarty little twinkle in his eye. Robin walked over to the wall where he was working, pretended to look at what he was doing. Yep, it was a twinkle, all right.

She moved until she was standing so close that her arm brushed his sleeve. "Still testing the layers?"

Jake looked down, smiled a crooked, *I-know-what-you-are-doing* kind of smile. "Yep."

"What's that?" Evan called, forcing Robin to glance over her shoulder. He was watching her intently, his expression curious. "I thought you were going for a run?"

Okay. There were too many guys in her house, and his name was Evan. "Yes, I am. See you later," she said and walked across the foyer.

"Have a good run," Evan said, looking at Jake.

"Uh-huh," she mumbled, and walked out the door and proceeded down the street.

When the door shut behind Robin, Jake heard a heavy sigh and the rustle of newspaper behind him. "I swear to God she's going to be the death of me."

Good.

"I don't know what it is about women—one minute they can melt you, the next minute they make you want to jump off a cliff. Know what I mean?"

How about jumping off a cliff right now? "I suppose," Jake muttered.

The man's chair scraped against the floor; in the next moment, he was standing directly behind Jake. "So...what are you doing here?"

Man, oh man, he was destined to have a lousy morning, wasn't he? And he had such high (though admittedly asinine) hopes. "I'm testing the layers of paint to see what we're working with before I strip these walls."

"Ah," the dolt said. "I've dabbled a bit in this kind of work." When Jake didn't take the bait, he continued, "Redid my living room. Had that old-style paneling, you know what I mean? I took that out and textured the walls."

Yep, a bona fide expert with latent homosexual tendencies. "Hmmm," Jake answered.

The man turned away from the wall. "I should get to the office."

If he expected Jake to say something, he was going to be disappointed. Jake continued working as he listened to the sound of the man gathering his things, fought the urge to help him, and felt relieved when the door finally shut behind the guy. If there was one thing he hoped for this job, it would be that *that* guy would not be around too often... but wait a minute, there was that dipshit thinking again. Jake paused to wipe the brush he was using, shook his head again at his own great foolishness. He really had to shake the thought of Robin from his mind as he worked. Or at

least the memory of her scent when she had stood so electri-
fyingly close to him this morning.

Meanwhile, Robin was pounding the jogging trail in slow,
leaden steps, her hangover forgotten in favor of thinking about Jake. What it was about him she couldn't be
entirely certain, other than the fact that he was so rug-
gedly male. And handsome. Very nice coppery eyes. And
as she turned around the corner and headed up North
Boulevard again, she thought about the care he took with
the antique brick, his fingers stroking it—okay, enough
already. What was she doing? Wasn't it bad enough that
she had fallen into bed with Evan? Now she had to go
and fantasize about a perfect stranger, and a contractor
at that?

God, she really needed a hobby. Or a boyfriend. A boyfriend who had nothing to do with her house or her work,
completely disengaged from her life, existing simply to
adore her and buy her gifts. That way, she wouldn't be sleeping with Evan or fantasizing about some hired Hammerman
who was working on her house. There was only one small
problem—she really had such putrid, rotten luck when it
came to guys. And boyfriends bored her.

When she opened her front door, her gaze immediately
swept the entry and dining room, but there was no sign of
Evan.

"He went to the office," Jake offered.

Robin colored slightly, came in and shut the door, and
stood there with her back to it, feeling very uncertain. And
fat. Oh, man, she felt FAT in running shorts. She stole a

121

glance down the hallway to her room, mentally calculating the distance—she could make a mad dash for it, but then, he'd see the jiggle in her butt.

Jake looked at her expectantly.

Robin chuckled, thought she sounded an awful lot like Olive Oyl. "Well. Well, well."

"Pretty humid out, huh?" he asked, turning back to his work.

What did that mean? Did she...oh Lord, help her— *smell?* "It's not too bad," she lied and suddenly pushed away from the door. "I've run in much worse. *Much* worse." What a ridiculous thing to say.

"Well, you must be a pro," Jake said, looking pretty dubious. He paused, went down on his haunches next to a tool bag, and fished inside. Robin ended up at the dining table, acutely aware that she was, once again, trying very hard to look at Jake without actually *looking* at him. God. She went to the kitchen, scrounged up a bottle of water, then wandered back into the dining room. Her gaze fell on the box of doughnuts. The lid was up, the box was empty. *Damn.*

"So...what else do you do, Robin Lear?" Jake asked as she drank her water.

"What do you mean?"

"I mean besides run and steal doughnuts. You into sports?"

Ahhh...*sports.* So not her thing. "I tennis when I can." Which meant never. "And golf—"

"Oh yeah? Where do you play?"

"River Oaks."

"Oh." He continued digging through his tool bag. "Never played there."

Well, of course not—River Oaks Country Club was the most exclusive club in all of Houston and not just anyone could play there. Actually, very few people could play there. *He* certainly could not play there. "Uh...what about you? Any sport?"

"Baseball."

"Oh, me, too!" Robin quickly responded, pleased to have found something in common. She walked into the foyer, her shorts forgotten. "I love the Astros—"

"No kidding?" he asked, obviously surprised. "I try to get to all their home games."

"Really? I wish I could get to more of them, but I travel so much. I go every chance I get when I am in Houston. We have a box."

"Lucky you," he said, sounding truly envious. "Who do you like?"

"Moz," Robin said, propping herself precariously on one rung of a ladder he had brought into the foyer.

"I should have known. All the ladies like Moz, huh?"

"He happens to be the best pitcher they have!"

"He's too old and he's overpaid, and that's about the best you can say about him."

"Ha! Shows what you know—he's as good as any of those skinny little twenty-year-olds they have on the mound," Robin said indignantly on Moz's behalf.

Jake snorted. "Please. He's a washed-up has-been and he's ruining the salary caps."

"Oh, so *now* I get it. You're one of those guys who doesn't like anyone to make more than he does, right?"

"Excuse me? Moz makes more than Midas, and he can't even pitch his way out of a paper bag. You must be one of those who thinks money is an entitlement instead of, heaven forbid, earning your keep."

That struck a raw nerve in Robin and she instantly retorted, "I do so earn my keep!"

Jake laughed. "Okay. But we were talking about Grandpa Moses, not you."

Oh. Right. Robin's face colored. Feeling terribly self-conscious, she jumped down off her perch on the ladder. Only she didn't go very far—her running shorts caught on a screw or something behind her.

Jake laughed, which only made her face flame. "What *is* that?" she exclaimed, suddenly twisting and turning to dislodge herself, rattling the ladder in the process.

"Hey, what are you doing? You're scarring the brick!" he warned her.

But Robin was too mortified to care about brick. "I'm stuck!"

"Serves you right, Hotpants," Jake said. "Moz!" He put down his brush and stepped forward.

But when Robin realized he meant to help dislodge her, she panicked, and was suddenly twisting like a dervish, trying to free herself before he could touch her.

"Careful, Peanut, you're going to scar that great brick. Just calm down and let me…" He leaned over her, clucked his tongue. "How did you manage to do that?"

Humiliated. That was the only word she could think of, and Robin squirmed again, wild to get off the ladder, but Jake put a steady hand to her hip to lean around her. Robin instantly froze, sucked in her breath, and held it—his touch was like the moment between the realization one has touched fire and is about to feel the burn—only this was a burn she wanted to feel. Unnerved by it, by the nearness of his body, she hung paralyzed, felt his hand at the base of her spine and on her hip, felt his fingers pull up and dislodge the fabric of her shorts, his knuckles kneading her flesh. And then she was free.

Jake stepped back.

Robin slid off the ladder—unthinkingly, her hand went to the spot he had touched her, her fingers feeling for the scar he had surely left behind.

Jake's gaze followed her hand, then flicked back to her eyes, seeping right into her and filling her to the rim before he turned back to his work. He picked up a paint scraper and attacked the wall, muttering that he should get to work.

Robin stood there a moment, unable to move. "Thanks," and walked blindly through the dining room, groping her way to her bedroom through a fog as dense as it was unfamiliar.

In the privacy of her bath, she wondered what in the hell had come over her. He was a man, just like dozens of men she knew. Why should his touch galvanize her so thoroughly? Whatever the reason, it made her feel a little shaky inside.

Robin finished her bath, dressed quickly, and stood looking at herself in the full-length mirror, thoroughly disgusted by what she was seeing. She had chosen a brand-new pair of chocolate-brown Prada slacks and a crème-colored Christian Dior silk blouse. Okay, really, she had enough trouble without getting all dressed up to do her renovator, which was exactly where this was headed. What about the consequences? She would have to work in the same space with him for several months. What would she do then? Barricade herself in her bedroom? Had she not experienced the pain of working alongside someone she had slept with as recently as, oh say, last night? *Stupid, stupid, stupid...*

Still, Robin slipped on a pair of Ralph Lauren sandals, but paused when she heard the unmistakable sound of a woman's laughter. She froze, tried to pin the sound down, until it hit her—*that* was Lucy Ramirez's laugh.

And the thought of Lucy with Jake sent Robin lunging for the bedroom door and struggling with the porcelain handle, thanks to the sweet-scented Chanel lotion she had put on her hands.

CHAPTER NINE

Still laughing, and leaning against the same ladder Robin had hung herself on, Lucy looked surprised when Robin came spilling out of her room and down the hall. "Hey, it's about time," Lucy said.

"And a cheerful good morning to you, too, Lucy. What's going on?"

"Jake and I were just telling a few tales while I waited for you to get out of the shower," Lucy said, sliding off the barstool. "You take a really long shower. Really long. You could probably track it on Doppler radar."

Robin glared at her assistant, but as usual, Lucy was oblivious. She was studying Robin's pants. "Are those new?"

"No."

"I haven't seen them before."

"You haven't seen all my clothes, Lucy."

"That's because I can't keep up."

"Could we just please get to work?" Robin asked through clenched teeth, and thank you, Lucy, because now Jake was looking at her pants.

"Sure," Lucy responded cheerfully, as if suddenly remembering why she was there. "Your dad called. He said I was to bring you the names of these people to call.

Then Evan said you needed to see the accounts for Peerless Packing and Wirt Supplies and Packing. Don't ask me what is up with that, but thank God this is all in the computer, because I'm telling you, there is nothing left of that office except ashes. Remember all those files on your desk? Gone! And then Darren called and asked if you were free for dinner—"

"Oh, hey, hey!" Robin interrupted, laughing nervously as she stole a look at Jake's back while shaking her head furiously at Lucy.

Lucy cocked her head to one side. "What? Why are you shaking your head like that?"

"I'm not shaking my head—"

"Yes you are. If you don't want to go, I'll call him, but I thought you liked this guy."

Robin cringed. "Why don't we go to lunch and go over this stuff?"

Lucy looked at her watch. "It's ten o'clock."

"I meant coffee."

"Okay, but I think Evan's coming back—"

"He can get his own coffee!"

"Okay, all right!" Lucy said, eyeballing her suspiciously. "We'll get coffee!" With another hard look at Robin, she swung around, snatched up her giant designer knockoff shoulder bag and marched toward the kitchen. Robin was right behind her, picking up her new little kate spade purse in her near sprint to get out of the house, following Lucy out the back without so much as a *ta-ta* to Jake.

Ahead of her, Lucy abruptly stopped and turned, almost colliding with Robin. "Am I insane, or am I seeing things right?"

Oh shit. *Shit shit shit,* it was obvious. Robin's heart started beating like a drum; she looked everywhere but at Lucy.

"I mean, have you ever seen anyone so *cuuuuute?*" Lucy squealed and grabbed Robin's wrist in her excitement.

"Huh?"

"The worker guy, Jake! He's gorgeous!"

"Really?" Robin asked and self-consciously tried to tame a curl at her temple. "I didn't notice."

"Oh, come on!" Lucy demanded, incredulous. "Why didn't you tell me you had a man like that tucked away in your house? I would *love* to work at home if I had a guy like that stuck inside. I'd set it up like Hotel California. Once he came in, he would never come out—"

"Come on, Lucy, he's just a contractor," Robin reminded her as they headed for the car.

"Just a contractor—what does that mean? Well, whatever, he's gorgeous. And he's so nice. And funny. Girl, he is *funny.*"

Okay, Robin thought, he might be nice, but he wasn't particularly funny. And he was stingy with doughnuts. "I haven't really talked to him."

"Yeah, well, with a guy like that, you really don't need to talk," Lucy said with a not-so-subtle elbow in Robin's ribs.

"Can we just talk about the files you brought?" Robin insisted, trying hard to change the subject.

But Lucy continued to wax dreamily about Jake at the coffee shop, even through the ordering of two skinny double mocha cafés au lait with nutmeg. Robin was finally able to shut her up by blurting out the news of her demotion.

At first, Lucy was stunned. She gaped at Robin. "Are you kidding?" When Robin shook her head no, she contorted into a howl of laughter. Looking around at everyone looking at Lucy, Robin didn't exactly appreciate her reaction and said so.

"I'm sorry," Lucy said, wiping the tears of laughter from beneath her eyes. "But the thought of you and Eldagirt Wirt is too much!"

"Who is that?"

"Eldagirt owns Wirt Supplies and Packing—she's one of the people your dad wants you to call. I'll just say this—she eats concrete-and-barbed-wire pie for breakfast and asks for seconds." Lucy giggled, reached for one of the two thick files she was carrying, leafing through them until she found one paper in particular, which she shoved across the small table to Robin. "Here's her number. If I were you, I'd wait 'til after lunch to get in touch. Definitely not a morning person."

Robin scoffed at that, proclaimed she wasn't afraid of Eldagirt, and turned her attention to the file's contents while Lucy very helpfully put forth her theories about why the office had burned. Which boiled down to her pinning it on nonexistent transients.

When Lucy finally headed back to the freight yard, where she'd set up a temporary office, Robin stayed on at the coffee shop a while longer, reviewing the fascinating and titillating account files. The way she saw things, she had two choices. Either she could mope about her rotten stupid luck, or she could prove her father and Evan wrong. How hard could it be? She could learn everything there was to know, just plunge right in and show them that she had what it took. Starting with an understanding of exactly how Styrofoam peanuts were made. She was so excited by the prospect, it was all she could do to keep from skipping back to her house.

While Robin was trying to mine her way through the information about the two packing materials companies, Jake was learning it would be the following week before Zaney would be back to work. At least that's what Jake thought he said—the music was blaring so loudly in the background, he could hardly hear him.

He was still brooding about that and how he was possibly going to stay on schedule when Robin came sailing through the door, tossing keys, purse, and files onto the already overloaded dining table. If she saw him, she certainly didn't acknowledge it. She thrust one leg to the side, cocked her hip, and flipped through the mail she held in one hand, then carelessly tossed the envelopes onto the pile on the table. Only then did she turn, hands on hips, and face him. "Hey."

"Hey."

She shifted her gaze to the window frame. "What are you doing?"

"Stripping the old paint on this casing."

Robin wrinkled her nose. "Shouldn't you do the walls first?"

"The casing needs to be stripped before I put the chemical peel on the wall," he said patiently, as if she required any explanation at all, even if she was so goddamn gorgeous.

She moved forward to stand beside him. "It just seems like the windows would be last."

In spite of the distraction of the faint scent of lilac, Jake couldn't let it go. "That may be the most uninformed thing you have said yet."

"*Yet?*" she protested. "That would imply I have said other misinformed things, which I have not, Handy Andy. I haven't found the stained glass I want yet."

"Handy Andy, huh?" All right, lilac scent aside, he was going to have to establish some ground rules if he was ever going to complete this job. "Okay. How about we have a deal since we'll obviously be working so close, Miss Burned-Down-My-Office. I won't tell you how to buy a packing materials company, and you don't tell me how to renovate this house. Deal?"

She laughed. A dark curl wrapped itself around her eye. "If that isn't so typically male, I don't know what is—'don't tell me how to do my job,' *blah blah blah*—"

"Well, that's a pretty typical female response if you ask me, the old I-know-how-to-do-everything-better-than-you attitude. I bet you're used to having everyone at your beck and call."

"And just what is that supposed to mean?" she asked, squaring off.

The woman did not lack for confidence, which, in spite of her being a little off her rocker, he found appealing. "Well, in a word, you're bossy."

She gasped. "Bossy!"

"Bossy."

"So a woman offers you some sound advice and you see it as bossy? Doesn't that seem kind of sexist?"

"No. A woman butts into a project when she doesn't have a clue what she is talking about and starts offering free advice. I see that as bossy."

"You are obviously confusing bossy with assertive. I just want the job done right, of course."

"I can't help but wonder why, if you know so much about renovation, that you hired out to begin with. Which reminds me—I've been meaning to ask you about that huge hole in the wall upstairs."

That shut her up. Her brows burrowed into a frown. "Oh gosh, look at the time," she said, looking at her watch. "I've got to get to work." She walked on, leaving the scent of lilac behind.

"Just as long as it's your work and not mine," he said, and with his back to her, smiled broadly when she muttered something about a goat.

For a while, she worked, occasionally mumbling under her breath. Then she got up, started walking around the table, lost in thought. And just when Jake thought she might actually walk through to the basement, she snatched up the phone and punched numbers. "Yes…Robin Lear calling for Eldagirt Wirt, please."

Jake almost choked.

"Robin Lear," she repeated. "Lear Transport Industries."

That was followed by a wait of maybe five seconds before Robin began to tap her foot. Patience was definitely not her strong suit. Suddenly the foot tapping stopped. "Yes! What—excuse me? Robin Lear of Lear Transport Industries. I would like to speak with Eldagirt Wirt about an opportunity I think she will find very exciting—no, she didn't win a cruise. Look, could you just ask Ms. Wirt to come to the phone?"

Whatever the other person said seemed to throw her for a loop. "Huh?" she asked, sounding terribly confused. "No, wait—hello?"

Robin held the phone out from her head and looked at it. "What the hell?" she said, and put the phone down.

Jake kept his back turned, trying hard to pretend like he hadn't just heard every bit of that. After a moment, he heard the click of her heels into the kitchen, the sound of a variety of doors being opened, and then the click of heels back into the dining room.

"I'm ordering out, do you want anything?"

He assumed she was talking to him and glanced at his watch. Twelve thirty.

"But vegan," she added. "Do you like vegan?" He turned to look at her. She arched a dark brow. "You know, vegetables and plant-based. No dairy, no meat."

"How does a person live without dairy or meat?" he asked.

"That's precisely the point," she said, and pushed that dark curl from her face. "You can live a much longer, healthier life without clogging your veins with animal fat."

"Lots of people eat meat and live long lives."

She blinked. "Well, yeah. But it's not that healthy. Look, you don't have to eat it. I was just asking."

"No thanks," he said. "I've got to go out later. I'll pick something up then."

"Fine," she said absently, and picked up the phone, dialing from memory. "Hi, this is Robin Lear on North? I'd like delivery, please. Eggplant wrap and salad—EGG-PLANT WRAP AND SALAD! Eggplant—okay. Thanks. Wait—one question. I ordered an eggplant wrap two weeks ago, and I could swear it was mozzarella and not tofu. Are you sure it's tofu? What? Well…okay…just make sure its tofu, will you?"

Now he knew for a fact he didn't like vegan and was about to say as much when his cell rang. Lindy. He clicked on the phone and walked to the front door. "Lindy, what's up?" he asked as he stepped outside and walked to his truck.

From the dining room window, Robin watched him. She could imagine what Lindy looked like—probably tall and willowy and blond. Jake probably asked her out for a pizza and the movies on the first date. She could just hear it now—*Do you like piña coladas, long walks in the rain, puppy dogs, and old movies?* They deserved each other. He was the kind of guy who probably needed a woman to hang on his every word, and anyone named Lindy was probably the woman for the job. A match made in heaven.

Dammit.

A match made in heaven had completely eluded her. It seemed like everyone she knew had one. Well, everyone except Rebecca, who was married to Dirtbag Bud. And Rachel—you could hardly count Myron as a match made in heaven. And Lucy, although she kept a string of guys around. And Evan damn sure didn't count, in spite of her atrocious lack of judgment last night. Okay, so Mia and Fix-Em Fred had matches made in heaven. It bothered Robin that she was even thinking this way. It wasn't as if she was looking for some long-term relationship.

She liked her freedom.

Thrived on it.

Who was she kidding? She'd love to have a long-term relationship. But she picked the wrong guys (Evan), and the ones who picked her never stayed long. Why was she so obviously

unlikable? "*You'll chill out someday.*" Mia's remark came screaming back at her, then Jake's observation that she was bossy, and
Robin wondered if it were possible that she was just now figuring out what everyone else already knew. Robin didn't want to
be unlikable. She really meant well. But she knew that she had
a slight problem—every thought that popped into her head
came tumbling out her mouth. And the thought that popped
into her head in that moment was *loser.*

That sent Robin into an even blacker mood.

Jake wasn't faring a whole lot better out on the drive.

"I was thinking we could study together for the exam
Thursday," Lindy was saying.

Why did that sound like an after-school malt date?
"Lindy...I think you should know—I'm not really looking
to date just now."

"Date? Who said date?" Her laughter was stilted. "Just
friends!"

"Okay. So we'll study—"

"Sure!" she said brightly. "I'll meet you at the campus
café around eight, okay?"

"Okay," he said. "See you." He clicked off, wondered why
he wasn't into her more than he was. She had all the pre-
requisites—nice, fairly attractive, could cook...not mouthy
like some women...Jake shook his head, didn't really want
to go there.

When he returned to the house, Robin was seated at
the dining table and was chewing on the end of a pen, her
brow furrowed as she pored over paperwork. Not wanting to
disturb her, Jake passed through to the kitchen and checked
out the plumbing beneath the sink, making a list of things
he needed to price later this afternoon. But when he looked

under the cabinets, he noticed a leak, and crawled in as far as he could to have a look.

As he worked, he could hear Robin in the other room. She left two messages for one Lou Harvey in a tone that Jake figured was going to get her nowhere fast.

When he at last located the source of the leak, he crawled out, came to his feet, and made a few notes. The sound of Robin's heels on the tile floor clicked to the front door; he heard it open. After a moment, the door shut, and the *click-click-click* returned to the dining room.

"Hello, this is Robin Lear," he heard after a moment. "I ordered an eggplant wrap over an hour ago and it hasn't arrived. Yes, North Boulevard."

Jake finished making the notes he needed and walked into the dining room.

"But I ordered it an hour ago!" she insisted, doing the loop around the dining room table again. "What do you mean you don't have a record? I asked the guy if it was cheese instead of tofu, and he said it was definitely tofu, and—what? How long? No. No, that's okay. Never mind," she said and put the phone down. "Pathetic. I can't even order lunch right!"

She actually sounded sincerely forlorn. And looked it. She glanced up as Jake walked in, ran her hands through her wild hair. "I keep calling these people and they won't call me back, the lunch guy forgets he even talked to me, and I don't understand half of what I'm reading in these papers. I can't be an acquisitions specialist and I am starving. I'm talking like five or six hundred calories worth of starving."

Jake didn't know about calories, but he knew where there were good eats. "You should check out Paulie's sometime," he suggested.

Robin turned, blinked big blue eyes at him, and Jake felt a curious draw from the pit of his stomach. "Where?"

"Paulie's. Best food in Houston."

Her blue eyes lit up. "Give me a minute to get my things."

That startled him. "What? Wait—I just meant you ought to *try* it."

"I know, but I don't have my car."

"Well, I…" What had he done? "I guess I could pick up a few things while I'm out."

"Where?"

Jake shrugged, looked away from those blue eyes, and rooted around in his backpack. "Over to Smith and Sons."

"I love Smith and Sons!" she said brightly.

He didn't believe his ears; he looked up, but Robin was busy smoothing out the wrinkle in her slacks. "This sounds like a great idea."

But it wasn't an idea, it wasn't even close. It was a gum-bumping mistake on his part.

"Just give me a minute, would you?" she added, but she was already halfway down the hall in the opposite direction.

Great. He was going to cart the barracuda around with him. Jake watched her disappear into the bedroom, then walked straight outside.

Whatever had just happened, however he had come to actually invite his client to lunch at Paulie's (*Paulie's!*), he hoped that her string of bad luck had ended and he was at last safe.

But a tiny little voice in the back of his head said that he wasn't safe, not even for a minute. From what, exactly, he really wasn't sure.

CHAPTER TEN

Robin appeared a few moments later, her hair brushed back and tucked neatly behind her ears, and sporting a pair of sunglasses that looked like sideways triangles. Jake peered at her closely as she climbed into his two-ton truck and sat gingerly on the dirty bench. He glanced at the stain she was avoiding and leaned over to have a better look. "Mustard. It looks like mustard." How could he know? A ten-year-old truck was going to have a stain or two. Robin just inched closer to the passenger door.

He started the truck, glanced at her again from the corner of his eye. "Can you actually see out of those things, or are they for decorative purposes only?"

"Of course I can," she said, with a roll of her eyes that he clearly saw above the tiny little lenses, "these are *Guccis.*"

"More like gotchas," he muttered under his breath.

"What?"

"Nothing." He backed out onto the street and headed west. They rode in silence at first; Robin folded up in the corner, careful not to touch anything, he with one arm slung carelessly across the back of the bench seat. When they turned onto Park Lane, he turned on the radio, forgetting that he had last listened to hard rock, which damn near shattered the windows. He quickly moved to change it, but Robin said, "Oh hey, I *love* these guys!"

Jake blinked. "The Dead Sorcerers?" he asked, incredulous. "I wouldn't have pegged you as hard rock."

"Oh yeah? What would you have pegged me?"

He shrugged, adjusted his Oakleys. "New age, maybe. Yanni, definitely."

That prompted a very unladylike snort; she folded her arms beneath her breasts and adjusted in her seat to look at him. "For your information, I listen to all kinds of music and always have, but mostly rock."

"Like?"

"Like the Foo Fighters, the Stones, Celine Dion—"

"Celine Dion?" he said on a bark of laughter. "She's elevator music!"

"She is not!" she cried indignantly. "Okay, Smartypants, who do *you* like?"

"First, no one's called me Smartypants since the third grade. Second, I just bought the new Red Temple CD. You heard of them?"

"I went to their concert in New York!" she said excitedly. "That singer guy is to *die* for—what's his name?"

She looked entirely too dreamy to suit Jake, so he feigned ignorance, saying only, "All I remember is that he looks like a girl," and switched over to the Astros game.

"So did you play as a kid?" Robin asked, leaning over to turn up the volume like she owned the truck.

"Yep. Grade school, junior high, all the way through high school and beyond."

"Beyond? What's beyond?"

That was territory he hadn't really intended to open up, particularly since the wounds were still a little raw after eighteen years, and he wasn't exactly keen to admit his failure. But damn it, she was looking at him with her mouth pursed in a way that could, conceivably, make a man move a mountain or two. "Minor leagues," he said cautiously.

"Really?" She looked happily surprised. "What team?"

Jake hesitated. "Baytown Sharks."

"*Oooh!* Very cool! What position did you play?"

"Right field."

"Must have had a good arm."

Huh. Amazing, but she seemed genuinely interested, so interested that Jake began to talk, albeit reluctantly, about his stint in the minors. It surprised him—in all these years, he hadn't actually spoken of it to anyone other than to mention it occasionally in the course of conversation. But Robin was engrossed in his telling of it, asking pertinent questions, seemingly impressed. *Impressed.* With him. It wasn't that Jake thought poorly of himself, it was just that…he was a practical man, and practically speaking, women like Robin Lear were not usually impressed with guys like him. Nevertheless, by the time they arrived at Smith and Sons, he was telling her about the Sunday men's league he played in Hermann Park.

"Hermann Park? I jog there! Maybe I'll just run by and watch sometime," she said as she flung open the door of his truck, nicking the car next to him. "I'll yell if I see you." She stepped out and marched off toward the garden area, her little purse swinging confidently in her hand.

Jake watched her hips moving in those nice tight pants a moment before he got out. By the time he'd locked his truck, Robin was bent over a stack of gargantuan ceramic pots. He walked past, told her he had to grab a few things and would only be a moment. Distracted, Robin waved him away.

Smith and Sons was one of those eclectic little mom-and-pop shops that had grown from hardware to just about everything else except groceries: a huge jumbled array of goods that took several minutes to navigate and even more to find anything. Once Jake had the couplings and pipes he needed, he paid—being careful to keep the receipt for Her Highness per their contract—and wandered back outside.

Robin was nowhere to be seen. He asked the guy watering the rosebushes, who shook his head. "She got a cart, man, and took off," was all he could offer. Jake walked around the garden, didn't see her, thought maybe she'd gone to the hardware section. But she wasn't there, either. He made his way through the kitchen area, house decor, and lumber, then outside again among the native plants and trees. That's when he saw the flash of curly black hair two aisles over.

Ducking through the saplings, he strode to where he had seen the top of her head and stopped dead in his tracks. It was Robin, all right, with a cart piled high and full with a dozen or more plastic pink flamingos, one gargantuan ceramic pot, and an azalea bush.

She looked up as he strode forward and stopped to survey the contents of her cart. Robin followed his gaze to the pink flamingos and flashed a cheerful smile. "For my pool."

"Ah," he replied, nodding. "Except that you don't *have* a pool."

"Oh, I know, but I think I might get one," she said with all sincerity. "Maybe some ferns, too. You know, for the corners," she added thoughtfully, and pushed the cart forward, between two neat rows of ferns, while Jake wondered *what* corners. He stood with his bag of couplings and watched her look at first one fern, then the next, and realized, much to his horror, that they were shopping. *Shopping!* For a pool she didn't even have! He eyed his watch, then Robin again, bent over another fern as she was, and his gaze was drawn to the tantalizing bit of purple he could see beneath her silk blouse.

He adjusted his stance slightly, saw that it was purple lace, barely covering what he guessed might possibly be the perfect breast. If it hadn't been for the bit of purple lace, Jake would have walked on to his truck and called her a cab. But there he was, following that piece of lace down the aisle between the ferns, saying things like *there's a good one* and *not that one, the tips are brown.*

A half hour later, the azalea and ceramic pot were stuffed in the bed of his truck, next to two ferns, a stack of lumber from an old job, and fourteen pink flamingos that bobbed along in their strange little gaggle as Jake sped down Kirby toward Paulie's.

Robin was talking about pools. She was so wrapped up in imagining where exactly she might put this pool (and of course, those stupid pink flamingos), she did not notice she was the only one conversing. He glanced at her from the corner of his eye, wondered if he'd lost his mind. What in God's name was he doing in the early afternoon, running around town with this woman? He had work to do, plenty of it, really did not have time for shopping at Smith and Sons, much less a bite to eat at Paulie's.

No time for it, but hell, he was only human. After all, she was an exceptionally good-looking woman. And she had a strange sort of refined, elitist mud-wrestling thing going on that he was finding disturbingly intriguing. And even though she held herself out as being in another stratosphere, beneath that slick exterior (and it *was* a kick-butt exterior), there was a funny little girl with a mess of black curls and the prettiest blue eyes he had ever seen.

Yep, he was intrigued, all right.

Even more so when they went into Paulie's. He liked Paulie's relaxed atmosphere, liked the wide variety of what he considered to be really good, really cheap food. But when Robin began to peruse the menu, rattling off the caloric content of each entry like an astrophysicist, Jake instantly realized his dumb mistake.

The waiter, who looked like he'd been pulled off the set of *Planet of the Apes,* chewed his thick lips as he stood, his pencil poised and pressed against the little notepad, waiting for her to order something. *Anything.* Robin ignored him, took her own sweet time to flip through the menu and wrinkle her nose at every entry. She finally sighed wearily and asked, "Do you have anything without grease?"

"Yeah, right," the waiter snorted. "We're into rabbit food here, carrots and tofu—"

"Tofu? Perfect!" Robin cried and handed him the menu. "Just bring me a Not Dog, please."

Grok the Apeman paused in the scratching of his big head to exchange a look of confusion with Jake. Robin folded her hands primly in her lap and looked first at Jake, then the waiter. "Oh!" She laughed sheepishly. "And a glass of water. With lemon. And not too much ice, maybe half full. The ice, that is, not the water."

Grok blinked, looked at Jake for help, but seeing that he was going to get none there, looked uneasily at Robin again. "Uh...what did you want again?"

"A Not Dog," she said, articulating.

"A what?" Jake asked.

"A tofu Not Dog. He said they have tofu."

"I think he was kidding," Jake said, to which Grok nodded violently. "And they don't have Not Dogs." He looked at Grok. "Just bring her a couple of dogs."

"*No!* Do you have any idea what's in a hot dog?"

"I've eaten plenty of hot dogs in my lifetime and I haven't died yet."

"That's a miracle, Jake. Hot dogs are as disgusting as they are fattening."

"Yeah, well, if you'd quit worrying about calories, you might actually enjoy some good food now and then," he countered, and looked again at Grok. "A couple of dogs, a bacon mushroom cheeseburger with fries, and two cokes."

"Wait!" Robin cried. Grok stopped writing. Robin looked at Jake, saw his scowl, and looked at the waiter again. "Okay. Hot dogs. But water!" she insisted. "And don't forget the lemon!"

Grok nodded furiously, made some mark on the paper, and loped away before she could change her mind.

Robin sniffed. "I never eat junk, especially when I'm trying to drop a few l.b.'s."

Now that was just plain stupid. Robin Lear was about as perfect in body as a woman could get, and in fact, upon further reflection, that perfect little ass of hers wasn't quite so perfect—it could use another pound or two. "That's ridiculous," he said with a snort.

"What do you know?" She folded her arms across her middle and in doing so, pushed her breasts dangerously close to the opening of her blouse.

"I know what looks good on a woman, and you look good," he blurted.

Robin blinked her surprised, and then a slow, seductive smile spread across those lips. "Well, *thank* you," she said, looking entirely too pleased with herself.

With a sigh, Jake leaned back in his chair and looked up at the greasy ceiling.

"You're not so bad yourself," she added.

He instantly lowered his head and eyed her with all due suspicion.

"In fact, if it wasn't for your general lack of humor—"

"Well now, that's the pot calling the kettle black," he said. "You're the don't-talk-to-me, you-must-be-a-pervert girl."

"That again?" She flicked her wrist dismissively. "I said I was sorry. You're too sensitive. And you need to take some responsibility for your part in it."

"My part?" he choked. She shrugged casually and gave him a pert little smile. She was teasing him. Jake shook his head. "You are one piece of work, Peanut."

"Priceless art," Robin said, and when Jake lifted a brow, she giggled.

Damn it if a smile didn't spread across *his* lips. He didn't think that was the direction he needed to be heading, so he changed the subject. "So...how's your dad?"

Robin's smile quickly faded. She shrugged, picked at a seam on the table. "I guess he's okay. Mom says they are going to California to see a spiritualist. My mom is really into homeopathy and Eastern philosophies."

"I knew a guy who had Lou Gehrig's disease and chose Eastern treatment," he offered.

Robin lifted a very hopeful gaze. "And?"

And he should have kept his mouth shut. Joe Powell had died. "He, ah…he did all right," Jake lied, grateful that Grok chose that moment to come back with the drinks. Jake asked her about where she'd grown up. She told him how her parents left West Texas cotton farms behind for Dallas, and how her father had been a line-haul driver for years before branching out on his own and creating the shipping company that was, judging by her trappings, extremely successful.

By the time Grok brought the food, Robin was actually making Jake laugh with stories of her childhood. "We lived in a two-bedroom house next to the railroad," she said as she carefully separated the two hot dogs to opposite ends of the plate. "We'd sneak out and go put pennies on the tracks so trains would smash them." She picked one hot dog and opened the bun wide.

Interesting—Jake and his brothers had done the same thing, only with objects far more interesting than pennies. It was almost impossible to think of Robin living in the same kind of place, particularly as she scraped the cheese and relish from the dog. But there she was, going at it with gusto, as if it were a perfectly natural thing to do to a hot dog.

"My mom caught us one day when the train was barreling down the track," she said, pausing in her task to lick her finger. "Needless to say, that was the end of that." She pushed the discarded toppings to one side, then pushed the wienie from the bun, and proceeded to cut the hot dog into bite-sized pieces. Fascinated, Jake watched her destroy a perfectly good hot dog as he shoved three and four french fries into his mouth.

"She didn't like what she called our 'experiments,'" Robin said and forked a clean, bite-sized piece of wienie into her mouth.

"Ah. Reminds me of a similar experiment gone awry. My little brother, Todd, had a stuffed Bullwinkle that he dragged everywhere. My other brother, Ross, had this idea that if a train were to run over Bullwinkle, he'd just flatten out and spring right back to shape. Well, Bullwinkle did not spring right back to shape. There was cotton batting scattered from Houston down to the Gulf."

"Ooh, poor Todd! What happened?"

Jake's memory soured, but he forced a smile. "My dad whipped the dickens out of me and Ross." In truth, the whipping had left horrible welts on them.

Robin smiled. "You have two brothers? I have two sisters. Where are you in the lineup?"

"The oldest."

"Me, too!" she cried in delight. "So what do your brothers do?"

This is where all similarities ended. Jake took a big bite of burger, chewed thoughtfully, pondering Robin's reaction, then wondering why he cared. She had hired him to do a job, not father a child. He swallowed. "Ross was killed in a drunk-driving accident," he said, omitting the small detail that Ross was the drunk driver. "And Todd is in prison."

To her credit, Robin did not balk or faint or scream in terror. She said nothing, just picked at the last two bites of the hot dog. "Really?" she asked after a moment. "Maybe I know Todd." She lifted her gaze; her blue eyes were shining with empathy. "Hardy har har."

Jake smiled, grateful that she had tried.

"So what's he in for?"

"Armed robbery."

She nodded. "And how long has he been gone?"

A lifetime. "About three years now. He's got another twelve to do. Maybe less if he can keep out of trouble."

"And Ross? When did he die?"

Jake looked out the front window at the sunlight dappled on the hood of his truck and wondered just exactly when the spirit had left Ross. "Two years ago."

"You must really miss him."

Her voice sounded odd; Jake looked at her, saw the sadness deep within him reflected back in her eyes, and knew she was thinking of her father. "I miss him a lot," he said solemnly.

They sat just looking at one another for a long moment, until Robin's fair skin colored an appealing shade of pink, and she abruptly attacked the second hot dog, scraping the condiments from the meat.

"Wait," Jake said, shaking his head. "I can't watch you do that again."

"Do what?"

"Destroy a perfectly good hot dog. Eat it right."

"I *am* eating it right!"

"No, you're not, you're eating it like a tea cake." Jake impulsively grabbed her wrist with one hand, then reached for the dog with his other. "This is how you eat a hot dog," he said firmly, and let go her wrist, swiped up the catsup bottle, and poured a respectable pile onto the dog. Then he shoved one end in his mouth, took a bite, and put the rest of the dog back on her plate. "Try it! You'll like it!"

"No!" she exclaimed, looking at her plate in horror.

"Come on—"

"It's gross."

"Chicken."

"What? What did you say?" she gasped, her brows forming a sharp V. "Did you just call me a chicken?"

"Bok bok bok—"

It worked. She picked up the dog so fast he almost didn't see it. She put the dog to her lips, stretched her mouth open to carefully accommodate it, and slowly slid it between her teeth. Her eyes rounded. "*Umm,*" she said.

Jake thought he was going to faint, right then and there.

Robin chewed slowly and thoughtfully as if tasting meat for the first time ever, while Jake squirmed and silently begged her to take another bite. She swallowed, looked at him in great surprise. "Not bad!" she admitted, and put the dog to her mouth again in such an innocently seductive way that Jake feared he would melt all over the damn floor.

She finished the dog, drained her water. "So? Are you going to sit there and critique my eating habits all day? We need to get back," she said. "I've got a lot to do." She popped up from her seat.

Yes, yes, yes, they needed to get back to reality right away. Jake dug in his back pocket for his wallet, lifted out a twenty, and tossed it on the tabletop as Robin fussed with her unruly hair. He followed her out, noticed how smoothly she slipped into the truck when he opened the door for her. He came around to the driver's seat, started her up, and was adjusting the radio again when he caught her looking at him.

He lifted a brow in question.

Robin smiled. "Is the game still on?"

As a matter of fact, the Astros game was now in its seventh inning, and he and Robin drove down Kirby listening to the game while the pink flamingos danced in the rearview mirror. When they turned onto North, the Astros drove a run in, and both whooped, high-fiving it like old friends.

"You know," she said coyly as they neared her house, "I meant what I said today. You really aren't half bad." She gave him a grin so wicked that it made his pulse pound. He smiled and turned toward her, waiting for the punchline.

Robin arched one sculpted, devilish brow.

A silly grin spread across Jake's lips, and he felt exactly like he had in the fifth grade when Maria Del Toro said she liked his shoes. He could have leapt tall buildings in those shoes after that. "Is that right?" he asked.

"You're surprisingly much better than a pervert."

"Thanks. That means a lot coming from you, Peanut."

"But I have to take off points for your advocacy of processed meat snacks and the nasty things you said about Moz, who is the greatest pitcher ever."

"Fair enough," Jake agreed. "And I'm taking points off for the Fu-fu Not Dogs."

"That's not fair, Jake. You can't take points off for being healthy."

"No, the points are being knocked off for being wacko," he said, laughing, fully intent on telling her that she still wasn't half bad in spite of her grave error in judgment, and in fact, pretty damn good, but Robin's gaze was drawn to a point over his shoulder and her smile suddenly faded.

Jake dragged his gaze from Robin to look over his shoulder, to where Lindy was standing at the window holding an insulated lunch bag.

CHAPTER ELEVEN

How odd, Robin thought, as she sat staring at the girl with shoulder-length mousy brown hair, that she detected the faint smell of fried chicken. She and Jake opened their doors, stepped out at exactly the same moment, and he said, "Lindy, what are you doing here? How did you find me?"

Robin almost dropped her purse. Lindy? This was *Lindy*? This little chicken-fried jailbait was Jake's *girlfriend*? What happened to blond and willowy? What happened to adult? What was she, maybe twelve? Unbelievable! Robin could kick herself—*I meant what I said, you know*—Damn it! She could just die of humiliation right here and now!

"Your mom. Hey, I brought you some fried chicken. Are you hungry?" Lindy was asking.

"That was nice of you, but you probably should have checked with me me before coming down to the job site."

"Oh," she asked, looking curiously at Robin. "I just thought you might need a break and a chance to eat before we hooked up later."

Hooked up later? Robin frowned at Jake's back, grabbed one pink flamingo and stuffed it under her arm. Jake took the insulated bag from Lindy, clasped her elbow, and turned

her away from the truck and Robin. As Lindy smiled ador-
ingly up at him, Robin grabbed another flamingo and
started for the door. She could be such a dolt sometimes.
She glanced back to see if Jake was coming or making out
with Lollipop Lindy behind the garage, and in the course of
doing so, she collided head-on with Evan, who stepped out
the door at the precise moment she was stepping in.

One flamingo fell to the ground.

"Oops...are you all right?" he asked, catching her elbow.

"I'm fine. But what are you doing here?"

Evan stooped to get the dropped flamingo. "I'm happy
to see you, too," Evan said with a wry smile and handed her
the flamingo. "And I'm here because we've got work to do,
kiddo. What are these?"

"Well...they're pink flamingos." Obviously. She stepped
past Evan into the house and on to the dining area, where
she deposited the two flamingos against the wall.

"Why?" Evan asked, following behind.

"Why what?" Robin tossed her kate spade bag onto a chair.

"Why the pink flamingos?"

"I am thinking of getting a pool," Robin said, and before
he could question her endlessly about that, she marched
to her computer, hit a button, and watched her e-mail pop
up. Four messages. One from Darren at Atlantic (*Hope you're
okay!!*), one from Bob (*Was it something I said?*), and two from
Lucy (*1. Insurance guys*; and *2. Re: Insurance guys*).

"Did you look over those accounts?" Evan asked, pink
flamingo in hand.

"Yes. And I made several attempts to speak to those
accounts, and I am dying for someone to clue me in on what
sort of name is Eldagirt Wirt—"

The smell of fried chicken interrupted her train of thought. Jake had strolled in, the insulated meals-on-wheels delivery in hand. Robin looked back to her papers. "Are we still on to meet with the insurance guys?" she asked Evan.

"As a matter of fact, I talked to the agent earlier—it looks like it was probably faulty wiring."

That momentarily drew Robin's attention from the smell of fried chicken. "Faulty wiring," she repeated, thinking it was a trap to get her to admit she'd left the coffeepot on.

"A short in the alarm system."

"Not arson?"

Evan chuckled. "No, not arson."

Flooded with relief, Robin instantly, unthinkingly, looked at Jake. He gave her a thumbs-up behind Evan's back and flashed a smile that raced right down to her toes.

"—probably ten months or so before the office is inhabitable again." Evan was still talking, Robin realized. "They'll talk to us about it. But we're covered and I let your dad know."

Well, wasn't that cozy, Evan reporting to her father. Perhaps he mentioned to Dad that he got her drunk on very expensive wine last evening and then had sex with her. Perhaps Dad and Evan toasted his success over the phone.

"I asked Lucy to make the arrangements for our travel to Minot," Evan blithely mentioned.

Robin paused. She looked up at him. "Excuse me?"

Evan paused in his casual perusal of the pink flamingo. "You don't think we are going to acquire a company over the phone, do you?"

"We?" she said, stealing another glimpse of Jake, who had, thankfully, put the stupid lunch bag in his backpack and resumed work.

"Yes, *we*," Evan said, looking at Jake, too. "I'm not going to leave you hanging, Robbie. Of course I am going to go with you. At least to Minot."

Oh no. That was much, muchmuchmuch too convenient. "Thanks, but I prefer to do this on my own."

"Robin—"

"Evan, if you want me to learn, shouldn't I just jump in and do it?"

"Maybe I need to remind you that I tried to let you do it before, and now Aaron is holding me responsible for that little Atlantic deal you cooked up. Face it, Robin, you could stand a little guidance, and your father has charged me with giving it to you. It's just to Minot, so don't get your panties in a twist. Once I show you how to handle this sort of thing, I'll go on to New York and you can go to Burdette and try your hand with Ms. Wirt."

Robin's face was flaming—she was certain Jake thought her a complete boob now, thanks to Evan.

"I told Lucy to set something up for next week. In the meantime, why don't you try and get Ms. Wirt on the phone?"

Oh, brilliant idea! Why hadn't she thought of that before?

"And there are some local accounts that need your review. They're out in the car—I'll be back in a jiff."

She watched him stroll out of the dining room, dressed to the nines as usual, his Italian leather loafers almost soundless on the tile floor. As he walked past Jake, Robin was momentarily distracted by the tattoo peeking out beneath the arm of Jake's T-shirt as he reached high above his head. She was dying to see it, imagining it was something like a heart, with a name scribed in flowing letters across it. *I heart Lindy.* Better yet, maybe it was a skull and crossbones. Whatever, it sent a peculiar little shiver down her spine, just like the rest of him.

Oh God—was she really doing this? Was she really lusting after Jake? Robin abruptly turned away, walked out of the dining room and down the long corridor to the master suite. Since when had she become so...so aroused by the sight of a man? Irritable now, she shut the door behind her and stood, hands on hips. What she was doing was avoiding work. It was so obvious. She was avoiding work because she felt like a fish out of water. Not only did she not have the foggiest clue how to go about acquiring a company, she was so inept she couldn't even get the likes of Eldagirt Wirt on the phone. And the only person who could teach her was her ex-lover Evan. (*Definitely ex! One gigantic slip in judgment did not constitute a re-relationship! Ex, Ex, Ex!*)

She supposed she could at least be happy that she hadn't burned down her office.

Robin fell backward onto her bed and stared morosely at the ceiling. Dad was right; she was arrogant and useless and nothing but window dressing. But she was going to change that. All Robin had ever wanted was to follow in Dad's footsteps, to become a viable, integral part of the company, his legacy. One she hoped would be her legacy one day. The thing to do was to pour herself into this job and do it right. She had to stop avoiding it with this fruitless, impractical, stupid flirting with Jake. She could not let her fear of failure derail her.

Robin suddenly sat up. She had work to do. She was going to out there and start researching bubble wrap. And when she proved she could do it, Dad would see how wrong he was about her and everything would go back to normal. Assuming she could figure out what normal was. Okay, well, one thing that was definitely abnormal was lying on her bed and fretting in the middle of the day, and she didn't want to face the fact that maybe she was just a little bit, teeny-tiny bit afraid.

That did it.

Robin sat up, shook her fingers through her hair, and walked out of her room to do what she did best. Work.

Jake noticed the change in Robin's demeanor the moment she came back into the dining room and plopped down at her computer with a determined look on her pretty face. She ignored him, was even a little stiff with Romeo (which didn't bother Jake in the least), and punched the computer keys like pop-up weasels. That was all just as well, because he had decided that intriguing or not, this flirting thing was dangerous business. The last thing he needed was to have some sort of fling with a client, because nothing would come back to bite him in the ass faster than that. And there was no question in his mind that this flirtation could never be more than a fling, period. He harbored no illusions otherwise.

A fling would be an enormous irritant right now. He had enough going on with school and Cole, and there was the constant distraction of work, and Zaney, and his mom's health, and Lindy's infatuation. He hated telling women he didn't want to see them, and generally tried to avoid those situations altogether. Which meant he hadn't dated seriously in a long time, mainly because of a lack of money and time. But things were a little different now. After all, he wasn't getting any younger. He had bought the house in the Heights with the vague notion that he might want to settle down someday, and someday was staring him in the face. Lindy was a great gal—what more could a guy want?

Something. This guy definitely wanted something more. He just didn't know what it was, and thinking about it only made his head hurt.

So Jake forced himself to ignore his little problem, and ignore the conversation going on behind him between Robin and Romeo. Actually, he had no idea what they were talking about, but whatever it was, he really did not care for the way Romeo spoke to Robin, his tone condescending, like she was stupid. Robin was anything but stupid. Crazy, maybe—but not stupid. The man sounded like a patronizing buffoon.

Jake moved upstairs to work so he couldn't hear them any longer, and was actually beginning to make some headway when his cell phone rang—Mom.

"Jacob, where are you?" she asked when he answered.

"At a job. What's up?"

"It's Cole. The principal called and said he wasn't in school again today—"

"Goddammit, I'm going to kill him if I find—"

"He's home," his mom quickly interrupted him. "He just came wandering in like he always does after school. He doesn't know that I know he ditched school today. I thought you might want to be here when I talk to him."

"Yes, I definitely want to be there," he said through clenched teeth. "Look, Mom, it's time he came to live with me," he blurted. "I've been thinking about this—he needs to learn how to be a man, and I'm going to have to be the one to teach him. It's too hard on you."

"You know how I feel about that, Jacob. You aren't home enough as it is."

"I'll be home more."

"How are you going to do that? Are you going to give up school? You were so hellfire bent on it, even though I told you it'd take away from your obligations. Now you don't have the time to give to him. I'll grant you he needs to learn to be a man, but he needs someone who can devote his full attention to it. You can't do that."

"Maybe not, but you can't deny he's running roughshod over you, Mom," Jake insisted. "He needs a firm hand. He needs to be jerked up by the short hairs once in a while and know he's going to find his butt on the end of my boot when he cuts school."

She paused, lit a smoke, and exhaled wearily. "Are you coming over or not?"

Jake sighed, looked at his watch. "Yeah. I can be there in an hour," he said and warned her to keep an eye on Cole before he got there. He clicked off the cell phone and stared blindly out the casement window at the thick, lush lawn surrounding Robin's house. Maybe his mom was right. Maybe his vow at Ross's funeral was just a wish, not really a promise. He didn't have time for Cole; he barely had time to breathe. He was working hard, trying to make something of himself…but for what? So he could be a rich and lonely old man some day? He was thirty-eight years old and had so far managed to avoid a long-term commitment. Cole was in desperate need of one, and Jake worried if he was even capable of giving him his full commitment.

Whatever the answer—and Jake really wasn't sure he wanted to know the answer—he had the immediate problem of Cole's cutting school to deal with. Lost in thought, he walked down the curving staircase to the entry, packed up his things, and left to fight Houston traffic to have yet another heart-to-heart with a lost kid.

Robin never heard Jake leave, and in fact, was a little surprised he'd managed to get out without her noticing. Perhaps she was actually able to focus on her work. Or perhaps it was because Evan had talked and talked and talked until her head was pounding. Who could even hear themselves think in all that racket? And then he was pacing about the dining room, complaining that he was hungry, and somehow convinced her to try a new restaurant with him.

But when they got there, Evan was smiling in that familiar way of his, like he knew something about her that perhaps Robin didn't know herself. She hated that look; it implied an intimacy that just wasn't there. She decided, over appetizers, that this was the perfect opportunity to explain that they were *not* getting back together again, and if he ever brought wine to her house again, she just might clock him one. She owed him at least that much—after all, she had slept with him last night. She could understand where a man might misconstrue things.

But when she told him, as nicely as she could, that last night had been one huge, monumental mistake, Evan got a little pissy. After he insisted she'd liked it, Robin said again, "I had too much to drink, Evan. I got carried away when I should have showed some restraint. But I need to tell you that even though we did…it…that it really has no bearing on my feelings about…about…"

"Wanton and meaningless sex?" he snapped.

"About us," she had said, ignoring his jab. "I haven't changed my mind."

Evan slowly leaned back in his seat and glared at her, finally managing to say (through a jaw that was clenched tightly shut), "You can be pretty damned arrogant at times, Robin. And cruel. I wonder why you think it is okay to toy with people like this."

There was that arrogant thing again, and it pricked her hard. "I am trying to be honest," she said. "You should try it because I think you've been trying to rekindle something with me for several weeks—"

"You ran off to London. How could I try and do anything? Okay, fine. You made some huge mistake. But we have to work together and I don't want to screw that up."

"Me, either," she said softly and contritely.

Evan downed his wine and said, "I won't go so far as to say I understand you, but okay. Colleagues only, right?"

"Right," she said, only she didn't feel right at all. Not at all.

While Robin was sipping Chianti, Jake was concentrating on what the instructor was saying about load balances. Engineering II was not his favorite class to begin with, but it was a hell of a lot harder with Cole on the brain. When he'd confronted Cole at his mom's, the kid had sat slumped down on the couch, his spindly legs spread wide apart, glaring. "You're going to school, Cole," Jake had said. "If I have to take you myself every single day, I will."

"When are you gonna stop acting like you're my father? You ain't my father! You don't have no say over me!" Cole had instantly shot back.

"Like hell I don't have any say over you. I may not be your father, but I am your uncle, and like I told you, I'm all you've got."

"Everyone's always telling me what I don't got," he'd complained.

"Maybe what I need to do is have a visit with your school to see if something else is going on that causes you to skip class and not learn proper English," Jake had snapped.

Cole's brown eyes had grown wide at that threat. "I don't want you to go to my school."

"All the more reason to go then," Jake had said. "If you won't go to school like you're supposed to, then I'll go down there and find out what's up."

"I don't have to take this shit!" Cole shouted and had vaulted off the couch, bounding up the stairs two at a time.

"You watch your mouth!" Mom had shouted up after him. They heard the slam of his door, and Mom had sighed wearily. "I might as well be raising Ross all over again."

Jake had left before she could start her litany of complaints.

He was late for class, sneaking into the last seat. "Thanks for deciding to join us this evening, Mr. Manning," the grad student instructor drawled. Jake frowned as the rest of the class turned around to have a look. Smirking, the instructor resumed his lecture, and Jake tried to concentrate. But by the end of the class, having lost most of what the instructor had said, he waited impatiently for last week's assignments to be handed out. When the instructor at last came to Jake, he shook his head, handed him a paper that had a bright red D scrawled across the top. "You're going to have to apply yourself, Mr. Manning, if you want to pass this course. There are names of students who will tutor for a fee in the library. I suggest you call one."

Jake pushed down the desire to deck the pompous smart-ass, and went to find Lindy.

She had picked a table in the corner of the café, had spread her papers wide so no one would join her. Her face lit up when Jake approached. "I finished the assignment for Planning Three," she said happily, "so I'm all yours. I figured you didn't have much time to do the assignment, but I think between the two of us we can work through it tonight."

He couldn't help but wince inwardly at her smile. Lindy was the kind of girl that could make a man very happy, such a nice girl that he thought he really ought to have his head examined. But the surprising and alarming truth was, he found an overbearing, stuck-up prima donna more interesting than the June Cleaver scene. He sighed, dropped his backpack, and folded his arms on top of the table. "Lindy, we really have to talk," he said and watched the smile fade like a light from her attractive face.

CHAPTER TWELVE

Evan drove her home, barely managed a good night. Robin let herself in through the kitchen, paused there to toss her doggy bag of ravioli into the fridge (she was not the type to leave food behind when her cupboard was Sahara-desert bare), then walked through a house as empty as she felt inside.

She didn't like the feeling of emptiness. She didn't like hurting Evan, either, or the fact that she couldn't seem to form decent relationships. It always felt like there was some hard and high wall she was struggling to climb, but to what? God, who knew? She was too tired to think about it, thought it funny that a day of accomplishing absolutely nothing could exhaust her so. The moment her head hit the pillow, she fell into a deep sleep, interrupted only by one of those pesky dreams in which she was drowning.

When she awoke the next morning, she felt very strange, as if someone else had stopped by to inhabit her skin. The antsy feeling was so unlike her and so uncomfortable that she hurried out to the dining room to work, anxious to *do* something, anything, to make the feeling go away. She was still in her Curious George pj's, engrossed in her research of bubble wrap when Jake let himself in the back door, carrying three pink flamingos and an Igloo lunch box.

"Morning," he said stoically, put the flamingos down, and walked to the foyer. Robin gathered her robe more tightly around her, took a sip of very blah coffee, and attempted to focus on the information on her screen. But then Jake climbed up the ladder, reached high overhead, and began to pry old trim from the top of the paned glass windows that graced the top of the eighteen-foot entry.

All thoughts of bubble wrap flew out of her head. Robin surreptitiously watched him over the rim of her coffee cup. As he strained to reach the trim, she could see the outline of his hips fitting snugly in a pair of faded denim jeans, his broad muscular back beneath a very thin T-shirt, and the flash of that tattoo she was dying to see.

Okay. She had been around the world more than once, had dated more men than she could remember anymore, and rarely, *rarely*, had the physical presence of one man gotten under her skin like this. She was attracted to Jake Manning, big-time. She continued to covertly watch him from behind the cover of her laptop, and miraculously, for the first time, she began to see past his butt to what he was actually doing. It fascinated her—he moved smoothly, working quickly and evenly, as if the dismantling of her home was the easiest thing in the world to do. She admired the way he didn't waste a moment, how everything was done with maximum efficiency.

She watched until it became apparent she was going to get nothing done again today if she kept it up, and retreated to her bedroom for a shower and a little regrouping. She dressed in a denim skirt and pale blue raw silk blouse, then slipped on some sandals, figuring since there weren't going to be any high-powered meetings on North Boulevard this afternoon, she might as well be comfortable.

When she returned to the dining room, Jake was gone again and her answering machine was blinking. She returned calls to Lucy and the account rep in the valley. She made calls to her attorney and her old college roommate, Cecilia Simpson-Duarte, who was hosting a charity event. She even took a phone call from Lou Harvey's secretary, who called to confirm a meeting in Minot, North Dakota, the following week, which, even though it was only Minot, made Robin oddly ecstatic.

Now if only Eldagirt Wirt would call. From the looks of the LTI and Dun & Bradstreet reports, the Wirt company was probably the best option of the two. With a groan, Robin picked up the phone, dialed the number to Wirt Supplies and Packing that she now knew by heart, and got the receptionist again. "Wirt. How may I direct your call?"

"Robin Lear calling for Eldagirt Wirt, please."

The girl sighed wearily. "She's not in at the moment. May I leave a message?"

Okay, Eldagirt's work habits—as in never—were really beginning to annoy Robin. "Do you expect her in *today*?"

"Yes, I expect her in *today*," the girl said. "Girt is a very busy person, Miss Lear."

"I am sure she is," Robin hastily agreed, wondering just how busy a person who made bubble wrap could be. "But I've been trying to get hold of her for two days now."

"One and a half. You've called her four times in twelve work hours."

Well, hell, bite her head off, then. "Is there a convenient time to call?" Robin asked, trying to put the image from her mind of a woman named Eldagirt blowing up each individual bubble in the rolls of wrap she made.

"It would be better if she could call you this afternoon. She's in and out a lot with her son. Is there a number she can reach you?"

Oooh, her *son*. Now she got it—the woman was not committed to her job. "Why, yes, there is a number. It is the same number I have left four times now. Shall I repeat it?"

"No," the girl said coldly. "I'll be sure and tell her you called."

"I just bet you will," Robin muttered as she hung up the phone. "And while you're at it, tell her to get a real name!" she added petulantly, heard a strange scraping sound, and jerked around. Jake was standing under the archway, holding a stack of drop cloths. "And may I just add for the record that I don't know how she runs that show if she's never there!" she added testily.

"Ah well, you know what it's like to be a busy executive," Jake said as he strolled into the foyer and began to spread the drop cloths. "A long lunch, a round of golf with your client, then a meeting with the sales force to assure yourself that the business didn't get up and walk out the door while you were screwing around."

Robin snorted at his warped perspective. "Please. When I actually have an office, I can hardly grab lunch most days because there is so much to do." She did not add that most days, she was busy trying to set up deals that were doomed from the start.

"Yeah, well, I've worked in enough executives' houses to know it's not exactly nose to the grindstone all day, either."

"Oh yeah?" she asked, following him into the entry.

"Like this heart doctor's garage apartment I did a few months ago. This guy's wife went to the gym every day at two. And every day at two oh five, he came home with his girlfriend. God's honest truth," he added at Robin's dubious look. "And every day at three fifteen, they scooted out of the drive just before the wife came home from the gym."

"I don't believe you. Where was this, anyway?"

"River Oaks."

"River Oaks?" she asked excitedly. "I grew up there!"

"I thought you said you grew up in Dallas."

"I said that's where we started out. Then we moved to River Oaks. So who was it?"

"Marvin Hanes."

With a shriek, Robin slapped a hand over her mouth. "Dr. Marvin Hanes? *The* Marvin Hanes? Dad used to play tennis with him! Oh my *God*! What is it with men?"

"With those men, it's a power thing," Jake said nonchalantly, bending down to examine several cans.

"What do you mean, a power thing?"

"The more women, the more powerful they feel."

Robin collapsed against the brick wall, her arms folded across her middle. "It's just so…disgusting. Why can't men be faithful?"

"Wait, wait," Jake said on a laugh. "Don't lump us all in with the sorry lot of dogs! There are men who can be faithful."

Oh yeah, right, like Dad. "Name one," she challenged him.

"Me," he said in all earnestness.

Robin blinked; he steadily returned her gaze, and funny, she desperately wanted to believe if there was any man on the face of this earth who would honor one woman, it was Jake Manning. "Really? So if a better deal came along, are you saying you would not dump your girlfriend in a heartbeat?"

The color seemed to drain from his face so quickly that her heart skipped a beat. "I don't have a girlfriend if that is what you are after. And what do you mean, a better deal?"

Robin snorted. "I mean better—as in better looking. More money. That sort of thing."

"So you think it all boils down to money and looks?" he asked disdainfully. "That's more of an indictment against women, if you ask me. They look for money, power—"

"Oh, and men don't look for those things? It's just the truth, Jake. There are certain inalienable facts about life, and one of them is that money talks."

"Wow," he said, looking her up and down now. "That's really cold."

"It's not cold," Robin said dispassionately, "it's just the way of the world." But Jake was now looking at her as if he pitied her somehow, and Robin felt suddenly and strangely lost. She wished she'd never started this conversation. She wished she'd never mentioned girlfriends. She could feel herself flushing.

Jake looked away, squatted down by the cans again, picked one, and withdrew a screwdriver from his hip pocket to flip open the lid. "So you know what I think about this Eldagirt Wirt?" he asked, artfully changing the subject as he grabbed a paint stick and began to stir. "I don't think she exists."

Robin laughed. "Well, maybe if I'm lucky, Wirt Supplies and Packing doesn't exist, either. Maybe this is just some huge joke my dad is playing on me."

"If it is, it's a good one, because it sure has you going," Jake said, and then wondered aloud what Eldagirt must look like, insisting she was a little old lady with a cowskin handbag.

Robin disagreed. "A bulldozer," she said. "Army boots, flak jacket. She has to be, with a name like that."

They were laughing, talking like old friends as he began to strip away old paint and dirt from the brick in the entry. They talked about last night's Astros game.—*See your boy Moz last night? He gave up three runs in the eighth.*—*You can't blame the loss on him! Those fielders had huge holes in their gloves!* They argued about the relative value of tofu in society.—*Tofu is made by people who want your money, that's all there is to it.*—*Oh yeah? Why don't you just open up your veins and pump in some forty-weight?* Robin explained how bubble wrap was made by pressing two sheets together then inserting the bubbles, and was bowled over to find out he already knew.—*How did you know?*—*I'm just real smart.*—*Why, yes, and modest, too!*

Robin wondered if Jake liked her company as much as she liked his. It felt comfortable between them shooting the breeze, and for a moment or two, Robin could believe she had known Jake all her life. But then again, she was aware that she had never known anyone like Jake.

Jake showed her what he was doing, ushering her in front of him, telling her to look at the brick as he painted the cleaner over it. Framed by his body, Robin watched, but she was much more aware of his body so close to hers, the very titillating sensation that their bodies fit like hand and glove.

"See the brick?" he asked, his breath soft on her ear. "See the color of it? And the little mark right there? This brick is worth a small fortune."

"It's beautiful," she said, and insanely, intentionally, leaned backward, into him, on the pretense of looking up at the paned-glass windows above, until her hair was brushing his shoulder. "The stained glass is going to be gorgeous."

"Yeah, this will be one beautiful house...with a beautiful owner."

Robin's breath caught in her throat; she froze for an instant, debated madly whether she should turn around and kiss him, but quickly decided against it. Because she didn't have the guts. And because Mia chose that moment to come strolling in.

"Robin?"

Robin spun out from beneath Jake's arm and into the middle of the entry, her heart pounding.

Mia's eyes narrowed with suspicion; she looked at Jake, then at Robin. "I thought I might find you here," she said, in that all-knowing, all-seeing way of hers. She walked into the entry, the heels of her Prada pumps clapping loudly on the tile floor. Perfectly dressed as usual, Mia's blond hair was pulled back in a sleek ponytail and her capri pants were skintight. "*What* are you doing?" she demanded.

"Learning about brick," Robin said quickly and walked through the archway into the dining room. "What are *you* doing?"

Mia was eyeing Jake as if she expected him to pull out a gun. "Shopping. I thought maybe you'd want to get some lunch."

"Lunch? Ah…" *Think fast, think fast…* "I can't. I have a lot of work to do."

One of Mia's blond brows arched high above the other as she coolly shifted her gaze to Robin. "Oh really?" she drawled, and took one last up-and-down look at Jake. "What are you going to do for food?"

"Leftover ravioli."

"You must be kidding."

"From Santiago's."

"*Ooh*, I've heard Evan talk about that place. Was it as good as he says?"

Acutely aware that Jake was listening to every word, Robin picked up a paper on which she had scribbled some notes and pretended to study them, muttering, "It's okay."

"Speaking of Evan," Mia said, "he called this morning and said his new boat is down in the marina again. He wants to do a dinner out there."

Robin jerked her gaze to Mia. "*Evan* called?

"We talked about it last weekend, remember?"

Like Robin could ever forget last weekend.

Mia sighed impatiently. "Michael and I are free this weekend. Are you?"

"No," Robin said quickly. "I can't. Anyway, I thought Evan was going to New York."

Mia shrugged. "What's the deal with all these pink flamingos?" she asked, picking up Robin's kate spade bag and having a look inside. "And where did you get this bag? Is it last year's?"

Thankfully, the conversation deteriorated from there into Mia's general obsession with handbags. Robin loved Mia, but she had never wanted her friend to be gone as badly as she did at that moment. She felt like a frumpy wallflower in her jean skirt next to her perfect friend, and worse, she could have sworn she saw Jake looking at Mia more than once. But Mia, true to form, seemed to have forgotten he was even in the same room, for which Robin was grateful. Which begged the question—since when did she feel so ridiculously and profoundly stupid and gangly? *What was happening to her?* She was out of control, so out of control that she suddenly informed Mia she had changed her mind about lunch. "I don't really like ravioli," she said to Mia's look of surprise, grabbed her handbag from Mia's grip, and marched out through the kitchen without so much as a glance backward.

Jake watched the Porsche pull out onto North Boulevard, his nostrils still full of the sweet smell of lilac. Robin's scent. He frowned; whoever the blonde was, her timing couldn't have been worse—he'd been about to kiss Robin. Which wasn't exactly the brightest idea he'd ever had. In fact, it ranked right up there as the dumbest. The woman as much as admitted that money and power mattered, neither of which he possessed. No wonder she thought that—she'd grown up in River Oaks, probably in one of those gated mansions with a security guard. What would she think if she knew he grew up off Telephone Road? She'd think he was too far beneath her, that was what, a working man trying to latch on to the better deal, as she so eloquently put it. She didn't need someone like him hanging around.

On second thought, maybe her friend had excellent timing.

But damn it, that black curly hair and figure that was all butt and legs, and those blue eyes and those lips... *Get a grip.* Those were River Oaks lips that drank wine he couldn't pronounce and ate at Santiago's. Okay, so he *had* lost his friggin' mind. Thank you, God, he hadn't kissed her.

Jake stared at the wall in front of him. Next week, Zaney would be back to work and he'd have the demolition crews come in. Yeah, he'd have the crews come in, go do something else for a couple of days, and clear his mind of this stupid, crazy notion that anything could come from having a couple of things in common with a beautiful woman who lived in the Village.

He was revving up to abuse himself for being such an idiot all over again when he heard something that sounded like a body being dragged across the floor. What the hell was that? He turned abruptly and unexpectedly came nose to forehead with a round baldpate. Startled, he reared back a couple of steps.

"Well, what's your name, son?" the old man standing before him asked.

"Uh...Manning. Jake Manning," he stammered.

"You must be the contractor."

"Yes," he said, taking in the man's siesta shirt and Forrest Gumperals.

The old man scratched his chest and peered up at the paned-glass window. "How much you charge?"

"*Elmer!*" A woman's voice pierced Jake's eardrum; she came rushing into the dining room from the kitchen. "Stop bothering that man!"

Elmer shook his head and shuffled out of the entry on a pair of enormous white sneakers. The old woman smiled and adjusted her thick glasses. "Mr. and Mrs. Stanton." When Jake didn't react to that, she added, as if he should already know, "We're Robbie's *grandparents*."

"Ah. I thought you were burglars."

Mrs. Stanton blinked. Then she laughed, her eyes crinkling very pleasingly beneath her cola-bottle specs. "Did you hear that, Elmer? He thought we were burglars! Ha!"

"It's not us he needs to worry about, is it? By the way, where is our little convict?" Mr. Stanton asked, then laughed loudly, as if that was the most hilarious thing a body could have possibly uttered.

Jake liked the Stantons. "She went out with a friend."

"Lucy?" Mrs. Stanton asked as she set the grocery bag down on the dining table.

"No. A tall, blond woman."

"Oh!" Mrs. Stanton clucked and shook her head in disgust. "Mia Carpenter!"

"Oh now, Lil, that's been a good twenty years ago. You got to let bygones be bygones."

A *humph* was all Mr. Stanton got in response. Mr. Stanton, incidentally, had already made his way back to where Jake was working. He stood, his hands clasped behind his back, peering closely at the solution Jake was using to clean the brick. "Did a little renovation myself when I was younger. Never had much talent for it. Now *you*, you've got talent. I guess you noticed that Robbie's just like me, dumber than a hammer when it comes to stuff like this. I told her she couldn't do this herself, and see if I wasn't right. She damn near put a hole in every room before she finally gave up and hired you to do it." The old man chuckled softly. "That girl's been trying to tackle the world since she was a baby, and this is exactly what happens when she gets some wild hair up her—ah, nose. She leaves a mess a mile wide."

Jake could definitely believe that was true.

"Elmer Stanton, come away from there and leave that man alone!" his wife insisted.

"Insufferable woman," Elmer Stanton said cheerfully and shuffled away a second time.

When Mia saw the Ford Excursion in the driveway, she wiggled her fingers, engagement ring and all, toward the passenger door. "Hurry up and get out. I don't want your grandma to see me."

"God, Mia, that was twenty years ago," Robin groused as she gathered her purse and bag from Jaeger, the shop to which Mia had forced her to go.

"It could have been a hundred years ago for all I care," Mia snapped impatiently.

"You *did* wreck her new Buick," Robin reminded her.

"Okay, but who in their right mind buys a *Buick?*" Mia argued. "Hurry up, hurry up! I don't want to be late to the gym," she added and shot Robin a sidelong glance. "You should really try and pay a visit to the gym, too."

"Oh, *thank* you. Nice to know you are watching my butt for me," Robin said and hoisted herself out of the Porsche, slammed the door, and adjusted her brand-new Hugo Boss shades to better glare at Mia. "I'll call you later," she said.

But Mia was already backing out of the drive, trying to get out before Grandma appeared in her Easy Spirits to kick a little ass. Robin watched her drive off, wincing at the screech of her tires, then turned and made her way up the drive.

As she approached the back of the house, she could see Grandpa on his knees in the backyard, his butt high in the air, busily digging. And there was Grandma, just around the corner of the guest house, pruning one of four azalea bushes they had obviously planted while she was gone, right where Robin imagined her pool would be.

"I was going to put my pool there!" she shouted at them.

"Hi, honey!" Grandma called cheerfully. "We planted some azaleas!"

Grandpa looked up from his digging. "Say, Robbie, how much is that fella in there charging you?"

"Okay! Well. Gotta get to work," Robin responded nonchalantly and adjusted her grip on her shopping bag.

"I brought you some pineapple upside-down cake," Grandma called after her as she walked on to the kitchen. Inside, Robin dropped her bag—the Jaeger linen pantsuit already forgotten—glanced at the cake, and continued on to the dining room.

Jake had made some amazing progress over the last few hours—he had managed to strip most of the brick wall in the entry and had removed all the trim. When she came in, he flashed that warm smile of his. "Aha. The prodigal granddaughter returns."

Robin could feel her grin was ridiculously huge. "I take it you met Lil and Elmer."

"Yep. Nice folks."

They were certainly that, even if they did drive her absolutely nuts. She punched a key on her computer, scanned the half dozen e-mails from Lucy, then leaned over to look at the answering machine. No messages. Apparently, Eldagirt couldn't be bothered to call her today. This was really beginning to annoy her to no end—this was business, not a social call. How could she just ignore her like that? The more Robin thought of it, the more inept she felt, which she didn't need, which only made her madder.

"Okay, that does it," she said aloud. "I've had it." She angrily snatched the phone off its cradle. "I am going to give this Wirt chick a piece of my mind! I may never get in to see her, but I'll feel much better."

"Going in with both barrels, huh?" Jake asked, chuckling.

"Got a better idea, Hammerman?"

"No. But you know what they say."

"No, what do they say?" she muttered absently as she began punching the numbers.

"You catch more flies with honey."

Robin paused in her abuse of the phone's number pad. "Huh?"

"You are going about this deal all wrong."

Okay, he was a hunk, but not hunk enough for that. "Excuse me?" she asked, ignoring the beeping of the phone.

"Oh my—" He made a sort of groaning sound, then was suddenly striding forward, his hand out. "Give it over. *I'll* do it."

That was such an absurd suggestion that Robin burst out laughing. "What, you'll call Eldagirt?"

He motioned impatiently for the phone. "Hand it over."

"You don't know what you're doing!"

"Well, it's obvious you don't, either. Come on, you have nothing to lose at this point. Hand it over."

Grinning, Robin put the receiver down in his open palm.

Jake grinned triumphantly. "Got a number?"

She grabbed the phone back from his hand, pounded the numbers she now knew by heart, and handed the phone back to him.

With a far too superior wink, Jake put the phone to his ear. Robin folded her arms and grinned in anticipation of his failure; Jake's smile only broadened.

"Hey, Jake Manning here," he said suddenly. "How ya doing?" He pointedly turned away from Robin. "Oh, I'm doing pretty good. Could stand a little rain down here in Houston though. What's the weather over there?"

Robin rolled her eyes, slid into one of the dining room chairs, and counted the seconds until they hung up on him. *One-one thousand, two-one thousand...*

"Oh, is that right?" Jake asked cheerfully, turning to give Robin a wink. "We've been pretty lucky, but I'd be glad to get a little rain before everything dries up."

It had rained buckets last week.

Jake laughed easily. "You got that right. Say listen, let me tell you why I called...er, what did you say your name was? Carol. So anyway, Carol, I'm down here with a shipping company that is growing by leaps and bounds, and we're starting to ship freight all over the world. The thing is, we don't have a reliable packing materials company to serve us."

He paused, nodded his head. "That's what I'm saying," he agreed. "You start shipping all kinds of stuff, and you don't have a reputable packing supply company with a proven track record, and you're sunk. So we're trying to find us a partner who can make sure we have the materials we need to be competitive."

He paused again; his brows lifted at something Carol said, and he flashed a grin at Robin that indicated he had hit the right spot. But just as quickly, he frowned. "Umm… *leartransportindustries.*"

He paused; then his frown deepened. Robin leaned forward.

"Yeah, I know, I hear you—No, you're right about that. Not good. What? Ah…" Jake glanced over his shoulder at Robin and quickly strolled farther away, into the entry. "*Robin,*" he muttered. At least Robin thought that was what he'd said, and felt a sharp stab of panic. She stood up, followed him into the entry.

"Uh…sure. Yes, I think we can fix that, sure. Not to worry. What? Hey, whatever works for you—okay, great! That's great, Carol. I really appreciate it," he said and turned to smile again at Robin. "Thanks again and we look forward to hearing back."

With that, he hung up and grinned at Robin. "Ms. Wirt will call you in the morning."

Was she imagining things, or did his chest puff up an inch or two? "You're kidding."

"I'm not."

She gaped at him.

Jake laughed, strolled into the dining room, and replaced the phone. "You have to pay your respects. That's something you're going to have to learn."

Now he was just showing off. "Pay my respects to who, exactly? I can't even get Ms. Wirt on the phone, and neither could you!"

"To *Carol.* Carol is the one running the outfit, just like Lucy runs your office—"

"Lucy does *not* run my office—"

"You can't deny Lucy keeps things humming," he said. "Those girls are the front line. You have to get past them to get to the decision-makers. They're busy, and they don't have time for a lot of crap, and they are going to be the one to decide if a cold call goes on up the chain. If Carol can't tell Eldagirt Wirt what you want, then Eldagirt Wirt isn't going to waste her time with you. And if Carol doesn't like you, then it's a pretty sure thing Eldagirt isn't going to be overly fond of you, either. See what I mean?"

"Sort of," she begrudgingly admitted.

"Everyone has a role. You just have to understand what it is."

That actually made a lot of sense. It was true that Lucy never passed someone along to her without telling her what the person wanted so Robin could decide what to do with the call. It was also true that if Lucy got a bad feeling about someone, Robin tended to trust her instincts. And it was painfully true that she had treated Carol abominably, attempting to pass over her like a doormat.

"Now the bad news is," Jake said, wincing slightly, "Carol's not real fond of you. You might need to…well, you know…eat a little crow."

"Ugh," she said, frowning. "I hate crow." Man, she had a lot to learn. Maybe Dad was right. Maybe she was arrogant. Robin groaned, shoved her hands through her hair. "How do you know so much?"

Jake shrugged. "Just been around, I guess."

Robin nodded, considered the easy set of his mouth and imagined that he was probably a good friend to those lucky enough to know him. "Thanks," she murmured. "I think I needed that." She extended her hand to him. "Really."

Jake looked at her hand as if he didn't quite know what to do with it. Thinking she might have somehow offended him, Robin started to withdraw it. But Jake suddenly took her hand in his, holding it gently, like a feather, turning it over slowly to look at the back of her hand. His hand dwarfed hers, made hers look like a delicate thing.

His rough, callused palm skimmed the surface of her skin, creating a burning friction. The effect was absolutely electrifying; Robin drew a breath and held it as he very carefully turned her hand over, so that her palm was facing up, and with one blunt finger, wordlessly traced the path of her life line to her wrist, scoring her with his touch, sparking a river of fire that ran down her arm and straight into her heart.

Jake looked up, his liquid brown gaze meeting hers, and she felt it seep into her, past the carefully constructed wall, down into the very pit of her. His hand closed tightly around her fingers, and Robin took a step forward, drawn like a magnet to the circle of his arms, attached by a powerful, physical current running between them.

"Well now, what's going on here?"

Hello, Grandpa.

CHAPTER THIRTEEN

Yep, Jake liked Old Man Stanton—he cackled upon catching them doing the hand thing, pointed out Robin's furious blush, and thereby flustered his granddaughter so bad that she fled into the dining room and plopped down to stare at her computer.

She tried her best to pretend it didn't happen, but couldn't do it, not with a blush like that, hot and fierce, just like the one Jake felt under his own skin.

Damn.

Whatever had just happened between them, he couldn't really say. Maybe it was her genuine, innocent surprise at hearing someone might not like her, a glimpse of a secreted purity in her that went racing through him like fire. Something he had said had softened her in a way that was totally incongruent with the fast-moving, hardened rest of her. Robin was tough, she was arrogant. She was the proverbial material girl, collecting more things in her quest for the better deal. But at the same time, there was an innocence about her, an untouched part of her that so very much appealed to the man in him.

And when she had offered her hand, that delicate, nail-bitten hand sparkling with a sapphire that matched the color of her eyes, desire had surged through Jake on a tsunami wave, crashing through him and pushing him down to the bottom of it. The lure of forbidden territory had compelled him to take her hand in his; he had been only a moment away from taking her in his arms.

What alarmed him was not the handholding, or even the discovery by Mr. Stanton. It was that he was even having these thoughts about Robin Lear, and the very real fear that next time, he wasn't certain he could restrain himself. Which was why he was going to work very hard to obliterate all thoughts of Robin Lear, grit his teeth, and force these absurd images he was building in his head, images of her in various locations, like the back of his bike, or in his truck. In his bed.

Man, he needed to put some buffers between him and the house on North Boulevard before it was too late.

In the dining room, Robin was having similar misgivings about what she considered a near disaster, and while she could hardly tolerate Grandpa's ribbing, he had saved her from a horrible, terrible mistake. She did not need any entanglements right now; she had enough trauma in her life as it was. Nonetheless, she couldn't seem to let the hand incident go, and spent a fair amount of time studying the wall where Jake had been working, imagining his capable hands skillfully and carefully removing years from the brick.

And she wondered why this...this thing with Jake felt impossible, or what exactly it was she was afraid of. It baffled her—but Robin generally preferred to avoid any real introspection because she rarely liked what she saw. And men, well...they either wilted around her or tried to corral her. Usually, after the first few dates with a guy, she would begin to feel like she was searching for something. Something the guy probably didn't have. But Robin never had understood *what* she was searching for.

She tried not to think about that, and tried to focus on the wacky world of packing materials. But when she drifted off to sleep that night, in that conscious point of no return, the curious question of why she couldn't do this thing with Jake clouded her thoughts.

When she slept, she dreamed of pink flamingos and pickup trucks.

The next morning, she hauled herself out of bed at the ungodly hour of six a.m., put on her running gear, and headed outside before it got too muggy, determined to put this strange infatuation firmly behind her.

She did not succeed.

Coming back from her lame attempt to run and think about anything else but Jake, she entered the house through the back door, and damn near walked over a man she had never seen before, down on one knee, scraping up what looked to be the remnants of a breakfast taco on the floor. At least she *hoped* that was what it was.

The man looked up, jerked backward with surprise when he saw her, then said cheerfully, "Oh hey, how you doing?"

Only then did she notice his arm was in a sling. "Who are you?"

"Me? Oh! I'm Chuck Zaney. But you can call me Zaney."

Zaney, Zaney...did she know him? Robin racked her brain, tried to remember where she had left the phone.

Before she could remember, the man offered, "I'm the dude behind Manning. Get it? Well...not behind him like *that*," he quickly clarified, "but you know...like *with* him."

"Zaney," she repeated, the name registering in some deep recess.

"Yep. Spelled just like it sounds." He suddenly laughed. "You know what they used to call me in school? Zany Zaney." He waited a beat or two, then laughed in loud Foghorn Leghorn fashion. When Robin did not join in his jocularity, his laughter trailed off. "Yep, those were some crazy guys," he said and wiped the back of his hand across his mouth.

"Where's Jake?" Robin asked quickly before he detoured down memory lane again.

"Oh man, he had to go talk to his nephew's teacher. The kid keeps running off, so Jakie, he's gonna go knock some sense into him." Zany Zaney finished cleaning up whatever it was and struggled to his feet. "I'm still trying to figure this out," he said, waving his sling about. "Hard to manage the tacos."

"I can see that," Robin said and walked past him to the dining room. The clump of Zaney's work boots followed directly behind her. "So when is Jake going to be here?" she asked.

"Dunno," Zaney said, shaking his ponytailed head. He held up his good hand. "He's gotta go see about the kid," he said, folding one finger over, "and then he has to make up his class," he added, bending the second finger, "and then..." He paused at the third finger.

Robin waited for him to finish his thought. Until she realized that he had. "His class?" she prompted, trying not to sound too interested.

"Oh, yeah! Jakie, he's gonna be an architect! He'll be done next summer if Cole don't mess it up for him."

This news surprised her. "He's studying to be an architect?"

Zaney nodded again. "He's real good."

The unexpected information pricked her conscience—for some reason, Robin had assumed Jake was streetwise but uneducated. That snap assumption on her part, however vague, struck her as unfair...and maybe even a little arrogant. "So how is it this Cole is going to mess it up?" she pressed further, her curiosity running rampant now.

"Well, see, Cole, he's Ross's kid. But Ross died in a car wreck. Cole was just a punk kid then, still is if you ask me, but Ross's old lady, she wasn't really planning on raising the kid, so she took off, and Cole's been living with his grandma ever since, but now he's a little older, and he keeps getting hisself into trouble. So Jakie, he says he's gonna teach him how to be a man." Zaney paused, adjusted the tool belt around his slim hips with his good hand, then struggled to withdraw a measuring tape. "'Bout how big is this room?"

"How old is Cole?"

"Fourteen. See, my idea is we start upstairs and gut those rooms first."

"Does anyone else live there? I mean with Cole?"

"His grandma's all. Jake's dad ran off a long time ago. Then Ross died, and Todd the Toad—that's what we used to call him, the little fart—oops, beg your pardon," Zaney said, his face turning crimson. "Well anyway, Todd, he's gone for a while, so no, there ain't no one there but Cole and his grandma." He looked down at his measuring tape. "Okay, I'm gonna go upstairs and check it out," Zaney said.

"Sure," Robin muttered. Zaney clumped up the stairs as she headed for the shower.

She mulled over the information Zaney had so happily given up. It fascinated her that the three Manning sons had turned out so differently. Jake must have faced a lot of adversity. But...*wow*. What fragments she knew about Jake's life were a little on the mind-boggling side. It was hard to understand how he could be so...so sane. Yet he had somehow managed to overcome it, was building a solid clientele among Houston's elite families, and while he was doing that, he was attending school.

Pretty damn remarkable. And highly admirable. She had really underestimated him.

Robin finished dressing, donning gray slacks, white shirt, and black sandals. As she came out of her bedroom, she heard a familiar voice, and groaned softly to herself at the sight of Grandpa in the entry. He was wearing his coveralls. And he was with Jake.

"Hey, El, you want to hand me that crowbar?"

El? *El?*

Grandpa shuffled over to the toolbox, found a crowbar, and hurried to hand it to Jake. Then he stood there, hands on knees, watching closely as Jake pulled the baseboard from the wall.

"Grandpa, what are you doing?" Robin demanded as she came into the dining room.

"Hey, Robbie-girl."

"He's assisting me," Jake said, giving her the once-over with a lopsided smile. "Me and El, we're a team."

That was all the world needed. Robin was about to protest, but the phone started ringing, and when she went to answer it, she couldn't find the damn thing. On the fourth ring, she found it, said breathlessly, "Hello?"

"Ms. Lear?"

Instantly, she knew the gravelly voice on the other end belonged to none other than Eldagirt Wirt. "Yes! Robin Lear, here!" she said excitedly.

"Eldagirt Wirt. I hear you been trying to get hold of me." She sounded like she had smoked a pack of cigarettes just moments ago.

"Thank you for calling!" Robin said, and almost added something entirely too smart, like *this year*, but then remembered: flies with honey. "I know you are very busy. Ah... Carol, ah, she's been a great help," she said, surprising herself. "I'll try not to take up too much of your time, but I'm with LTI in Houston, and we've been looking at different packing supply companies, hoping to form a partnership."

Eldagirt responded with a phlegm-laden cough.

"Ah...your company has an excellent reputation—"

"The best," Eldagirt interjected.

"Yes. Yes, that's right, one of the best! That's why I wanted to talk to you. I thought perhaps we could explore a future collaboration between LTI and Wirt—"

"LTI...is that Lear Transport?"

"Yes, it is!" Robin exclaimed. "So you've heard of us?"

"Nah. Carol told me once, I just couldn't remember. She says we've stocked you before. So, this LTI runs all classes of freight?"

"All classes. I'd love to come and talk to you about what we transport."

Robin could hear the click of a Zippo lighter and the draw of smoke into Eldagirt's lungs. "The thing is, Ms. Lear," she said, exhaling, "I don't got a lot of time. I've increased my accounts by about fifty percent over last year, and I'm a single mom, so I am running from one thing to another all the damn time."

"Oh," Robin responded, disappointed. But wait...this was business—surely the battle-ax had a babysitter or something. "Well...I promise not to take *too* much of your time," she said uncertainly. "I'd just like the opportunity to tell you what we've got in mind."

Another draw of smoke, a lazy exhale. "Tell you what. I'm not so busy on the weekend. Come up on a Saturday and we can talk a little."

Oh *yeah*! Saturday in Burdette! "Sure," Robin said instantly. "Burdette. Is there, like, a local airport there?"

Eldagirt's laugh was one long wheeze. "You ain't never been out this way, have you? It ain't but a two-hour drive from Houston."

"Yes, but—"

"There's a little landing strip just outside of town, but it don't get used much. I'll plan on making time next Saturday. Get here around noon. I'll meet you at the—" A sound in the background interrupted her; Eldagirt shouted to the side, *"Do you mind? I am on the phone!"* After a moment, she said, "Like I was saying, just come next Saturday at noon."

"Okay," Robin said, feeling even more uncertain. "How will I find you?"

Eldagirt wheezed again. "You'll be able to find us, don't you worry," she said and dragged on her smoke again. "Burdette ain't no bigger than a tick on a dog's butt. All right, I gotta go. See you next Saturday."

"Wait!" Robin exclaimed, frantically trying to think of some reason she could not go to Burdette next weekend, but caught sight of Jake standing there, watching her.

"Yeah?" Eldagirt asked, the impatience in her voice evident.

Nothing. Not one reason came to mind that would keep her from going. "I just wanted to say"—*something!*—"thanks. Thanks a lot. I really do appreciate this," she said, and felt, strangely enough, as if she really meant it.

"Oh!" Eldagirt said, her voice lighter. "Well, okay, see you then." She hung up.

Robin slowly put the receiver down, stood completely still, feeling something...after days of fuddling about like a blind man, she had done it; she had gotten through to the elusive Eldagirt Wirt! She suddenly threw her hands up in the air and, with a *wheeeee*, whirled about. "I did it! I got Eldagirt Wirt on the phone, and she invited me to Burdette next Saturday!"

"That's my girl," Grandpa said happily, having no idea what she was talking about.

"You see?" Jake said. "Somehow, I knew you could do it."

"I know it's only a trip to Burdette—"

"Might as well be a presidential visit, as hard as you've tried," Jake reminded her as he handed Grandpa a hammer and pointed him upstairs. "Way to go, Peanut." He winked as he started up after Grandpa.

Grinning like a fool, Robin gave him a thumbs-up, watched until he disappeared upstairs, then reminded herself it was only Burdette. She sat down and began reviewing the files Evan had brought her, trying hard to keep her mind from Jake, trying harder to learn about the profit/loss ratio of Wirt Supply and Packing.

When Jake, Grandpa, and now (oh boy) Zaney reappeared near the noon hour, she was distracted by Zaney's protracted monologue about how he was going to form a band, playing one-armed air guitar as he talked. The man definitely wasn't quite right, and she couldn't help admire Jake for appearing to be interested in what Zaney was saying when lesser men (like Grandpa) were made comatose.

Grandpa looked exhausted, actually, and she asked if he would accompany her to the grocery store, where he filled her basket with cookies and sodas, which Robin took out and replaced with peanut butter, yogurt, a head of romaine lettuce, a handful of frozen dinners, and a giant Hershey bar. When Grandpa wandered off to the home appliance aisle, she perused the cereals, trying to remember if she ever actually ate cereal, and if so, what kind.

There was something not quite right about her life, wasn't there? Most people knew if they ate cereal or not, didn't they?

Finally worn out with the task of keeping track of Grandpa, Robin figured she had enough so that she'd live another week or so, and returned home.

Jake had left, Zaney said, and therefore, Grandpa decided to go home, too. Robin left Zaney tearing out the trim upstairs and put away her groceries, hating the barren look of her refrigerator. It was like a giant metaphor staring at her, the only thing missing was the big flashing neon arrows pointing to the empty box. She phoned Lucy to check in—that call was always good for a bitchfest. Lucy had no messages for her, other than the news Evan had had a long talk with Darren at Atlantic, and the account file was now closed.

So Evan had appointed himself her cleanup man. How humiliating was that?

By late afternoon, when someone came by and honked and Zaney flew out the door, Robin was restlessly stalking about her house, wondering why she had bought such a big residence when there was no one to go in it.

It occurred to Robin that perhaps her mom was right— she *did* flit from one thing to another, never letting a moment go by that wasn't sucked up in some frantic activity, and now that her life had been turned upside down, she wasn't quite sure what to do with herself. Her dad's illness, her job, this general emptiness, was making her feel as though her life was slowly unraveling into one long nothing. All she had to show for thirty-four years of living was just a lot of things and more things, as if the quantity of possessions made up for the dearth of meaning in her life. She just kept moving faster and faster until everything was just a blur, running and running, searching for...*what?*

There it was again, that question. And she did not like the clammy, almost sickly feeling it gave her, this realization that she had been searching for something all her life, but it was a feeling that would not leave her. By the time Sunday morning rolled around, she was crazed with determination to change things in her life. Toward what end, though, she had no clue. One thing was certain, however—it was a glorious day for a stroll through Hermann Park, where she heard a men's baseball league played.

At an exclusive resort in Newport Beach, California, Aaron and Bonnie sat side by side, cross-legged, on a tatami grass mat. New Age music played softly in the background, the smell of incense wafted through the air. Bonnie held her hands on her knees; her spine was straight, her eyes closed, and her face lifted upward, toward the soft blue light. Her lips moved with the murmuring of the chant, but she made no sound.

Next to her, Aaron had forgotten the chant they were supposed to be repeating and was admiring Bonnie's neck. He was trying to remember the last time he had kissed the smooth skin there, recalling with vivid clarity the taste and feel of it.

Bonnie's eyes fluttered open; she stole a glimpse of Aaron sidelong and smiled. "You aren't practicing the chant," she whispered.

"I know," he whispered back, and leaned over, so that his lips were just inches from her neck. "Why, Bonnie?" he breathed.

His question startled her; she put a hand against his chest, looked at him with wide blue eyes. "Why what?"

"Why are you with me? Why still? Why haven't you gone back to your life? I was an ass to you, Bonnie. I don't deserve this."

Bonnie looked stunned. Her gaze drifted from his face to her hand against his chest. Aaron covered her hand with his, pressed hers tighter against his heart.

"You're right," she whispered, her gaze still on their hands, "you don't deserve it. You don't deserve me."

CHAPTER FOURTEEN

At the bottom of the seventh, Jake's vision was so blurred he could hardly see the ball without squinting. He was getting old—he used to party all night and still be as good as new, but now, if he stayed up late doing nothing more exciting than cramming for a test, he was a wreck the next day. What really pissed him off was that he was the only one in this league who seemed to be suffering from age.

"*Strike!*" the ump called, and with a sigh, Jake stepped out of the batter's box, headed for the dugout, completely disgusted with himself. Tossing the batting helmet into the corner, he dropped heavily onto the bench, avoiding anyone's gaze.

"Hey, you did pretty good, considering that pitcher was throwing crap."

That voice shot through him like mercury rising; Jake jerked around, saw Robin standing at the fence on the end of the dugout, smiling prettily. She waved cheerfully, as if it was perfectly natural for her to be at his game. It wasn't natural at all, and moreover, neither were those legs. Good God, he had never seen such long and shapely legs in his life. She was wearing a T-shirt that sported the American flag, a stretchy red miniskirt, and a different pair of funny-looking sunglasses than he had seen before.

Beside him, the podiatrist Bob Richards squinted in Robin's direction, giving her the once-over. "He's throwing crap all right," he agreed.

Jake was instantly on his feet, but not fast enough.

"You didn't look like you were stepping into your swing. You know...like this." She stepped back from the fence before Jake could reach her, demonstrating exactly how he might step into his swing.

"That's very interesting," he said loud enough for the guys to hear, and, reaching the fence, added in a loud whisper, "*What are you doing?*" as he stole a glimpse of the others over his shoulder.

"What do you mean?"

"What do you mean, what do I mean? What are you doing *here?*"

"I told you I might run by. Anyway, it looked like you had your weight on your back foot."

Unbelievable. It wasn't enough that she should tell him how to do his job, but now she was going to trot down to the ball field and tell him how to bat? "Thanks, but I think I know how to swing a bat," he said, frowning. "I thought you meant run by like in jogging shoes and spandex. How long have you been here, anyway?"

"Long enough to see you swing at three perfect strikes," she said, tossing her head pertly.

Did she not understand that women did not advise men on sports? Of any kind? *Ever?* Especially and foremost in front of other guys? "Thanks for the batting lesson."

"Just trying to help," she said cheerfully, stepping back from the fence.

"Right...but remember our rule? Don't help me."

She blinked big blue eyes at him. Then lifted her chin. "Fine," she said. "Strike out if that's what floats your boat." She marched off in the direction of the bleachers.

Jake paused for a moment to watch that very fine ass of hers march away, then turned around, saw the rest of the bench crowd staring at him. He glared back and stuffed himself up against the fence.

When the inning was finally over (thank *God*), he trotted out to right field, and let his gaze wander to the bleachers while the pitcher warmed up. Yep, there she was, couldn't miss her, and somehow, she had managed to park herself right next to the surliest person in the crowd, young Cole Manning. Slumped down, the kid was lost in denim pants with legs so wide they looked like one of those ballroom gowns, and a T-shirt that hung to his knees. In stark contrast, Robin was sitting on the edge of the bleacher.

The first batter up hit a lazy fly to left field, an easy out. The second batter hit a sharp liner back through the box, which, had it been a mere six inches to the left, would have lodged itself in the pitcher's forehead. The third batter hit a drive in the gap, between center field and right. The image of Robin sitting up, stretching her slender neck to see, suddenly flashed across Jake's mind, and he realized he was running, feeling the stretch of scarred tendon in his ankle, knowing he should let the center fielder call it. But insanity gripped him; he dove through the air, caught the ball in the tip of his glove, then wrenched his arm clean from the socket throwing the ball to second. The stunning result, much to his amazement, was two outs and the end of the opposing team's bat.

He hadn't done that in a hundred years. A thousand, maybe.

As he jogged back to the dugout, still a little dazed, he forced himself to look at the bleachers.

Clapping wildly, grinning broadly, Robin gave him a thumbs-up. The gesture made him, oddly, strangely happy. Okay, maybe even a little delirious. She had seen him play, and play well, which, these days, didn't happen as often as Jake liked. Acknowledging her thumbs-up with a subtle wave of his own, he disappeared into the dugout and smacked his glove down on the bench in the international male signal for *I still got it.* But as they called the lineup, and he was looking around for his batting helmet, he heard again, "Hey, Jake!"

All right, this was just too much—she was back. He put his foot down, turned slowly toward the fence. "*Yesss?*" he drawled.

"Honestly, if you got up on the balls of your feet, it would help you step into the swing."

In case he wasn't certain what she meant, she demonstrated for him. Ruben Sanchez, a NASA software engineer, and an astounding zero for twenty-one in the league, watched her from the on-deck circle, then mimicked her technique a couple of times.

"See?" she said to Ruben. "Balls of your feet."

"*Yeah,*" Ruben said, as if Barry Bonds himself had suggested it.

"Robin?" Jake asked politely.

"Yes?"

"Go sit down. Over there. Way over there."

She frowned. "You are really stubborn."

"There you go again, attributing your own faults to me."

The first batter stroked a single; they both paused, watched him get to first.

"All right, try this on for size," she said. "Pigheaded. Pig. *Head*," she repeated, using her hands to sketch a pig's head in the air.

"I think I might know a little bit more about baseball than you," Jake continued, climbing the steps of the dugout to the on-deck circle as Ruben advanced to the batter's box. He flashed a smile at her over his shoulder, and stepped onto the on-deck circle. To prove just how stupid it was for her to give him advice, he took a couple of hard swings that made his shoulder burn.

Ruben, on the balls of his feet, slapped a single on the first pitch, stunning himself and the team. He could hardly run, but he was so elated that he actually rounded first and made it all the way to second when the left fielder bobbled the ball. Firmly on base, he beamed, panting, chest puffed, yelling at Jake to bring him home.

"Oh yeah, what do *I* know?" Robin called out.

Jake ignored her. At the bottom of the eighth, Ruben was the go-ahead run on second. All Jake had to do was get a single to pull the team ahead. Hey, no pressure there. He stepped up to home plate, assumed the position, and let the pitcher throw him a ball, then stepped back, knocked the dirt from his cleats with his bat. When he was good and ready, he very casually stepped into the batter's box again, taking all the time he needed to position.

The next pitch was a slider; he swung hard, wrenched his back again, and hopped out of the batter's box on one foot as the ump called, "*Steeee-rike!*"

"Jesus, *what* are you *doing?* Step into your swing!"

This had to be his worst nightmare ever. He was going to step into it, all right, and take a swing that would knock her butt all the way into next week. He survived one ball, then another, and followed those two pitches up by stupidly swinging at a lousy curveball in the dirt.

"Ah *jeez*," he heard Robin moan.

"Got your batting coach here today?" the catcher asked, snickering.

"I got your batting coach right here, pal," Jake growled. With a full count, he crouched down, anticipating the pay-off pitch. The pitcher wound up and uncorked a sinker. By some divine miracle, Jake managed to get under it; the ball went sailing high toward right field. He dropped the bat and raced toward first, rounded it like an old pro as he heard a cry go up from the crowd. The ball had sailed well over the right fielder's head; the go-ahead run was rounding third and headed for home.

As Jake hit second base and ran for third, Bob Richards looked like a contortionist, jumping up and down and waving him home. Jake did not break stride, rounded third without knowing where the ball was, and in the last few feet, hurled his entire body through the air, diving headfirst into home, his hand outstretched, his fingers reaching the plate just ahead of the catcher's tag.

The small crowd went wild; the team rushed out to home plate to help him up. Every fiber in him burned, but he grit his teeth, spit the sand from his mouth, dusted off his pants, then laughed at his great luck with the team, high fives all around.

As he turned toward the dugout, he saw Robin pressed up against the fence, her hands loosely tangled in the chain links above her head. She grinned at him with such admiration that Jake actually felt himself grow an inch or two. He grinned right back, sauntered toward her, his smile as wide as Texas.

"Now *that* was a nice at bat," she said as he neared the fence. "You finally got up on the balls of your feet."

Jake laughed. "So, are you going to hang around for the last inning, or are you going to go coach some other team?"

"Oh, I don't know," she said, dropping her hands to her hips. "There's really not much around here to work with. Besides, after that performance, I wouldn't miss the end of this game for the world!"

"Good," he said, earning another winsome grin. With a little wave of her fingers, she turned toward the bleachers. He watched her walk away (could never see enough of that), then stepped into the dugout and collapsed on the bench. He was pleased when Victor Hernandez put them up another run before the inning ended. The opposing team could not muster even a base hit in the last inning, and thereby ended the game.

As Jake headed for the dugout to get his gear, Robin and Cole stood at the same time, both making their way down the bleacher steps. In his extra-wide pants, Cole had trouble negotiating the bleachers. On the ground, Robin walked about three feet ahead of Cole, who was doing his usual reluctant shuffle, head down, hands stuffed in pockets. The kid had to be exhausted—it was hard work to stay that miserable.

"Hey, you're really *good*," Robin said brightly as she walked up to the fence.

Jake did not confess that his performance today had more to do with lucky pride than any skill. "Thanks. So do you often hang out in the park watching old men play baseball?"

Robin's laugh was rich, warm. "I *told* you I was going to come by."

"I didn't believe you," he said, latching his hand to the fence and leaning toward her. "I think you probably say lots of things you don't really mean."

"I'm wounded."

"So how did you find my nephew?" he asked as Cole shyly slunk over to them.

"Your nephew?" Robin made a sound of surprise as she shifted her gaze to Cole.

"Meet Cole Manning. Cole, say hello," Jake said, and the kid pulled one hand out of his pocket, stuck it sort of half-way to Robin.

Robin graciously accepted it. "It's very nice to meet you, Cole. I'm Robin."

"Hey," Cole muttered, quickly withdrawing his hand.

"Robin is…she is…"

"His batting coach," Robin interjected when Jake could not seem to think of an appropriate word.

Cole squinted up at Jake. "She said you were a big baby."

"Jeez," Robin said, blushing. "You could have at least mentioned that you knew him!"

Cole shrugged, but dammit if Jake didn't see the hint of a smile. "I didn't say anything because he *is* a big baby."

"Very funny," Jake said, reaching into his pocket for some change. "Here, go get a couple of sodas. I'll meet you at the truck."

"Bye, Cole," Robin said as Cole took the money and started to slink away.

Cole gave her a lift of his chin. Jake waited for him to gain some distance, then looked at Robin. She was smiling, blue eyes shimmering, eyes that could pull a man into a world of trouble.

"So...it turns out that instead of being a pervert, you're actually a man of many talents," she said, playfully punching him in the arm. "Baseball, school, renovations."

"Ah. Zaney's been talking, has he?"

"A little. Isn't it a glorious day? I was walking through the flower gardens earlier, and it's just gorgeous. Do you do that? I mean, when you're happy, do you ever want to just get out and see flowers?"

Yes. Oh yes, there were definitely those moments. Like now. "Would you like to see some of the prettiest wildflowers in all of Texas?"

"Here at the park?"

"No—about an hour outside of Houston. There's a place I found a few years ago where the wildflowers bloom like you've never seen them. If you want, I could take you."

A smile slowly spread across her luscious lips, one almost as brilliant as her sapphire eyes. "That," she said, "would be very cool."

Robin heard Jake's motorcycle on the drive and checked herself one last time in the mirror. She had changed to jeans and (just in case) matching bra and panties. One never knew when one might end up splat on the highway.

Instead of letting himself in as he normally did, Jake knocked. Robin flung open the front door, all smiles, but her breath lodged in her throat. Leaning against the scaffolding, one leg crossed over the other, Jake was wearing Levi's that were faded in just the right place, boots, a plain white T-shirt, and a bandana tied around his head. He looked about as hot as any man she had ever seen. Hotter.

He grinned at her like he knew what she was thinking, and casually took in her hair, her patriotic flag shirt, and her jeans. "I was going to ask if it was okay to take the Hog, but you look like you're ready for it."

She was ready for it, all right, and grabbed a jacket and backpack from the stair railing. "Let's go."

Jake's laugh made his whiskey eyes dance. "Then come on, gorgeous."

On the drive, he showed her where to sit on the bike and where to put her feet. Robin donned a baseball cap and straddled the Harley. And when Jake took his seat in front of her, she confirmed what she had believed—that their bodies fit perfectly together. He was nestled deeply between her legs, and the breadth of his back, the strength of his legs, the whole package was just...perfect.

"Hold on to my waist," he instructed her as he started the bike up.

No problemo. She put her hands on his waist—*very* solid, no love handles—and inched them around farther, until she was practically lying on his back. As they coasted down North Boulevard, she couldn't help but imagine lying in bed with him like this, drifting off to sleep against the warmth of his strong back. He told her to hang on and enjoy the ride.

Oh, if only...

They were out of Houston in no time at all and the day was perfect—the trees a vivid green against a brilliantly clear blue sky, a perfectly moderate temperature. Robin could not have had a better day if she had painted it, and with his firm control of the bike, she could relax with her hands on his waist, enjoying the rush of wind on her face.

They rode out toward San Antonio and turned onto an old ranch road and headed north for a time until Jake slowed and turned onto a dirt road lined with live oaks and cypress trees. Robin couldn't see where they were going, other than to know that pasture stretched on either side of the road. When they crested a small hill, Jake slowed to a stop above an amazing vista that rivaled any Robin had seen around the world.

Just below, the Brazos River meandered lazily among gently sloping hills. An old frame house, long abandoned, stood in empty disrepair, a tattered curtain flapping in the breeze the only sign someone had once lived there. Live oak trees with their long branches shaded the grassy sprawl on the banks of the river. The fields were carpeted in riotous color: violet bluebonnets, vivid red Indian paintbrush, sunny yellow buttercups, black-eyed Susans, lilac verbena, and pristine white rain lilies. A small herd of longhorn cattle grazed peacefully on the opposite bank; only one lifted its head at the Harley's intrusion.

"It's *beautiful*," Robin said in awe when Jake turned off the bike. He stood up, helped her off. She walked forward, taking in all of the serene little valley. It made her long for... *something*. "How did you find it?" she asked.

"Just riding," he said as he unbuckled one saddlebag and reached inside. "When I can, I like to get away and clear my head."

Get away from what? she wondered. Had he come here looking for solitude? Or had he brought others here? Like Lindy?

He pulled an insulated cooler from the bag. "Come on," he said, and reached casually for her hand.

She loved the feel of her hand in his, loved being dragged down the incline by him, loved seeing his hips move determinedly in Levi's that were so worn in the back that she could actually see the blue checked pattern of his boxers underneath. She wanted to believe they had done this before and would do it again, that she would always feel this warm sense of contentment.

When they reached a barbed-wire fence, Jake dropped her hand and stretched the wires to make an opening big enough for Robin to get through. When she was on the other side, he handed her the bag and climbed over. "Your eyes are the exact color of bluebonnets, did you know that?" he asked, taking the bag and her hand again, as if he had done it a thousand times before.

"I didn't know that," she said laughingly.

They walked through the field of wildflowers until they reached the long boughs of a very old live oak. Beneath it was a rickety old wooden picnic table.

"Who owns this place?" she asked as Jake set the insulated bag down.

He winked, gave her a sly grin. "Who knows?"

"You mean we are trespassing?"

"I prefer to call it passing through," he said, opening the bag.

"What if someone comes?" she asked, surreptitiously admiring his body.

"No one ever comes out here."

"Okay, well…I just sort of promised myself I wouldn't go to jail anymore."

"I'll do my best to keep you from it, but you know, there's only so much a man can do," he said with a chuckle. "I've got beer and peanuts. You like beer?" he asked, reaching into the bag and extracting a longneck.

"I haven't had a beer in years," she said, as he twisted the top off and handed her the bottle.

"Live dangerously," Jake suggested and helped himself to a beer.

Robin felt like she was living pretty dangerously just being out here with him. Robin took a sip of the beer, felt it slide cold and wet down her throat, soothing her mouth made dry by the ride out. With a smile, she lifted the bottle in mock salute to him. "Excellent vintage."

He propped himself against the table, one arm across his chest, and took a generous swig of his beer, his eyes never leaving her. "So what do you think of this little field?"

"It's beautiful."

"You've probably seen a lot better, but it's pretty nice for this part of the world."

"It's pretty nice for any part of the world."

He glanced at the field of wildflowers. "It is beautiful, but it all seems to fade next to you."

The compliment caught Robin off guard; she slowly lowered her beer, arched a curious brow.

"Okay, I'll confess," he said, lifting one hand in surrender. "I think you are about the most beautiful woman I have ever laid eyes on."

Robin was ridiculously pleased to hear it, and her smile grew very wide. "Really? I can't remember the last time anyone said something so nice to me. Thank you."

"You're welcome. And if you weren't so damn bossy, I'd say you were just about perfect."

Robin laughed. "Well, if you weren't so damn pigheaded, I'd say *you* were just about perfect."

He laughed with surprise. "You can't seriously think *I'm* pigheaded."

"Oh, please. Impossibly so."

"Give me an example."

"Like someone tries to give a you a tip or two on batting—"

"Princess, you must be joking. What could you possibly know about batting?"

"Hey, I've batted before! Just because you're a man doesn't mean you have a lock on *batting*, and frankly, the way you were swinging away today, I'd say you could use a lesson."

He laughed. "I think you're missing the big picture here."

"Ookay, just what do you think I am missing?"

"What you are missing," he said, putting his beer aside, "is that you and I keep dancing around the obvious."

A funny, warmly delicious little shiver shot right through her. "What obvious?"

Without warning, Jake lifted his hand and stroked her cheek with his knuckle. "It's obvious," he said, leaning forward, "that you want me. *Bad.*" And before she could protest, he caught her by the hand, jerked her forward, and covered her mouth with his own.

At the unexpected touch of his lips, a sweet wave of hysteria roiled through Robin; her heart was suddenly slamming against her chest. His hand was on her nape, pulling her closer, caressing her neck while the other hand found her shoulder, drifted lower, skimming torturously over her breast to her waist. His lips moved languidly on hers, savoring the taste of them, softly shaping them to his own.

The sensation rocked her; Robin heard herself whimper, and his tongue flicked across her bottom lip, sweeping inside, entwining with her own.

Her beer slipped through her fingers; her hand went around his waist, and she stepped more closely into the circle of his arms, wedging her leg between his. He cupped her face; his rough thumb stroked her cheek while he pressed her harder into him, anchoring her to his solid body.

A delicate pressure began to build in her, filling the space around her pounding heart. Jake delved deeper, caressing her, drinking her in, and Robin slipped unconsciously into a pool of shimmering desire, a throbbing that spilled into her breasts and her groin. She grabbed Jake's wrist, clung to it so that she would not melt right there, into the wildflowers, and was numbly aware that he effortlessly held her up and buoyed her.

At the very moment she thought she would disappear in his kiss, he lifted his head, gazed into her eyes, traced her swollen bottom lip with his thumb, and said, "Yeah. You want me."

Robin blinked, dragged a shaky hand across her mouth. "Do not," she muttered breathlessly.

"*Liar,*" he murmured and kissed her again, kissed her so hard that Robin's blood began to boil. Kissed her so thoroughly that she was suddenly flat on her back on an old, rotting picnic table, amid beer bottles, beneath a live oak tree and the most virile, absolutely-wrong-for-her guy she had ever met with a tattoo of barbed wire sneaking around his bicep.

And it felt *glorious.*

CHAPTER FIFTEEN

How long they lay there, Jake had no idea. He had slipped into a dreamy, sensual world where his imagination and his hands ran wild, until at last he decided she might be uncomfortable on that hard wooden table. Reluctantly, he pulled her up and handed her another beer. Robin smiled a little deliriously toward the sky. "Isn't it a *glorious* day?"

It was glorious, all right.

They sat side by side, their fingers entwined, talking about everything and nothing, listening to the rustle of the spring breeze in the trees around them and watching the sun dapple the river.

They talked about baseball, Robin continuing to insist, for reasons that seemed insane to Jake, the merits of the pitcher Moz, who had not delivered a game since opening day. They talked about peanuts, the edible kind, with Robin reporting the fat content in an average serving.

"Why do you do that?" he asked as she cracked a peanut and studied the contents. "Life can't be too much fun if you worry about every bite you put in your mouth."

"Because," she said, popping two peanuts in her mouth, "there is a fat girl in me dying to get out. And the world does not like fat girls. Especially men. Admit it."

"Men like women with some meat on their bones. They like someone they can grab hold of and not be afraid of breaking in the heat of the moment."

Robin looked at him from the corner of her eye, a dubious smile on her lips. "So…the chunkier the better?"

"Yeah. Sort of." He imagined having hold of her, driving into her warmth while she gripped him with all the strength she had.

Jake had to look away.

Robin cracked open another peanut, oblivious.

They talked about music.

"I guess my all-time favorite has to be the Rolling Stones. What's the name of that song?" Robin asked through a mouthful of peanuts, her concern about the fat grams apparently forgotten. "You know…*I saw her today in my reflection, a timeglass in the sa-aa-and*," she warbled in the most godawful, tone-deaf voice Jake had ever heard.

He burst out laughing. "You're butchering the lyrics."

"I am not!"

"Yes, you are. It goes, *I saw her today at the reception, a wineglass in her ha-and…*"

Robin frowned thoughtfully and tossed another peanut shell into the little pile she had created, and then tried to pretend she was mad when he pondered aloud how someone could get such simple lyrics so terribly wrong.

They talked about his school, how he had come to study architecture, how he hoped to expand his business. "I admire you for it," Robin said. "It must be hard with work, and Cole, and you know, everything else."

He wondered briefly what everything else meant, but the talk turned to her work, why her father had demoted her the way he had. "I used to travel all over the world as an ambassador for LTI. Now I am sitting in my house trying to get Eldagirt Wirt on the phone."

"Yeah, well, I bet the Eldagirts of the world have more impact on what LTI does than a bunch of VIPs looking for a party."

They talked about Zaney, with Robin looking genuinely distressed for the injury that Zaney had suffered in the oil fields many years ago, which left him with a mind about as deep as a birdbath. "He's a good man. No sense at all, but a good, well-meaning man," Jake said.

"It's so…I don't know…laudable the way you take these people under your wing, like Zaney and Cole."

Jake shook his head. "I didn't take on Zaney and Cole, they just happened to be in my life. I bet you'd do the same."

"Really?" Robin asked laughingly. "I don't know if I would."

When the beer began to run low, they walked over to the old house and through the empty rooms with old pine plank floors and big windows, and imagined who might have lived there. When they entered the main living area, Jake could not tear his gaze away from Robin's; he was mesmerized by the color and the depth of expression in her eyes. She held his gaze, then took his hand, turned it palm up, and traced the crevices and calluses that had formed from a lifetime of hard work. He tried to pull away, embarrassed that no matter what he did or where he went, his hands revealed the truth about him—he was a laborer, always had been, always would be. Yet she wouldn't let him pull away. "I love your hands," she said. "I love the way they feel—so real."

When the beer was gone and the sun had started to slide off to the west, it was time to end one of the most pleasant afternoons Jake had ever spent in his life. He gathered up the empty beer bottles, looked at Robin, and smiled. "I really enjoyed the afternoon."

"Me, too," Robin said. "You know what? In spite of all appearances to the contrary, I kind of liked the look of you when you showed up on my drive."

Jake put his arm around her shoulders and inhaled the scent of her hair. "As long as we're confessing, I'll admit I thought you were one fine-looking ex-con." She laughed; he kissed the top of her head and slipped her hand into his as they started up the grassy slope to his bike.

But for Jake, the end of a perfect spring afternoon was beginning to cloud over with mild confusion. What had started out as a lark had moved into something more intense and the opposite of what he intended, leaving him feeling uncharacteristically perplexed. "Robin," he said as he stuffed their trash inside his saddlebag, "I'm not sure where we are."

"You don't remember how we got here?"

"What I mean is, I'm not sure about all this," he said, gesturing toward the river and picnic table. "It sort of changes things, doesn't it?" He shifted his gaze to the old house. "I don't imagine Mr. GQ would like it much."

"Mr. GQ? Who, you mean Evan?" Robin exclaimed with a snort. "I don't care what he thinks. We are not...you know, *together*."

Jake didn't believe that. If he hadn't seen Evan in his boxers that morning—

"All right, we *used* to date," she said, blushing furiously. "And I...I...okay, I'm not the only one with ghosts here—what about Ms. Kentucky Fried Chicken?"

Jake couldn't really say anything. Lindy was a ghost all right, and he couldn't seem to rid himself of the thought that he was making some huge mistake.

"It's complicated, isn't it?" Robin finally asked on a soft sigh.

"Yeah," he said, sobering with her.

The ride back was subdued, the mention of their respective lives a damper on the perfect afternoon. It was almost dark by the time they pulled into Robin's drive. She climbed off the Harley and glanced conspicuously at her front door. "Thank you," she said, shifting her gaze to him again. "This was perfect. Really perfect."

Jake grasped her hand, brought it to his lips, and kissed her knuckles.

"I'd ask you in, but I really have to get up early tomorrow. We're off to Minot."

He hadn't expected to be asked in, if that is what she thought, and wondered what she *did* think he was after. "Hey..." He faltered, unsure of what he wanted to say, feeling awkward, as if he shouldn't be sitting here holding her hand.

"Yes?"

Jake felt an unexpected tug of deep regret, and let go her hand. "You don't have to worry. I mean, don't think just because of today that I..."

Her smile faded.

Shit. "Today was really nice, Robin, but don't...don't think that I'm going anywhere with this. I've got a job to do here. I enjoyed your company."

Something flitted across Robin's pretty blue eyes that he couldn't quite read. She nodded, shoved her hand in her back pocket. "Oh. Okay. Well...thanks for the ride."

"Sure." He debated if he should try and explain that he knew he was out of her league, that she would never settle for someone like him, and that because he knew it, he wasn't going to push it, and he damn sure wasn't going to try and take advantage of her.

But Robin was already walking away. At her door, she shoved the key in the lock, pushed it open, then gave him a quick, pithy wave as she stepped inside and shut the door.

It was a moment before Jake could move, frozen by a blast of cold confusion. He finally decided he should have his freaking head examined for taking her out there in the first place.

His mood turned foul on the way over to Telephone Road, and the Manning family was determined to whip it into a hurricane. When he arrived, Cole was slumped on a sofa in the living room, staring at the TV.

"What's up?" Jake asked.

"Nothing," Cole responded without looking at him.

"What are you watching?"

"Can't you see? It's baseball."

"I mean, who's playing?" Jake tried again.

"Two teams," Cole said, the disdain dripping in his voice.

"Don't be a smart-ass."

"I'm bored!" he cried. "This place sucks! There's nothing to do!"

Jake's patience was wearing thin. "How about homework?"

Cole suddenly moved for the remote, clicked the game off, and stalked upstairs without so much as a glance at Jake. Man, the kid had a lot of animosity.

"Thought you'd be here for supper," Jake's mom called from the kitchen.

"Sorry, Mom," he said, walking into the kitchen. "I ended up going out of town today."

Mom looked up from the magazine she was flipping through and exhaled a cloud of smoke at him. "You had a job?"

"No. Just took a ride."

With a snort of disapproval, Mom ground out her smoke, stood up, and went to the fridge. "I got some leftover tuna casserole. I'll fix you a plate."

It was pointless to decline, he knew, so Jake sat down at the old Formica kitchen table, looked around at the yellow painted cabinets and the faded pineapple wallpaper. "Why don't you let me redo this kitchen, Mom?"

"You got your hands full as it is. I knew you wouldn't have enough time for Cole, and I guess I was right."

"What, I'm not supposed to have time to myself?"

"Not when you got responsibility for a kid. I never had any time to myself."

"I know, Mom. You never did anything but sacrifice," he groused, not wanting to hear the broken record tonight.

But Mom gave him a pointed, you-know-better look over her shoulder as she fixed his plate. "That's right. I did nothing but sacrifice for you so you could play baseball. Lord knows your dad wasn't going to give you that."

True. But then again, Dad was an asshole.

"That girlfriend of yours called here again today looking for you. At first I thought you'd gone off with her," she said as she put his plate in the microwave. "Don't know why you got any interest in her anyway."

And now they would move right into a critique of his love life. "She's nice. But it was an accident that she found your number at all."

"Some accident," Mom muttered.

"Got any beer?" he sighed, and heaved himself up, went to the fridge to have a look for himself. He pulled out a can of generic beer, went back to the table and popped it open.

"Ever since you left here, you been hooking up with gals who ain't got enough sense to come out of the rain," Mom continued, oblivious to his impatience.

"Jesus, Mom, why do you have to do this?" he said, shoving a hand through his hair. "Do you have to point out everything you think I'm doing wrong? Give me a little credit—at least I'm here! At least I'm not dead or in prison!"

Mom removed his plate from the microwave and put it in front of him. "I'm not complaining about you, Jacob," she said. "Maybe I don't got all the right words to say it, but I'm trying to get across that you hook yourself up with these gals that you don't care nothing about. Now you got your nephew and he needs you, and he needs a woman in his life. He's learning from you, so if you're gonna go with girls, go with one who's got some substance to her. That's all I'm saying."

A vision of Robin, instant and uninvited, flashed across his mind's eye. He took a bite of the casserole—tuna, cream of mushroom soup, saltine crackers—and thought it was delicious. His kind of food. Not fusion cuisine, or whatever bullshit Robin had talked about. And why "fusion cuisine" should irritate him so, he didn't know. Jake ate quickly, nodded absently as Mom ran down a list of all Cole's faults, then put his plate in the sink and gave her a quick kiss on the cheek. "I'll talk to him," he said wearily and went to find him to try again to reach him.

CHAPTER SIXTEEN

The phone rang so loud in Robin's ear the next morning that she about had to peel herself off the ceiling. It was Lucy, telling her a car would be around to pick her up at nine to take her to the airport. "Splendid. Go away," Robin croaked, hung up the phone, and stared bleary-eyed at the clock. Seven a.m. Christ Almighty, where was the fire?

She rolled onto her back, blinked up at the bare ceiling above her, and thought of Jake. The stupid jock had been in her thoughts and dreams all night, from the moment he basically told her that he would make out with her, but that was about it. How very charming. And really, who did he think he was, anyway? But then again, what did she expect? She wasn't a teenager—one outing did not constitute going steady, dammit.

Robin pushed herself up on her elbows and looked around the room. The sun was spilling in from the east windows, casting large squares of irritatingly cheerful light over wood floors. Clothes were strewn everywhere because she had tried on several outfits yesterday to find the perfect, get-on-a-motorcycle-with-him ensemble. Bastard. It wasn't as if *she* liked *him*.

Oh hell yes, she did.

With a heavy sigh, she sat up on the side of the bed and frowned at the wall. He really had his nerve. She didn't know which stung worse—that she really did like him and he didn't like her quite so much? Or that he might prefer the Lindy-type over her? Ouch. Nothing against sweet little virginal bake-sale Lindy, but that was really a bite. To hell with it—she wasn't going to spend the day crying over some guy who wore steel-toed boots for casual wear. No sir, *she* was going to Minot, North Dakota. Hallelujah!

When Robin finished her shower and had packed, she dressed in classic St. John and stumbled out of her bedroom, in desperate need of coffee. In the kitchen, she heard creaking above her, and took two sideways steps so that she could see out the kitchen door. *Grrrreat!* There was his truck. The jerk was up there right now, probably with his pal Doofus—hell, probably even Grandpa—ripping out the walls and turning her Tudor-style mansion into a showroom of her empty life.

Robin flipped on the coffeepot, tapping her foot while she waited for it to brew. When she had her cup of coffee, she marched into the dining room, dug out her computer from the mound of paper that was beginning to build, and punched up her mail.

Aha, there was a surprise. A note from Bob (*Last chance, Ms. Lear, LOL!*), one from the insurance agent, the usual thousand from Lucy, and one from Cecilia about the Spring Tulip dance. While she was perusing those, someone came clumping down the stairs. Robin refused to look up, refused to give him even the slightest hint that she—

"Hey hey, if it ain't my cellmate!"

Robin jerked her gaze to a grinning Zaney, gathering tools at the foot of the stairs.

"I beg your pardon?" she demanded hotly.

"I said, HEY, IF IT—"

"I *heard* you. So what, is he blabbing it to everyone now? Does he think it's funny?"

"Well, it ain't nothing to be ashamt of," Zaney said, looking more bewildered than usual. "It happens to damn near all of us."

Oh God. Dear God. "No, actually, it does not happen to damn near all of us."

Zaney heaved up the bundle of tools. "Don't have to get so bent outta shape," he muttered under his breath and trudged back upstairs.

Robin tried to focus on her e-mail. *New safety regs, mandatory read. DOT inspection next Thursday…* The house was suddenly stifling and full of too many fools, herself included. When was the car coming? When could she escape this place for Minot? She stood abruptly, marched back to her bedroom, retrieved her stuffed Coach duffel bag, and lugged it to the entry. A glance at her watch said that it was only eight forty, but Robin opened the door and walked out onto the drive, peering up and down North Boulevard for any sign of the car. Seeing none, she turned on her heel and shrieked with alarm, clamped a hand over her heart at the unexpected sight of Jake standing directly behind her.

He grinned.

She frowned. "What?"

He lifted a brow. "You hurt Zaney's feelings. He thought you two were going to be cellmates for life."

"Very funny," she said, and tried to step around him, but Jake matched her step. "Do you mind? I'm about to leave."

"Since when are you so anxious to get to Minot?"

Since you said what you did, you big jerk. "I have to work."

"Okay," he said, nodding thoughtfully. "But if you don't mind me saying so, you seem a little pissed off. As in royally."

Pissed off, ha! "Pissed *off?*" No, nononono, she wasn't PISSED OFF. "Why would I be pissed off?" That would imply that he meant something to her, and before he could answer, her mouth opened and her tongue began to wag. "You know, you have your nerve," she said, punching her fists to her hips. "That little thing you're doing, you know, the—'oh, I'll be very charming and take you out to a field of flowers and kiss you, but don't expect me to be around'— *that* thing—is pretty maddening, and it's just really rude."

The second brow rose to meet the first. "What are you talking about?"

"What you said!" she cried, furious he could be so thick skulled. "You said, 'hey, I had fun, but I'm not going to be around,' or something like that, probably because you and Betty Crocker are all lovey-dovey, but still, I think it was really...well, it was just *mean*, that's what it was—"

He startled her by catching her upper arms and pulling her close. "Robin—"

"Oh no," she said, her hand coming up between them, "don't think *I* am into this or anything, because I don't want you around, but still, the presumption—"

"Oh, okay—it's fine for you to mess around, but not me," he said, dropping her arms. "So do you use a ladder to get up on that high horse, or what?"

Now she was pissed. "What I do is none of your business."

"Pardon me, Bubbles, but I thought there were *two* of us out there—"

"Big mistake! Trust me!"

Jake stopped, glared down at her. "Thanks for clarifying. All I was trying to say last night, and pretty badly, it seems, is that I am not trying to take advantage of you. I don't know where this is going—at least I didn't, but I guess I do now. You don't want me around? I understand—it's not like we come from the same planet, is it? I am reminded of that pretty constantly."

"*Ooh...*" Robin muttered. Her heart began doing that funny skip thing again. "Jake..." she started, but the sound of gravel crunching beneath tires startled them both.

"Madam, your broom has arrived," Jake said as the limo coasted into the drive and rolled to a halt right in front of them. Robin groaned as the driver got out and walked back to open the passenger door.

Evan was already climbing out before the driver could pull it completely open; he stared at Robin and Jake across the hood of the car. "Rob? What are you doing?" he asked, eyeing Jake.

"What do you mean?" she asked, self-consciously taking a step away from Jake.

Evan kept looking at Jake. "I mean, are you ready?" he asked, his voice cool.

Other than the fact she didn't want to leave now, not until she could say...*what?* That she was sorry, that she really liked him, that she had a great time yesterday. "I'll just get my things," she muttered, more to herself, and walked quickly to the house to retrieve her computer, overnight bag, and her new, thanks-to-Mia Hermès purse.

When she walked back outside, Jake hadn't moved, was still standing there, his weight on one hip, calmly regarding Evan. Evan had come around to this side of the limo, was leaning up against it, one leg crossed over the other, his arms folded across his chest. Both men turned as she walked out onto the drive.

"Ready?" an unsmiling Evan said, stepping aside so the driver could open the door.

"Yes." Robin shifted the bag on her shoulder and looked at Jake. "I'll be back in a couple of days."

"Don't rush on my account," he said and glared at Evan again.

The driver quickly relieved Robin of her overnight bag and computer; Evan held the door open for her, then climbed in to sit beside her. As the limo pulled out of the drive, she caught one last look at Jake over her shoulder. Although his head was down, he was watching her leave, methodically pushing a tape measure in and out, in and out, until she could no longer see him.

Robin faced forward. Evan smiled. "Your handyman seems like a nice guy."

"He's not a handyman."

"Oh, *sorry*," Evan chuckled. "What is the politically correct term for handyman?"

"So who is going to meet us at the airport?" she asked, changing the subject.

Evan opened his Tod briefcase and presented her with a sheaf of papers. "You need to review this before we get there," he said, and as Robin took the stack of papers, he buzzed the driver and instructed him to find a Starbucks.

That the company jet made a very bumpy descent into Minot should have been the first clue, but nothing could have prepared Robin for the gale-force arctic wind that almost knocked her on her butt and did quite a number on her hair. Mr. Lou Harvey was on hand to meet them, dressed in a blue polyester sport coat, a very thick polyester-ish tie, and a white button-down shirt. His salt-and-pepper hair was slicked down under an impenetrable shield of Brylcreem, and his black tortoiseshell glasses drew immediate attention to his watery amber eyes.

"Lou Harvey! Glad to meet you!" he boomed, popped a Rolaids into his mouth, and vigorously shook Evan's hand, then Robin's, wincing outwardly at her hair. "Do you want to visit the ladies' room before we get started?"

Once they were safely ensconced in his Oldsmobile Cutlass, Lou insisted on giving them a tour of the town. Robin tried to claim the backseat, but Evan was too quick for her, smirking when she maneuvered her way into the front next to Lou. Her skirt was too damn short—not only was she freezing, but she could hardly keep the thing from riding up. It was a wonder they didn't drive head-long into someone, since Lou couldn't take his eyes off her legs.

They drove past the Grizzly Grill and Saloon, the municipal center (where, Lou said to her knees, and through a mouthful of Rolaids, they would have lunch tomorrow at the Lion's Club), and past Sears twice before heading to the outskirts of town. Lou was hauling ass now, and came barreling to a stop in front of a red, corrugated steel building, proudly labeled *Peerless Packing Supply* in big yellow letters. He jumped out, ran to the glass doors leading into the offices of the building, and flashed a gap-toothed grin at Robin's breasts as she hurried past.

Inside, Evan shoved his hand through his hair in an attempt to repair it and lied, "Great-looking place!"

"Yep!" Lou said, beaming. "Same since 1972."

No lie, Robin thought as they walked into the middle of a small suite of offices and cubicles. A brillo pad of hair popped up above one cubicle, beneath which a pair of humongous frames peered at Robin. The woman who owned them stepped out of her cubicle—she wore red pants, a sweatshirt that had a moose painted across the chest, and black Easy Spirits. She eyeballed Robin up one side and down the other, taking in her hair (still atrocious), her St. John suit (ridiculous choice for this weather), and her Feraggamo pumps (already killing her). Then the woman affixed her gaze to Robin's Hermès purse.

"This is Barbara Gates, head of our accounts payable section!" Lou said loudly. Barbara nodded as she tried to read the little gold tag on Robin's purse. They moved through the accounting section, and two more Jack-in-the-box heads popped up in the cube farm. Barbara followed closely behind, her eyes on Robin's purse, as if she thought it might disperse a Jolly Rancher or two.

In the warehouse, they stood amid giant spools of bubble wrap, cardboard wrapping, pallets, and conveyor belts while Lou explained what they were seeing. In the course of it, Barbara leaned into Robin and said, "I like your purse."

"Thanks."

"What kind is it?"

"Hermès."

The woman nodded knowingly. "Seen that at Penney's."

They moved on through the warehouse, finally reaching Lou's office, where they began to talk numbers. Robin had to hand it to Evan—he was as smooth as he was smart. He managed to get the most pertinent information out of Lou about gross sales and receipts, sales volumes, and the details on the larger accounts. Lou, who in spite of appearances to the contrary, was pretty savvy himself, openly sizing Evan up, skirting his more delicate questions with a joke. At the end of the afternoon, however, Robin had a pretty good handle on Peerless Packing.

Lou drove them to a low-slung highway hotel later that afternoon. Robin lugged her bag to her room, shut the door against the howling wind, and noticed, with a shudder, the big, hand-lettered sign: *Please do not clean game or fish in room.* An hour later, she was in the lobby where the free complimentary breakfast would be served the next morning, dressed in linen slacks and jacket.

Evan came a moment later, wearing jeans and a more serviceable navy-blue blazer. "You don't have anything more substantial?" he asked, checking out her outfit. When she shook her head, he cracked a smile and threw an arm around her shoulder. "Then I'll just have to keep you warm." At her withering look, he laughed. "I'm just kidding. Can't you take a joke? Come on, I called a cab."

Their destination was The Hunter's Lodge, which Evan said he chose for local flavor. Local flavor was right—blanketed by a thick haze of smoke, various parts of elk, moose, and longhorn sheep adorned the walls, and in the middle of the dining area, a stuffed wild turkey welcomed them. They were shown to a booth by a very cheerful young woman who reminded Robin of Lindy. Actually, everyone reminded her of Lindy. Even the cheeseburger she ordered reminded her of Lindy.

"*Cheese*burger? What's gotten into you?" Evan scoffed after ordering the salmon (*lightly* sautéed in butter).

Jake Manning, that was what. It appeared that he was completely, totally, and firmly lodged under her skin. "What's wrong with a cheeseburger? When was the last time you had one?"

"Nineteen seventy-four," Evan said disdainfully.

"And fries, too," she defiantly told the waitress, and thought again as the Lindy-clone walked away that she felt a little guilty for letting this infatuation with Jake go so far as it had. But when she thought of *why* she felt guilty, it made her crazy. It all boiled down to one thing: she was not supposed to like a guy like Jake. It was not in the path she had loosely charted for herself. Her life was supposed to be one of acquisition and achievement, including men with pedigrees and buckets and buckets of money. She was following in the old man's footsteps, wasn't she? Jake was a great guy, but by the looks of things, he wasn't going to be the one to provide her the lifestyle she was used to, and wow, that was shallow, wasn't it?

"I think Peerless is a good operation," Evan said, and as he began to talk, Robin was acutely aware of the fact that she was supposed to like a guy like Evan. He was accomplished, he was a self-made millionaire, he was handsome. He was the guy she was supposed to be head over heels for. And as Evan droned on about the pros and cons of Peerless, she could see why Dad was so in love with the guy. He was very good at what he did, and he had the rare ability to adapt, which was something she did not do very well (case in point: Minot). He was pleasant, he was considerate, and he'd been crazy about her once. As Evan checked out the

Lindy-clone's ass, she decided that there really was nothing wrong with him. He was the perfect man for a woman like her. She just couldn't help wondering what that said about her.

But it didn't really matter, because the sad truth was, Evan just did not float her boat. Robin did not feel the rush of blood when he walked into a room like she did with Jake, or think about him like she did Jake. Like today, with just a memory of his kiss to go on, she had thought constantly of Jake, wondered what he was doing, remembered the feel of his lips on hers, the rough texture of his hands on her skin, the warmth of his smile. The harsh words she had spoken, which made her wince. When she looked at Evan, she wondered if he still sorted the underwear in his drawer by color, or if he had ever mowed a lawn in his life.

"So what do you think?" Evan asked, interrupting her thoughts.

"Think?"

He frowned lightly. "About Peerless? The thing I've been going on and on about for the last fifteen minutes? What's the matter, Robin? Why are you so distracted?" he asked, leaning across the table to grasp her hand.

Robin looked down at his hand, his perfectly manicured hand, and thought of Jake's scarred one. "Evan…"

Slowly, he withdrew his hand. "Oh," he said with a heavy sigh, reading her thoughts. "*That* again. Look, Robbie, I told you, I'm through. You've made your wishes perfectly clear. You don't want a relationship in spite of your curious lack of judgment in sleeping with me—"

"Hey—"

"Uh-uh, no 'heys' this time," he said. "It was a damn stupid thing to do. But okay, what's done is done. *I'm* done. I'm not trying to get in your pants, I'm not trying to do anything but make you an executive in this company. A *good* executive. So you can quit reading something into everything I say or do. Let's at least be adults about this for the sake of the company. Just…just get over yourself, will you?" he said and picked up the martini he had ordered and took a deep drink.

"Okay," she said weakly, feeling his irritation. "I won't mention it again."

"Good," he said gruffly. "Now, about Peerless. I want to hear what *you* think of their potential," he said and stabbed his elbows onto the table, looking at her with gray eyes so cold that she shivered in her linen jacket.

In spite of the wind and chill of the night's hard freeze, the day dawned sunny and pleasant in Minot. Lou Harvey was at the motel at eight a.m. sharp. He shook Evan's hand (SLEEP ALL RIGHT? he boomed with a wink and a nudge), smiled at Robin's breasts, and ushered them out into the Oldsmobile Cutlass. They sped across town to Bubble Wrap City, where they spent the morning until it was time to go to the Lion's Club.

They careened to a halt in front of the municipal center and entered an open room where round tables had been set for lunch. Robin thought she had walked into a sea of Q-tips. A string of lady blue hairs and geezers—some actually too young to be geezers, but what the hell—advanced to introduce themselves. Lou Harvey was beside himself, practically bursting at his polyester seams with pride over his sophisticated guests.

It had all the markings of being the longest hour and a half in her life, but a funny thing happened at that Lion's Club luncheon, something that both astounded Robin and touched her. It wasn't the Pledge of Allegiance, with Evan saying it louder than any of the Q-tips. Or the invocation. It wasn't even the singing of the Lion fight song that stirred her, or the surprisingly pleasant conversation with Barbara, who declared Robin's very expensive Hermès purse inadequate in the compartment department (which it was) and told her about her softball team (the Peerless Pretties). It wasn't the bland salad or blander chicken, or the amazingly insightful and surprisingly amusing luncheon speech by the local medical examiner.

It was, Robin decided over yellow cake with red, white, and blue icing, the sense of camaraderie, the feeling of belonging. These people gave awards to one another for the most mundane things and little personal accomplishments in their unimportant lives. They asked each other about their loved ones, seemed interested in the details of gout, legal troubles, or softball scores. It was the fierce way in which they pledged allegiance to the flag—so fiercely, one could believe that they would pick up arms in a moment and form a battalion if challenged. It was that they seemed to really care about one another. As Robin watched the members around her trading jokes only they found funny, she felt the strange empty feeling come over her again. She actually *envied* these people, she realized. She envied their belonging. She wanted to belong. To someone. Something. Anything.

On the flight back to Houston, Evan settled back in his seat and chuckled to himself. "Could you believe that crowd?" he asked with a roll of his eyes. "The Pledge of Allegiance? Shit, I haven't said that since I was ten!"

Neither had she. Maybe that was what was wrong with people like her and Evan. They had no allegiance.

Evan drifted off to sleep; Robin stared out the window, mulling over the surprising fact that she actually *liked* Barbara. She even liked ol' Lou Harvey for reasons that were not completely clear to her, but something about him made her suddenly sentimental. She picked up the phone, dialed her mother's cell. "Mom? It's Robin," she said when her mother answered. "How's it going?"

Mom sighed. "Hi, honey. Your father isn't feeling too well. We're going back to New York tomorrow to see his doctor."

The news unleashed a dull panic in Robin. "Is he there? Can I talk to him?"

"Sure. He's right here."

"Robbie? What are you doing?" Dad asked after a moment.

"How are you, Dad?" she asked, her eyes misting.

"Oh...I don't know. Kind of tired, I guess. Where are you, Minot?"

"We're on our way back to Houston now," she said, remembering that she had specifically *not* told him she was going to Minot, and gave Evan a frown that would have made him wince, had he been awake.

"How did it go?"

"Pretty well. I'm not sure Peerless is who we want, but they seem to have a good solid operation."

"What did Evan say?"

Robin closed her eyes, tried to swallow the disappointment.

"Pretty much the same thing. I'd let you talk to him, but he's asleep."

"Yeah, let him sleep. I'll see him in New York this week anyway."

"So how do you feel, Dad?"

"Don't worry about me, Robbie," he said gruffly.

But she wanted to worry about him. She wanted to be part of his crisis. "Dad, I've been thinking about you, and I—"

"I hope you've been thinking about what I said. I hope you have slowed down a little and taken stock of your life."

"I was going to say that I have been thinking about how you are doing, and I thought maybe I could come to California, or New York, if you are going to be there. You know, spend a little time with you."

There was a noticeable hesitation; she heard Dad sigh. "No, that's not a good idea. I may have to have more radiation, and I don't want you around for that. I'd rather you stay in Houston and find your footing. You need to focus on your issues, not mine."

His rejection stung and as tears welled, she resented him deeply for it. "Sure. My issues. Gotta whip them into shape."

"What? Okay, well...you and Evan getting along?"

She was too stung to even notice the question, really. "Fine. Just fine."

"Good. Tell him to call me about Minot when you get to Houston, will you?"

Right. He needed a *real* report. Not one from someone with issues. "You bet. Hope you get to feeling better. I guess I'll talk to you later."

"Yep."

She had no idea what else to say. "Well then, bye."

"Bye-bye, baby," he said, and hung up the phone.

Robin put the airphone back in its cradle and stared blindly at the pale blue sky through the little portal, feeling more lost than ever. Her relationship with her father had never been exactly rosy, but this was just hurtful. Since the astounding news of his cancer and the loss of her job, nothing seemed right anymore, nothing *felt* right anymore. It was as if she had nothing to lose, nothing to find, that her life was just a series of moments wasting away. In fact, the only thing that was clear to her was that she wanted to see Jake's smile and feel its warmth wash over her. *Now, please.*

In California, Aaron put down the cell phone and grinned at Bonnie. "I think we're seeing some progress, Bon-bon," he said cheerfully. "I think Robin is seeing Evan again."

Bonnie frowned lightly, picked up her fork, and stabbed at the pineapple on her plate.

"What's the matter?" Aaron asked, confused.

"I'm not sure if Evan is Robin's choice or yours, frankly," she said. "You may think you know what's best for everyone, but you're not always right."

"Well, I am right about this," he said with a snort. "Evan is a good man. He's thoughtful and will take good care of her and he knows the business inside and out. I could not ask for more at this point."

Bonnie put her fork down, stared across the table at him. "Would you stop that?"

"Stop what?"

"Charting your daughter's life. You sound like you are more interested in the business than you are Robin. She will find her own way without you dictating the course for her—just let her choose her own path."

Aaron waved a hand at her, looked down at his plate, and saw several strands of his hair. "Robbie could do a whole lot worse than Evan Iverson. Trust me, this is the right thing for her," he said and pushed up from the table. "I'm sorry, but I've got to lie down."

He walked out of the room, but not without hearing Bonnie utter, "That is so like you, Aaron. You know better than all of us put together. It's the same arrogant attitude you accuse your daughter of having, you stubborn bastard."

CHAPTER SEVENTEEN

J ake had not known until today that one could catch up to
four episodes a day of *Wheel of Fortune* on cable TV. This
information, courtesy Elmer Stanton, who had brought a
little portable TV and set it up so he'd have something to
do while Zaney was working. Shortly thereafter, Jake could
hear Zaney shouting out the wrong answers (*Can't take it
with y'all! Can't TAKE IT WITH Y'ALL!*). He had finally convinced
them to turn the damn thing off, but it was too late—he
figured they had lost at least an hour to Vanna. Since Robin
wasn't due back until tomorrow, Jake decided to work late
and catch up.

A demolition crew had come in and taken out the two
walls upstairs, another crew had stripped the paint and
wallpaper in the house. There were two old fixtures in the
upper master suite that needed to be disconnected, and the
wiring was so old and corroded that he had to carefully peel
them apart before pulling it all out.

That's what he was doing when he heard the kitchen
door open and shut. He thought it was Zaney, but then he
heard the unmistakable click of heels and his heart did
a funny little flip in spite of his disappointment. He had

known what she was from the beginning, and still he had allowed himself to get caught up, to hope she was different.

Jake quickly wiped his hands on his workpants, then shoved one through his hair for want of a comb. The heels were on the stairs now, and he walked out of the master bedroom just as Robin reached the top landing. The sight of her stopped him—she looked absolutely gorgeous, even more so than when she'd left yesterday.

"So you're still here," she said, ruining the effect.

"I didn't think you'd be back until tomorrow. I was trying to catch up on some work."

She took a measured step toward him, seemed not to know what to do with her hands, and finally letting them settle on her waist.

"How was Minot?" he asked.

"Cold and windy."

"So…did you acquire anything? Like a packing supply company?"

Robin laughed, shook her head. "No. But I said the Pledge of Allegiance." She took another careful step forward. "And I ate a cheeseburger. With fries."

"Wow. Better call Ripley's. Pretty soon we'll have to tether your legs and arms so you won't float away before the parade."

She laughed lightly, her teeth snow white in the early evening light. "So what about you? Did you renovate anything?"

"You mean, did I manage to accomplish anything between your grandpa's jokes and Zaney's new addiction to *Wheel of Fortune*?"

"Oh no," Robin groaned.

"I'm really glad you're back," he blurted, surprising himself with the admission.

"Yeah, I know—I'll call Grandma tomorrow. I bet she doesn't know he's over here."

She missed his point completely, and Jake had noticed she had a real knack for doing that. They stood awkwardly. There was so much Jake wanted to say about yesterday, so much he didn't know how to say. Deep conversations about his feelings were not exactly his forte. But then he remembered something. "Come here," he said, unconsciously extending his hand to her. "I want to show you something."

Robin glided forward, slipped her hand into his. He liked the feel of it—small and soft. He led her to the big bay window. "I found this earlier," he said, pointing to a scratch in the woodwork. "Looks to be pretty old."

She leaned forward, peered closely at the inscription:

LH and DD
Forevermore

"Oh my," she whispered. "Forevermore." She looked at it wistfully, then shrugged. "Kids, I guess."

"Kids? I thought maybe it was a man who loved a woman very much." And since when had he become so sentimental?

"Then it's a wonder he didn't come back and scratch it out." She glanced up at Jake, and laughed. "You don't really believe it *was* forevermore, do you?"

Funny, but Jake felt like the concept of "forevermore" was a notion that lurked on the edge of his consciousness, forbidden to enter. He shrugged self-consciously. "Don't you believe in it?"

"No." She laughed as if that were preposterous. "I don't know anyone who has made it—do you?"

Good point. But he wanted to know someone who'd made it. *He* wanted to make it.

Robin leaned forward to look at the inscription. "I don't really think in terms of forever. I don't think of anything other than where I am going next. Lately I've begun to think that I haven't been doing anything except running around in big circles. Maybe that's my forevermore—caught on one big loop going nowhere and I can't get off." She laughed again and moved away from the window.

Jake wondered what had happened in her life that would cause such a beautiful woman to have no more hope for love than Robin did.

"Have you eaten?" she suddenly asked him. "I was sort of craving Thai food—I'd love to take you along. You know, payback for watching *Wheel of Fortune* with Grandpa."

Say no, he told himself. He needed to study, needed desperately to study before he fell further behind. Not to mention his vow to himself to never repeat what had happened Sunday. It was a bad idea, very bad, given their yo-yo dance. "I've really got—"

"It's still pretty early—we can swing by your house," she interjected. "Zaney said it was in the Heights, right?"

Jake did a frantic search of his brain to remember if he'd left anything objectionable lying around his house. God, he wasn't actually considering—"Yeah...sure," he said out loud, feeling like a monumental fool the instant the words slipped off his tongue.

Twenty minutes later, as Jake made his way through the streets of Houston to the Heights (Robin following in her Mercedes), he said aloud, "You are a goddamn *idiot*. You are going to get all wrapped up in this and then what? Wait for her to tell you she doesn't want you around? Because she will, you stupid asshole."

His brain was obviously clueless, his groin was clearly running the show, and that annoyed Jake to no end. The more he knew Robin, the less he wanted that to be a reason to be with her—he did not want to lust after her, but she was so gorgeous that a man could hardly keep from it. It was all too complicated for his peabrain to understand, and, he thought as he pulled up to his house, slammed the truck into park, and got out, he wasn't going to try and understand it. Not right this moment, anyway. He had the more immediate problem of making sure there wasn't any dirty underwear in plain sight.

Parking behind him, Robin stepped out of her car and looked up in awe at the old Victorian house. "Ooh, this is *beautiful!*" she said, coming around the front of her car.

"I'm doing some work, so it doesn't look too great inside," he warned her as they ascended the old steps onto the wraparound porch. He was painfully aware that his house, while charming, did not even come close to comparing with hers. His was a house that was attainable—hers was a house straight out of a Hollywood movie. He fumbled with the lock, opened the door and stood aside, letting Robin precede him. She walked in slowly, admiring the ten-foot ceilings, the elaborate crown molding, and the old floor-to-ceiling brick fireplace.

"This is wonderful," she said, walking deeper into the room. "Cozy, cheerful...much more warm and inviting than mine. Mine could double as a museum, don't you think? Mind if I look around?"

"Help yourself. I'm gonna grab a shower. There's some beer in the fridge if you'd like one." As he disappeared into his room to shower and change, he watched her wander into the dining room, glance at his homework strewn across the table, then on, to the kitchen.

Jake reappeared twenty minutes later, showered, shaved, wearing khakis and a crisp white shirt that, thankfully, he'd found hanging in his closet.

Robin was sitting in his one chair—a recliner—flipping through the pages of *Architectural Digest*. She glanced up as he walked in the room, flashed an instantaneous smile that made him warm all over. "Well, *well*, Mr. Manning," she said, coming to her feet.

"Okay, I'll admit it. I have more than jeans and T-shirts."

"Yeah," she said, walking closer. "You're really cute."

"*Cute?*" he groaned, rolling his eyes as Robin laughed. But it pleased him enormously. Definitely more than it should have. "Come on, Princess, before your turn my head."

The restaurant was a small place, decorated like an Asian river delta, with grass thatching, warm colors, and waiters in Saipan hats. Jake had never had Thai food, or any other international cuisine. Unless he counted Mexico. The menu might as well have been printed in Chinese for all he could make of it. Robin very artfully suggested some dishes he might like without making him look like a clod.

"Great," Jake said quickly to their waiter as she pointed out the spicy peppered shrimp, which, she claimed, went well with beer. She ordered chicken with red curry and pineapple. That sounded wholly unappetizing to Jake, but what the hell, he was game for a little experimentation. Of any kind, come to think of it.

When the waiter brought him a beer with a funny red label on it and Robin a glass of rice wine, he held his breath and drank and asked about her trip to Minot. She confessed to feeling out of place, but seemed really taken with the Pledge of Allegiance, which he found amusing. It was funny how she could speak of a regular old run-of-the-mill American town like it was another planet. He supposed that was because Robin did occupy a whole other planet than most regular folk. *Robbieville*, he thought as he watched her hands moving, sketching in midair the various people she had met, *where money is consumed like water and people flit in and out with no apparent purpose or destination.* It was a world most could not fathom and a few could only dream of, yet there were moments he had the sense that Robin wanted off her planet, wanted to be down here with the mere mortals.

Over what he hoped was the main course, Robin made him very happy by telling him that Mr. Slick had gone to New York for several days. If Jake never laid eyes on that ass again, it would be too soon.

"And I have to go to Burdette Saturday," she moaned. "Evan is *soooo* much better at this than I am. He knows how to put people at ease. I seem to make them uptight."

She stared at her plate for a moment, then suddenly gasped and looked up. "*You* can go with me!" she exclaimed. "Yes, yes, say you will, Jake! This Saturday—it won't take long, I promise. We'll just jet up there, spend a couple of hours and come right back—"

Bad idea, extremely bad idea. He held his hand up, shook his head. "Wait, wait…I can't go to Burdette with you. I don't know anything about—"

"You don't *have* to know anything! Just come with me, I'll do the talking."

He had no doubt about that. "I've got my own work to do. Besides, what am I supposed to do while you are wheeling and dealing?" he asked, helping himself to some of her chicken. "Just sit there and twiddle my thumbs?"

"Oh, come on, you're my pal, aren't you?"

A pal. They were *pals*. Great. Okay, as long as he knew the ground rules. "I'll think about it," he said.

They continued to chat like old friends, at least until the check came. When the waiter put it down, Jake reached for his wallet, but Robin slapped her hand down on the leather case. Jake instantly covered her hand. "Let go," he said gruffly.

"No. It's my treat. I invited you, remember?"

"I remember, but I don't like women to pay my way."

"Excuse me? We're on caveman rules? Come on, step into the twenty-first century." Robin tried to yank the check toward her, but Jake held fast.

"I'm serious," he said, and he was—*very* serious.

Robin smiled sweetly. "Don't be silly, Hammerman— you're my contractor, so I buy, and besides, I already had dibs."

"No," he said. "Let go."

Robin shrugged. "Okay," she said and relaxed her hand. Jake reached for his wallet again, at which point Robin suddenly snatched the check up and fled to the front of the room, damn her. And then she brought him home, just like he was a girl, driving the entire distance singing the wrong lyrics to the radio, refusing to listen when he tried to set her straight.

She was exasperating and pushy, this one, but Jake did not want the evening to end. The Thai food had been, well...informative...and the company had been, oddly, the best he had had in years. She had a way about her, a spark, a unique view of the world. And it seemed that over dinner, the more Robin talked—her illustrative hands moving wildly in time with the tenor of her conversation—the more enchanted he grew.

When they reached his house, he glanced at his watch—ten o'clock. He had a crew showing up at eight in the morning. Today had been grueling; he really needed to sleep. "I've got a new Red Temple CD. Wanna come in for a little while?" he heard himself ask.

"Are you sure? It's getting late," Robin said, but she had already turned off the car.

Inside, he offered her a beer, and wished he had something a little more sophisticated when she declined. She was standing in the middle of the room as he put the CD in the player, and as a haunting strain of a violin lifted from the speakers, he turned around, intent on making her sit in the one chair he had while he fetched another from the dining room.

But Robin surprised him. Shocked him. Put him back on his heels and floundering like a rodeo clown as she came striding forward, slipping into his arms as if she belonged there, tilting her head back and going up on her toes to kiss him.

That knocked Jake for a loop, sent him reeling, his heart tumbling and pinging off the wall of his chest. Her lips drifted across his like a whisper of silk, tantalizing him. Her arm slipped around his waist, pulling him closer, and she nestled against his chest. With her breasts pressed against him, he could feel the heat of her body and the shot of fire straight to his groin. Mentally, Jake stumbled; he was unaccustomed to being the recipient of bold ardor, always the one to initiate. Her hand was now on his rib cage, moving up, slipping around to his arm, then his neck, until she cupped his face.

Jake recoiled as if he had been burned by fire.

Robin opened her eyes, smiled so seductively that he believed for a split second he might literally collapse to his knees. If she touched him again, just *touched* him, he feared how he might react, how swiftly he might sweep her into his arms, carry her to his bed.

"What's the matter?" she said in a throaty whisper. "Don't you like it?"

Oh, he liked it all right—liked it so damn much he couldn't find his tongue to tell her to stop.

With her finger, Robin lightly stroked a trail across his lips, then kissed the corner of his mouth, trailing a row of feathery light kisses to his ear. "*Don't you want me?*" she whispered, and the dam burst, flooding every part of him, hardening his cock to the point of aching. The rock music was blaring in the background creating a white-hot noise to surround them.

There was only one problem—she had invited him to dinner, she had paid for it, and she had driven him around like someone's granny. He'd be damned if she was going to take this from him, too. Jake suddenly grabbed her hands and pushed them behind her back. "You're gonna have to learn that you can't always just take what you want," he said low.

"What's the matter?" she purred, smiling seductively.

"Sometimes, it's sexy for a woman to be aggressive. But most of the time, its sexier if she just lets herself be a woman. Relax."

Robin arched a brow. "Wow. That sounds like a another chapter from *Confessions of a Neanderthal.*"

"No," he said, shaking his head, inhaling her scent. "It's a chapter from *I'm Gonna Make You Scream.*"

"*Ooh,*" Robin said and laughed low, letting her head fall back, exposing the creamy white skin of her neck.

Jake pulled her into his chest, and with his mouth, he found her neck, devoured the flesh there before lifting his head so that his lips were against her ear. "I want you," he said gruffly. "I want you so bad I just might explode."

She sighed, wrapped her arms around his neck as his lips grazed the curve of her throat. His hands had started a slow ascent up her rib cage; as he drew her earlobe between his teeth, he sought her breasts, finding them, cupping them, rubbing his thumbs across the flimsy fabric of her blouse. He could feel her body tense with his touch, and that only made his desire burn. His hand moved again, to her bottom, kneading it, holding her tightly against his rigid shaft while his tongue dueled wildly with hers.

His mind, his eyes, every orifice, every fiber, was filled with the scent and the feel of her. He didn't even realize he was moving, until they bumped into a wall. God, he was melting, dangerously aroused and piteously desperate for her body. His hand slid from her cheek, fluttered to her collarbone, and drifted down over her breast, cupping it in his palm to feel the succulent weight of it. His mouth, hungry for the taste of her, followed his hand, dipping to her neckline, touching the swell of her breast. Robin's hands splayed against the wall behind her, and she rose on her tiptoes, lifting her breast to him, whimpering softly when his lips closed around her nipple through the sheer fabric of her blouse. Aware that he was devouring her like a madman, without care to her expensive clothing or anything but the need to feel her, touch her, be in her, he could not keep his hands from roaming her body, could not stop his mouth from suckling her.

"Where?" she whispered hoarsely. "Where is your bed?"

With a groan, Jake swept her up, carried her through the darkened door beside them, and deposited her at the foot of his bed. She smiled in that wicked way of hers, reached up to wrap him in an embrace as she kissed his mouth, his eyes, his cheek.

And then she pushed him down on the bed. Hard. She crawled over him, straddling him, holding herself victorious above him. "You are making me crazy," she said hoarsely, as she slowly unbuttoned her blouse. With the speed of a snail, she pulled the flimsy blouse open, revealing a dark red, lacy bra that barely covered her breasts. She tossed the blouse aside, reached for his hand, and pressed it against her breast.

Something primal and deep kicked Jake hard in the balls; blood was surging through him like a raging river, ripping through his veins. He had never desired anyone or anything so completely in his life. The need to fill her was so overpowering that he couldn't stop now even if he tried. With a surge of strength, he toppled her over, moved her onto her back in one movement, then covered her with his body, pinning her hands above her head.

Robin laughed.

"You never learn, do you?" he asked, kissing her.

"So I've heard."

He pressed his mouth against hers, thrust his tongue inside, sending them both into the dark of his oblivion.

Somehow, he managed to free her breasts of the bra she wore. The touch of his fingers across her taut nipple undid him; he gripped her wrists tighter above her head. Her chest was heaving; she looked up at him with a glint in her eye, and he chuckled deep in his throat while his eyes feasted on her body, awed by how the curvy shape of her formed his desire. "Be still," he murmured.

"*Touch me,*" she whimpered breathlessly.

Turned on like a bolt of lightning, Jake growled as he unbuttoned her pants, slowly unzipped them, and slipped his hand inside. She wasn't wearing any panties. Ah hell, he *had* died and gone to heaven. He slipped a finger into the space between her pants and her crotch, just barely brushing the wild curl there, and Robin squirmed. He then slipped his finger between the wet folds of her sex.

"*Oh God,*" she moaned, tossing her head back, baring her long neck to him. Jake let go of her hands, kissed her bare belly, and moved lower, catching her pants in his teeth and, with help from his hands, pulling them from her hips, his mouth brushing the spring of curls, inhaling her feral scent.

She was writhing now, kicking off her pants and opening her legs wider, giving him access. When his tongue slipped between her damp lips, her hips bucked and she made a guttural sound of pleasure that sent the blood pounding through Jake, engorging his heart and his penis. But he held on, and with painstaking consideration, he began to explore her with his tongue, laving every crevice, flicking airily across the core of her desire, then deep into the recesses of her body.

Robin's response was explosive; she was moving against him, gasping for breath, the little cries of pleasure coming quicker and quicker in anticipation of release. He stroked her, sucked her, nibbled as if she were a delicacy until she almost came, then backed away, tried another delectable portion of her, and would have been happy to continue for hours, he thought, until Robin came with such force and unapologetic pleasure that he almost came with her.

She raked her fingers through his thick hair before jerking him up and smothering him with a profoundly deep kiss. Jake groaned, felt himself very close to losing it. She was panting now, tugging at his belt, frantically pulling the tail of his shirt from his trousers. Jake stroked her breasts with his hands as she worked, content to shape the hardened nubs between his fingers and his mouth while she clawed his shirt from him.

"*Jake*," she whispered anxiously when she at last got his shirt from his back. "Your *pants*," she hissed. And in a gymnastic move worthy of Olympic consideration, unzipped them and shoved them down his hips while Jake groped in his nightstand for a condom. She managed it, leaving only a pair of boxer briefs between her and the Biggest Erection Ever. Robin attacked the boxers and was hardly gentle about it, and gasped with pleasure as he sprang free. "*Oh*," she exclaimed in a rare moment of calm, admiring his body, "you're *beautiful*."

Jake lowered himself to her. "Not as beautiful as you," he said sincerely.

Robin buried her face in his neck; her hands swept down his belly, swirled around his throbbing erection, and cupped his testicles.

The moan Jake heard was his; he realized that he was straining to maintain control, that he was dangerously, deliriously close to spilling himself all over her. He brushed against her damp heat, a slow, back-and-forth movement that was so tantalizing he was actually torturing himself while her hands and mouth sought every other inch of him. When he couldn't stand his own teasing another moment, he slipped into her.

Shit, she was so hot, so wet, so *tight.* Her body opened for him, wrapped firmly around him, and hell, she was beginning to move in all the right ways, stroking him, squeezing him, and threatening to send him to the moon. "You're gonna make me lose it, baby," he groaned.

Robin's dark brows dipped into a vee. "I can't wait."

Neither could Jake. He lowered his head to kiss her, devouring her lips and tongue, and before he lost the last little bit of reason he had left, he began to move, withdrawing, sliding in again, picking up the rhythm with each new stroke. His hips circled, stroking her a little differently each time. They were both panting now; he was struggling to hold back, struggling to reach for the biggest and brightest orgasm of his life.

Then Robin began to move, circling to meet each thrust, tightening around him each time he withdrew. Jake clenched his teeth—between the swell of her breasts rubbing against his chest, the pout of her lips, and the way her body coiled around him and drew him in, he had no direction or thought in mind but to reach home, to reach the very core of her.

His body thrust deeper, faster, and harder into her, angling her legs in a way that he could reach her, pressing his body against her, slipping in and out so fast and hard that Robin had given up trying to keep pace with him. She had buried her face in his shoulder, moaning her pleasure, her fingernails sinking into his back. And when he thought he could not take another moment of it, he felt her body contract tightly around him, felt her shudder violently, felt the bite on his shoulder as she tried to muffle the cry of her orgasm.

He lost it.

Completely, totally, his life spilling in quick, burning spurts at the end of savage thrusts, until he was numb with exhaustion and contentment.

He slowly lowered himself to her, kissing the arch of her neck and burying his face in her hair as she tried to regain her breath. When he was convinced his breathing would return to normal and he would not expire, he rolled to his side, gathering her in his arms.

Neither of them spoke.

Jake watched her—she lay with her eyes closed and her lips slightly parted, her breasts lifting with each saturated breath. Robin Lear made love like a woman who had been shipwrecked for a thousand years.

And he had never been so completely, so wholly satisfied.

In the dark, she reached for his hand, clung to it tightly as she tried to regain her breath. And when she had caught it enough to talk, she opened her eyes, smiled up at him, and said, "Let's go again!"

CHAPTER EIGHTEEN

That might have been the best sex she ever had, but nonetheless, Robin tiptoed out after Jake had fallen asleep, then worried that she had really screwed things up. She hoped he wouldn't think it was one of those wham-bam-thank-you-Sam deals, because it certainly wasn't that. It was more a generalized fear of what she had gotten herself into, because just thinking about what had happened between them made her all warm and mushy inside and sent a delicious little shiver up her spine.

This would not do—she wasn't about to embark on some protracted fling with her contractor. Surely he understood they were pals. Sort of. Okay, so they'd hung out a little bit. They were in close quarters—it was natural. But surely he knew, like she knew, that everything would return to normal when the job was done.

But when Jake arrived at work, he was carrying a bouquet of lilac and bridal veil flowers. "I've got a couple of bushes growing around my house," he said, sort of apologetically.

Uh-oh. The man had gotten up, discovered she had left, and still had gone outside with a knife to cut her fresh flowers. In the rain. *Damn.* Yep, they were just about the most beautiful flowers she had ever seen. And Jake...well, Jake just made her sigh. Which was why this whole thing had all the markings of a complete disaster.

In fact, Robin was so preoccupied with those thoughts as she arranged the flowers in an old cut-glass vase that she was oblivious to the crews stomping about, or Zaney singing the new song he had penned (it was *sooo* bad), or the rain, or the phone, or the herd of pink flamingos, which, for some inexplicable reason, had been moved to her kitchen in her absence.

She put the arrangement smack-dab in the center of her dining room table, then repositioned her computer so she could surreptitiously see Jake through the flowers as he moved in and out of the entry. Then she proceeded to watch him instead of working on the figures she had picked up from Minot like she had promised Evan she would do.

And that is precisely what she was doing when Lucy arrived an hour later, sporting two cups of coffee and a thick file. "Where'd the flowers come from?" she asked as she dumped the file onto the dining table.

"An admirer," Robin said coyly.

"Ah, come on!" Lucy whined. "Who from?"

Robin shook her head, thankful for once that the doorbell rang.

"Come on, who, who?" Lucy begged as Robin moved to answer the door.

"Forget it. I'm not saying," Robin said as she picked her way through the scaffolding. She winked at Jake as she went by, opened the door, but could not see the delivery guy behind the huge spray of yellow baby roses in a crystal vase. "Robin Lear?"

"For *me?*" she asked with delight. Jesus, she was going to have to write *Time* magazine and insist he be named Man of the Year.

"*Two* bouquets?" Lucy said from the dining room. Taking the huge bouquet, Robin thanked the deliveryman, shut the door, and stepped around the scaffolding to where Jake was standing. "I should be sending *you* flowers," she whispered low as she carefully stepped by him.

But Jake's smile was not nearly as cheerful. In fact, it looked more like a frown. And Robin suddenly had the rotten feeling that perhaps Jake had not sent her another bouquet of flowers, which left only one valid possibility as to who did send them. Damn it all to hell! Robin marched into the dining room, put down the flowers, and reached for the card. *You did a great job yesterday. Keep up the good work! Evan.*

Butthead!

"Who are they from?" Lucy asked.

"No one," Robin said, barely able to contain her exasperation. She picked up the flowers and strode to the kitchen, opened up the trash, and tossed the flowers inside.

"God, what are you doing?" Lucy cried, watching her.

That would teach him, the asshole. Robin turned, marched back into the dining room and glared at Lucy. "Men can be so stupid."

Her buoyant, day-after-great-sex mood effectively doused, she hunkered down over her computer and began to review the figures they had gotten from Peerless Packing Supply. Robin did not look at Jake—she *couldn't* look at Jake. Embarrassed, humiliated, and altogether put out with Evan's high-handed ways, she blocked all men out and delved into the numbers before her. Meanwhile, Lucy went through some paperwork, snorting at Zaney's many verbalized observations about life.

And frankly, no one could have been more amazed than Robin when, in forcing herself to be productive, she began to see a pattern emerging in the numbers. She was so sure about what she saw that she placed a call to LTI's financial manager, who, based on what she told him, helped confirm her suspicions. Peerless Packing Supply was losing money. No wonder Lou Harvey was so anxious to sell.

Feeling pretty good about her analysis—or rather, her ability to *do* the analysis, something she had secretly feared, given her status in the company as Senior Window Dresser, her better mood was restored by the time Mia showed up.

"Okay, I'm outta here," Lucy said when she heard Mia's *Yoo-hoo* from the kitchen. Robin could hardly blame her—Mia treated Lucy like she was inconsequential, but then again, Mia treated everyone as if they were inconsequential, even Robin. Lucy believed Mia thought she was somehow better than a Mexican secretary, but Robin knew that Mia disliked Lucy because she was exotic and very attractive. If there was one thing Mia could not abide, it was competition.

She did not, and had never, considered Robin competition. And to this day, Robin didn't quite know how to take that.

Mia was wearing a pristine white linen dress with black Manolo Blahnik sandals that were totally inappropriate for the rainy spring weather. Oblivious to the workmen, and moreover, their ogling of her, she came in, flopped down in a dining chair as Lucy gathered her things, and propped her chin on her fist. "I hate men," she announced.

Behind Mia's back, Lucy gave Robin an exaggerated roll of her eyes. "Later."

Robin waved; Mia acted as if she hadn't even seen Lucy. "Any man in particular? Michael, perhaps?"

"*Especially* Michael."

Nothing new there. Robin sighed wearily, accustomed to Mia's frequent breakups with Michael. "Okay, so what happened?"

Mia flipped her hair back, turned slightly to pass a cool glance over the workmen, then slumped in her chair. "We went to Juanita's last night. You know, the artist?"

Some artist. She painted blobs on canvas. Wait—that wasn't doing Juanita's *art* justice. She painted *colored* blobs on canvas and she was, for reasons that completely escaped Robin, all the rage in Houston.

"Anyway, there was this girl there, *little* girl, like eighteen. Someone said she's related to the Bushes. Michael couldn't take his eyes off her. He couldn't stop *talking* to her. In fact, he practically crawled down her dress to have a look at her fake boobs."

"Ah." It was all Robin could say, knowing full well Michael's thirst for chasing skirts. Even she had been the object of his attentions on more than one drunken occasion, with Mia only steps away.

"We had a huge fight about it and I think I hate him."

"So, did you break it off?"

"What, the wedding?" Mia asked, surprised. "Of course not!"

257

Robin stopped what she was doing. "You're kidding, right? He's already got a wandering eye and you're still going to marry him?"

Mia nodded matter-of-factly, then rolled her eyes at Robin's look of surprise, as if Robin were somehow taxing her. "Oh, shut up. *All* men do it, you know that. But it doesn't mean we have to like it."

"*All* men do *not* do it, Mia. Why would you settle for anything less than perfect love?" she blurted, instantly wondering where that had come from.

Mia blinked. And then she shrieked a laugh. "What planet did you come from? Look at your dad, Rob! You can be so naive sometimes. There is no such thing as perfect love. There is sex, and there are joint bank accounts. And once the 'falling in love' business wears off, you better hope you have married the biggest bank account."

"God, that sounds so mercenary."

"Oh please," Mia said, dismissing her with a flick of her giant amethyst ring, "the only reason Evan never showed any outward interest in other women is because he was scared to death of you and what you could do to his job." She said it as if it were a proven fact.

That hurt. "Evan was not and is not scared of anything, especially me," Robin shot back. "And Evan has never been afraid to look at other women."

"*Everyone* is scared of you, especially guys. You eat 'em head first, like gingerbread men."

It was moments like this Robin wondered why she and Mia had remained friends these twenty years.

"Pretty flowers—where did they come from?"

"The ground," Robin said defensively. Mia shrugged, picked up a magazine.

Eventually, she got bored. Since she couldn't coax Robin to go shopping, she picked up her cell phone, got in touch with Cecilia, who convinced Mia they should have a massage first. Mia thought that sounded grand. "See you," she said to Robin, and sailed out of Robin's house, leaving more than one slacking jaw behind.

Robin was glad she was gone. Sometimes, Mia was more than Robin could deal with.

She turned her attention back to Peerless. The more she looked at it, the less it seemed like a good deal. By late afternoon, she was surprised to see how quickly the day had gone, and looked at the list of questions she had made for Evan. She thought about calling him, but it was late in New York; he'd probably left the corporate offices by now. Besides, with work on her house starting to wrap up for one day, she had lost interest in anything having to do with bubble wrap and had focused all of her attentions on Jake Manning.

Zaney was the last one out after the crews, waving his cast. "Yo, *heeey*, lookin' good!"

"Thanks!" she said brightly.

"Yep, that's some pretty flowers, all right. Hey!" he said, a lightbulb coming on in his brain. "Those came from Jakie's! Jakie brought you *flowers*!" he exclaimed, as if she didn't know that, and continued merrily out the door.

Jake was the last one down. He paused in the entry, shoved his hands in his pockets. "So...you doing all right?"

She nodded, leaned back in her seat, and folded her arms across her middle. "What about you?"

"Better than I have in a long time," he said with a lopsided smile. "But...I'm sort of wondering why you left."

Robin felt the old twist in her gut. She glanced uneasily at the flowers. "You didn't really expect me to stay, did you?"

"Well, yeah," he said, sounding surprised. "Why wouldn't you?"

Why? Wasn't it obvious why? "Well...*because,*" she said weakly and wondered if it was so obvious that she couldn't think of why. Jake looked confused, almost ashamed. Which made Robin feel terribly callous as she struggled to reach the surface of her many thoughts. "Hey, I was wondering... since you did so good with the Thai, would you like to try some Cuban food with me?" she asked, hoping to avoid the discussion.

Jake grimaced. "Ah, well..." he started uncertainly, and Robin wanted to slide right under the table. Oh man, why couldn't she wait for him to make the first move? Why did she always have to direct everything? The heat was creeping into her cheeks so rapidly she didn't hear what he was saying at first and slowly realized he was asking her a question.

"I'm sorry, what did you say?"

"That Cole has a baseball game tonight. I promised him I'd come."

"Oh. Okay," she said, a little shocked by her overwhelming disappointment.

But Jake stood there, hands in pockets, looking uncomfortable. "I suppose we could get a bologna sandwich if you want to tag along," he suggested.

The mere mention of bologna had Robin wrinkling her nose.

"Hey! I tried Thai," he reminded her.

A kid's baseball game. A bologna sandwich. How very strange, but it actually sounded like fun. "Can I skip the bologna?"

"Robin," he said, shaking his head, "You sorely underestimate the great taste of meat snacks."

She wasn't going to touch that with a ten-foot pole.

It turned out that Jake was right about meat snacks—at least bologna.

Sitting under the night sky made charcoal by the ball field lights, and cooled by a warm breeze blowing in from the Gulf, the bologna-and-cheese sandwich on white bread with mayo, lettuce, and tomato tasted divine. The instant Robin sank her teeth into the sandwich she had vowed she would not eat (but was eating, thanks to a particularly stupid wager on the last kid up to bat), she was instantly transported back to the little house in Dallas, when Rachel was in a high chair, and she and Rebecca sat in giant chairs at the kitchen table, their legs swinging freely beneath them, eating bologna-and-cheese sandwiches, corn chips, and drinking Dr Peppers. She hadn't thought of that house in a long, long time, and though the memories were a little foggy now, she could remember Mom singing and how Dad would sweep her into his arms and dance her around the kitchen. They had been so happy with their little house and bologna-and-cheese sandwiches.

She paused in the eating of her sandwich; was her memory true, or colored by time? It seemed impossible, knowing Mom and Dad now (*especially* Dad) that there really could have been a time they were in love like that. But she *did* remember, and she remembered how she and Bec would giggle until Dad would pick each of them up and twirl them around the kitchen floor, too.

"For someone who swears off anything wrapped in red casing, you sure seem to be devouring that sandwich."

Jake's deep voice brought her back to the present, and Robin looked at what was left in the wax paper she held. She had, indeed, eaten two-thirds of her sandwich, and she laughed. "I *had* to eat it. You spent seventy-five cents on it."

"That's right," he said, puffing his chest, "I spare no expense when it comes to women."

She laughed again, felt Jake's smile radiate through her. They finished their sandwiches, watched Cole lose two fly balls in the lights in one inning.

When the game was over, they took Cole for a burger at Paulie's. "You need glasses, kid," Jake said as Cole devoured his burger.

"No, I don't!" he instantly protested. "Why?"

"Because you missed those two fly balls."

Cole shrugged and gulped down a couple of fries. "The ball was in the lights."

"What he needs is some of those cool shades the Astros' outfielders wear," Robin offered.

Cole immediately perked up. "Yeah!" he exclaimed eagerly. "They have those flip-down Oakleys! Can I get some of those?"

"Sure!" Robin answered, as if it was nothing to come up with a couple hundred bills for fancy shades. But Cole was beaming, suddenly talking about some shades he had seen on TV, and Robin was nodding, knew exactly what he was talking about, and even told him where she had seen them on sale. The two hundred smackers aside, Jake quietly watched her, admiring the way she could, without any discernible experience, relate to a kid who was otherwise so unreachable.

Later, when they let Cole off and he took Robin home, Jake asked her the question that had been burning in his gut all day. "Why did you run away last night, Robin?" he asked as she gathered her things.

She blinked, surprised. "Run away? I didn't run away, I just went home."

"It's just that the nicest part is, you know, *after.*"

Robin flashed an irrepressible grin at that sentiment. "Coming from a guy, that's pretty remarkable. Okay, look, I'm sorry if I upset you," she said, and picked up her purse.

But Jake wasn't through; he put his hand on her arm. "Robin, is there something you're not saying?"

She looked out the front window, avoiding his eyes. "Like?"

"Like it sort of feels we're dancing around the maypole here, doesn't it?"

Robin clutched her purse tightly and laughed, a high-pitched, nervous laugh. "Come on, Jake! We're having a good time, right? Why do we need to analyze it?"

He didn't have an answer for that—he couldn't disagree with her, but at the same time, he couldn't seem to put his mind and heart around what he was really feeling. The part of his brain that actually thought about stuff like this was so rusty as to almost be unusable—but he knew, instinctively, that something was not quite right. Yet without being able to say what, he finally shook his head and laughed. "Nothing's wrong with it," he said, and meant it.

At least, he was pretty sure he meant it. He leaned over, kissed Robin good night, kissed her until he had to let go, and reluctantly watched her walk up the drive. And he wondered, as she stepped inside her house, if he hadn't been caught up in a cosmic storm or something, because at that moment, he was feeling extremely crazy to be dancing around the maypole with her, being pulled in a direction he wasn't sure he wanted to go.

He drifted off to sleep that night thinking of being with Robin, and was having a very pleasant dream along those lines when the phone began to ring, rattling him. He came up on his elbow and blinked, realized it wasn't the phone but the front door, and glanced at the clock. Two a.m. Unbelievable. Zaney was the first person to pop in his mind, but as he shoved the bedcovers aside and got up, he realized even Zaney wasn't stupid enough to come knocking at two in the morning.

Wearing only his boxers, Jake stalked to the door and threw it open. The flashing red and blue of a police cruiser on the street blinded him; he blinked, held up one hand against the glare, and focused on the cop standing there.

"This your kid?" he asked and pushed Cole forward. Unfortunately, yes, and Jake feared he might literally go right through the screen door in his haste to get his hands on his kid.

CHAPTER NINETEEN

The knock on Jake's door in the middle of the night did not bode well for the next day, which began with a major argument with Mom when Jake insisted it was time Cole came to live with him. *You don't want that, Jacob. It's your guilt talking, nothing more, and that ain't no way to do Cole.* When he had demanded to know what in the hell that was supposed to mean, she had hemmed and hawed, but had finally said what some vague part of him already knew. *You feel guilty for having left us behind and not being here for your brothers.*

He swore he didn't feel guilty. He accused his mom of wanting to be miserable and of wanting to keep everyone around her miserable. Both fuming, they had ended the conversation. Only Jake's fuming turned to fury when he took Cole to school and discovered he had been suspended two days for cutting class.

So he showed up at work in a very foul mood with one surly teenager (who was in danger of getting popped if he mouthed off to any of the guys the way he mouthed off to Jake). When he talked, that was. Which was never, at least not to Jake.

They spilled out of opposite sides of the truck, slamming their doors in almost perfect unison. "I'm going to put you to work, son," Jake said as they stalked toward the house.

"I'm not your son," Cole shot back, slinking along behind Jake. "I don't even want to be around you!"

"Tough shit," Jake said through gritted teeth.

Zaney was in the kitchen as the two burst through the door, and said brightly, "Hey, it's the Colester!" To which Cole snorted his obvious disdain. "Hey, little dude, who pissed in your Post Toasties?" Zaney demanded.

"Don't ask," Jake said, and motioned Cole forward. They proceeded through the dining room to the entry, where various tools and drop cloths were scattered. Jake pointed to the mess. "You're going to clean this up."

Cole looked at the mess of tools, sawdust, and drop cloths and moaned, "*All* of that?"

"All of that. And when you are finished, come upstairs, because I have more." And then he left the grumbling kid and ascended the curving staircase. When he reached the first landing, he glanced out the portal window and saw Robin in her running clothes, standing, hands on hips, on the greenbelt that ran down the middle of North Boulevard, waiting for traffic to pass. Gazing at her, he felt his anger with Cole growing.

The problem was, he had feelings for Robin that went far beyond the usual lusting, and deep into that dark, musty tunnel of really caring about someone. Like he'd never cared in his life. He cared what she thought, how she felt, who she was. He cared what she thought of *him*. Cared so much that he was angry with Cole, mortified that she might see how inept he and his mom were at raising him. And panicky that Cole's troubles might make her shy away. He had enough strikes against him. He didn't need any more.

When Robin caught a break in the traffic and jogged across the street, he stalked up the stairs, forcing himself to more urgent matters. The demolition was in full swing; Jake made sure the crews were not taking the job too far. Then he went downstairs to check on Cole and say hello to Robin.

Cole had picked up the drop cloths and folded them, and was out front, hosing down the buckets. Jake opened the door, stuck his head out. "How's it going?"

He received a shrug in response from Cole, but Zaney was much more exuberant. "*Great!*" he shouted at Jake. "Me and the Colester are having a *grrreat* time!" Jake gave Cole a glare sufficient to remind him he was still in a world of trouble and shut the door.

He found Robin seated at the dining room table, showered and dressed in a linen skirt that drew attention to her long, shapely legs. She was on the phone, but smiled warmly and waved him over. He came around to where she was sitting, and she mouthed the word *Grandma.* "Okay, Grandma. Okay. Okay," she said, and looked up at Jake, her blue eyes laughing. "Grandma…Grandma! I gotta go. I'll talk to you later, okay?" She clicked off the phone. Then she bounced up to her feet. "Good *morning.*"

An inevitable smile spread. "Morning."

"Hey, I'm going out for some coffee. Want some?"

Jake looked out the window at Cole. "Yes."

"Great! I'm dying for a doughnut."

"I thought doughnuts were off-limits."

"Oh, they are," she said breezily, ignoring the incongruity in that, and grabbed her purse. They went out the back door, got into Jake's truck, and pulled up next to the curb where Zaney and Cole were working. "Keep an eye on him," Jake called out the window to Zaney.

As Jake rolled up the window, Robin asked, "Is school out today?"

"For Cole. He's been suspended for cutting class, so he's getting a taste of the real world today."

"Oh," she said and looked back at Cole. "I hope everything is okay."

He feared nothing would ever be okay for Cole. "The kid has problems," he said flatly.

"Like what?"

"Like you don't want to know."

"Yes, I do! I like Cole."

Jake glanced at her as he turned north, headed for Kirby. "You're kidding. He's surly, he's rude, he's impossible to reach—"

"All kids are like that. Anyway, he's not rude to me."

"*I* wasn't like that," he protested. "Were you?"

"Of course!" Robin laughed. "Rebellious and moody and very uncertain where I fit in this world. Some might argue I still am."

"Oh, come on," Jake scoffed. "You lived behind some huge gate in River Oaks. Are you trying to tell me you were uncertain of where you *fit*?"

"Are you trying to tell me you are one of those who think money can buy happiness?" she demanded with a snort. "Money just makes everything worse!"

"Right," Jake exclaimed impatiently "I sure would have liked the chance to have money make everything worse when I was a kid. My folks never had two nickels to rub together, and believe me, it was not a happy time. A little money would have gone a long way toward improving the situation."

"You think so? My parents fought all the time and would fly off and leave us there with some nanny-type person who called Rachel *Raquel.* Dad never saw me play softball, he hardly knew the asshole Rebecca ended up marrying, and Rachel, well…she was in some little dream world with her drama club. Believe me, I was a miserable kid and I can relate to Cole. So what did he do to get suspended? I bet I can top it."

She wanted to know? Jake told her. Let the whole, ugly thing come tumbling out. Ross's troubles, the woman who gave birth to Cole. It was a new and disconcerting experience to talk about things so personal—he'd never been much of a talker to begin with. He had learned with his dad early on that words always came back to wound you. But with Robin, words rolled out of him from somewhere deep inside. Articulate words he didn't know he had in him, that described his frustration with Cole and his own complete ignorance and ineptitude with a fourteen-year-old brain, in spite of having had one at some point in his life.

But Robin instinctively put him at ease, didn't interrupt, except to ask thoughtful questions. More important, she didn't seem to judge him or his family as he had secretly feared. She just seemed genuinely concerned for Cole.

"I can relate," she said when he told her about going down to the levee to retrieve him.

"You've been down there?" he asked, surprised.

"Oh no," she laughed. "I can relate because I ran away when I was seventeen." She nodded at his apparent surprise. "Dad was on my case about something—who knows what? And I had this boyfriend, Bo," she said with a roll of her eyes. "He lived down around the Astrodome—you know, on the *other* side of the loop."

Oh yeah, Jake knew very well.

"Dad couldn't stand him," she continued, "which is why I think I went out with him in the first place." She laughed at that, and Jake quickly put down the faint little flurry in the pit of his stomach that remark prompted. "So, Bozo had the great idea we could go to Austin to party. I was so stupid, I didn't even ask with whom. We drove the three or so hours to Austin, went to some house where there was a huge party going on. I didn't know anyone, of course. Anyway, we had been at this party for a while, and I realized I hadn't seen Bozo in a while. Like hours. I went looking for him, and couldn't find him anywhere. He'd left me there. Gone off with a girl, with friends, who knows?"

"Wow, that sucks. So what did you do?"

"Called Dad," she said, grimacing at the memory. "He said, '*I'm going to kick your butt from here to Kingdom Come, Robin Elaine! You get your ass back here right now!*'" Robin laughed at the memory. "Needless to say, I didn't rush right home."

"You *did* go home, though, right?" Jake asked.

"Oh yeah, Mom got me home—she sent a plane, and I got a cab to the airport. And then, I hid in Rebecca's room until Dad calmed down."

"What happened to Bozo?"

"Who knows? He's probably in the pen now," she said and immediately caught herself, her eyes going wide with mortification. "Oh, sorry…"

Not as sorry as he was. Jake waved a hand at her, dismissed it.

"Well, anyway, I guess I'm not the best judge of character."

She didn't seem to hear the irony in her statement, but it slapped Jake square in the face. He looked straight ahead, wondered about a home life in River Oaks that was so bad she would want to run from it. It occurred to him, as they turned into the parking lot of Java the Hut, that perhaps they weren't so different after all. Perhaps they were more alike than he could have hoped.

Inside, Robin ordered her usual quadruple foo-foo chocoloco skinny steamed nutmeg coffee, waited until he had ordered as close to Folger's as he could get, straight up, before putting a full-court press on him about accompanying her to Burdette. She laid out all the reasons he should go: (a) she was going, (b) she was going to Burdette alone, and (c) she did not want to go to Burdette alone.

"I don't know. I've got a class I'm trying very hard not to flunk out of."

"You can study on the plane."

"The *plane?* Burdette is a two-hour drive."

"Two hours you and I don't have." She smiled, and a dimple appeared in one cheek.

"And I promised to make baseball practice this week—"

"See? I'm saving you time. Anyway, you don't need to practice! Sheesh, you practically handed them a win with one hand tied behind your back!"

Jake laughed. "It wasn't *quite* like that."

"Come on, Jake," she said, and lowered her head, looking up at him through her lashes. "Don't you want to be a member of the mile-high club?"

That idea kicked his testosterone levels up a notch or two. "Okay," he said instantly, felt his heart melt with Robin's smile, and was painfully aware that the more he was with her, the more impossible it was to be without her. Damn. He was in for a fall.

Later that afternoon, when Jake went looking for Cole, he had a moment of panic when he couldn't find him anywhere. His first thought was that Cole had run off again—he'd been sour and resentful all day. And the kid's mood had not improved with the double whamoburger Jake brought him. If he'd run off and was wandering around *this* neighborhood, someone had probably already called the cops.

When Jake couldn't find him upstairs, he searched the bottom floor, then went out onto the front lawn. No Cole.

Now the panic was beginning to swell in him. He walked around the east lawn and saw no one. He proceeded to the back, certain now that Cole had taken off, but what he saw on the back lawn drew him up short. It wasn't that Cole was with Robin, or that they were busily rearranging the pink flamingos like maniacal little beavers. What shocked him was that Cole was *talking*, and from where he stood, it looked like a blue streak. Robin seemed to be adding a comment here and there, but for the most part, Cole talked while she made a herd of flamingos in the corner of her lawn.

Jake watched for several minutes, then backed up, turned around, and went back the way he had come. He was awestruck. No one had been able to connect to Cole, not his teachers, not Mom, and certainly not Jake. But there he was with Robin, talking like they had known each other a lifetime. She had that effect on people, could breathe life into the world again, make you want to open up and let her in. It was an effect that he really adored, so much so that it sort of frightened him.

He wondered if it frightened Cole, too.

That night, before class, Jake ran into Lindy. She politely asked after him, but Jake felt like an ass. She smiled, but he could see that wounded look in her eye, and Jake wondered for the thousandth time—was he really going to pass up a woman like Lindy for this fling with Robin? The question ate at him; he could hardly focus on the calculations the instructor was reviewing on the board. He finally realized what was bubbling inside him was fear—fear that he was out of his freaking mind, that he was playing with fire that could destroy him, and his business, too.

Come Saturday morning, it was the stark evidence of the Lear family wealth that frightened him.

He should have suspected what he was in for when Robin answered her door wearing a cool, milk-chocolate pantsuit and turquoise blouse and jewelry that made the color of her eyes radiate. "*Wow*," she said, eyeing the one decent pair of tan trousers he had, a white button-down he had had for God only knew how long, and a navy sport coat. "You look great!"

That was nice, but he was totally inadequate next to her. What he knew about women's clothing could be put on the head of a pin, but he knew expensive clothing and accoutrements when he saw them. Expensive clothes, expensive woman.

And still he was not prepared for what greeted him at Hobby airport.

Robin couldn't help but laugh, because he was, like any mere mortal, blown away by the so-called company plane. It was a Lear family jet, the implication being, of course, that there was more than one. It came complete with a small kitchen and eating area, a sleeping bunk, and four thickly padded leather seats that faced each other for cozy tête-à-têtes in the sky. Even the pilot—Pete, Robin called him—was wearing a uniform that reminded Jake of the air force.

"Help yourself to any chair," she said as they entered the cabin. "I'm going to put some coffee on."

Jake lowered himself carefully into one of the Corinthian leather seats and looked around. There were fresh roses in a secured vase on the dining table; he could see into the compact bathroom in the back where towels monogrammed with an L were hanging over the basin. The finishings around the windows and trays were brass and mahogany. This was something he had only seen at the movies, never in real life. At least not *his* real life.

Robin returned from making the coffee and settled into the seat directly across from him. "Have you been on one of these before?"

She asked in all seriousness, and sometimes Jake wondered if she wasn't just flat-out nuts. He'd only flown a few times in his life to begin with. "No," he said simply.

"Dad has two of them. He started flying lessons a year or so ago—"

"Miss Lear, we're ready for taxi, so if you and your guest would please fasten your seat belts," a voice boomed above them.

Robin instantly fastened her seat belt, then leaned across to help Jake when he couldn't find his. It was rolled up and tucked away in a little pocket.

"We should have invited Cole. He'd like this," she said as they settled in and the plane started to move.

Yeah, he'd like it all right. Any mere mortal would like it. "You and Cole seemed to be getting along pretty well yesterday," he observed.

Robin nodded. "He's really a cool kid!"

Which just went to show, Jake thought, how clueless she really was. "Hard to see it."

"No, really! When he talks about something he likes, he's very animated. It's kind of funny, actually. His voice gets really high."

Jake had never heard Cole's voice get really high. And he'd certainly never heard Cole say he *liked* anything. "So... what does he like?"

"Well, a girl named Tara, for one."

Bowl him over with a feather—a girl? Cole showed no interest in the opposite sex; he showed no interest in *anything*. "You're kidding," he said flatly.

Robin shook her head.

"Since when?"

"Since the third grade. But he didn't think she liked *him* until she sat with him at lunch one day. That apparently put a spring in his step. Unfortunately, the very *next* day, she sat with Randy Somebody, and Cole didn't know what that meant. So he cut class."

"Are you telling me that he cut class because some girl didn't sit with him at lunch? That's it? That's the whole stupid reason his world collapsed?"

"That's it!" Robin said cheerfully. "He's really sensitive, you know."

Oh God, it was worse than he thought. He had a *sensitive* nephew. Nooo, nooo…not good. Sensitive boys made for very strange men.

"What's that?" Robin asked.

"What's what?"

"*That.* That sort of grunting sound you're making."

"I'm not making any *grunting* sound."

"See there? You did it again. What's the matter, haven't you ever had a devastating crush on a girl before?"

Actually, he had one so devastating at the moment he thought he might just crash and burn with it, thank you very much. But Jake snorted at her question, leaned back, looked out the window as they taxied down the runway. That idiot kid—so what if his girl sat with another guy? It didn't mean anything. And he'd remind himself of that the next time Mr. Pompous Ass showed up at Robin's, instead of thinking how to rub the smirk off his face.

The plane lifted, the sharp ascent pushing his stomach back to his spine.

"So?" Robin asked, oblivious to the plane's laboring up the incline. "Have you?"

"Yes, as a matter of fact, I have had a crush on a girl. But tell me something—were you able to get all of this out of him in one afternoon?"

"Yep. And the thing about how you don't listen to him."

Great. Fantastic. Not only did they have time to discuss all of Cole's insecurities, they had time to discuss Uncle Jake's shortcomings, too. "I probably don't," he admitted curtly. "Because he whines all the damn time."

Robin clucked at him. "He's fourteen. Fourteen-year-olds whine."

"Okay, you want to know the truth?" he asked, irked that she could have divined so much information from Cole when he could barely get him to respond. "I don't like Cole. Don't get me wrong—I love him. He's my nephew. And I would give my right arm to see him happy and to escape the life we had growing up. But I don't *like* him."

Instead of gasping with shock and indignation for saying such a horrid thing about his own nephew, Robin chuckled and shook her head. "Jake, you're so funny! He's *fourteen.* Everyone knows that fourteen-year-olds are very hard to like. Believe me, I had two sisters who were fourteen after me and they were *impossible* to like. But the difference is, I think, that they were so full of themselves they were in danger of bursting. Cole doesn't seem to know where he fits in and doesn't feel like he belongs anywhere or to anyone. I think he's kind of lost. Which is understandable—he said you and your mom argue about who has to take him."

"No, we argue about who *wants* to take him," Jake angrily clarified.

"See? He doesn't like himself, so he sees it all upside down. It's tough for anyone to feel unwanted, but especially for a teenager, you know."

He knew. He looked at her in wonder. "How'd you get so smart?"

Robin shrugged, flicked an imaginary piece of lint off her jacket. "I don't know...I guess I'm just extra brilliant. Or maybe because twenty years later, I *still* feel that way. I really do relate to him," she said and glanced up at Jake. "Do you think that's strange?"

"No. What I think is strange is that I am struggling to relate to him, but I don't really understand why. He's just like my brothers and I were growing up—angry, defiant, rebellious...but for some reason, I can't seem to see the world through his eyes."

"That's because you had hope," she said matter-of-factly and studied a cuticle as if it were the most obvious conclusion in the world. Yet the suggestion clanged like a bell in Jake. It was so plainly obvious, so simple, that he was stunned he had not realized it before. Of course Cole had no hope— he had lost his father and his mother, his grandmother was a disciplinarian, one uncle was in prison, and the other...well, the other yelled at him for the most part.

It was a thought that lodged deep in Jake's brain and his heart as their discussion turned from Cole to what Ross had been like as a kid, how Jake could see so much of his brother in Cole. By the time Pete came on the intercom and announced they were descending toward Burdette, Robin was laughing at the tale of Jake's first date ever, and a double one at that, with Ross and the Dewley twins. He had been maybe fifteen at the time, and yes, he had been obsessed with Sara Dewley.

The plane landed on an old, pitted runway, bouncing like a rubber ball as it shuddered to a stop. Robin leaned forward again, looked out the portal window, and winced. "It's worse than I imagined." They saw a dilapidated old metal building, and beyond that, the stacks of a smelting plant. When the plane shuddered to a stop and Pete opened the door, they were instantly assaulted by the smell of sardines or something very much like it.

"Processing plant," Pete offered helpfully at their twin grimaces. Exchanging wary glances, Jake and Robin waited for a young man with a red baseball hat to push the stairs up to the plane.

Robin made a careful ascent to the bottom of the stairs. The young man eyed Jake as he came down behind her. "Where y'all from?"

"Houston," Jake responded while Robin straightened her clothing and glanced around.

"You the ones for Wirt?"

"Yes," Robin said, eyeing the man. "How did you know?"

"Oh, 'cuz Girt sent someone to pick you up." He pointed in the direction of the metal building. Jake and Robin turned their heads.

Robin gasped.

Jake instantly put an arm around her waist and muttered, "Don't panic."

CHAPTER TWENTY

L ike hell she wasn't going to panic!

The…*conveyance*…was an ancient pickup, which appeared to have been white at one time, but was now a fleshy color with a red fender, a silver hood, and a steel bumper. A man was sitting in the driver's seat with the door open, one leg propped on the running board, an oily baseball cap pulled down over his eyes. He spit on the tarmac, looked up, and waved lazily at Jake and Robin.

"That's Bob," the kid said. "Girt sent him for you."

But Robin had already moved past Bob and was paralyzed by the sight of the two salvaged captain's chairs, propped up in the bed of the truck against the cab, facing backward. "*Ohmigod*," she muttered, frantically wondering how in the hell she would ever get in the back of that truck, much less *ride* in it. There was no amount of bubble wrap in the world worth ruining her Versace suit, and Styrofoam peanuts damn sure weren't worth the humiliation. Oh no. Nononono—

"Deep breaths," Jake reminded her.

"No way," she said, shaking her head. "I won't ride in that. I won't get *near* that!"

"Come on, it's not the end of the world—"

"*Yes, it is!*" she whispered, frantically grabbing his arm. "Yes yes *yes*, it is! I can't do it! I *can't*! I'm wearing VER-SA-CE!"

"I am sure you can dry-clean fur sashi," Jake said in all earnestness as he attempted to peel her fingers from their death grip of his arm.

"I am not riding in that," she said again. "I won't do it!" She whipped around to the kid in the red baseball hat. "YO! There has to be another way into town. A taxi service? A rental car?"

"Bob don't mind taking you."

"You don't understand," she said, letting go of Jake's arm and marching to where the kid was standing. "I can't ride in that truck." He looked confused. "Okay, look at that," she said, gesturing insistently to the truck, "and look at me. Do I look like I belong in that truck?"

"Lady, you don't look like you even belong in this state!"

"That's right!" she cried, relieved. "So how else can we get into town?"

"Bob's all we got."

Robin gaped at him, unable to absorb it, unable to see herself in the back of the pickup truck, no matter how hard she tried, not even on acid. Never. Not doing it.

"Robin, you're making a bigger deal out of this than it is."

Oh *fine*. Fix-it Fred thought she was just being a big baby. What did he know? "Jake. I am not dressed to ride around in the back of a pickup truck."

"Before you get your panties in a wad, I'm sure ol' Bob intends for you to ride in the front with him. I'll ride in the back."

He had to be kidding.

"It's not that big a deal," he continued. "This isn't Houston. Sometimes you gotta go along to get along. And I'm not afraid of ruining my fur sashi."

She wished he'd quit saying *Versace* like it was some sort of synthetic fiber.

Bob, a long and lanky fellow, was now walking toward them, his hands in his pockets.

"Now listen," Jake added, wrapping his hand around Robin's wrist as the kid started to drag the stairs away from the jet, "let me offer a little piece of friendly advice. If you don't have anything nice to say about a man's truck, then just don't say anything at all. If you dis the truck, you dis the man. Got it?"

"Huh?" she asked, but Bob was upon them and Jake was already extending his hand in greeting.

"How you doing? Jake Manning. And this is Miss Lear."

Bob took his hand, shook it vigorously. "Bob Lamke. Girt asked me to give you folks a ride into town." He shifted his gaze to Robin. "Bob Lamke," he said again, offering his hand.

Grease was caked beneath his fingernails; Robin quickly hid her hands, ignored Jake's dark frown, and said, "Thanks for coming to pick us up."

"Oh…" Bob dropped his hand. "Well, if you're ready," he said, motioning to the truck.

Robin nodded mutely. Jake slipped his hand over hers, gave her a hard squeeze, leaned over as they fell in behind Bob, and whispered, "You better step down off your little pedestal, girl."

Whatever. She was not going to start making deals in the bed of an old pickup truck, no matter how natural that might seem to Handy Andy.

Surprisingly, Bob's truck was not nearly as filthy as Robin had imagined—Jake was right; it appeared Bob took great care of it. On the inside, there were two different captain's chairs with a large console between them, which, judging by the look of it, had been modified in someone's backyard. From Bob's rearview mirror hung a Christmas tree odor eater, and on the dash, a bobble-head New Orleans Saints football player smiled at her. The seat was actually clean, and Jake complimented an openly proud Bob on his redo of the bed before jumping effortlessly over the side and settling into the captain's chair directly behind Robin.

Bob pumped the gas a couple of times, then started the thing up. "Girt asked me to drive you through town," he shouted over the muffler-less engine. "We'll take a little tour of the plant after we're through this afternoon."

"Through? Through with what?"

Bob looked at her in surprise. "She didn't tell you? Saturday's bowling day!"

No, it wasn't a cruel joke the universe was playing on her; she wasn't even hallucinating—she was, apparently, alive and well and standing in the middle of a bowling alley. This, of course, after the scenic route through town, which included a drive-by of the smelting plant, the new Super Walmart, and the town square, where Christmas decorations were still hanging. "They save money that way," Bob informed her.

But the Rock-n-Bowl was the town's crowning glory. The moment Bob opened the tinted glass doors, a rush of air smelling like stale smoke and popcorn permeated her brain; and the sound of balls and pins was so loud she could hardly hear Bob tell her to get her shoes. It took a moment for that to sink in, the hilarious notion that he actually expected her to bowl. She started to shake her head, but felt Jake's hand on the small of her back pushing her forward, to the counter.

"Tell them what size," he said gruffly. "Remember, when in Rome…"

Rome, hell! Too stunned to even think, Robin muttered her shoe size. The man put a pair of red-and-purple bowling shoes on the counter, then red-and-green ones for Jake, which he promptly picked up. "And *smile.* Stop looking so damned horrified."

But she *was* horrified. She had expected to breeze into town, have a short but intense discussion with Eldagirt—who had yet to make an appearance, by the way—and be home in time for cocktails with Cecilia in River Oaks. Not once, astonishingly enough, had the thought of *bowling* crossed her mind. Worse, Jake seemed completely unfazed by it, and much, *much* worse, looked as if he was actually excited by the prospect.

He nudged her with his elbow to follow Bob. "Lookit, you're going to piss everyone off if you keep looking so miserable," he muttered low.

What about her? What if *she* was a little pissed off about this sudden turn of events?

"Now come on, Robin. This Burdette and it's Saturday," he reminded her.

"You cannot be serious," she whispered hotly as they descended into the lane area. "You cannot possibly think that it is all right to do business like this!"

"Why not? It's just one step removed from doing business on the golf course."

Ahead of them, Bob stopped at a plastic picnic table bolted to the floor. Around it, three women were seated.

"It is fifteen golf carts and five thousand caddies away from doing business on a golf course!" Robin said testily and stopped behind Bob, plastering a smile on her face. The three women, all in plus sizes, gave Robin a cool once-over as Bob explained she was the person Girt was expecting. But their eyeballs pretty much bulged two Torn-and-Jerry feet out of their sockets when Bob introduced Jake.

"Ladies," Jake said with a smile, "I hope you don't mind if we crash your game."

"Honey, you can crash whatever you want," one said, and they all laughed.

Bob lackadaisically motioned to the women. "This is Sylvia and Sue, and that's Reba."

"As in McIntyre," Reba said, putting a pudgy hand to her hair.

"Pleasure to meet you. I'm Jake, and this is Robin."

Not one of them took their eyes from Jake. Sue dragged long on a cigarette she held between two sausage-like fingers, eyeballing him up and down. "Are you gonna bowl?"

"If you don't mind letting a hack join."

"We don't mind!" Sue and Reba chimed at the exact same time.

"Where's Girt?" Bob asked.

Sylvia barely spared him a glance. "Running late. David's not feeling well today, I guess. But she said to get started without her."

"Y'all better go on ahead. I imagine Girt's gonna need some help," Bob said and turned and walked away, leaving Robin and Jake with the three Humpty-Dumptys.

"I'll find a ball," Jake offered, shedding his jacket, and walked to racks of bowling balls.

The three women managed to drag their gaze from Jake's butt to Robin and eyed her curiously. "What'd you say your name was?"

"Robin."

They all waited for Jake to come back.

He was back in a jiffy, plopping himself down next to Sue with a devastating smile, which charmed the skintight, butterfly-appliqued stretch pants right off of her. She giggled at something he said about the shoes, and turned red as a beet when he declared that he couldn't possibly hope to beat someone who came with her own bowling shirt. Sylvia and Reba were drooling, too. Well, at least she shared one thing in common with these women, Robin thought—they all thought Jake was a hunk. And when the hunk had finished changing shoes, he stood up, announced his intention to help Robin find a ball, grabbed her by the elbow, and marched her forward.

When they were out of earshot of the women, he said, "All right, it is *definitely* time to get over yourself. Are you going to be miserable all afternoon, or are you at least going to attempt to hide your loathing?"

"I don't loathe them!" she protested.

"Oh yeah? Well, you look like you'd just as soon drive head-on into a brick wall. Now put your shoes on and stop acting like you're above bowling, because you're *not*. You put on your shoes one foot at a time just like everyone else in this joint," he said sternly and picked up a ball. "Here. Stick your fingers in there."

"I'm going to ruin my nails," she pouted as she stuck them inside three holes.

"You can buy more. What do you think, does it feel okay? Not too heavy?"

She shrugged. He groaned, pointed her back to the table with her ball, her shoes, and her handbag. Robin sat gingerly next to Reba and forced herself to smile. "You bowl a lot?" Reba asked.

"Ah...no."

"Have you *ever* bowled?" Sylvia asked, grinning at Sue's horrified little snicker.

Okeydokey, here they went. "Once," Robin said. The three women looked at each other. Robin bent over, slipped off Cole Haan flats, and, with a grimace, forced herself to slide her foot into one bowling shoe, then the other.

"Can we take a couple of practice rounds?" Jake asked as he breezed by.

"*Sure!*" Sue all but shouted, and bounced to her feet and hurried to the carousel, where she picked up a flaming pink ball.

"This oughta be good," Sylvia said, sniggering with Reba.

It *was* good. Jake brought the ball up to his nose, gracefully glided to the edge of the lane, one leg sweeping long behind him as he went down and let the ball roll from his fingers. Much to Robin's surprise, he knocked all the pins down.

"*Strike!*" shrieked Reba.

Jake turned around, grinning from ear to ear, *sooo* pleased with himself. "Ladies, I do believe I am ready to go," he said proudly, and smiled as the three of them came clamoring forward to bowl their practice rounds.

Surprisingly, the women bowled as expertly, and almost as gracefully, as Jake. Reba was the last to lumber up to the line, and in a movement that seemed to defy physics, knocked all the pins down except two, which she managed to hit with the next ball.

Then all heads swiveled, *Exorcist*-like, toward Robin. Jake motioned for her to come up. *Damn.* Robin had bowled once in her life, and that was only because she'd had one too many beers, and it had been a public persona disaster. As she really was not one to relish making a complete ass of herself, Robin swallowed a lump in her throat, stood, and walked stiffly in the funky shoes to where Jake was standing.

Jake put his hands on his hips. "You'll need a ball."

Well, he didn't have to smirk when he said it. Robin pivoted like a robot, went to the carousel, and picked up the blue ball he had selected for her, and walked back to the line.

"Relax," Jake said. "This isn't Chinese water torture. Just line it up and let go."

"I think I can figure out how to bowl," she said with a roll of her eyes.

Jake frowned, leaned over her shoulder. "Do you want this company? If you don't, then let's just ask one of these nice ladies for a ride back to the airstrip and get the hell out of here. If you *do* want this company, then I strongly suggest you get that chip off your fur sashi shoulder and *lighten up.*"

"And just who are you, my conscience?"

"Fine," he muttered and stepped back. "Be a bitch about it. You're up."

Bitch. *Bitch!* Oh yeah, she was up, all right. So far up that when she was done with him, she was going to leave his dismembered body all over Louisiana. Robin lifted the ball, eyed the pins down the lane, took two steps forward, and let the ball fly.

Only it flew across the lane, popped up out of the gutter, and went sailing down the next lane, where it ricocheted off the pin gate and disappeared into a hole on the side. Dumbfounded by her incompetence, Robin stood there, wondering if this latest episode of *The Twilight Zone* was ever going to end.

"Serves you right," Jake said. "But don't freak out," he added, his voice a little softer. "We'll find you another ball and hopefully you'll get it right next time. It would help if you'd loosen up and bend your knees a little."

"I *did* bend my knees," she whimpered.

"No, baby, there was no bending of any knees anywhere on this lane. There wasn't even a bend of an arm. Or a waist. That was a Frankenstein bowl if I've ever seen one."

Great. Robin turned around to get her ball and noticed that none of the women made eye contact. So it was that bad.

Her second bowl wasn't much better—but she managed to keep it in her gutter. Robin quickly made her way back to her seat on the bench and fell into it, wondered if Sue was talking about her when she leaned over to whisper something to Reba. What a nightmare! If it made any difference to the Tweedledees, she had no more desire to be in this bowling alley than they desired her to be here. All she wanted to do was discuss a little bubble wrap and get the hell out of Dodge, but *noooo*. She glared at Jake, wondered how he did it so easily, grudgingly admiring how he seemed to adapt to everything around him.

When she stepped up to the lane for her next turn, barriers suddenly popped up on either side of the lane, startling her. The howl of Sue's laughter behind her was almost her undoing. She turned slowly, looked at them looking at her, obviously enjoying themselves at her expense. All except Jake, who came striding forward. "What the hell?" she softly demanded.

"Bumper guards. To keep your ball in the right lane."

"I've never seen anything like that!"

"Well...they're usually for little kids," he said, wincing a little.

Robin's eyes narrowed; so this was how it was going to be. "Oh yeah? And whose bright idea was it? Sylvia's? Sue's?"

Jake bit his lip. "Reba's."

Something snapped like a twig in Robin's brain. She stepped around Jake, waved at Reba. "Thanks for the help!" she called cheerfully and growled beneath her breath when Reba nudged Sue in the side. Laugh at her, would they? She turned a murderous gaze to the lane in front of her. She'd show them—she was going to learn how to bowl, by God, right here, right now, or die trying.

Her first attempt wrenched her back, but the ball stayed in the lane and hit two pins.

"Hey! Well, okay!" Jake called, clapping, his voice betraying his surprise. "*That's* what I'm talking about! This time, bend your knees!" he encouraged her.

Robin bent her knees. She bent her knees so deep she damn near kissed the polished wood lane. The ball still bounced, but it wobbled down the lane, knocking over five or six more of the milk bottles. She stood up, slapped her hands together, and turned around, her chin high as she marched back to her seat.

By the eighth frame, free of her jacket and jewelry, Robin was arguing with Reba about how many pins she had knocked over (until Reba pointed out the system automatically counted them), pumping her fist with each bowl, and having (okay, very hard to admit) a *good* time. She had lightened up. She had learned to bowl. And on the home stretch of the second game, she was spanking Sylvia.

Jake was having a good time, too. He had fetched a bucket of beer for everyone, was going for a game of 200, which he seemed to think was pretty outstanding. He also seemed to enjoy the opportunity to flirt, yet another sport at which he appeared to be naturally gifted. And he *was* great fun to be with. In spite of their rocky beginning, Jake was joking about the way she bowled, high-fiving her when she managed to knock the pins down, and encouraging her when she didn't.

But her personal victory in conquering bowling did not make Robin any less irritated that Eldagirt Wirt had not even bothered to make an appearance. She was beginning to wonder if she had been taken for a ride when Sue's cell phone rang. She handed it to Robin. "For you."

"For me?" she asked, surprised, and took the phone. "Hello?"

"How'd you bowl?" Girt asked in her gravelly voice.

"I managed to eke out a couple of games," Robin said irritably. "Did I misunderstand our meeting?"

"Nah." Girt paused to drag on a cigarette. "Sorry about that, but my son's sick. Bob's on his way to pick you up and bring you on out to the warehouse."

"Umm…okay. May I ask if you are going to be there?"

"'Course I'm gonna be there!" Girt declared in such a huff that it sparked a serious coughing spell. "He'll be there in about ten minutes," she said hoarsely. "Now could you hand the phone back to Sue?"

Robin handed the phone to Sue. Sue put the phone to her ear. "Hey," she said, but whatever Eldagirt said in return caused Sue to look at Robin, then quickly turn away so she could not hear her.

Fine. She just hoped that when Sue gave her report, she would note the strike Robin had in the seventh frame of the second game, thank you very much.

"We're going to the warehouse," she informed Jake as he came back from returning his shoes. She jabbed one arm into her jacket. "I think Wirt is giving me the runaround."

"Why, what did she say?"

"She said her son was sick," Robin responded with a roll of her eyes.

"Seems plausible."

"Seems lame! I don't know about your business, Jake," Robin said as she slipped off her bowling shoes, "but in mine, you learn not to trust too much. Someone is always trying to get one over on you."

"Is that your business? Or just you?" he asked glibly and proceeded past without her answer so he could say good-bye to the ladies.

Robin followed suit, primly extending her hand to Reba. Reba's green eyes were sparkling with mirth as she accepted it. "Hope we get a chance at a rematch."

That seemed unlikely, but Robin smiled all the same. "Me, too—next time, I am taking you down."

Reba laughed heartily, the flesh on her bosom jiggling with the exertion of it. "Hell, I think you mean it!"

Sue and Sylvia likewise thanked Robin for bowling with them, and eyeballed Jake's butt one more time as he said his good-byes to Reba. "You're lucky there, girlfriend. Don't keep him up too late," Sylvia said.

"I'm not promising," Robin said with a wink, much to the delight of Sylvia and Sue.

She and Jake waved good-bye and walked out into the sunshine to wait for Bob, where heat was radiating off the parking lot at a cool five thousand degrees. Jake was pretty pleased with his 200 game, and even reviewed some of the frames for her while they waited.

"Yeah, yeah," Robin said, laughing. "You're a stud."

"I know," he said with a grin. "So come on, that wasn't so bad, was it? You looked like you were having a pretty good time."

She folded her arms and peered up to the main road in search of Bob's pickup truck. "Okay, I will admit it was fun. But I really didn't come to Burdette to go bowling with three women I've never met and will never see again."

"Life's an adventure if you'll let it be, Robin."

"You sound like a John Denver song."

"Baby, I *am* a John Denver song," he laughed as Bob came barreling around the corner, the sound of his engine drowning out any further conversation. He came to a hard stop, leaned over, and pushed open the passenger door. Robin guessed that meant to get in.

Bob pointed his truck toward the opposite end of town from the smelting plant, and they were off again. With the radio tuned to a country western station, they hurtled down the main drag, picked up speed on the outskirts of town, flew past trees draped in Spanish moss, and finally slowed to turn down a poorly paved road that obviously saw a lot of truck traffic, and coasted up to three white warehouses at the end of the road.

Bob stopped the truck, got out, and went inside.

Jake climbed out of the bed of the truck at the same time Robin stepped out. She brushed off her pants, then glanced up, and immediately burst into laughter at the sight of Jake's hair.

"Watch it," he said good-naturedly as he tried to comb it with his fingers.

"Y'all getting on okay?"

Robin would recognize that voice anywhere and whipped around. But it surprised her to see that the body did not match the voice. Eldagirt Wirt was not a ball-busting former Nazi bodyguard as Robin had imagined, but a very thin and wiry woman with lots of curly black hair, who looked to be about the same age as Robin—definitely *not* an old hag. She was wearing a red-and-white striped sleeveless T-shirt, and her arms were buff. The T-shirt was tucked into a pair of black Wranglers that looked as if they had been painted on, and at the end of two skinny legs were a pair of classic Doc Martens—just like the pair Robin owned.

"Call me Girt," she said, and stepped forward, smiling, revealing stained teeth.

"I'm Robin Lear."

"Oh yeah, I knew who you was right away," she said matter-of-factly. "What I want to know is, who is he?"

"My friend, Jake Manning."

"Well, now I'm really sorry I didn't make it to the bowling alley," Girt said with a grin. "Hope you don't mind a little bowling, Mr. Manning."

"Are you kidding? I bowled a two hundred."

"No lie?" Girt asked, clearly impressed.

"No lie," Jake said, his chest still puffed.

Girt shifted her gaze to Robin. "I take it you don't bowl much."

"I don't get the opportunity," she lied.

Girt started toward the building. "That's what we do in Burdette," she called over her shoulder. "You might think about that if you're serious about buying this place."

That remark caught Robin off guard—she had never mentioned purchase to Girt. "What makes you think I want to buy?" she asked, hurrying to catch up.

"Mr. Iverson told me. He's called down here twice now."

Robin stopped in midstride, trying to grasp the notion that Evan had called Eldagirt Wirt, confused as to *why* he had, and moreover, why he hadn't told her.

Girt held the door open for them. "You coming in?" she asked before disappearing inside.

"I see what you mean about not being able to trust anyone," Jake said as he put his hand on her back and gave her a gentle push forward. Confused, Robin stumbled forward.

Wirt Supplies and Packing was a much larger warehouse than Peerless, but without the fuss of offices up front. There were only two that she could see, each with two desks and stacks of papers piled high on the floor, the filing cabinets, and the desks.

"Hope you'll forgive the mess," Girt said and proceeded to show them through her operation. She explained where the packing materials were made and stored, the various types of bags, plastics, and boxes they made and sold, the different strappings, the wooden pallets, the storage units, the cushion products.

It was plain Girt was proud of her operation. She said that her father had started the company, that she had bought him out when he got sick with cancer. Bob helped her manage the operation, they employed thirty-two people, most of whom were longtime employees.

"That's quite an accomplishment," Jake observed.

Girt beamed at him. "We pride ourselves in being good to our employees. That's one thing I'd have to know, that my people were going to be taken care of."

"Does your father get involved anymore?" Robin asked.

"Oh, he died," Girt said matter-of-factly. "He's been gone two years now."

The casual way she said it was like a fist to Robin's gut; unconsciously, she put a hand to her stomach. Jake quietly took her hand and held it.

They moved through the last warehouse, where the cushioning products were prepared for shipping, but Robin wasn't paying much attention. She was too engrossed in the number of similarities between her and Girt. When they finished the tour, Girt invited them up front for a soda. On the way, Robin asked why she would consider selling a business of which she was so obviously proud.

"Not sure I will," she admitted. "But you people and American Motorfreight—they've made noises about buying me out, too—it's just all made me think about things a little different."

"Like life?" Jake asked.

"Yeah," Girt said with a laugh. "Like life. I'm a single mom, you know, and I have to think of my son."

"But can't you keep this and look after him?" Robin asked, suddenly and strangely convinced she did not want Girt to sell.

Girt smiled as they walked up to the main office. "Not really," she said and motioned for Robin to precede her. "Meet my son, David," she said as Robin stepped across the threshold.

Seated in a wheelchair, his head strapped to some godawful contraption and his arms and legs horribly twisted at odd angles, David grinned at her. Next to him, Bob was mixing something up in a Slurpee cup.

"David's got cerebral palsy," Girt said and walked over to her son, ran her hand along the top of his head. "If I sell Wirt, I'll never have to worry about taking care of him again. I keep thinking about that."

"*Oh God,* "Jake murmured softly, and Robin silently echoed his plea.

CHAPTER TWENTY-ONE

They had lifted off, en route to Houston. Robin was still lost in thought about Burdette and Girt and her son. She looked at Jake sitting across from her, his legs crossed, his sandy brown hair wildly disarranged by his tour of Burdette from the back of a pickup truck, reading a local paper from a convenience store. Amazing, how easily he seemed to fit with people from all walks of life. She couldn't seem to do that. Why? Why couldn't she befriend Reba and Sue and Sylvia right off the bat? *Because you're arrogant.*

"What are you thinking?" Jake asked without looking up from his paper.

Startled that he had sensed her retreat, Robin shifted uneasily in her seat. "Nothing."

"You're awfully quiet," he said, looking up. "That's so unlike you."

"Very funny." She grinned, looked at her hands. "I was just thinking about Girt."

"She's good people," Jake observed, putting aside his paper.

"Yeah, but I didn't think so before today. I assumed all sorts of things about her."

"That's just human nature. You get impressions of people over the phone or e-mail that get blown out of the water when you actually meet them."

"But it's more than that. I don't know…I don't understand how *you* can walk into a room and be so easy, but I can walk into the same room and feel like…like my back is against the wall. Like I am surrounded by the enemy." She winced at that, glanced out the window. "I think Dad is right. I think I really *am* arrogant."

Whatever she expected Jake to say, she did not expect him to laugh. He moved forward, braced his arms on his thighs. "Robin. I don't know what kind of trip your old man has laid on you, but you are not arrogant. You are strong-willed and you know what you want. And you're aloof; you have a tendency to hold yourself out. But you're confusing fear with arrogance."

"*Fear?* I'm not afraid!"

"Like hell you're not. You were afraid to ride in that truck today. When we walked into that bowling alley, you stiffened up like an old dead cow."

"Not because I was afraid," she argued. "I just don't get along with people like you do. I don't seem to connect like you do."

"Are you nuts? Look how you treat my nephew when no one in my family can stand the kid. And Zaney—God knows Zaney can be a pain in the ass, but you don't seem to mind him. And what about Lucy? And Elmer—"

"You can't count him, he's my grandpa."

"The point is, you get along fine with anyone you allow past that wall you put up."

"What wall?"

"You know, the rich princess in the tower routine. You can be a little standoffish."

His remark, surprisingly, did not offend her. She knew exactly what he meant. "See? I'm arrogant, not afraid."

"You're afraid."

"Okay, Certified Genius, what am I so afraid of?"

"That they won't like you."

His answer stunned her—she'd never thought of it, but knew instantly that it was true.

"But you are in luck, sweetheart, because I'm going to help you conquer your fear," he said with a devilish grin and moved across the small aisle toward her.

"Oh really? And just how are you going to do that?" she asked, putting her hand on his chest as he braced his arms on either side of her to kiss her forehead.

"I am going to take you to meet my mom on Easter Sunday."

Robin laughed. "I'm not afraid of your mom!"

"You should be," he said lazily, kissing her lips. "Hey, by the way...you're not afraid of flying, are you?" he asked, kissing her again. "I mean, *really* flying?"

"Are you kidding?" she asked and welcomed Jake as the charter member in her mile-high club.

They spent that evening in her bed, languidly making love, watching TV, and eating popcorn, the only food Robin had in the house. Jake made a point of not leaving, and on Sunday, when he left to go get Cole, Robin called her dad in New York.

"I'm doing fine!" he said gruffly when she asked. "Stop worrying about me!" But Mom told her that Dad was going to have to go for more radiation. They hadn't quite gotten it all.

"What does that mean? Why didn't they get it all?"

"It's a very aggressive type of cancer. But we're still very hopeful."

Robin closed her eyes. "Mom, how are you holding up after all these weeks?"

Mom laughed. "Well, he's as impossible as he ever was… but he needs me."

It must be nice, Robin thought. He certainly didn't need her.

That afternoon, she treated Jake and Cole to an Astros game from box seats, courtesy LTI. They ended the day with pizza and Cole talking about how much he hated algebra. Jake seemed fascinated, and the two of them had a legitimate, civilized, conversation. And for some reason, algebra made Robin think of the work she was doing.

The next morning, she phoned Evan in Dallas.

"Robin!" he said, surprised to hear her voice.

"How's it going, Evan?"

"Great! Just great!"

"I was in Burdette this weekend. Girt said you called her."

"Oh yeah?"

"Yeah. Why did you call her? I thought you were going to let me handle this."

"I am! I tried to get hold of you. When I got back to Dallas Friday, I ran into the sales manager at American Motorfreight. He mentioned in passing that they were thinking of acquiring Wirt. When I couldn't get hold of you, I called down there, told her not to make a hasty decision, that we wanted to talk to her, too."

Robin pondered that—it sounded reasonable. It was true she had been out of pocket Friday afternoon, and Girt had confirmed American Motorfreight's interest.

"So what did you find out?" he asked.

"Well, she's got a larger operation than Lou Harvey, which we knew. And it's definitely more diverse, which I like. Lou's deal bothers me because it looks like he's been losing money the last couple of years."

"Right. I saw that, too," Evan agreed.

"But I don't know if I understand everything I see with Lou's operation. On the other hand, Girt says she hasn't seen a huge increase in profit, but she's been steadily growing."

"That's right. Let me tell you a couple of things to look for," Evan said and proceeded to list things Robin could check as crews began to trickle in to work on her house. He confirmed her instincts about Peerless and Wirt, which both surprised and pleased Robin. She had not reached the point where she actually trusted herself; it helped that Evan seemed to think she was right on target.

They were talking about the Wirt profit-loss statements when Jake came in. He grabbed her hand and brought it to his lips, then, with a wink, disappeared into the kitchen. When he returned, Robin was still on the line, laughing about the infamous office politics in New York and one particularly notorious secretary. Carrying a circular saw, Jake paused to put it down as Robin laughed at Evan's telling of the secretary's latest escapades, picturing the whole scene in her mind.

"Okay, well, look, I'm going to be in Houston next week. I'm pretty booked, but maybe we can get together for dinner and talk about Wirt, all right?"

"Sure," Robin said and switched her computer screen to her calendar. "Wednesday night would be great."

"Okay, got you down. Take care and I'll see you next week."

Robin put down the phone, put Evan on her calendar, and looked up. Jake hadn't moved. He was standing there, looking at her with an odd expression. She held up a magazine she had been reading. "Hey," she said cheerfully, "I found the perfect place for your house—Retro Hardware. I'm going over there this afternoon to look at the stained glass. Have you thought about what you want?"

Jake had thought about what he wanted, all right. Had thought about it pretty much for the last month. One thing he knew for certain, as he walked over to see the pictures Robin was poring over, was that he didn't want Iverson in her life or anywhere near her.

He was not a jealous man by nature, and in fact, he rarely allowed himself to get involved deeply enough to have cause for jealousy. But there was something about Robin that appealed to the deepest parts of him, and there was something about Slick Evan he instinctively did not trust. Evan had a thing for Robin. He could tell just by the way the dude looked at her. At the same time, Jake recognized Evan's role in LTI, understood the interaction with Robin was inevitable. He just had to figure out how to handle it if he was going to pursue something meaningful with Robin, which certainly was his intent.

And as the next few weeks unfurled, Jake spent as much time with Robin as he could, trying to balance school, Cole, and his work with the very real need to be with her. His reaction to her, both physical and emotional, overpowered all normal operating procedures. Somehow, she was pushing him from the shallows into the deep, so deep that he felt he was treading water when they were apart. He could feel her when she wasn't with him, could feel her hair on his face, her breath on his chest.

That was exhilarating, but it was plenty disturbing, too. He didn't *want* to feel that. He never wanted to get used to any kind of happiness because it never lasted, and he felt safe in that assumption. This was a silly dream he was living, and while it was one thing to have silly dreams, it was much worse to actually believe they were attainable.

Yeah, something amazing was happening to him. Funny little dreams of fulfillment were beginning to creep into his thoughts, dreams that practically had a white picket fence around them, dreams that included a degree, Robin in his house and his bed, and even Cole, flourishing in high school, preparing for college.

But okay, he wasn't so far gone that he didn't know their evolving relationship wasn't entirely a bed of roses. He was never sure of Robin's feelings, for one thing, didn't know if when the job ended, her feelings wouldn't end right along with it. And while he could feel her affection, there were also certain barriers between them. Like money.

That was an aspect that deeply bothered Jake—he couldn't abide her shopping habits. Robin had no concept of money. She would go to the grocery store but come back with a bag full of shoes. Like one day, when he happened to see the price tag on the end of a shoebox and almost had a coronary—up until that point, he hadn't known it was possible to mortgage a pair of shoes. "That's insane!" he had blurted. "There are people starving in this world and you are paying *that* for shoes?"

Robin was immediately indignant. "So? I give plenty to charity. I can buy a pair of shoes if I want."

"Of course you can…but it's the principle of spending that much on shoes, Robin."

"Oh man," Robin cried, "here we go again! Doughnuts, shoes—you have too many damn principles, Jake."

"And you obviously don't have enough."

That stunned her—she gasped, then abruptly picked up her shoes. "I don't have to listen to this!" she snapped and went into her bedroom, slamming the door behind her.

Okay, maybe he was out of line, but she went through money like water, unfazed by the enormity of what she was spending. For a man struggling every month to keep his business afloat, it was a hard thing to watch.

Truthfully, a lot of his discomfort was wrapped up in his pride. No matter how hard he tried, he couldn't get used to the fact that Robin had so much more than he did. He liked to think of himself as an enlightened guy, definitely a player in the new millennium, but the cold hard truth was when it came to men and women, he was pretty traditional in his beliefs. Men protected and provided. Women…well, women did whatever women did. Nurture. Raise kids. Bake and decorate. Actually, it didn't matter to him *what* they did, as long as he was the one doing the providing.

He wasn't even close to providing on her scale, wasn't even in the same galaxy. That quiet frustration led to more than one argument between them. Like the day she had the idea that they would "pop up to New York" for dinner. The suggestion was so ludicrous to him that he didn't think much of it, until he overheard Robin calling in for the Lear jet.

"You're kidding," he said flatly. "You are not thinking of ordering that jet up just so you can eat sushi in some New York bar."

It was very obvious she was not kidding, and furthermore, did not like the way he asked that question. "Why not?" she demanded. "It's my jet."

"It's not *your* jet, it belongs to LTI, and you have a responsibility to that company to be fiscally prudent. Can't you see the unnecessary expense to your father's company of jetting around the country on your personal whims?"

"News flash, Handy Andy—it's none of your business what I do."

He hated when she said that, like he was some second-class citizen, unaffected by her decisions. But at the same time, it *was* none of his business. "Well then God help LTI the day you're at the helm."

That remark had infuriated her.

They didn't go to New York that weekend. Robin was mad for a full day, but did at last own up to being spoiled. And in return, Jake owned up to butting in where he didn't belong. But he would have been less than honest if he didn't admit that her endless resources were a source of distress to him, pointing out to him in many different ways that he was playing way out of his league.

And it sure didn't help matters that Mr. Ever-Present Evan seemed to have the same disregard for money as she did. It seemed he was forever showing up to take Robin to dinner at some swank restaurant Jake could only afford to read about. It was all done under the guise of business, of course, and Robin was naive enough to believe it. Yeah, well, Jake saw Evan for what he was: a master at the game of wooing women, and in this case, Jake didn't have the resources to compete.

But he had to hand it to Robin—his lack of resources never seemed to bother her. Other than an occasional exasperation when she tried to pay for something and he wouldn't allow it, she never seemed to want more from him than he could offer. She seemed perfectly at ease at Paulie's or at the junior high ball fields, and never seemed to lament the fact that she wasn't at some fancy restaurant. Nevertheless, *he* was conscious of the differences between them, and perhaps even more acutely aware of the differences between him and Evan.

Jake might have considered throwing in the towel had it not been for the connection between him and Robin that transcended the money. When they were together, the lovemaking between them was ethereal. Robin had a healthy appetite and was an eager participant, willing to try almost anything a man could imagine. Every time she found her fulfillment with him, it was so open and unabashed that it sent a shiver down Jake's spine. He was more than fulfilled; he was infused with a primal hunger for her.

There was so much to like about Robin, so much to enjoy, so much to admire, that Jake realized he was, inexplicably, and against his conscious will, falling in love with her.

Which was why, therefore, it was with some trepidation that he took her to meet what was left of his family when Easter

Sunday finally came around. If anyone would send her running, it was the Mannings, and Norma Manning in particular.

In New York, Aaron sat in the Naugahyde lounge chair, his baseball cap on backward, hooked up to IVs in both arms that were pumping a shitload of cancer-fighting crap into him. He could see through the little square pane of glass in the door that Bonnie was just outside, leaning up against the wall, her head bowed. He could imagine the rest of her—one leg crossed over the other, her arms folded tightly against her middle as if she, too, might get sick. It was a pose he had seen more times than he wanted to count.

He owed her his life if he could manage to keep it. How funny that time could erase all the things he had once known about her, all the things he had once adored. But it had all come back to him these last grueling weeks, every little thing about Bonnie Lou Stanton that he had once loved so dearly. And he still loved her, he realized, maybe even more now. But it had taken an ugly cancer for him to remember.

He supposed this was God's way of shaking some sense into a man who thought he was stronger than Him. That afternoon, he felt the sickness slowly moving through him, and he vowed on his very own life that if God granted him another chance at life, he would make it up to her. He would honor and cherish her like a queen.

He did not allow himself to think that he might have already squandered all the chances God was willing to give him.

CHAPTER TWENTY-TWO

Easter fell unusually late that spring, and that Sunday morning dawned clear and beautiful, the air still cool from a night of Gulf breezes. But it was Houston, so by the time Jake arrived at Robin's, the humidity was setting in to stifle the day.

Robin didn't seem to notice—she was awfully bubbly. She had been in Burdette yesterday, working with Girt, and when she'd returned to Houston around six, she'd phoned to tell him that Reba had reached Bowling Nirvana, just like him, having scored a 200. Then she had added that she was having dinner with Evan to go over some figures.

"On a Saturday night?" Jake had asked, despising himself for sounding so needy.

"He's got to go to New York tomorrow, so this is the only time I can catch him. I'll call you when I get home, okay?"

Except that she didn't call when she got home, didn't call until this morning, apologizing profusely for having gotten in so late. Jake did not ask why, didn't really want to know why. No, actually he did, but he didn't think he had the right to know, and he damn sure didn't think he could stomach it. His relationship with Robin felt as if it was on unstable footing. On the one hand, Robin seemed to enjoy each moment with him as much as he enjoyed spending time with her and seemed to *want* to be with him. But he never felt the same level of commitment from her. In fact, there were times it felt as if she might flit away at any moment. Then the next moment he'd believe wholeheartedly she wanted what he wanted—a family, a house. A life.

Robin came bouncing out the door with a large paper bag, her face a wreath of smiles. "Look—Easter eggs! Grandma made them for me."

Jake peered into the bag, saw what looked like a dozen hard-boiled, painted eggs. "Ah…great."

She stuffed the bag and her purse behind the truck's bench seat and got in. "Do I look all right?" she asked.

"You look beautiful," he said, meaning it.

She beamed. "Thank you. But what about the shoes?" she asked, wiggling a pink sandal at him.

For a man who could count the pairs of shoes he owned on one hand, it seemed a rhetorical question. "What about them?"

"I mean, do they go?"

He looked at her slim-fitting capri pants and fitted blouse and shrugged. "I guess."

She groaned, rolled her eyes. "Jake, a little help here? I'm really nervous."

"Nervous?" He laughed. "Why?"

"Because I want to make a good impression!"

"Oh my—baby, you'll knock 'em dead." He laughed again, baffled how a woman like Robin Lear could possibly be worried what his family would think of her. The likelihood was much greater that Robin would be the one to be appalled.

But in fact, his trepidation was misplaced—it was his mom who seemed almost appalled when they arrived and Robin climbed out of the pickup truck and came striding forward. She smiled warmly, one hand gripping the paper bag with the Easter eggs, the other extended in greeting. "Mrs. Manning, it is a pleasure to finally meet you!"

Mom looked at her extended hand, took it gingerly. "Pleased to meet you," she mumbled, and quickly let go. "Jacob? Ain't you gonna take her bag?"

Jake bent to kiss his mom's leathery cheek. "Happy Easter, Mom," he said, taking the bag from Robin.

"I brought Easter eggs," Robin announced hopefully, motioning to the brown bag.

Mom, in usual fashion, frowned. "We're having ham," she said. "Hope you like ham."

"Yes!" Robin proclaimed, perhaps a little too enthusiastically. "Yes I do!"

"Well. We better get them eggs inside," Mom said. She paused to pull a smoke from her pocket, lit up, and exhaled as she gave Robin a quick once-over before turning toward the house. Jake held out his hand to Robin. "Jacob says you work for a freight company," she said over her shoulder.

"Yes. Lear Transport."

Mom had nothing say to that.

"Do…do you work, Mrs. Manning?"

"Not anymore. It's all I can do to watch after Cole nowadays," Mom said wearily and labored up the steps of her porch, opened the screen, and went inside, letting the screen door slam behind her.

God. Jake noticed, as he opened the screen door for Robin, that her smile was a little thin as she stepped across the threshold. He worried if she noticed how threadbare the carpet or dated the furniture was, or noticed the smell of turnips and stale smoke in the air.

"Yo!" he heard Zaney shout. Jesus, he was glad to hear that voice for a change. The guy had no family, and had become a permanent fixture at Jake's family gatherings.

"Hi, Zaney," Robin said with a shy little wave.

"Robin! Look what I got!" Cole said excitedly as Jake shut the door behind them. He came rushing toward her with a new pair of sneakers that looked like spaceman shoes, definitely an appropriate addition to his already bizarre wardrobe. "Grandma got 'em for me," he said, proudly holding them up, and Jake marveled how, in moments like this, Cole could still seem so childlike.

"Hey...*sweet!*" Robin exclaimed. "And huge!"

Cole grinned broadly, a rare sight.

Jake glanced up, saw his aunt Wanda and cousin Vickie, and made quick introductions. Thank goodness for Vic— she was, as usual, all smiles. "Hi, Robin! We've heard an awful lot about you!" she said, nudging Jake playfully in the ribs.

"Oh, is that right?" Robin asked, stealing a look at Jake.

"These are my kids, Elissa and Nicholas"—she paused, barked, "*Kids! Get over here and say hello to Robin!*" The two kids hurried to their mom's side, looked at Robin warily as she smiled down at them and wiggled her fingers in a childlike wave.

"Robin, look what else I got!" Cole called, oblivious to the introductions being made, bursting in on them so quickly that little Nicholas stumbled backward. Cole was holding a supersized T-shirt with bright red flames licking up from the hem.

"Now *that* is cool," Robin said admiringly.

"It cost twenty dollars!" he added, then disappeared again.

"Would you like something to drink, Robin? Some iced tea?" Vickie asked.

"Thank you, I would love some."

"That's a real pretty jacket you got on there," Vickie said as she motioned Robin to come with her. "What is that, linen?"

"Yes," Robin said and looked over her shoulder helplessly at Jake as she followed Vickie to the kitchen.

"I saw something similar at Target I thought was real cute."

As Jake watched Robin disappear into the kitchen behind his cousin, he placed a mental bet with himself how long it would be before she bolted.

"I think they've got some real nice stuff now," Vickie was saying in the kitchen, still talking about Target. "They had their Easter sale last weekend, and I got Elissa a real cute little Easter dress," she continued as she fetched ice and tea from the fridge. "But you know, Elissa's at that age she doesn't like dresses. She's sort of a tomboy."

"Ah," was all Robin could think to say, but she didn't have to look far to see where Elissa had gotten those tendencies. After all, her mom was wearing a KFLX Radio T-shirt, blue denim jeans, and caveman sandals. Her brown hair was pulled back tightly in a long ponytail that reached halfway down her back, and her bangs looked like they had been shellacked around an orange juice can.

"Now Nicholas, he's the one who's into clothes," Vickie blithely continued. "It has to be Nike or Reebok before he'll even look at it. Do you know those sneakers cost seventy-five dollars on sale? Can you imagine paving that much for *shoes*? Well, his daddy said to him, said, 'Son, when *you* start paying the rent around here, you can buy whatever shoes you want'—Sugar?"

"No, no thank you."

"—'so just forget it.'" Vickie paused to hand Robin the glass of iced tea. "Kids are so silly," she said cheerfully. "So. How long you been dating Jacob?"

Talk about getting right down to brass tacks. Robin sipped her tea. "Just a little while now."

"Is it *serious*?" Vickie all but whispered behind her glass of tea.

Oh *man*. "We enjoy one another's company," Robin said pleasantly and mentally patted herself on the back for being so smooth.

"No, but I mean, are you thinking about making it permanent?"

"Permanent?" she echoed dumbly.

"Like marriage," Vickie prompted her.

"*Marriage?*" Robin squeaked, choking on her tea.

"Jacob's never been married, can you believe that? He's thirty-eight years old and never been married. But I have to tell you, I am so glad he didn't get hooked up with that Lindy—oh my *God*!" she exclaimed with a roll of her eyes.

Gossip. Well, all *right* then—now Robin was on familiar ground.

"She was just…*stupid*, you know what I mean?"

Yes, yes, she knew *exactly* what Vickie meant. "So you met her?" Robin asked carefully.

Vickie shrugged, sipped her tea. "She came by here one day looking for him, carrying a pie, if you can believe that. I mean, you don't start right off making *pies* for Chrissakes until you at *least* got him a little interested, because then he's just gonna expect it. You know what I mean?"

Robin nodded earnestly that she did, and decided she and Vickie were going to be great friends. "So he wasn't really interested in her, huh?" she asked, dredging for all the dirt.

"Ah, hell no," Vickie said with a dismissive flick of her wrist. "Just trying to be friendly is all. He hadn't really been interested in anyone since Gloria a couple of years back."

"Oh *really*? I never heard of Gloria."

Vickie's eyes lit up like Christmas trees, but before she could tell her anything about Gloria, Mrs. Manning called from the other room, "You ain't talking out of school, now are you, Vic?"

Vickie's eyes widened under her shellacked bangs. "No, ma'am!" she called, then smiled ruefully at Robin. "I'll catch up with you later during horseshoes," she whispered conspiratorially and didn't even seem to notice that Robin was speechless at the mere mention of horseshoes, yet another sporting event for which she had no talent or desire.

Robin followed Vickie into the adjoining room, noticed that Jake had abandoned her—through the sheer drapes, she could see him outside with Zaney and Cole under the hood of Zaney's battered truck. She was, she realized in a moment of panic, alone with Mrs. Manning, Wanda, Vickie, and the two kids. Wanda was working on a piece of embroidery or knitting or some craft thing. Vickie picked up a magazine and began to leaf through it. And Mrs. Manning smoked.

She motioned to a high-back wooden chair with an old, stained embroidered seat as she eyed Robin. "Have a seat," she said. "Is it all right I call you Robin?"

"Sure!" Robin said and sat, folding her hands in her lap.

"So…how did you meet Jacob?" Wanda asked.

"Ah…he's renovating my house."

"I've been trying to get him to come fix a door in my house for six months," Vickie said absently as she leafed through the magazine.

Mrs. Manning continued to stare at Robin. "Where do you live?"

"North Boulevard. It's near the Village."

She nodded. "Nice house, I'd say."

"It will be when Jake is done. He's excellent at what he does."

If she wasn't mistaken, a hint of a sardonic smile flashed across Mrs. Manning's face, but disappeared quickly. "Ain't the first time I've heard that."

"What kind of work do you do?" Wanda asked.

"I, uh…I work for a shipping company. We ship freight around the world."

"Oh…do you work in the office?"

"The corporate offices."

"Doing what?"

Well, I was my father's lackey for a while, but then he demoted me to bubble wrap…"I am an acquisitions specialist," she said, wincing inwardly at how stupid that sounded.

"A what specialist?" Vickie asked unabashedly.

"I, uh…well, like right now, I am looking at acquiring a couple of packing material companies. We buy packing materials to pack our freight. If we buy a packing supply company, then we'd make our own and not have to rely on someone else's supply."

"I don't know what you mean when you say packing materials," Mrs. Manning said.

"You know...stuff that goes in boxes."

"You mean like them Styrofoam peanuts?" Vickie asked, incredulous.

Robin could feel herself coloring. Of all the things she had envisioned for herself, peanuts definitely had never been in the picture. Neither was Telephone Road, for that matter. "Yes. Like Styrofoam peanuts."

Vickie looked at her mother. Wanda looked at her embroidery.

"I'd best see to the potatoes," Mrs. Manning said, heaving herself out of the recliner.

"Can I help you?" Robin asked, coming to her feet.

Mrs. Manning's eyes flicked the entire length of her before she slowly nodded. "I imagine there is something you can do."

Well, that was debatable, but Robin followed Mrs. Manning to the kitchen anyway. Jake's mom pointed to a cabinet next to her ancient fridge. "You'll find some plates in there. There will be twelve of us for dinner if Derek ever gets back from fishing. I don't know why he's got to go fishing on Easter Sunday, but he ain't my husband." She proceeded on to the stove and lifted the lid on the potatoes.

Thank you, God—setting the table, something she could definitely do. "Okay!" Robin said, pleased with her task. "Where's the dining room?"

Mrs. Manning looked up. "This ain't quite the Village, you know." She nodded at the kitchen table. "You're looking at it."

"Oh." *Wooonderful.* Robin proceeded stiffly to the cabinet Mrs. Manning had indicated, withdrew twelve old pottery plates decorated with brown and orange leaves, and walked back to the table, wondering if she should remove the used coffee cups there.

"You know," Mrs. Manning said as Robin pushed the cups aside for the moment, "my son has a lot on his plate right now, what with his work, and school, and trying to help me manage Cole."

"Yes, he's a very busy man," Robin agreed as she began to lay the plates.

"You must be busy, too, with your packing stuff."

Her job certainly sounded glamorous when put like that, didn't it? "Sometimes. I travel a lot."

"Just wonder how you have time to see my son at all."

Okay, maybe she was being a touch PMS-ey, but Robin did not like the way Mrs. Manning kept saying *my son.* Like she owned him, had a say in him or something. "We make the time," Robin said simply. "I really enjoy his company."

"Oh, I'm sure he enjoys yours, too," Mrs. Manning said with a laugh that sounded dangerously close to a snort. "But Cole needs him right now."

What did *that* mean? Robin picked up the used coffee cups, marched to the sink, put them on top of an already huge pile of dirty dishes. "If you will show me where the silverware is, I'll put it out."

Old lady Manning pointed to a drawer. Robin yanked it open, started counting forks.

"Now, I'm not trying to make you mad," she continued.

"Please, Mrs. Manning, you aren't making me mad."

Still, the old bag chuckled, paused in her ministrations over the stove to light a smoke. "You can call me Norma," she said, as if that was some huge favor. "All I'm trying to say is, I look at a pretty, rich girl like you, and I wonder why you'd be running around with my son when you could be with just about any man out there. I wonder if you aren't out just having a little fun at his expense. If you are, he don't need that right now."

Of all the unmitigated, uncalled-for *chutzpah*! "Having fun?" Robin echoed, a little more sharply than she intended, and wondered what Jake would say if he knew his mom was essentially telling her to get lost. "I don't know what you see when you look at me, Norma," she said pointedly, "but I really *like* Jake. And he seems to like me. We are seeing each other when we can, and I guess we're both content to just see where it goes."

Norma Manning chuckled. "Good. Glad to hear you at least like him."

Astounded, Robin gaped at the woman's back. She was hardly accustomed to justifying her dating habits. Okay, maybe to her father, but never to the mother of her dates. Funny thing was, while Robin was fuming, Norma seemed amused, and even got a little talkative. As if she had never accused Robin of using Jake, she asked her to baste the ham (without anything obvious that Robin could see) and check the beans (which she assumed meant stir). Norma mashed the potatoes and began to tell Robin what Jake was like as a boy—apparently one who slept with his bat and never went anywhere without his cleats or his baseball jersey. Though the stories were humorous, they were also poignant to Robin. It had to have been more devastating than she could know when Jake tore his Achilles tendon and ended a dream that had begun when he was a boy.

But he did sound like an adorable little boy, almost as adorable as the man. By the time the food was on the table, Robin was actually laughing with his mom.

Vickie's husband, Derek, had arrived by the time Norma called everyone in for dinner, and they all crowded in the small kitchen until it looked as if it might actually burst at the seams. They squeezed in around the table, sitting in a hodge-podge of chairs. Jake dutifully said grace when his mother asked, his deep voice resonating in the room. With the *amen*, everyone attacked the food, startling Robin by grabbing bowls and passing them in every direction, talking on top of one another as they asked for various dishes, laughing at the things one another said, and enjoying the home-cooked meal. Norma played hostess, groused at every request, but nonetheless jumped up and down to fetch whatever was needed.

The loud, raucous free-for-all was not like anything Robin had ever experienced. Even the food was a complete departure from the carefully balanced, light meals her mom instructed the cook to make on the rare occasions they were all together, and she wished for a glass of wine instead of iced tea...but nevertheless, it was *fun*.

There wasn't a stiff air of formality around the table, nor did anyone seem to mind the lack of proper manners. The emphasis seemed to be on the companionship instead of rules; no one seemed out to impress the other. At her family gatherings, they often engaged in subtle contest over the price of a bottle of wine (actually there was *no* alcohol here, which some people—well, Robin, anyway—found disconcerting). As someone shoved a basket of rolls into her hand, Robin couldn't help but think of the last meal she had had with her family, the one served with bone china, crystal glasses, and real silverware while her father berated her and her sisters about their inadequacies. This gathering was missing the finery, but it had something much more valuable—a real sense of belonging and closeness.

It felt wonderful.

As Vickie heaped a large spoonful of mashed potatoes onto her plate, Robin thought this was what family was supposed to be, and when Derek asked what Robin did for a living, for the first time since she had been demoted, she laughed. And proclaimed that she was a bona fide expert on bubble wrap.

Sitting across from her, Jake quietly watched her, feeling awfully proud as she extolled the virtues of well-made bubble wrap. It seemed funny now that he had worried she would find his family and their ways a little barbaric for her refined tastes, or that Mom would manage to chase her off before dinner was even served. Robin was a champ; if she was appalled by the free-for-all, he couldn't see it, and furthermore, she actually seemed to enjoy the back-and-forth banter with Derek about the size of bubbles in bubble wrap.

In truth, as he looked at Robin, gorgeous Robin, he could admit that he had seen a change in her over the last several weeks. She had gone from the sort of highbrow woman who had a habit of looking through people like him to one who now looked directly at him, into him. One who could let him look back without squirming.

That afternoon, Elissa and Nicholas and even Cole hunted for the Easter eggs Robin had brought as the adults prepared for the traditional game of horseshoes, played every Easter without respect for age, gender, or ability. They formed teams of two, Derek and Jake ganging up on Vickie and Robin. Robin was as hapless at horseshoes as she was at bowling, but Vickie, bless her, laughed louder than anyone when Robin threw a horseshoe and broke the humming-bird feeder Vickie had given Mom. When the game was fin-ished—Derek and Jake winning an unapologetic twenty-one to four, and with four ringers to his credit—Jake took a seat on the back porch with Mom to watch Robin and Cole play against Zaney and little Nicholas.

When Wanda got up to go in and make a pot of coffee, Mom lit up a smoke and inhaled deeply. "She's real nice, Jacob," she said as she watched Zaney do one of his famous shot-put horseshoe tosses that scattered Cole and Robin to opposite ends of the yard. "And real pretty. I can see why you're crazy about her."

"Mom, don't start," he warned her. "Don't make a big deal out of this."

She exhaled, looked at him from the corner of her eye. "You think I don't know you? You think that your mother can't take one look at you and know you're gaga about that woman?"

Man, he hated when she did that. "You're imagining things," he said dismissively.

"The hell I am," she said with an air of motherly supe-riority. "And you'd be a fool *not* to be crazy about her. I just hope you're not so foolish that you get hurt."

"Hurt? What are you talking about?"

Mom paused to tap the ash from her smoke, then inhaled deeply again. "Just what I said. I hope you don't get hurt, Jacob. She's real pretty and she's real nice, but it's real obvious she don't belong down here. She might as well be from the other side of the world. One day, you might just wake up and find her gone back to that side of the world. That's all I'm saying."

God, but Mom had a way of bluntly stating the truth that grated on him. Like he hadn't thought of that every day they had been together. Like that didn't haunt his growing and deep attachment to Robin. Nonetheless, he snorted at her suggestion. "You watch too many movies, Mom. I'm having a good time right now, nothing more, so there's no need for you to worry about me."

She laughed. "How dumb do I look, Jacob?" she asked, and still laughing, ground out her cigarette before going inside to help Wanda.

CHAPTER TWENTY-THREE

They left the Easter gathering with Robin promising an exuberant Vickie that she would come again. Cole followed them out, wearing his new space shoes, and carrying the remaining painted eggs, trailing Robin. He waited until Jake took the bag from him and went around the other side to put it in the truck before speaking to Robin in a near whisper. "There's a dance at the school next week," he said, looking at his feet.

"Oh yeah? Are you going to ask Tara?" Robin asked.

Cole shrugged, scuffed the toe of his shoe on the curb. "I don't know. Maybe."

"I think you should. I bet Tara would be thrilled if you called her."

Cole seemed to think about that, then shrugged again. "She'd think it was really sweet if Dustin asked her. Not me."

Robin cuffed Cole on the shoulder and made him look up. He had beautiful brown eyes and long dark lashes, just like his uncle. "Don't be so sure about that. I'm a girl, and I'd want you to call."

He flushed, grinned sheepishly, and looked at the ground again as Jake came around from the back of the truck.

"Are you ready, Robin?" he asked, opening the door for her. Cole shoved his hands in his pockets and stepped back so Robin could climb into the passenger seat. She winked at Cole, mouthed the words *do it*, then said, "Have a good week at school, Cole!"

Jake shut the door, gave Cole an affectionate hug. "Be good and mind your grandma." He walked around the front of the truck to the driver's side. "See you," Robin called as Jake turned the ignition, and noticed as they drove away how Cole just stood there, watching them leave. A person couldn't see that kid standing there without feeling something, and Robin's heart winged out to Cole so fast that she couldn't snatch it back.

At her house, they opened a bottle of wine (finally!), had a glass in the backyard on the wide, thickly padded loungers (her latest impulsive purchase), and gazed up at the stars. It reminded Robin of a time in the long distant past when she and her sisters would lie with their mother on a quilt in the backyard and look up at the stars. *You know why the stars are there?* her mother would ask. *To show you how high you can dream.*

Maybe she hadn't dreamed high enough. Maybe she had been so busy pretending to dream that she hadn't let herself actually reach for the stars.

"You know what I'm thinking?" Jake asked after a while, taking her hand.

She shifted her gaze to him, saw his lopsided grin. "That this wine would taste better in bed?" she asked, grinning, too.

He laughed, brought her hand to his mouth, and kissed her knuckles. "That's what I like about you—you can read a man's mind."

"Oh please—like there's anything to read," she quipped and let Jake drag her across the loungers onto his lap so he could kiss her passionately.

They made wild, buzz-induced monkey love, right there under the stars, finding fulfillment at the same moment, blissfully drifting into sweet oblivion in one another's arms. After a while, Robin stirred, buttoned her blouse, and woke Jake. They sleepily stumbled inside; Robin went in search of the wine bottle while Jake fell into bed. She returned with saltines and cheese in a can.

"Excuse me for a minute, I need to step outside and see if the world has actually stopped spinning," Jake exclaimed, pointing to the cheese substitute.

"I'm branching out! And it was the only thing they had at the convenience store the other night when I got back from Burdette." She put the tray between them, sat cross-legged, facing him, and sipped her wine as Jake squeezed a mountain of processed cheese onto a saltine and popped it into his mouth.

"Your family is nice," she remarked.

He frowned dubiously at that.

"But I don't think your mom particularly likes me."

Now Jake smiled. "She likes you. She's just hard to get to know."

Yeah, well, Robin hadn't gotten to the age of thirty-four without developing a woman's intuition about some things. Knowing when someone flat-out didn't like her was one of them, and she vigorously shook her head. "It's more than that. She thinks I'm messing with you."

Jake helped himself to another cracker, sans cheese, and munched thoughtfully. "Maybe. That's because she doesn't think I'm smart enough to know if I am being used. I don't know if you noticed, but my mom doesn't think too highly of me."

"You're kidding!" Robin exclaimed, genuinely surprised. "How could she not be totally proud of you? How could anyone not think you are the most capable man in the world? Jeez, if I had a son like you, I'd be prancing all over Houston!"

With a grateful smile, Jake reached up to tenderly stroke Robin's cheek. "You can be a real sweetheart, in spite of all appearances to the contrary."

"I'm *serious*."

Jake chuckled at her earnestness. "I'll let you in on a secret—my mom has never thought I measured up. I've never been able to do much of anything to please her. I pursued baseball and I was wasting my time. I started college and I was too old. I try to take Cole to live with me, and I am irresponsible. Honestly? Sometimes, the things she says—I think she believes I abandoned her like my dad did. And my Uncle Dan tells me I look a lot like the old man did at my age."

That piqued Robin's curiosity; she watched Jake take another cracker and pop it into his mouth. "Do you know where he is?"

"Dad?" He snorted derisively. "Haven't heard from him since he ran off, more than twenty years ago. He's probably dead. I'm sure Vickie will eventually get around to telling you the whole ugly story, but that...it's what's wrong with Mom. It colors everything."

"What do you mean?"

"She's afraid of loving—it hurts too much."

He said it so nonchalantly, like it was what anyone should expect, that it took Robin aback. What a sad, revealing thing to say. What an *awful* thing to say! But she knew exactly what Jake meant. "Isn't it funny how alike we are, you and me?" she asked. "My dad has never really thought I measured up, either. It seems like I have been forever trying to...to *please* him, to get him to say, hey, Robbie, you're a good daughter, or a good person. Or just something like, come on up and let's go out on the boat. But he never does. And when I do hear from him, it's usually to rant about something I've done wrong."

"Wrong? What could be wrong? You're a wonderful person, dedicated to your company, to him—"

Robin laughed at how pathetic that sounded, given the betrayal she felt at her father's hand. If only Jake understood how she had given him everything, only to be told she was basically mere window dressing to him. "Trust me," she said with a sardonic laugh, "I'm wrong. You want to know his current complaint? I don't have any roots. I haven't pursued the right things in life." But the words, spoken with sarcasm, seemed to hang in front of her. They even sounded true. "I don't know why I care," she continued thoughtfully, "but for some reason, I keep trying to get him to like me." She shook her head at the lunacy of that, then smiled. "I guess I'm just stubborn."

"You really think your father doesn't like you?" Jake asked, surprised.

She nodded. "I think he loves me in some weird way. But he doesn't like me."

Jake pressed his lips together, stared at her for a long moment, then said quietly, "For what it's worth, I think you're absolutely amazing."

Robin gave him a grateful smile, cognizant that the way he was looking at her was making her heart skip, and tried to put a word to his look that she could cope with. "You're starting to make me feel like I have something strange on my head," she said, trying to make a joke of it, but Jake did not smile.

"I mean it. You are a beautiful, vibrant, accomplished woman. And genuine, someone who is way more down to earth than she thinks. I look at you, and I see someone I've been waiting for my whole life."

Robin gasped; her heart was now somersaulting, and she wanted to protest, wanted to stop him before he took this too far, and waved a desperate hand at him. "*Jake*," she whispered weakly, but he caught her hand and brought it to his chest, pressed it against his heart.

"I am falling in love with you, Robin."

Her physical reaction was so quick and sudden that the wineglass she had been holding so loosely went crashing to the floor. Jake let go of her hand, grabbed the tray between them, and saved it and the wine bottle from toppling over.

"I'm sorry," she said, flustered, as he put the tray on the floor. "I'm sorry."

Jake didn't seem to hear her—he grabbed both her hands by the wrists and pulled her on top of him as he fell back, landing on a cloud of pillows. "Me too, because I can't help how I feel or that you have managed to open a door in me that has been nailed shut."

She was skating on the edge of complete chaos—his words ripped through her like a scythe, opening ancient old wounds she didn't even know she had. It was too much, too many emotions erupting inside her. This was a man who

329

could speak like a poet, could make love like a real man, could make her laugh—she adored Jake, loved his company, loved to watch him work...but *love*? What did that really mean? Didn't that mean there were expectations that were far too great for either of them?

Jake suddenly let go of her, and she flopped over onto her side like a rag doll.

"I don't know how you did it," he said. "I don't know if it was the coffee, or the pink flamingos, or telling me how to bat, but somehow, you stuck one of those flimsy sandals in that door inside me and kicked it open without even trying."

Robin buried her face in the pillow, afraid she would say something stupid—even more afraid he would stop.

"And there I was, trying to mind my own business, but suddenly, I can't get you off my mind, I can't sleep without dreaming of you, I can't think without seeing you, I can't wait to get here in the morning, and I can't stand to leave at night. I didn't know what the hell was the matter with me, but I can finally admit to myself and to you that I know what it is that has been clanking around in me. I am falling in love with you, Robin."

"Oh God, I don't know what to *say*," she moaned into the pillow.

Jake leaned over her, kissed the back of her neck, then her shoulder. "Say, I love you, too, Hammerman. Say, me, too, or ditto, or you make me hot, you stud—"

"Oh, *Jake*," she whispered helplessly.

"Say you adore me, say you love me," he pressed.

But the words seemed lodged in her gullet—she couldn't force them out. Robin buried her face in a pillow. "I *can't*," she muttered helplessly.

"Oh God," Jake muttered somewhere above her, and she felt him draw away.

Robin sat up. "No—it's...I'm just not ready, Jake," she pleaded with him.

"Yeah, I see," he said, swinging his legs off the side of the bed.

"No, no, you don't. I *do* adore you. I just...I want to—I need to go slow..."

Jake didn't say anything for a moment, just gazed sadly at her. At last, he lifted his hand and stroked her cheek. "Okay," he said and gently pushed Robin down onto the bed. He kissed her softly. "Okay," he said again, as if to convince himself that it was okay, and kissed her eyes, her cheeks, her mouth, and then her breasts, pushing aside her blouse to explore her entire body with his mouth. Robin moaned, both from pleasure and pain. Pleasure from the expertise with which he brought her to the brink of a violent climax; pain from knowing that the man who did this to her had fallen in love with her, and that she didn't know how to return it, or what to do with it, other than to lie there, to let him say it, to let him show her. And when she came, she unconsciously called out his name as tender gratification rained down and covered her, creating a shroud beneath which she lay, feeling just barely alive as she tried to catch her breath and what was left of the bearings instilled in her a long, long time ago. Bearings that were fast slipping from her white-knuckled grip.

Jake was up before the light the next morning. He envied Robin her zombie sleep, with arms and legs sprawled everywhere. An A-bomb wouldn't have waked that girl. But he couldn't sleep, troubled by his stupid admission, blurted out like a teenage boy in love. Gaga, Mom had called it. What he wouldn't give to be able to deliver himself a good swift kick in the ass. What had he expected her to do with his poetic declarations? Announce her own undying love? Ask him to marry her?

You're a fucking idiot, man.

He was already working when the crews showed up and started banging around the house, trying to figure out how he had come to fall in love with a woman who was so far above him in economic and social stature as to be unreachable. It wasn't that he was intimidated by her wealth, exactly, or thought Robin above him in some way. It was just that it didn't seem…*practical.* Robin knew it, but oh no, he had gone and fallen deep into the magic and believed it. For a man who accounted for every nickel he made, Jake didn't think there would ever be a time he would feel good about spending money wantonly like she did, no matter how much money he had.

But then again, he harbored the insane notion that if he could just concentrate on getting his architect degree—he was so damn close, after all—that he could, conceivably, make the kind of money Robin was used to. He could support those things she was accustomed to, like fancy restaurants, trips abroad, even shopping sprees. Although he might eventually have to put his foot down about the shoe thing, because nobody, and that meant *nobody*, should pay more than fifty bucks for a pair.

It was that singular, faint hope of a potential future with Robin that made Jake even more determined than ever to finish school and expand his business, and it felt with every swing of the hammer against the brick wall that he was one step closer. And when Robin came out of her room that morning, dressed in a short skirt and a sheer blue blouse the color of her eyes, sporting a shy, dimpled smile, he was suddenly swinging the hammer with abandon, trying to remember when, if ever, he had been so captivated by a woman. And every time he looked at her—or caught her looking at him with the expression of confusion—or was it torture?—he felt an even bigger fool.

That evening, Robin arrived on his doorstep with a picnic dinner she had gotten from a very fine French restaurant. As Jake looked down at what was supposed to be lamb in a port wine glaze, he couldn't help wonder how much she had laid down for it. "Where did you get that?" he asked.

"Pierre's."

He knew that name belonged to a fancy French restaurant. "What did that set you back?" he asked, a little more sharply than he would have liked.

Robin frowned. "What difference does it make?"

Jake wished for a burger.

They spent a quiet evening, Jake at his drafting table, working on a design for class. Next to him, at the dining room table, Robin's fingers were fast and furious on the calculator as she reviewed some numbers from work. She was restless, muttering under her breath and bouncing up a lot. She would stalk about the dining room, brushing past him, her hand trailing down his back, or through his hair. Jake liked this—it felt comfortable, as if they had been doing this all their lives.

He had completed a major portion of his design when Robin's arms suddenly shot up in the air. "*Yes!*" she exclaimed, and smiled at him, eyes sparkling. "I got an e-mail from Girt. She said they just picked up a big seafood account that's going to pay for some box-pressing machines. Styrofoam boxes, here we come!"

"I remember when the word *Styrofoam* made you gag."

"Not anymore, not since I figured out how profitable the chunky white stuff is. Come on, ask me anything. I can tell you whatever you want to know about thickness, consistency, and how to color it. Styrofoam need not be only white, you know."

"First bubble wrap, now Styrofoam," he said, shaking his head. "Your talents are amazing. What's next, shrink-wrap? How will anyone compete?"

"That's precisely the point, Hammerhead. Did you think Queen of Bubble Wrap was just some silly title I had given myself? Oh no!" She laughed, leaned back in her chair, and stretched her arms high. "Girt said David's still got that bug thing he had when we were there a while ago. She's really worried."

A surprising shift in attitude about Girt, he couldn't help note. "Sounds like you guys are starting to be friends."

Robin looked surprised. "It does?"

"Well, yeah, when you start talking about her kid and what she's doing. What would you call it?"

Robin gave a little laugh; her eyes fell to her laptop. "I don't know…it's just that we've been talking on and off about her business, and these things sort of naturally pop up, I guess."

"That's how most friendships start."

Robin seemed to consider that for a moment, then firmly shook her head. "Girt and I have a lot in common, but not *that* much in common."

She said it as if it were out of the question, completely impractical, and it left Jake feeling cold.

And he wasn't the only one bothered by her remark—as Robin drove home that night (after being tempted to spend another night with Jake, but afraid of...*what?*), she thought about the evening, how natural it had felt, the two of them just being together. It seemed so *right*. So natural. So what was it she was afraid of?

Love?

No way. Love didn't scare her—she had loved before! No, she was afraid of getting tied down, of letting her heart do the talking instead of her head and ending up miserable because of a foolish mistake. And ending up with Jake would eventually prove to be a foolish mistake for them both, because the expectation he would have of her would far outstrip her ability to deliver. Wouldn't it? Yes. Yes, of course it would.

So why, then, was she so head over heels for Jake if he was so wrong for her? And he *was* wrong, no matter how much she liked him. All the warning signs were there—baggage (Cole, his family), instability (a fledgling business), bad choices (*Lindy*, whom Robin had accidentally heard on Jake's machine asking how he was doing, for Chrissakes), moneyphobia (turned white as a sheet when she suggested flying to Manhattan for the weekend). Oh yeah, he was all wrong, just like Girt was the wrong sort of friend for her, no matter how much she liked the old girl.

As Robin pulled into her drive, her head was beginning to ache, her stomach in knots. Every time she tried to think her stomach knotted up. It was too hard, too confusing, so she was just not going to do it. Nope, she was going to look on the Internet for flights to Acapulco, because she had the sudden and overwhelming urge to go somewhere.

And she might have just gone that moment, had the phone not been ringing when she came into the house.

Robin threw her bag aside and went diving for the phone. "Hello?" she asked breathlessly.

"Hi, honey."

"Mom! Where are you?"

"New York. We'll be here for another couple of weeks until your dad completes his treatment. Then I think we'll be heading out to the ranch."

Good; they'd be in Texas again, close to her. "How is he?" Robin asked.

"Cantankerous. Miserable. Testy. But I think the spiritual healing course we are doing is helping a lot."

Robin cringed; she could just imagine what Dad thought of that.

"I've been trying to call you for a couple of days and wish you a happy Easter. Have you been out of town again?"

"No. I was with a friend."

"What friend?"

What was that she heard, the wail of a locomotive headed right for her? "Just a guy," she said and immediately regretted the words.

"Anyone I know?" Nosey Parker pressed.

"No, Mom. It's just…no one you know."

Nosey said nothing, but Robin could practically hear the steam coming out of her ears. "Why the big secret?"

"Okay, exactly how old does a woman have to be before her mom stops giving her the third degree?"

"Oh, I don't know. One hundred and five?" Mom shot back.

Robin couldn't help herself; she laughed. "Oh man, I've got such a long way to go! Mom, it's really not that big of a deal. He's the guy I contracted to renovate my house. But he's a really nice guy! And we have a lot in common, so it's been kind of fun, that's all." Only a small lie. Really more of an understatement.

"What's wrong with him—is he an ax murderer?" Mom asked.

Robin snorted. "No!"

"Two heads?"

"Mom!" Robin cried, laughing.

"I'm just wondering why you sound so apologetic."

She *did* sound apologetic. Robin's smile faded; she sank into a chair next to the table and stared at the wall she had busted up. "I...I don't know," she answered truthfully.

"Well...I just wanted to check how you were doing, honey. I'll call you and let you know when we'll be at the ranch so you can come out and see your dad."

The mention of Dad rattled Robin. She unconsciously shook her head, tried to shake Jake from the forefront. "Does...does Dad want to see me?" she asked hesitantly.

"Of course he does, silly! He wants his girls around him, and I think after this round of treatment, he'll need to see you. It's been rough on him."

"Yes, of course. Just give me a couple of days notice, would you? Evan and I are in the middle of a couple of projects."

"Okay, sweetie. Give my best to Evan."

Yes, Evan. Safe, familiar Evan. Speaking of which, she needed to call him, and after hanging up with her mother, she dialed Dallas.

CHAPTER TWENTY-FOUR

The thing about Evan was, when he wasn't trying to get in her pants, he was actually a decent guy, and really very smart. They talked for a while that night about the account Girt had managed to snare, and ended the conversation with Evan promising to look into a couple of questions she had about Girt's new account. "I'll call you tomorrow," he said.

The next day, he called midmorning and walked Robin through the numbers she needed to complete her analysis. "Remember the calculation we used to look at Peerless? This should be pretty much the same thing, but you'll want to factor in the potential increase in revenue since she has that new account in hand."

"Right," Robin said.

"You're doing great, Robbie," Evan offered. "You're really starting to get the hang of this."

"Really?"

"Yes, really. Next time I'm down, we'll have to celebrate your success in acquisitions."

"Not just yet," she warned him. "I haven't actually acquired anything yet."

"But you will, I have no doubt. So it's a date—next time I'm down, we're going to celebrate the near close of this deal. All right? I'll be talking to you."

He hung up before she could really answer or at least ask him to call before he came down. With an unconscious shrug, she hung up the phone, then noticed a movement from the corner of her eye. It was Jake. "Evan," she said, waving absently at the phone. "You know, he is really very smart. I can see why Dad likes him so much—I've learned a lot from him."

"I'll just bet you have," Jake said and picked up a can of primer.

His tone surprised Robin; she paused in the gathering of her papers. "What's that supposed to mean?"

"It means he's more interested in landing you than some new plant."

"Jesus, how do you jump to such conclusions? You don't even know him!"

"I don't *have* to know him. I'm a man, he's a man, and I know exactly what he's after."

Robin frowned darkly. "That is so ridiculous. You don't know—"

"Apparently, neither do you," Jake said sharply. "Or maybe you do. Maybe you know more than I give you credit for," he said and continued up the stairs before Robin could tell him to keep his stupid opinions to himself.

A few days later, Lucy arrived with a thick file stashed under her arm.

"*Dude*," Zaney said as she sauntered inside. "Looking *gooood*!"

Lucy shot him a frown. "I'm not a *dude*, Zaney."

"I'll say!"

Lucy actually smiled a little at that before plopping the file down in front of Robin. "Evan said to bring you this."

"What is it?"

"Some stuff about Wirt. He said you should look into the age of the equipment."

"I already did that," she said and pulled the file closer, flipped it open. On the top was a chart showing the list of equipment in each shop, the approximate age, and the approximate cost of replacement.

Lucy took a chair across from her. "I am so ready to get out of that freight yard!" she exclaimed as she casually examined a nail. "You know Albert? He's about to get a swift kick in the balls if he doesn't keep his hands to himself. And it's so friggin' *hot* out there! They leave those bay doors open all the time, and it's like standing in an oven."

Robin scarcely heard her—the file Evan had sent over had several documents, covering both Peerless and Wirt. What she found a little puzzling about it was that it looked as if Evan had done much of the same work she had done, running through the same calculations. In short, duplicating everything she'd done. That he knew she was doing.

She was startled by the sound of a dropped hammer. Zaney had dropped it by Lucy's foot—well, kicked it, actually—and hurried over to retrieve it. He bent over, grabbed the hammer, then smiled up at Lucy. "Girl, you're a hottie, you know it?"

"Yes. I know," she sighed, barely sparing him a glance.

"You must be like, you know, a speeding ticket or something, 'cuz you got *fine* written all over you."

"Oh my *God*, is that the best you can do?" Lucy asked, smiling at her nail, her foot swinging carelessly.

"Well…" He paused to think about it, then nodded slowly. "Yeah. Yeah, that's about it."

Why would Evan have gone to the trouble to duplicate her work? Robin wondered. She had told him what she was doing at each step, had discussed it with him. She would have thought nothing of it, but this was several documents, several different cuts at the same problem, just as she had done.

"So anyway, I'm going back to the yard," Lucy announced, nudging the file Robin was poring over. "Evan's around today and tomorrow, and he said to tell you he'd probably stop by. Okay, call me!" she said and popped up out of her chair, strutting past Zaney with a very self-satisfied smile as he gave her his best wolf whistle, which really sounded more like a wheeze.

Robin put Evan's file aside, returned to the work she was doing on Wirt, but she couldn't concentrate. The more she thought of the papers in that file, the more it bothered her. Did he not trust her? What about all the encouragement he was giving her? Just lip service? It sort of felt that way, and Robin was trying very hard to give him the benefit of the doubt. She really had no reason to distrust him… did she?

Even if she had wanted to think about it, she couldn't when Grandma and Grandpa showed up. Grandma had made sandwiches for the work crews—"My famous egg salad," she announced proudly—and Grandpa had on his overalls. "Jake and me are gonna take down the last part of that wall," he informed her as he went shuffling by.

Grandpa and Jake did indeed try and take down a wall, making such a racket that Robin could hardly hear herself think. She finally gave up and joined Grandma on the terrace, where they sipped iced tea and watched Raymond cut the lawn by making lazy circles with his riding mower.

They discussed Dad and his last round of chemo for a while. But during a lull in the conversation, Grandma casually said, "That Jake's a nice boy, isn't he?"

Robin stole a look at her from the corner of her eye; Grandma adjusted her cola-bottle glasses. "He's all right," she said slowly.

"I think he's a *dish*. When I was a girl, he was exactly the kind of man we all dreamed about. Handsome, strong— clever enough to work with his hands and know how to build or fix things—and smart, too. I guess I should consider myself lucky that your grandpa had at least two of the three," she said, sighing.

Robin didn't dare ask which two.

"I stopped at the grocery store this morning to get some peas for my pea salad. You know that pea salad I make? With the eggs and celery? Elmer *loves* that pea salad and he's been after me to make it again. I swear, he could eat his weight in it. Anyway, the last time I made pea salad was the day before your office burned down, and it got me to thinking how far you've come since your...you know, getting arrested and all that—"

Robin groaned—her grandmother could not come to her house without mentioning that singularly spectacular event.

"—and I was saying to Elmer that it seems to me you are much happier than we've seen you in some time."

"What? Happier?"

"Um-hm. Without all the stress of that terrible job and a nice young man to keep you occupied—"

"Grandma, I am not seeing Evan."

"Well, I wasn't talking about him," she said slyly. "I was talking about Jake."

"Jake," Robin repeated.

"Oh, for Pete's sake," Grandma said with an impatient wave of her hand. "Your grandpa saw you holding hands, didn't he?"

"No, not exactly, he—"

"Well, it doesn't take a brain surgeon to figure it out. I can tell just by the way you look at him."

Robin was about to put an end to this budding rumor, but paused. "Wait—how do I look at him?"

Grandma laughed. "Oh, Robbie, you know...like you're in love, honey!"

That stung like salt in a raw wound. "I am not in love, Grandma, and don't you dare get on your hotline and start spreading *that* around town!"

"You can't fool me," she continued cheerfully, clearly enjoying herself. "Why on earth you would be ashamed of it is beyond me. He's such a nice-looking man."

"I mean it, Grandma—don't say that!"

"Touchy, *touchy*," Grandma said, and put her tea glass down. "All right, I'm not going to say anything. It's your business. Mum's the word." She made the motion of locking her lips and throwing away the key.

Robin's eyes narrowed. Grandma lifted her chin. "By any chance, did you mention something to Mom?" Robin asked, her suspicions shooting right up to high alert.

Grandma looked off in the other direction. "Raymond certainly does good work, doesn't he?"

"Oh, *great*," Robin groused and downed her tea.

Late that afternoon, after El had smashed his thumb with a hammer, Jake finally sent the crews home. They were almost finished with the upper floor and half of the bottom. There was some cleanup work that needed to be done—finishing out the archway they had just busted out, for one—but all that was really left was to move Robin's increasingly large spread of office upstairs so they could complete the dining room. As he walked through the upper floors to check one last time, he paused at the bay window of the master suite to look at the little inscription carved into the wood trim.

It fascinated him, because he understood for the first time in his life what would possess a man to do that.

Speaking of which, he called Robin up, watched her bounce up the stairs, took her hand in his, and led her through the various rooms, showing her what they had done.

"It's so beautiful!" she exclaimed in every room. "I can't believe this is the same house!" But when he walked her into the master suite, she caught her breath, twirled slowly around to take in the new wood floors, the ten-foot ceilings and new crown molding, the refurbished fireplace, the restored brick. And the large master bath had been remodeled into a den of luxury.

"It's *gorgeous.*" She turned around to face him, her eyes sparkling with delight. "It's all gorgeous, Jake." She slipped her arms around his waist and hugged him tightly. Jake could feel himself crumbling into that lovesick boy again.

They wandered through the rest of the second floor, then made their way downstairs, Jake explaining that when they finished the kitchen, they would be close to done with the work. And then Jake convinced Robin they needed to make a trip to Paulie's for a burger or he might very well expire. He promised to be back within the hour to pick her up.

Showered, shaved, and dressed in jeans and T-shirt, he was back by seven, pulling into her drive on his bike.

He let himself in and wandered to her bedroom. Robin wasn't ready, so he lay down on her bed and admired the very feminine motions of putting on makeup and combing her hair as she regaled him with the tale of Zaney's flirtation with Lucy. "He actually kicked a *hammer* at her," she said. They were still laughing about it when they emerged from her bedroom at a quarter past seven, strolling arm in arm down the long corridor.

Robin was the first to hear the knocking, and as she quickened her pace to answer the door, it swung open, and in walked Slick, dressed in strange, baggy striped pants, a white shirt open at the collar, and leather loafers without socks. Behind him was a man dressed in similar fashion, and Robin's friend Mia, who was wearing a little more than a pillowcase with straps.

"Evan?" Robin asked, walking into the entry. "What are you doing here?"

It was a miracle Cool Breeze even heard her—he was too busy staring a white-hot hole through Jake.

"I'm sorry, Rob," Mia said. "We let ourselves in since you didn't answer the door. You didn't forget, did you?"

"Forget what?"

"Oh God, Robin," Mia said impatiently. "I told you like five thousand times. We're going out on the boat."

"Well, you mentioned it, but I really don't remember you saying when—"

Mr. GQ cut her off with a condescending laugh. "Robbie, it's not a big deal. Sorry if we got our wires crossed. Mia and Michael and I are going out to the boat. I thought you were coming along. You and I were going to celebrate your success, weren't we?"

Robin's back stiffened. She pressed her lips together, looked at Jake, then at her three friends standing there like they were posing for some magazine ad.

Not one of them had deigned to acknowledge Jake.

Robin looked at Jake again, then her eyes narrowed as she swung her gaze back to Slick. "Sure. Jake and I will come along," she said, surprising the hell out of him.

"Robin—" he started, but she was quick to interrupt his protest.

"No, really, Jake. It will be fun! Evan has a big boat he likes to show off. By the way, have you met my dear friends Michael and Mia?"

At least Michael had the decency to come striding forward, hand extended. "Good to meet you, Jake...?"

"Manning."

"Manning." Michael pumped his arm. "Don't recall meeting your people."

That was probably because he didn't have any *people*.

"This is my fiancée, Mia—well, this week, anyway." Mia was so busy staring daggers at Michael that she couldn't be bothered to get up from the dining room chair she had melted into, and lifted a lazy finger in greeting.

"And you know Evan," Robin said.

Evan strolled forward, looking at Jake quizzically. "I'm sorry—I'm drawing a blank," he said, but the sardonic smile on his face told Jake he wasn't drawing a blank at all. "What did you say your name was?"

The bastard knew exactly who Jake was. "I'm the guy renovating Robin's house, remember?"

"Oh yeah. Yeah, that's right. The handyman," Evan said.

Indignation surged through Jake, but he clamped his jaw shut to keep from saying something he knew he would really, really regret.

Robin stepped between him and Evan to get her purse. "If we're going to go, let's go."

Mia and Michael were already out the door, an argument apparently underway. That was followed by a brief, polite little argument between Robin and Evan over which vehicle they would take. Robin marched to her Mercedes, jerked the door open, threw her purse in the back, and got behind the wheel. Evan slipped into the front passenger seat without even looking at Jake.

Against his better judgment—and in fact, ignoring a voice that told him to get the hell out of there while he could—Jake got in the back and tried to arrange himself where his knees didn't gouge his eyes. He finally gave in and sat crooked in the seat, feeling one step removed from moron.

The boat, as it turned out, was a yacht.

At first, Jake thought Evan's boat was one of those small commercial outfits they used for dinner cruises, but as Evan went striding up the gangplank, he realized that he had, once again, severely miscalculated the orbit of Robin's planet. As Mia went slinking up the gangplank after Evan on Michael's arm—their argument, apparently, put aside for the moment—Jake grabbed Robin's wrist. "What are we doing?" he asked quietly, so as not to be overheard by the others.

"Oh! Evan—he likes to have these dinners catered on his boat."

"Robin, this isn't a boat, it's a *yacht*."

"Boat, yacht, whatever."

"I thought we were going to go get a burger. Something really simple, something easy. I didn't anticipate sailing to Mexico."

"We're not sailing to Mexico," she said patiently. "We won't even leave the dock, which is really what's so absurd about it. He buys a boat with his bonus and doesn't even know how to operate it. Look, I know we were going for burgers, but Evan was really irritating me, and I said okay without thinking," she said, glancing up the gangplank. "I'm sorry, I shouldn't have done it. We'll just eat and go, okay?"

"I don't know why you want to have dinner with some-one who is irritating you," Jake said, a little irritably himself. "I damn sure don't want to dine with these people."

"Come on, it's not such a big deal. We'll just grab a bite to eat and get out of here, okay?" she asked and came up on her tiptoes, kissed the corner of his mouth. Jake frowned down at her; she lifted her hand in Boy Scouts' honor fashion. "Promise. One hour, no more."

Slick was waiting for them by the time they made their way up the little gangplank, a martini in his hand. Robin walked past him, into the main cabin, but Slick caught Jake with a clamp of his hand on Jake's shoulder. "You ever been on a yacht before, Jack?"

"It's Jake. And no, I haven't."

"Well, then this ought to be quite an experience for you," he said, and patted Jake's shoulder before preceding him into the main cabin.

Robin met him at the door, handed him a beer. He gratefully accepted it, but noticed that he was the only one with a beer bottle. Michael and Mia looked to be drinking martinis, presumably made by the guy standing behind the bar in a white shirt and black bow tie. Robin had a glass of wine in her hand.

Slick sat down on a bar stool, sipped his martini. "Come on in, Jake. Don't be shy."

Oh yeah, he was really beginning to dislike ol' Slick, a lot. And really, what self-respecting guy wore pants like that? Jake walked into the room, casually sipped his beer, and tried to take it all in without gawking like some low-rent tourist. The cabin was a huge room, lined with benches covered in thick cushions, the walls in mahogany and brass fixtures. In the center of the room was a rectangular table, covered with a tablecloth, sporting two vases of fresh-cut roses and a six-point candelabra. The table was set with gold-rimmed china, crystal wine goblets, heavy silverware. Each place setting—only four of them, thank you very much—had three plates, five forks, two knives and three spoons. It was enough to intimidate the most cultivated of souls.

Mia sat on one of the cushioned benches and sighed so heavily it was a wonder the yacht wasn't pushed away from the dock. "I'm sick of this heat already," she announced with all due petulance.

"It's only May," Michael chided her. "Are you going to start whining already? Just let me know so I can prepare myself for a long summer."

"Shut *up*, Michael."

Nice, Jake thought. A lot of respect flowing between those two.

"Oh Mia, I meant to tell you," Robin quickly interjected. "Lucy was down on Gray Street the other day, and she said Lily's is having a huge sale. I *love* that store!"

"Me, too," Mia said, perking up. "But what was Lucy doing there?" she asked and Jake thought the tone of her voice was a bit derisive—assuming, of course, he was accurately distinguishing this tone from her whine.

"Just shopping."

Mia snorted. "You must pay her pretty well. You know, I really don't like her very much."

"Lucy's okay," Slick said halfheartedly.

Mia shrugged; Robin frowned at her friend. "What's not to like about Lucy?"

"I don't know," Mia said on a sigh. "She's just...sort of *pedestrian*, you know what I mean?"

"Pedestrian? God, Mia, that sounds so elitist."

"I don't mean it to sound elitist, but you have to admit that there are differences."

"Do you mean in income?" Robin asked, clearly agitated. "Is that why you don't like her? Because she doesn't have as much money as you?"

"No, of course not," Mia responded with an irritable shake of her head. "I am talking more about how people like you and I have a different perspective of the world than people like her. I mean, we've traveled, we've been to lots of different places to shop or eat, or whatever...I just don't see how it can't create a difference."

"I know what she means," Michael said, nodding. "It's like, if you vacation in Paris and Lucy has never been to Paris, then it's sort of hard to relate."

"So if Lucy vacations in Mexico, is it hard for me to relate?" Robin countered.

"No, because you have traveled extensively. You have the ability to imagine."

"And Lucy doesn't? God, that is so arrogant!"

Those were Jake's thoughts exactly. If he hadn't heard the whole thing himself, he wouldn't have believed it.

"Whatever," Mia said petulantly. "And it's really not even that. I just don't much care for her."

"Maybe I should fire her," Robin shot back.

Mia laughed. "Would you?"

Robin turned away again to stare out the cabin windows at the harbor water.

"What do you think, Jake?" Slick asked.

Jake looked up, fixed him with a piercing glare. "Think about what?"

"Whether or not there are differences between people who have been accustomed to a life of privilege and those who have not."

"Don't, Evan," Robin said low.

But Jake didn't need or want Robin to stand up for him. "You want to know what I think? I think this conversation is ludicrous," he drawled, gaining everyone's attention. "If you want to believe yourself better than someone else because of a lot of travel or shopping, that's your deal. I prefer to choose my friends based on their character, not their income."

Slick's laugh rang false. He put down the martini glass, pushed it to the bartender for a refill without even looking at him. "That's awfully noble of you, making all your friends based on their character." He looked pointedly at Robin.

"When is dinner, Evan?" Robin sighed. "Jake and I need to get back soon."

"We can start whenever you are ready, princess."

The term of endearment cut through Jake like a knife, conjuring up unwanted images of Robin and Evan together.

"I'm ready if everyone else is," she said and walked to where Jake was standing, slipped her hand into his, and gave him a little tug so that he would join her at the table. Jake had the presence of mind to hold the chair out for her, but he was, again, the only one. Mia flopped down like a fish onto her chair. Michael sat as far away from her as he could get.

Slick turned to the bartender. "Let Drake know that we have one more guest than we thought," he announced loudly. "We'll need another place setting if he can dig one up."

Bastard. Jake took the seat next to Robin, the one with no place setting, and banged his beer down on the table. That earned him nothing but an amused smile from Slick as another man in white shirt and black bow tie came scurrying out of a door on the far end of the room, carrying a stack of plates, linens, and silver. He quickly and artfully set the place in front of Jake.

As he hurried out again, Robin looked at Slick. "By the way, thanks for sending the files over," she said.

"Ah…did they help?"

"Sort of. But I noticed you had done a lot of the same work I had done."

"Yes." He lifted his martini glass and sipped delicately.

"I was wondering why."

"Why? Well, I suppose because I have done that sort of thing before and you haven't."

"Yes, but you told me how to do it and I have been sending you all my analysis. It just seemed like a lot of work for you to duplicate," she said as a man and woman appeared, each carrying a tray laden with silver-domed dishes.

"Don't worry, Robbie. We're using your figures," he said dismissively and smiled an oily little smile. "I hope you have an appetite, Jake."

Could the guy be any more condescending? Jake was irritated for Robin, but whatever she thought, he couldn't tell. She just dropped it altogether as the woman leaned over her shoulder and asked, "Haut-Médoc? Or Margaux?"

Robin looked at the two wine bottles she held. "What is the vintage of the Margaux?"

"La tou de Mons, 1991."

"Thank you, I'll have that," Robin said. The waitress poured the wine then looked at Jake.

He might be a novice at this, but he was no fool. "The same."

"Are you a wine connoisseur, Jake? I thought you were a beer drinker," Slick remarked.

"I *am* a beer drinker," Jake said flatly.

"I can't drink beer," Mia said, and Jake figured that she couldn't do much of anything without whining about it.

The man paused on Jake's left, leaned over with a tray, and with his middle finger, pointed to one of two dishes. "Grilled shrimp with celery roots and remoulade, or asparagus and crab veloute soup?" he asked.

"Shrimp," Jake said gruffly, only to be dismayed that there were only four on the plate.

"And for your salad, sir, a brie and goat cheese empanada with champagne vinaigrette, or vine ripe tomatoes and mozzarella in basalmic vinaigrette?"

God, what he wouldn't give for a hamburger! "Tomatoes and cheese."

"And lastly, sir, for you entree: baked Atlantic salmon and lump crab in a bernaise sauce, tenderloin of beef with polenta and a port wine reduction, or lobster tail with beurre blanc?"

He figured the beef was as close to a hamburger as he was going to get in this crowd. "The beef."

"Really, Jake, you can get beef anywhere," Slick chimed in. "Why not try the lobster?"

Jake pinned him with a cold stare. "I'll take the beef, thank you."

Slick shrugged, turned back to his soup. "Suit yourself."

Yes, Jake thought, he would do just that, and spent the rest of the meal concentrating on using the right implement as the conversation turned to some little jaunt the four of them had taken to Vancouver one weekend. No doubt in the Lear jet, he thought miserably, wondering at the cost of that little excursion. He refused to let his imagination wander any further than that.

When dinner was served, Jake was too perturbed by the tiny little piece of beef to be interested in what they were saying, which had something to do with a mutual fund Slick thought was hot, and drifted in and out. He declined the port that was served with dessert, even though the Slickster insisted it was vintage, which he seemed to think should make a difference. Jake asked for another beer just to piss him off.

When the meal was (thankfully) over, and Robin excused herself and headed for the powder room, Jake got up and went outside for some air. It wasn't long before Slick joined him, with his hands shoved deep in his fag pants, staring up at the moon. "Beautiful out here on the water, isn't it?"

"Yeah," Jake drawled. "So do you actually take this thing out, or do you just dine on it?"

Slick glanced at him from the corner of his eye. "I take it out."

"Huh."

"So…you've been seeing Robin, is that it?" Clownpants asked, like Jake was going to subject himself to any questions on that front. And then he chuckled snidely at Jake's silence. "Let me give you a piece of advice, Jake. Robbie goes through men like water. I wouldn't get too comfortable if I were you."

Bastard. Asshole. "Do me a favor and keep your advice to yourself."

"Yeah, sure, I'll do that. But I guess you know her old man has cancer."

It was more of a statement than a question, and Jake responded nonchalantly, "So I've heard."

The asshole turned so that he was facing Jake. "Of *course* you've heard. That's why you're hanging around, isn't it?"

That implication caught Jake completely off guard. He slowly squared off in front of Slick, straightening to his full height, a good three inches taller than Weasel. "You're Robin's colleague, so I am going to give you the benefit of the doubt and pretend you aren't implying what I think you are implying," he said evenly.

Slick shrugged, looked out at the water for a minute. "I don't know if I am *implying* anything. But I *am* making an observation that it seems awfully coincidental to me that some handyman managed to get in Robin's pants about the time she found out her dad was dying. She'll probably inherit a huge fortune, won't she?"

Jake's reaction was pure instinct; he took a step forward, clenching his fists to keep from hitting the fool, backing him up against the rail.

"What's the matter? Truth hurt a little?" Slick asked and braced himself for the blow that was sure to come.

CHAPTER TWENTY-FIVE

Robin thought the evening already sucked, but this took the cake. She stepped in front of Jake before he could do something awful, like punch Evan, which is exactly what he appeared about to do. "What are you doing?" she cried, pushing hard against his chest.

"Oh good, a fight," Mia drawled behind her. "What did we miss?"

Must have been something good—Robin had never seen such fire as she saw in Jake's eyes, blazing down at her that very moment. His jaw was clenched as tight as his fist. "Let's get out of here," he said sharply and promptly turned on his heel, striding for the little gangplank.

"Yes, let's," Robin said, bewildered, but turned around to Evan, who straightened his shirt as he watched Jake stride away. "Are you all right?" she asked.

"Oh yeah, I'm fine," Evan said. "But I'm worried about you. The man has a temper."

"What happened?"

"*Robin!*" Jake bellowed from the yacht's gangplank.

Evan ignored him, smiled down at Robin. "A little too much testosterone, that's all. Do you want a ride? Let us give you a ride home. You don't need to go with him."

"No," she said instantly and stepped back. She did not fear Jake and never would. He would never touch so much as a hair on her head.

"I don't know, Rob," Mia said, glancing over her shoulder at Jake. "He seems sort of rough."

Which was precisely what made him so sexy. "I'll be fine!" she said angrily and turned away from her friends, walking to where Jake was impatiently waiting.

"I want off this tin bucket," he said low, and grabbed her hand, pulled her along, down the gangplank. But once they were on terra firma again, Robin yanked her hand from his grip.

His head jerked around; his brown eyes, still blazing, burned a hole right through her.

"What in the hell happened back there?" she demanded.

"Give me the keys."

"No—"

"Give me the fucking keys, Robin."

His voice was so low and cool that it left her speechless. After a moment's hesitation, she handed him the keys. He walked around the passenger side of the car, opened the door for her, motioned for her to hurry along. Once she was inside, he got in behind the wheel, and with his jaw clenched tight, revved the engine. They backed out on a squeal of rubber and exited the parking lot in much the same way.

They rocketed out onto the Gulf highway. Jake stared straight ahead. His expression sent a bit of a chill down Robin's spine, but she was too angry to let it go. "What in God's name were you doing? You almost *hit* him!" she demanded, folding her arms defensively across her middle.

"He's an asshole."

"He's not an asshole!"

"*Don't,*" Jake said, sparing her a very icy glance. "Don't defend him."

"Should I be defending *you?*"

"Just thank your lucky stars you stepped in when you did or I might have killed him."

"What did he say or do that was so horrible?"

Jake said nothing, just clenched his jaw tighter.

"Jesus, Jake, I want to understand, but right now, all my friends think you are some kind of fiend—"

"Your *friends,* as you call them, treated me like dirt all night."

"No, you don't understand—"

"That boy of yours was trying to bait me, Robin."

She couldn't deny that; it was obvious to her that Evan was jealous of Jake. "You have to understand, he's got an ego."

"And I don't?" Jake all but shouted. "He's an arrogant prick and a fucking coward!"

"Well, at least he's not a bully, forcing people to his way of thinking with the threat of his fist," she snapped. "What did he say, anyway?"

"You want to know? You want to know what that prick implied? That I was seeing you because your father was dying."

Robin gasped.

Jake careened around a corner, then punched it.

Clearly, he had misunderstood, Robin thought. Yes, of course he had misunderstood. There was no way Evan would have said such a thing. She knew him. "Is it possible you misunderstood—"

"I didn't misunderstand a damn thing."

"Well, even if he did, which he didn't, does that give you the right to *hit* him?"

"It damn near gives me the right to kill him. I won't stand for any man disrespecting me."

Oh great, it *was* a testosterone thing—Robin groaned with exasperation. "Could you try and give him the benefit of the doubt?"

"*Why?*" he roared. "Why do you insist on defending him?"

"Because he is my friend! They're all my friends!" she shouted back at him.

A red light flashed before them and Jake slammed his hand into the steering wheel at the same moment he slammed his foot into the brakes. They went screeching up the intersection, bouncing back with the force of the stop. Robin braced herself against the dash and slowly turned to look at him. "Calm down."

Jake laughed, shook his head. "I'm calm, baby. I'm real calm. I'm too numb to be anything else, because for the life of me, I can't figure out why someone as special as you would have friends as shallow as that."

That silenced her. Not because she felt indignant, but because she didn't know why.

When they got to her house—at a reasonable speed—Jake didn't say much other than good night, tossed her the keys, and walked purposefully to his motorcycle, taking off without even a glance backward.

Robin watched him disappear before wandering inside. She dropped her things on the dining table, made her way to the back terrace. There was a soft breeze blowing across the lawn, making the herd of pink flamingos bounce a little. She lowered herself into a lounge chair, pondering the evening.

Jake was right. Evan had been horrible, the jealousy practically oozing from him. And Mia, well, Mia had been a snob as long as Robin could remember. At the same time, while she could see Evan and Mia's faults as Jake saw them, she could also understand them. She could understand how they viewed the world because it was the same way she had viewed the world up until a few short months ago, and now...well, now, she was seeing things a little differently. She was seeing the world through Jake's eyes.

And she was beginning to really despise what she saw.

Which is why she changed into cutoffs and a T-shirt and drove to the Heights. When she pulled up into Jake's drive, she could see the flicker of a light deep in the back of the house. She tiptoed up the steps, rang the doorbell. After a moment, she could hear movement. A second later, the porch light flicked on, blinding her as the door swung open.

Bare-chested, barefoot, and wearing jeans that rode low on his hips, Jake stepped up to the door frame and leaned against it, one arm draped across his hard belly, the other loosely holding a beer bottle, the barbed wire tattoo around his bicep stark against his skin.

"Hi," she said.

"Hi."

"Can I come in?"

Jake inhaled deeply and released it slowly as he stood behind the screen, taking her in. "Don't know if I should," he said at last. "I think maybe I should send you back to your little group so you can sit around and laugh at the rest of the world with them."

Ouch. "Come on, Jake, you know I'm not like that—"

"Oh yeah? Does Burdette ring any bells?"

Ouch again. "Okay, that's fair. But I've changed—and before you list all my faults, let me please say I am sorry. I shouldn't have put you in that situation."

"Why? Because I don't belong with your rich and snooty pals?"

"No, because Evan was an ass," she said.

"Is," he said, his voice softer.

"Is." Robin sighed. "Come on, Jake. Let me in, please?"

He shoved a hand through his hair and released another long sigh. "I don't know, Robin. I'm not sure about things anymore."

That sent a shot of panic right up her spine. "You should let me in," she said, nervously tracing a line across the screen door, "because I owe you an apology for not seeing your side of it."

He nodded thoughtfully, took a swig of his beer, then pushed the screen door open a crack. "I think you really don't see how they are."

"You may have a point."

Jake pushed the screen door a little wider. "And maybe I'm a little biased—I haven't liked Clownpants from the get-go."

Robin couldn't help herself; she smiled. "Those were the *worst* pants I have ever seen."

Jake smiled a little. "Now we're getting somewhere."

Robin grabbed the screen door and pulled it wider still. "Prepare yourself, Handy Andy, because when I make an apology, there is no mercy."

And it was fabulous make-up sex, if Robin did say so herself. She made sure he understood just how sorry she was. Early the next morning, before the sun had completely risen, she felt his hardness pressed against her hip, and rolled over, into his arms. They made soft, lazy love as the sun rose to cast a shaft of light across the floor of Jake's bedroom, and then lay sated and drowsy in one another's arms, drifting in and out of sleep.

Jake was the first to rise, quietly disentangling himself from Robin's arms and kissing the top of her head. She opened her eyes long enough to see him stretch his arms high above his head and display his magnificent backside to her. He continued on to the shower and she rolled over, the sound of running water on the fringes of her consciousness.

He awakened her with a kiss to the cheek; he smelled of soap, had a towel wrapped around his lean waist. "I gotta get going," he murmured.

"Me, too," she said, sleepily, and yawned. "I have to go to Burdette today."

Jake stopped, turned to look at her. "To Burdette? Why? You were just there."

"We're going back to talk to Girt about a couple of things."

"*We?*" Jake groaned, and glared at the ceiling for a moment. "Why is he going? I thought you pretty much had this under control."

"Yes, but he's got more insight into this than I do and says there are some questions we need answers to before we can go further."

"So why doesn't he just tell you what they are and let you deal with it?"

This was beginning to feel very uncomfortable. Robin hugged the pillow tightly to her. "I guess because I'm still learning."

With a snort, Jake shook his head and proceeded into the bathroom. "Like hell. He's going to Burdette to make a play for you."

Oh Jesus, not again. "No, he's not!" she yelled after him. "God, Jake, I know he was an ass last night, but there is *nothing* between me and Evan! He knows it, I know it—it's been over, like, forever!"

Jake grumbled something in response that she couldn't quite make out. Robin got up, pulled on her cutoffs and T-shirt, and ran her hands through her hair. She was slipping on her sandals when Jake reappeared, his face lathered up for a shave.

"I gotta go," she said.

"I'm serious, Robin. I know how guys think, and this guy wants you back. He's not flying to Burdette with you because you need any help. He's flying to Burdette to win you back."

"Oh my God," she muttered. Jake's jealousy was a little much to take before coffee, and Robin snatched up her purse. "I don't know how to convince you," she said, rooting around in her purse for her keys, "You won't listen! You're so determined to be jealous of Evan—"

"*Jealous?*"

He said it like it was the most preposterous thing he had ever heard. Robin looked up, incredulous. "Yes, jealous! You don't like him, you think everything he says or does is some dig at you, and you keep reading a whole lot more into him than what is there. Jake, Evan and I *work* together. And we made a deal a long time ago that it was nothing more than that. Your insecurity keeps bubbling up and it's not necessary."

Jake gaped at her in obvious disbelief.

Robin rolled her eyes. "I'll see you later, okay?"

"Wait!" Jake said and came striding out of the bathroom. "Let's just back it up and assume I don't have this...this insecurity, and pretend for a moment that what I am saying is plausible. What if he wanted you back? How would he go about it? He'd take you to fancy restaurants, buy you gifts, send you flowers, and make sure he got every opportunity there was to be with you. And if he knew you were going out with me, someone he puts on a par with a slimy bottom feeder, he'd do everything to make you see he was the better deal. And he *is* the better deal, Robin, we both know that. He's got the means to support you—"

"Oh, for the love of God, this is not about *money*!"

"I hope not," Jake said. "Because if it is, I'm sunk. All I'm saying is that he knows the kind of luxury you are used to, the way you live. He knows how to play it to his advantage."

Jake was confusing her. She needed a cup of coffee, and slung her purse over her shoulder. "You're forgetting one thing. I don't need Evan to spend money on me. I obviously have plenty of my own. Honestly, I don't need anyone."

Jake sighed, rubbed the back of his neck. "That's sad, Robin. And not very reassuring."

Exasperated, Robin shook her head, strode toward him. "Can we talk about this later? I have to get some coffee." She pecked him on the mouth. "I'll see you later."

She left before he could say much of anything, hurtling down Montrose and right past Java the Hut without even noticing. Her mind was too full wondering what, exactly, she did need.

Jake was wondering, too, and by the time he got to work, he was beginning to think he had seriously overestimated what was between him and Robin. She didn't see what he saw so clearly, would not admit Slickpants' motives, and when it came right down to it, he was struggling to compete with the lavish attention that man gave Robin. He'd been ready to take her to Paulie's for a burger—not for lobster on some yacht.

Worse, the last thing she had said kept clanging in his head like some church bell. *I don't need anyone.* There it was, the big chasm between them. He needed her. He had told her so, had told her he loved her. But Robin had not once said she loved him. Which only made him realize that what he feared most of all—now that his heart was so tangled up in all this mess—was that she would, eventually, be lured away by the better deal. And when it happened (he figured it was inevitable), it was going to kill him, he could feel it. Just kill him.

Inside, Robin was nowhere to be seen. Zaney was busy finishing up the archway they had created upstairs, singing an old Monkees' tune. The paint crew was finishing up the last touches upstairs, and an electrician and plumber were working in the kitchen while the trim on the new cabinetry was installed. Jake started to strip the paint from the brick in the dining room, the last room to be renovated.

He had just gotten the veneer off the window casings when his cell phone rang.

"Jacob?" his mom wheezed into the phone.

"Hey, Mom. How are you doing?"

"Not too good. Your nephew has run off again."

Jake stopped what he was doing. "He's not in school?"

"Nope. Only reason I know that is because Billie Margoyle—her son Bill played baseball with you, remember him? Well, Billie's in that front office in the school now, and I asked her to call me if Cole was reported absent. He was reported absent, all right."

Jake immediately thought of the levee. God, he was going to strangle that kid. "I'll go find him," he said.

"You don't need to. The cops have him down at juvenile hall."

Jake groaned, closed his eyes, swallowing down the bit of terror that crept up.

"He and Frankie went down to the levee and got caught smoking a marijuana cigarette," Mom said, the disgust evident in her voice. "I'd sure like to know where those kids find that crap. Good Lord, what did I ever do to deserve this?"

"Mom, it's okay. I'll go down there and get him out."

"Don't try and tell me it's okay, Jacob. This is serious. I'm not going to have a pot-smoking juvenile delinquent dropout in my house."

"Okay, Mom," he said, his patience wearing thin. "We'll talk about that later. I'll handle it for now."

"I just hope you can. I hope it's not too late."

So did he.

Jake found Zaney, told him he'd be back after a while, and looked once more for Robin. Still nowhere to be found. Apparently, she'd already left for Burdette. Before he could say anything.

The Weasel was winning.

The juvenile facility was a zoo—parents, lawyers, and kind-hearted souls who apparently tried to work with troubled kids milled about, but no one seemed to know what was going on. Jake finally found a woman who, when he got her attention long enough to ask about Cole, pointed toward a courtroom. "Detention hearings are over there."

Detention hearing. He didn't like the sound of that.

Jake squeezed into the overcrowded courtroom, then watched as a string of children—babies, really—were brought before a judge. Some had stolen cars, others had been caught with drugs. But what astounded him was how many were brought in for more serious crimes, such as sexual assault and armed robbery. They were children, Cole's age, with no more sense or sophistication than a goat. For two hours, Jake sat watching the parade, growing increasingly frustrated and appalled. When he thought he couldn't stand it another moment, they brought Cole in.

The kid looked like hell, completely disheveled, his face white. He stood between two men in ill-fitting, cheap suits, nodding mutely as the judge asked him if he understood why he was there. Then the judge asked if there was anyone in the courtroom on behalf of Cole Manning.

Jake stood. "I am."

He peered over the top of his reading glasses. "Please come forward."

When Jake reached the table where Cole was sitting, the child would not even look at him. He looked beaten down. Frightened.

"Are you his father?"

"I'm his uncle, Jacob Manning. Cole's father is dead."

"Does he live with you?"

"He lives with my mother, his grandmother."

"Ah," the judge muttered, nodding, and looked down at the papers in front of him. "And where is the boy's mother?"

"Uh...no one knows, Your Honor," Jake said, despising how soap-operaish it sounded. "She took off a couple of years ago and we haven't heard from her since."

"How nice," the judge drawled and looked at the papers again, then at Jake. "Mr. Manning, this is Cole's first trip to juvenile court. He has been charged with minor in possession of marijuana. That's a serious offense. Nonetheless, I am inclined to hand him over to your care if I can be assured that you will pay close attention to this child's needs. He is in desperate need of adult supervision and guidance. Do you think you and your mother can provide that?"

Jake did not like being lectured like a delinquent father, and had to bite down hard to keep from arguing that Cole had plenty of adult supervision, that his problems had more to do with his search to find himself in this world than lack of supervision. "Yes, sir," he said tightly.

The judge had a lecture for Cole, too, telling him he would attend group counseling sessions once a week as well as drug counseling sessions until a date was set in juvenile court to dispose of the case against him. "I'm warning you, son, if you don't do exactly as I tell you, you are most certainly not going to like what we have in store for you. Mr. Perez, will you please set this young man up in the counseling classes I have ordered?" he asked, then looked at Jake. "Thank you for coming down, Mr. Manning," he said, dismissing him.

Jake waited another two hours for Cole to be processed out, angry that he had lost almost a day's worth of work, angrier that Cole had gotten himself into this mess. It was so damned frustrating—he wanted to take him and shake him until he heard some sense rattling around in there. He

370

wished there was some magical projector that could make Cole look at his future if he kept on this path. Lord, the child was only fourteen.

He stood around, growing angrier. But when Cole came shuffling out of detention hall, he approached Jake warily, his hands shoved in his pockets, his eyes downcast. He looked alone and frightened as he came to stand in front of Jake. And by some divine miracle, all the feelings of anger suddenly flowed out of Jake—he suddenly felt nothing but compassion for Cole, empathy for the harrowing day he had been through, sympathy for the rotten hand fate had dealt him. He looked Cole up and down. "You all right?"

"Yeah," the boy answered quietly, still unable to look up.

Jake put his arm around his shoulders. "Come on. Let's get a burger, you want to? I've had a hankering for a burger for a couple of days now."

Astonished, Cole peeked up, warily assessing Jake. But he nodded cautiously, and more importantly, didn't try to escape Jake's loose embrace as they walked out of juvenile hall.

CHAPTER TWENTY-SIX

Evan was resourceful, Robin would give him that. Just as she guessed, he refused to ride in Bob's truck and instead got on his cell phone. A used-car dealership delivered a 1985 pink Cadillac for their use for the day at a price they obviously could not refuse.

As they drove down the two-lane road toward the Wirt warehouses, Robin could see David outside under a cottonwood, strapped to his wheelchair, sitting next to a woman who was quietly reading a book.

"That's David," Robin informed Evan. "He's Girt's son."

"What's wrong with him?"

"Cerebral palsy. He apparently needs round-the-clock care, which is why Girt wants to sell the business."

"*Ah*," said Evan, as if that was significant somehow. "That's good to know. It might come in handy."

Puzzled, Robin glanced at him. "What do you mean?"

"Just that it's information we can use in the negotiations."

"Wait...you wouldn't use her son's condition against her," she said incredulously.

Evan laughed. "Of *course* not! Come on, let's go. If you want to get back tonight, we need to wrap this up." He was out of the car before she could say anything.

Robin followed, pausing to say hello to David, who half grinned up at her. Girt was waiting for them inside, her hair occupying two zip codes that muggy morning, and her black jeans, as usual, painted on her thin body. Robin instantly grinned. "Girt! How's it going?"

"Oh, I can't complain," Girt said, flashing her yellow teeth. "Nothing hurts or won't work, so I guess it's a good day, ain't it?" she asked and punched Robin playfully in the arm. She turned to Evan, stuck out a hand with fingernails gnawed to the quick. "Eldagirt Wirt. But you can call me Girt."

"Girt," Evan said. "Is there somewhere we might talk?"

"You bet." She pointed to one of the overstuffed offices on the perimeter of the warehouse. As they started in that direction, she tapped Robin's arm. "Guess what? Remember that nursing service I was telling you about? I talked to 'em last week, and they think they have a woman in Burdette who can care for David. Whoever she was staying with died. Now, I have to provide her room and board and all that, but it's definitely a maybe."

"That's great!" Robin said genuinely. It was huge for Girt to have found someone, she knew—Burdette was too small and too poor to keep qualified medical help in town, and Girt had confided that she might have to move to Baton Rouge to get David the care he needed—a possibility that had Bob in obvious distress.

Inside the office, Evan made a show of dusting off the one guest chair they had before offering it to Robin. She declined his offer to sit and stood against the wall as Girt settled in behind her desk and lit up a cigarette before she began to answer the questions Evan put to her.

Evan's style was easy; he spoke to Girt as if he were speaking to an old friend, peppering her with very subtle questions about profit and loss, account histories, and expansion into the fresh fish packing materials. Girt got out some of the same account books she had shown Robin, and Evan pored over them.

After an hour and a half of covering ground Robin had already reported to him, Evan put aside the books, locked his hands behind his head, and propped one Italian loafer on the edge of Girt's desk. "So… American Motorfreight is interested in buying you out, too?"

"That's right."

"No-good outfit," he said cheerfully. "Heard some stuff about them through the years. They go into operations like this and pretty much gut it. Replace everyone with cheap labor from Mexico. An outfit like that, the only thing they are interested in is the bottom line."

"Oh yeah?" Girt asked, her eyes widening slightly.

Oh yeah? Robin thought. That was news—she had never heard anything like that about American Motorfreight, and in fact, had heard they were a pretty good company, employee owned and operated.

"Yeah," Evan said, frowning as if he disapproved of that. "But you know, you could probably work out some deal with them where they wouldn't let these people go for at least a year, something like that. Of course, they'll try and get them to quit. You know how that goes."

Wide-eyed, Girt nodded.

"Well. I think we've got what we need. Do you have any questions, Robin?" he asked.

"No. Girt and I have discussed most of this in person and on e-mail."

"Great! Well then, why don't we think about getting back to Houston?" He came to his feet, extended his hand to Girt. "Appreciate the time. We'll be in touch."

"Oh! Well, okay...thank you," she said, and hurried to open the door for them.

Evan put his hand on the small of Robin's back and ushered her through. They walked with Girt to the front door of the building; Girt peered outside to where David and the woman were sitting beneath the cottonwood.

"Who's that?" Robin asked.

"My cousin, down from Shreveport for the week. She said she'd sit with him for a time so I could get some work done."

"So you're wanting to provide for your son, is that it?" Evan asked.

"That's it," Girt said, shoving her hands in her back pockets. "It's gonna cost me around three thousand dollars a month for live-in care."

Evan shook Girt's hand again. "We'll be in touch. Robin?" And he was already striding for the Cadillac.

Robin took Girt's hand, squeezed it affectionately. "If we make the offer, I promise, we'll keep the crew. You don't have to worry about that."

"Thanks, Robin," she said, the gratitude shining in her eyes. "I'll e-mail you!" she called as Robin followed Evan to the car.

Robin waved out the window as they pulled out of the gravel parking lot; Girt had walked over to where David was sitting, and she waved, too, then lifted David's arm in a mock wave.

"We can get this outfit for a fraction of its market value," Evan remarked as they pulled out onto the main highway.

"We can?"

Evan snorted. "She'd sell it for just about nothing to do something with her kid."

"Yes," Robin said, feeling suddenly and inexplicably queasy, "she probably would."

"The last thing she should have done was tell us what her bottom line was," Evan said, chuckling.

Robin didn't like that snide chuckle and never had. "Regardless of her bottom line, we would make her a fair offer, right?"

"Of course!" he said breezily, and reached for the radio, complaining that all one could get in Burdette was country western music.

Robin had thought that was part of the charm of the little town.

Back in Houston, she declined Evan's offer for a drink, but he drove to a swank little bistro anyway, insisting she could spare the half hour it would take him to knock back a gin and tonic. While he sipped at the drink, he talked absently about the work he was doing on his mansion in Turtle Creek of Dallas, then said, "You'd be better off in Dallas, you know. Your roots are there, Rebecca's there. Houston is an oil town, but Dallas is better suited to high commerce like you're trying to get into."

"Houston seems to work fine."

"I've been talking to your dad about moving the southwest regional corporate offices from Phoenix to Dallas. There would probably be a spot for a new VP in charge of acquisitions. We need to do this nationwide, I think, and with more than just packing."

The casual remark struck Robin as a bribe, and she was instantly reminded of what Jake had said just this morning.

Her eyes narrowed. "You wouldn't be trying to get me to come to Dallas because of…you know…*us*, would you?"

"Don't flatter yourself," Evan said with a snort. "I made that mistake once, but I rarely make the same mistake twice. I am just trying to consolidate. In case you haven't noticed, the economy has taken a nosedive."

Now, she just felt ridiculously full of herself. "Sorry," she said with a faint smile.

Evan tossed back his drink, pulled out his wallet, and fished out some bills. "Okay, let's go," he said abruptly. "I'm gonna run some final figures through our corporate finance and then we'll decide what we're going to do. In the meantime, I could use some help in looking at the number of missed pick-ups down here in Houston. The rate is about twice as high as it is across the country. You should really be on top of that."

"Sure, okay," she said, coming to her feet, and had to walk quickly to keep up with him as they left the bistro.

He dropped her at home, made no effort to come in. Robin walked inside, put down her purse. The house was silent—the work crews had left for the day, which she had expected, given the late hour. But she had sort of hoped that Jake would be waiting for her.

He wasn't.

She had a bath, thinking Jake would call anytime. When he didn't, she picked up the phone and called his house. No answer. Then she tried his cell. It immediately rolled over into voice mail. "Oh, ah…hey," she said, feeling suddenly awkward. "I, uh, I just got back from Burdette and was just calling to say hi. Well, okay, if you get this, maybe you can call me back?" Wincing, she quickly hung up. *Where was he?* Class, maybe, although the semester was drawing to a close.

His mom's? Who knew? At the moment, her stomach was growling, and she headed to her almost completed kitchen, rummaged around until she found a can of tuna and some crackers. A veritable feast, Batman.

She ate half of a bland tuna salad, then wandered onto the back terrace and switched on the porch fans. She took a seat on one of the chaise lounges, watched the pink flamingos swaying in the evening breeze.

When the phone started to ring, she almost killed herself trying to get out of that stinking chaise, and burst through the French doors of the dining room, grabbing the phone on the fifth ring.

"Hello?"

"Robbie, its Dad."

"Hey, Dad!" she said, brightening. "How are you?"

"I'm okay."

"How is the chemo going?"

He groaned. "The way chemo always goes—I'd rather jump off a cliff."

"But what are they saying? Are you going to be okay?"

"Robbie—" he paused, sighing. "I don't know. We'll see. They want to try this once more along with some drug therapy. Of course your mom is into the spiritual path and is threatening more herbal therapy if this doesn't work, so do your old man a favor and keep your fingers crossed."

She'd do more than that. "You know, I've been thinking a lot about you, wondering how you were."

"Yeah, well, I've been thinking a lot about you, too. I'm coming out to the ranch next week and I want you to come, too. We'll be getting into town next Wednesday after my last treatment. I want you there Thursday. Bring Evan if you want."

Okay, she'd let that one slide. "I'll be there. I am sure I can work it out."

"So you think that handyman will let you go?"

The question stunned her. "W-what? What did you say?"

"Don't play dumb. That handyman you're fooling around with."

"I'm not *fooling around* with anyone—"

"When I said I wanted you to stop and smell the roses, I didn't intend for you to take up with the first workman that walked through your door."

Robin's heart started pounding so hard she thought it might explode in her chest. "Thanks, Dad. Thanks for the clarification. You weren't explicit enough about who I was to date and when. So, what, does Grandma have a hotline in to your hospital bed?"

"Lil? I haven't talked to Lil!" He said it so gruffly that he started coughing, wheezing into the phone. "*Shit*," he said to himself.

Evan. Evan and his big damn mouth…Dad's cough grew violent, and though she was fuming, Robin could not bear to hear him like that. "Sorry, Dad," she said quickly. "Look, we'll talk when you get here, okay? Can we do that?"

"Yeah," he said, sounding noticeably weaker. "I'm looking forward to seeing you, Robbie-girl."

He had a very peculiar way of showing it, she thought bitterly.

Dad wheezed again. "I'll see you soon," he said hoarsely and hung up as another spasm of coughing hit him.

Robin ran through a few choice words for Evan as she carried the phone with her and wandered back out onto the terrace to resume her seat. A full moon, big as a platter, was just beginning to rise, and she thought of that lovely day she and Jake had gone to see the wildflowers.

The phone shattered her dreamy state of contemplation.

"Hey, baby." Jake sounded exhausted.

"Jake! How are you?"

"Okay. How was Burdette?"

"Great. I think Girt and Evan hit it off."

"That's good," he mumbled, obviously distracted.

"I didn't see you this morning before I left. Your truck was gone—"

"Yeah, I ran into a little trouble. Cole managed to get himself arrested."

Robin caught her breath; a flash of untold horrors raced through her mind. "What happened?"

Jake's sigh was heavy, full of emotion. "He and another kid cut class, went down to the levee and smoked a joint."

"Oh *man*..." Her disappointment was, surprisingly, quite intense. She hadn't realized she cared so much what the kid did. "Why? Did he say why?"

"No. He won't talk about it. I...I was hoping maybe you could help me out here. At least he'll talk to you."

Robin was already standing. "Are you at home? I'll come over."

"Thank you, Robin," Jake said, and she could hear the relief in his voice.

In truth, Jake was at his wit's end. He had gone round and round with Mom on the subject of Cole—her insisting it was Jake's fault for not paying more attention to the boy like he had promised, and he insisting she made matters worse in always trying to assess blame. That got them nowhere fast, and feeling the frustration of the situation, Mom next laid into Cole in that biting way of hers she had perfected through the years. The end result was a tight-lipped, surly Cole who refused to answer or do anything they asked of him. As a last resort, Jake had gathered up a few of his things, tossed them in an overnight bag, and ordered him to the truck. At least he wouldn't have to worry about Cole sneaking out—the Heights were too far from anything Cole knew.

"I don't want to go to your house! That's like another state!" Cole had complained.

"No choice, bucko. You made that decision when you smoked pot."

"You treat me like a kid. I'm almost fifteen!"

"That's because you act like a kid. When you stop acting like it, I'll stop treating you like one," Jake had shot back. They had ridden in frosty silence across Houston; when they reached Jake's house, Cole went to the room he used on occasion and slammed the door so hard that it almost came off its hinges.

When Robin arrived, she immediately asked where he was.

"In his room," Jake said.

Robin looked at the closed door. "Do you have a quilt or a blanket?"

"Yeah," Jake said, confused, "but what does that—"

"Humor me," she said.

Jake fetched the quilt.

Robin smiled, gathered it against her chest, then lifted up on her toes and kissed him. "Go get a beer somewhere."

"Are you kicking me out?"

"Yes. Go on. Come back in an hour or so."

Jake looked at the closed door, shook his head. "I don't know if that is a good idea."

"Do you have a better one?"

Touché. "Okay, fine," he said and grabbed a jacket and his helmet. "But I will be back in an hour—"

"and a half—"

"—and if he hasn't straightened up by then, I'll…shit, I don't know what I'll do."

Robin gave him a patient smile, motioned toward the door. "Go on."

"Fine," Jake muttered irritably and stalked out the door, feeling completely helpless. At the local watering hole, he nursed a beer and brooded about the situation, coming to no conclusion, other than the fact that he and Cole might as well be speaking Chinese. They were that far apart, on opposite ends of the world. And he hated involving Robin in this ugly little family matter—he would just as soon she never know how truly dysfunctional they were. But for some reason, she was the only one Cole seemed able or willing to talk to. Nonetheless, he didn't like the thought of her exposed to the surly little monster for too long, and left his beer unfinished, heading back home after one hour.

The house looked asleep when he parked his bike in the old detached garage. He walked around to the front door, paused there, listening for where the two of them might be. Silence. Robin's car was in the drive, so they hadn't gone anywhere. Jake wandered through the house, checking the various rooms and finding no one. Cole's room was empty. So was his. In the kitchen, he scratched his head, tried to think of where they might be, and then noticed the back door was ajar.

He walked to the door and pulled it open, peering out the screen door to the darkened backyard, trying to see in the shadows.

When he saw them, his breath caught in his throat and he felt a wave of intense longing come over him.

On freshly mowed grass, Robin had stretched a quilt, and she and Cole were lying on their backs on it, side by side, staring up at the stars, pointing to various things in the sky. Jake watched them, blinking back the sting in his eyes, wondering how she had known to bring Cole something so simple and so comforting, how she had lured a boy on the verge of manhood to a child's pleasure. After several minutes, he pushed open the screen door and walked outside, down the steps of the back porch, and across the lawn.

"I see it!" Robin exclaimed, pointing to the east. "See it? It looks like a hat or something, see it?"

"That doesn't look like a hat!" Cole scoffed.

"Then what?"

Cole considered it for a moment. "Uncle Jake's nose."

He and Robin laughed together. Jake said nothing as he reached the quilt, just lay down next to Robin. She gave him a gentle pinch in the side. "Your turn, Cole."

And Cole, either over his anger or oblivious to Jake, began to call out what shapes he saw. "I see a train...a basketball hoop..."

Jake slipped his hand into Robin's. She laughed at Cole claiming to see a Coke bottle, then said, "Okay, Jake. Your turn."

He looked up, saw a canopy of stars. "I see a moon," he started.

"No fair!" exclaimed Cole.

"Wait…it's coming to me. A Harley," he added, to which Cole laughed. "And a heart…"

The three of them lay there until the dew began to form beneath stars Robin said were there to show them how high they could dream.

It was over dinner several days later that Jake learned the root of Cole's distress was the girl, Tara, the object of his obsession. She had, once again, decided she liked another boy and it had devastated Cole. It was that slimy little Frankie who had given him the news, then had talked him into going down to the levee to smoke a joint. God, but Jake hated that kid.

"You have a way with him that I can't match," Jake told Robin. "He's lucky to know you."

She blushed prettily, absently twirled her spaghetti around a fork. "It's funny. I hardly know him, really, but I think I'd do just about anything to help him. He's such a good kid. A little lost, but a good kid inside. And sensitive." She glanced up at Jake. "Like you."

Now it was Jake's turn to blush. "He's not sensitive. He's senseless."

"You know what would be good for him? My family's ranch. He'd really like it—there are horses and cows and dogs. It would get him out of Houston for a long weekend, anyway. And it would give you a chance to bond with him a little. We could go this weekend."

"Yeah?" Jake said, mulling the idea over. He'd never been to a ranch, but he sort of thought it might do him a bit of good, too. "You know, that sounds like fun."

"Then you'll bring Cole and come with me?" she asked.

Jake nodded. "Yes. Yes, that sounds like a great idea."

"There's only one little catch," she said, dropping her eyes to her plate again.

"What's that?"

"My dad is going to be there."

Okay, maybe not such a great idea after all.

CHAPTER TWENTY-SEVEN

Aaron's insides felt gummy, like everything had melted together. Still battling the effects of the latest round of chemo, he tried to make himself comfortable in the over-sized wicker armchair on the veranda as he waited for Robin to arrive. But he wasn't having much luck—even the iced tea he was drinking made him queasy.

He really needed to lie down, but Aaron was anxious to see Robin, especially after talking to Evan. Of all his daughters, Robin was usually the first one to heed his advice and take it to heart. Evan said Robin was really coming along, pouring herself into her work and learning everything she could about the company she was about to acquire. Working from home was good for her—she wasn't traveling as much, and what traveling she did do was focused entirely on this acquisition.

Evan said she was growing as a person. Evan said she was doing great. Evan said the one thing that seemed a little off was her infatuation with the handyman.

When her Mercedes turned onto the drive, Aaron's heart did a little flutter of anticipation, and he hauled him-self to his feet, adjusted the baseball cap that hid a frighten-ing loss of hair. As the car drew nearer, he could see a man was driving, and he smiled to himself. Evan had made the trip after all. *Good.* That would give him the chance to review a few things with him.

But as the Mercedes coasted to a stop on the circular drive, Aaron's eyes narrowed. That wasn't Evan. *That* wasn't even *close* to Evan.

Robin bounded out of the car, came running up the steps to throw her arms around him, causing him to grimace with pain.

"Dad, I've missed you!" she exclaimed, and reared back, peering up at him, the shock of his appearance evident in her blue eyes. "Are you all right? You look tired. Do you want to sit down?"

"You don't need to baby me," he said gruffly and ran a shaky hand over the top of her dark head. "Good to see you, kid."

She smiled a brilliant, dimpled smile that reminded Aaron of his mother. He smiled, too, but it faded the moment he saw the man come up on the steps of the veranda.

Slowly, he turned his head, took the man in, from the tips of his steel-toed boots to the top of his sandy-brown hair. He was tall, an inch taller than himself, probably six feet two, maybe more. And a big man, muscular—Aaron would have guessed him a football player at some point in his life. He was also a good-looking fellow, there was no denying that. No wonder Robin had experienced such a tremendous lapse in judgment.

"Dad," she said, her voice betraying her nerves, "this is Jake Manning. And his nephew, Cole."

That was the first Aaron had even noticed the kid.

Manning stuck out his hand. "It's a pleasure to meet you, Mr. Lear. I've heard an awful lot about you."

Aaron's eyes narrowed. "That right? Just what did you hear?"

Robin laughed nervously. "Well he heard about you from me—you don't think he's fool enough to tell you now, do you?"

Aaron slowly shook his head, despising the man already. "No. I don't think he's a fool at all."

Manning was too smooth to let Aaron know what he thought about that. He was expressionless, just extended his hand again. Aaron reluctantly shook it, then gestured for Robin to step aside, away from his chair, so he could sit down again. He noticed the kid was staring at him, like he had two heads or something, and scowled at him to let him know he *did* have two heads.

"Robin?" Bonnie called as she came out the front door, Rebecca on her heels. She eagerly embraced her oldest daughter, kissed her on the cheek. "Oh, honey, I'm so glad to see you," she exclaimed, then looked at Jake, and damn her if she didn't smile broadly. Just as broadly as Rebecca. *Women.*

"Who have we here?" Bonnie trilled.

Jesus Christ, impressed with a pair of pecs.

"Mom, Rebecca, this is Jake Manning and his nephew, Cole."

"Pleasure to meet you, Mrs. Lear. Rebecca." He grabbed the boy by the shoulder and pulled him around. "Cole, you want to say hello?"

The kid muttered something unintelligible, but that didn't stop Bonnie and Bec from beaming ear to ear.

"Well, it's a pleasure to have you and your nephew at the Blue Cross Ranch, Mr. Manning," Bonnie said giddily.

"Please...call me Jake."

Please call me Jake, Aaron mimicked behind his back.

"Well then, you must call me Bonnie!"

"So you're the one who is redoing Robin's house?" Rebecca asked.

"That's me."

"I can't wait to hear all about it!" Bonnie exclaimed. "Why don't we sit down? Would you like something to drink? Iced tea? What about you, Cole? *Lupe!*" she called as she simultaneously ushered everyone to seats around a large wicker table.

"Jake, tell them about the brick," Robin said. Manning nodded like a good little puppy dog, Aaron thought, and began to tell them what he was doing to her house. Aaron sat off by himself, refusing to listen, miserably ill and even more miserably disillusioned. He watched his daughter's face as the guy talked, the way it lit up with laughter when they talked about someone named Zaney, the way she hung on every word the handyman said.

And he watched Manning, the easy way he used his hands to talk, the easy way he laughed. Evan was right—the guy was too blue collar for Robbie. She could have her pick, dammit, so what in the hell had possessed her to pick up with this guy? More important, how long would it be before she saw what he and Evan saw, what Bonnie and Rebecca would surely see once they got through drooling? That every time this Manning fellow looked at Robin, he saw one big fat dollar sign?

Too disgusted and too sick to think, Aaron finally got up to go take a nap. He gave the kid a good hard glare in the process. He thought it strange that the kid sort of smiled.

All the misgivings, all the anticipation of doom he had had before coming here had been right on. Aaron Lear made Jake feel about as welcome as a snake.

The man's total lack of hospitality pissed Jake off royally, no doubt about it. But at the same time, he could grudgingly understand it. If he were Robin's father, he'd want better for her, too. Only Lear was overlooking one very germane and fundamental fact—Jake *loved* Robin. Yet that couldn't make up for his feeling so uncomfortable at Blue Cross Ranch.

First of all, the place was immaculate, more of a castle than a ranch house. It was huge, sprawling along the banks of the river, with room upon room for which he couldn't imagine the possible uses. He'd never seen such rich furnishings in his life. Overstuffed leather chairs and couches, chandeliers suspended from longhorns in the ceiling, gold-plated fixtures everywhere. He was so nervous that Cole might break something he could not afford to replace that he dogged the poor kid, whispering at him not to touch, not to sit, not to do *anything*.

Robin's sister Rebecca—a very pretty woman with a soft countenance—took pity on Cole and borrowed him away from Jake for a while to take him down to the stables. Cole was eager to see horses, but even more eager to escape Jake's vigilant eye.

Which left Jake with Bonnie and Robin. They talked about the work on Robin's house, about Jake's efforts to earn a degree. He felt slightly embarrassed that he was, at thirty-eight, just now in school, but Bonnie seemed quite impressed by it and applauded him for his determination. Her praise stood in stark contrast to his own mother's conviction that it was too late for him.

When Rebecca and Cole returned from the stable—Cole's face upturned in a rare wreath of smiles (*"You can touch the horses!"*)—Bonnie announced they should prepare for dinner, which would be served in the south dining room at eight. Jake felt a moment of panic; but Robin quickly informed him that he needed only a collared shirt as she showed them to the guestrooms. Guest *rooms.* Adjoining rooms connected by a huge bath he and Cole would be sharing. "If that's a problem, I can borrow one from Dad," Robin said about the shirt.

Jake quickly threw up his hand. "That won't be necessary." That would *never* be necessary. He would die before borrowing anything from Aaron Lear, especially a shirt.

Robin looked at Cole and frowned slightly. "Do you have anything but T-shirts?"

Cole shook his head. "No. That's all I got."

"Come on," she said and took him by the hand, led him down the huge corridor, disappearing in a room beneath a large portal window. When they returned, Cole was wearing a salmon-colored button-down shirt tucked into his oversized cargo pants. He looked ridiculous, like a mango stuffed atop a cantaloupe.

But Robin seemed awfully pleased with herself, and smiled admiringly at Cole. "There are a few things various guests have left behind. It's a little big, but it will work, won't it, Cole?"

He turned a mortified gaze to Jake.

"Be sure and wash your hands," Robin blithely continued, then glanced at Jake. "You, too. I'll see you downstairs," she said and left them to finish dressing.

Jake and Cole looked at one another.

"It's *pink*," Cole said helplessly.

"I know," Jake said, just as helplessly, and the two of them stared at each other in dismay.

Jake somehow convinced Cole he could stand to wear it this one time, made a mental note to get the kid a white button-down shirt as soon as possible for emergencies such as this. They worked on Cole's cowlick for a time, but both of them finally conceded there was nothing to be done for it. Jake was wearing a black polo, tucked into a pair of off-white Levi's, which he hoped wasn't some dress code faux pas. The two of them proceeded nervously downstairs, careful not to touch anything.

They had to wander around a bit to find the south dining room, past huge rooms with even more leather furniture and thick rugs and rustic furnishings that looked as if they had walked straight out of a magazine. "We already came this way," Cole complained once. Yes, Jake *knew* that, but he wasn't about to admit he was lost. It was the sound of polite, distant voices that finally led them to the right place, and they entered the room like two wayward children.

The room was paneled in white, the windows hung with heavy floral chintz drapes that matched the upholstered chairs. The table had been laid with china, crystal goblets of varying sizes and shapes, mounds of silverware, and real, honest-to-God linen napkins. Bonnie, Rebecca, and Robin, all dressed in expensive-looking summer dresses, were milling about a sideboard where there looked to be appetizers of some sort. Mr. Lear was seated at the table wearing clothes that instantly reminded Jake of Slickpants (save the baseball cap), his shoulders slumped, staring at a veritable pharmacy lined up in front of his plate. He glanced up as

Jake and Cole walked in, gave Jake a cold once-over, then looked again at the array of bottles, scowling mightily.

Feeling extremely out of place, Jake put his arm around Cole's shoulders and nudged him forward.

"Look who's here!" Bonnie sang happily, hurrying over. She stopped midstride to admire Cole first. "My, don't *you* look handsome!"

Cole blushed furiously.

"And so do you, Jake," she added, with Robin beaming over her shoulder, and damn it if *he* didn't blush.

"We're eating light tonight, I hope you don't mind," she said airily and took Cole's hand, leading him to a seat next to Mr. Lear. "It's already so hot, isn't it? Here, Cole, you sit here, sweetie."

Robin slipped her arm through Jake's and forced him to the table, too, seating him between Cole and Bonnie. She sat directly across from him, Rebecca next to her. Bonnie smiled happily at the group. "What a wonderful treat!"

"Get on with it, Bonnie," Mr. Lear said gruffly.

Bonnie sighed, picked up a little bell, and tinkled it. Instantly, like genies out of a bottle, a man and a woman appeared, the man with a bottle of red wine, the woman with a bottle of white, and for Cole, a bottle of Coke. They moved gracefully from person to person, asking wine preference in a whisper as Bonnie launched into a tale, for Jake's benefit, of how they had come to acquire Blue Cross Ranch many years ago. "We were so lucky to have found it. I always wanted to get back to this area," she said, after telling Jake how they had stumbled on the property. "My father's people come from around here."

"El?" Jake asked, perking up a little. "I thought he was from Houston."

Bonnie gasped with delight. "You know my father?"

"Mom," Robin groaned. "How could he not? Grandma and Grandpa might as well live with me, they're over so often."

"Oh, Robbie, you know how they adore you."

"Actually, El has been a great help to me," Jake said, earning a frown from Robin and a giggle from Rebecca. "He's been helping out with the renovation. In fact, he helped me take down a wall just the other day."

"Elmer Stanton?" Mr. Lear asked, disbelieving.

"Really?" Bonnie asked, clearly delighted. "Oh, Jake, that's so wonderful of you. You can't imagine how much that means to my father—he's so desperate to be of some help," she gushed.

"Mom, stop. It's embarrassing," Robin protested. "Grandpa is not a charity case!"

"He comes closer to being a basket case," Mr. Lear said.

"Dad!" Rebecca chastised him.

Bonnie glared at her husband, then turned a smile to Jake. "You'll have to forgive my husband, Jake. He and my father have fought like two old yard dogs for thirty-five years. And Aaron's a little cranky these days."

"You'd be a little cranky, too, if you were drinking this shit," Mr. Lear snapped.

Beside him, Cole giggled at the cuss word, which made old man Lear scowl at him, and in turn, made Cole giggle more.

"Just goes to show you what trouble Grandpa stirs up even when he's not here," Robin said and took a long, fortifying drink of wine.

Once the food was served, Mr. Lear lost interest in everything around him and concentrated on the eating. Jake noticed he took small bites, then would put his fork aside and close his eyes, chewing carefully. His expression was so pained that Jake had the image of knives sliding down the man's esophagus. Speaking of pained—Jake spent most of his meal nudging Cole to sit up, to remove his bare hand from the food on his plate, to wipe his mouth (with a napkin!), to take smaller bites, and for God's sake, say nothing about what Jake was fairly certain was a part of a pheasant, which apparently was what Bonnie considered light summer fare.

Bonnie did most of the talking, peppering her daughters with questions they both seemed terribly disinclined to answer (*Have you talked to Bud, Rebecca? So, Robin, have you and Jake been to visit his parents?*). By the end of the meal, it seemed to Jake that everyone was exhausted from trying to make conversation or avoid it.

When the genies reappeared to clear their dishes away, the family retired to the front room—a huge bay centered on a massive limestone fireplace, over which a longhorn steer's head hung. The paneled walls were lined with bookshelves, a smattering of leather couches, and big overstuffed pillows were grouped around the cold hearth. A large, furry white rug lay atop polished wood floors. To one side there was a large oval table—a gaming table, judging by the green felt covering and the chessboard shoved off to one side.

Mr. Lear headed straight for a long, narrow cabinet and a silver tray with several crystal decanters filled with amber liquids. The women filed in behind Jake, choosing various seats. Cole stood at Jake's hip, and as Jake moved, Cole moved, shadowing him. Jake chose a couch. Cole sat directly next to him.

"Anyone for a scotch?" Mr. Lear asked gruffly, unstopping one of the decanters.

"Aaron, do you really think you should?" Bonnie asked and shook her head when Mr. Lear glared at her. She held out her hand to Cole. "Come here, young man—I want to show you something."

With a furtive look to Jake, Cole got up, head down, and allowed Bonnie to lead him to the gaming table. She went to a hidden cabinet in the paneling and extracted a box. "I hope you like games!" she said cheerfully. "Robin? Rebecca? Think you can beat your mom at a game of Yahtzee?"

Yahtzee? This was beginning to look a little like Beaver Cleaver land. But then Mr. Lear finished pouring drinks and plopped down across from Jake holding two glasses. And here was Ward Cleaver on acid, Jake thought wryly.

Mr. Lear leaned forward with some effort and handed him a glass of amber liquid. "You're man enough to drink scotch, aren't you?"

Now! In this corner, the contest of the biggest balls! Jake smiled wryly, took the drink, tossed it down his throat, and handed the empty glass to Mr. Lear.

Mr. Lear smiled. "Good for you—now you've shown me you can be a jerk. That's one-hundred-fifty-year-old scotch; it should be savored."

Prick. "Is that what you were trying to accomplish?" Jake asked calmly.

Lear shrugged, sipped at his scotch. "I'll pour you another—"

"Don't bother. Wouldn't want to waste any of that fancy scotch on someone like me, now, would you?"

Lear's clear blue eyes—Robin's eyes—sparkled with twisted glee. "At least you're man enough to admit it."

"Admit what?"

"That you aren't good enough for her."

"I'd be the first to say it," Jake agreed and leaned back, casually slinging one arm across the back of the couch. "No one is good enough for her. But at least I'm willing to do whatever it takes to try."

"Ah, poetic," Lear said, nodding appreciatively. "Nice touch."

No, this wasn't going to work, old man. Jake had lived far too long on the streets of Houston to be a man who was easily intimidated, not even by the lofty likes of Aaron Lear. He glanced across the room, to where Robin was sitting. She was looking at them, a worried frown on her pretty face.

He smiled reassuringly.

"You're good at this, I'll give you that," Lear continued. "But you damn sure aren't the first one to come sniffing around my daughter looking for a free ride. Sadly enough, you probably won't be the last."

"I'm not looking for a free ride," Jake said evenly. "Robin and I have a relationship—"

"Right," Lear interrupted him. "A relationship that goes something like this: You spend every dime of your pathetic little paycheck on her, make her feel like a princess with your presents and compliments, maybe even manage to move into her house for all intents and purposes. And all the while you are dreaming about the day she and all of her money agrees to be your wife, and you figure your bonus is going to be a good one, seeing as how her old man is dying of cancer. That sound familiar?"

"Yeah, as a matter of fact, it does," Jake said, smiling at the look of surprise on Lear's face. "Sounds exactly like what your boy Evan is up to."

That caught Lear off guard; his eyes narrowed and he slowly took another sip of scotch. "You better watch yourself, hotshot. You're not nearly as slick as you think."

Robin stood up, started in their direction. "I never thought I was slick, Mr. Lear. I'm an honest man who happens to love your daughter—"

"Spare me your crap."

Jake shrugged. "You don't want to listen to what I have to say? Fine," he said and turned a blindingly false smile to Robin.

Whatever her father had said to Jake, she was not going to have it from Jake, that much was obvious. They had stopped talking when she'd joined them, and in fact, Dad had complained of nausea and had retired early. But she had seen the look on her father's face, knew that look all too well.

Jake would only smile when she asked. "Your father loves you," was all he would say.

The next day, after a cowboy breakfast Mom insisted on serving on the veranda (all to impress Jake, hello), they piled into the Jeep with Rebecca and drove to the far side of the ranch to see if any new calves had been birthed. There were two, still wobbly on their legs, bleating at their mothers.

Cole was mightily impressed. "Can we ride the horses now?" he breathlessly asked Rebecca when they piled back into the Jeep.

"Yes! Want to come along, Jake?" Rebecca asked, looking at him in the rearview mirror.

Jake laughed. "No, thanks. I've never ridden a horse, so I'm not sure it's a good idea to start at my age."

"You've never been horseback riding?" Robin exclaimed, punching him playfully in the arm. "Then you *must* go!"

"No, no, no." He shook his head. "Maybe some other time."

"Now's as good a time as any," Robin disagreed. "To the stables, Bec."

And over Jake's protestations, Rebecca drove them down to the stables.

There were three horses in the stables; a half dozen more were out grazing. They began in a paddock, where Rebecca and Robin showed them how to approach a horse, how to get on, how to dismount. Cole was far better at it than Jake, swinging up like an old pen rider. Rebecca showed Cole how to rein the horse and took him around the paddock a few times until Cole was doing it on his own. In the months Robin had known Cole, she had never seen him smile so broadly, had never seen him enjoy himself so much.

Jake, on the other hand, was not enjoying himself quite so much. In part because he was inexperienced, but also because they had saddled up old Belle for him, a mean old mare who was one step away from becoming a bottle of Elmer's Glue. Belle was supposedly manageable, a prime consideration as far as Jake was concerned. Only Belle did not like to be ridden, and she made that very clear the moment Jake sat on her back.

Naturally, being 110 percent male, Jake refused any help from Rebecca and insisted on trying to persuade Belle to trot around the paddock. Belle was having none of it; she danced and tried to switch him off with her tail. Then she began side shuffling, trying to rock him off. But Jake held fast.

Robin and Rebecca exchanged looks, both stifling a laugh, watching as Jake desperately held on to the old girl. Finally, in a fit of frustration, Belle did the unthinkable— she bucked. Having no clue it was coming or how to hold on, Jake went toppling off her like Humpty Dumpty, landing squarely on his butt. Robin shrieked and tried to climb over the rail; Rebecca went rushing over to help him up, and Cole laughed hysterically from atop his horse.

Jake was up before Rebecca could even reach him, waving her off. "I'm fine," he said cheerfully. "But I'm going to kill that old nag," he said and went striding forward, prepared to do battle.

Jake won.

Belle was riding beneath him after another hotly contested match between the two, and even looked a little happy. As for Jake, well, the Cheshire cat had nothing on him. That was so like Jake, Robin thought—when life kicked him in the teeth, he got up, brushed himself off, and went at it again. She so admired that about him.

Rebecca next took them out of the paddock and into the adjoining pasture. Robin watched from atop the railing. She turned when she heard the sound of an approaching golf cart, thinking it was Mom. But it was Dad, wearing a safari hat, khaki pants, and Maui Jim sunglasses.

He stopped the cart and got out, walking carefully in a sort of lopsided way to where she was sitting.

"Hey Dad, how are you today?"

"A little green."

"Jeez, shouldn't you be feeling a little better now?"

"You'd think," he said and draped his arms over the railing.

"What if it doesn't get better? Will you go back to New York?"

Dad sighed, adjusted his hat. "I don't know. Your mom has some Eastern doctor lined up. They do some mumbo-jumbo deal where they supposedly treat the whole you, and cure the cancer while they're at it. I figure it's worth a shot at this point."

The sound of dejection in his voice was heartbreaking. "Don't give up, Dad," she muttered helplessly.

He squinted up at her on the rail and reached out, covering her hand with his. "I'm not going to give up, baby girl. I'm going to fight this with everything I have. I have too much left to do." He patted her hand, shifted his gaze back to the riders again. "I just hope you don't make it any harder on me," he said, his hand slipping away from hers.

"How would I make it harder?"

"I want to talk to you about this guy."

Robin's gut contracted; she steeled herself against his assault. How strange, she thought, that her body seemed to react defensively so naturally. But then, Dad had never been an easy man to deal with. She had been steeling herself against one thing or another for as long as she could remember, and swallowed down a lump now. "What about him?"

"He's not right for you."

No surprise there. They'd had this conversation a dozen times in her life about a dozen different guys. "Dad...you don't even know him."

"Oh yes, I do—I know what kind of guy he is. I know what he wants."

"No, you don't—"

"Robin, don't be foolish," he said angrily. "That man is after your money, sure as I am standing here."

"Don't insult me," she said, just as angrily, and jumped off the fence. "Do you think I am so stupid I don't know when someone is trying to take advantage of me?"

"In a word? Yes."

"Oh, thanks a million, Dad. Nice vote of confidence. Again."

"For God's sake, Robbie," he said, his voice a little gentler, "I'm not saying you are stupid. But you have a tendency to think with your heart, not your mind. Anyway, I don't know why you'd be interested in a guy like him when you have someone like Evan Iverson wanting you."

"Oh my God. I don't want to be with Evan! He's *your* choice, not mine. You told me to make my own way, Dad, and that is what I am doing."

"I told you to take some time to discover what is important in life, to stop and smell the roses. I did *not* tell you to take up with some broke handyman!"

"Well pardon me—I didn't understand that I had to be with who you chose. For some asinine reason I thought that for once in my life, at least *this* choice would be mine!"

"Robin," he said, gripping the rail, "the Lear name is a powerful one. There is an awful lot of money tied up behind that name. I will be damned if I am going to see you robbed blind because you got the hots for some construction worker."

Furious anger blinded her. No matter how much she tried to care for this man, he seemed to knock her down at every opportunity, and Robin had had enough. He might be a powerful man, but he was a prick. And Jake—well, regardless of who he was or where he came from, Jake would never do that to her. Jake would hold her up on a pedestal, treat her with respect. Maybe *that* was what she had been searching for. Respect. Acceptance. She suddenly realized that was worth far more to her than her father's money.

Robin squeezed through the railing, started walking toward the Jeep.

"Wait a minute! Where are you going?" Dad demanded.

"Home! I've had enough of your criticism, Dad. I'm not your window dressing anymore! I am not going to be some doll you can pose however you want!"

"Robin Elaine, stop right where you are!" he bellowed.

She stopped. Debated. And slowly turned around. Over Dad's shoulder, she could see the three riders had come to a halt, too, were looking back at her and Dad. "If you walk out of here with that man, you can kiss your inheritance goodbye. I'm not playing around here. You go, and that's final."

He might as well have kicked her in the gut. Every word snatched her breath like a sucker punch. What had she done? Fallen in love? That was her crime? The very idea, the very thought that she might give up everything the Lear name brought her because she loved…*loved* (it *was* love, wasn't it?) was unbelievable. And strangely liberating.

She stared at her father, keenly aware that for the first time in her life, she was going to do what *she* wanted to do and not try to please a father who could not be pleased. She smiled. "Okay, Dad, have it your way. You keep it, every last cent. I don't want as much as a dime. You want me to make my way in this world? Then I'll go start at the very bottom if I have to, because there is nothing you can say, no threat you can make to force me to give him up. Buy yourself another ornament."

With that, she turned on her heel and went striding to the house to pack her things, almost laughing at the sound of her father calling her back.

Aaron watched his oldest child leave from the windows of the master suite, wondering if the nausea he felt this time was from the drugs or from losing her. Stubborn little fool. Yeah, but she'd come back. She always did. She'd say, *I was wrong, Dad, you were right.* Stubborn, but able to own up to it when she was wrong. And she was wrong about this, dead wrong.

She'd come back.

He just hoped it wasn't too late.

As the Mercedes rounded the corner up the drive in a cloud of caliche dust, a door slammed behind him.

"You asshole. You never change, do you?" Bonnie seethed.

Aaron winced, turned halfway to look at her. She was standing in the foyer of the master suite, her legs apart, her hands braced against her hips. He could almost see the steam coming out of her ears and fire out of her nose.

"How...*dare* you?" she barely managed to get out.

"How dare I? How dare I try and help my daughter with my last dying breath?"

"I am not going to stand here and listen to your dying bullshit," she said and marched forward to the dresser, yanked open the top drawer, and started jerking out various articles of underclothes, tossing them on the bed.

"What are you doing?" he asked, gingerly lowering himself to a chair.

"Leaving."

A flame of panic raced up his spine. "You can't leave—"

"Like hell I can't."

"Bonnie, for Chrissakes, stop it!" he said sternly, but she stared fiercely at him, daring him to try to stop her before she turned on her heel and marched to the closet. Aaron struggled to his feet. "So you're just going to march out of here because Robin doesn't like what I told her?" he asked incredulously.

Bonnie stopped what she was doing, slowly turned to look at him, and he was shocked to see that she was crying, tears streaming down her face. "How dare you judge that man, Aaron? He is kind, he is considerate, he is...is obviously and wildly in love with our daughter! What do you find so objectionable?"

"I don't find anything about him—he's not even worth my consideration. Evan is a much better choice for her—"

"She didn't choose Evan!" Bonnie cried to the ceiling. "Why can't you get that through your head? She loves Jake! God, Aaron, when are you going to learn? She did what you told her, she went her own way, and you still manage to find fault. You can't let go of their lives, why should you expect them to do for themselves? To live for themselves?"

Aaron shook his head, sighed heavily. "Bon-bon, he doesn't have the means—"

"What means? Money? Is that the yardstick by which you measure everything? Well, you have money, Aaron, and it hasn't made you a better person."

"What's that supposed to mean?" he demanded.

"It means," she said, swiping angrily at the tears on her cheeks, "that you were that young man once. You didn't have a dime to your name when you asked me to go to Dallas with you. My father despised you for it, remember? But you promised me—" A sob choked her; she looked helplessly at the ceiling. "You promised me what you didn't have in money you would make up in love, tenfold. You *promised.*"

Aaron sank helplessly onto the massive four-poster bed, staring at Bonnie, rudely reminded of a vow he hadn't thought of in years. But oh God, but he remembered it now, just as clearly as if he had made it yesterday. The two of them, lying on a quilt in the backyard of that little house, looking up at the stars. *You see those stars, Bon-bon? I love you all the way to those stars and back. Look up there and see how high we can dream...*"I gave you everything," he said, knowing the moment the words escaped his mouth how empty they were.

Bonnie looked at him with an expression so hurtful that he inwardly cringed.

She pulled a bag out of the closet, stuffed several things into it, and as Aaron watched, picked it up and walked to the door.

"Don't go, Bonnie, please! I need you," he said helplessly.

Bonnie paused, her hand on the doorknob. "I know, Aaron," she said. "And the sad thing is, I need you, too. I always have. But you haven't changed and…and I tried, I really did. But I just can't do this."

And she walked out the door, leaving him on the edge of the bed, another wave of nausea filling his throat, mixing with the acrid taste of his tears.

CHAPTER TWENTY-EIGHT

The drive from Comfort to Houston was interminably long and silent. From the backseat of Robin's Mercedes, Cole attempted to talk about the weekend, particularly the horses and Rebecca, but didn't get much response from the front seat where Robin and Jake rode in frosty silence. He finally gave up and popped his Walkman on his head.

The frostiness stemmed from an argument Jake and Robin had over leaving in the first place. Robin had expected Jake to be outraged at her father with her, but instead he surprised her by urging her to stay, to work things out with her dad. "He's a sick man. He's got a lot on his mind."

"He's sick all right," she'd muttered. She wanted to leave right away, to go home to her empty house and her empty life and just sleep because she was so damn exhausted from a lifetime of trying to please her father.

"He just wants what is best for you, baby—you can't fault him for that," Jake continued as Robin angrily stuffed her bag.

"He doesn't know what is best for me!" she snapped. "He doesn't know me at all! I'm just another fixture to him, like a car or a boat—"

She broke off, tears welling in her eyes again. Jake came up behind her, slipped his hand around her stomach and pulled her back into his chest. "He's right, you know. Not about my being after your money, I don't mean that. But he's right that I can't provide for you in the same way he has. At least not yet, and maybe never. He knows that, and you're his daughter. He wants the very best for you. I would, too, if I were in his shoes."

"God, Jake," she said, wrenching free of his arm, "you can't seem to get it through your head that I don't need anyone to provide for me!"

"Oh, really? So you are willing to give up all this?" Jake asked, sweeping his arm to the house around him. "You've lived in the lap of luxury for a very long time. Do you think you can just turn your back on it? Because that is what you are about to do."

"*Stop*," she said, choking on a sob. "Stop defending him. Stop pretending that money is so important."

"Stop pretending that it's not," he quietly countered.

Robin sniffed, wiped her nose with a used tissue, then methodically finished packing her bag while Jake watched. When she finished, she hoisted it over her shoulder. "Are you coming?" she asked, looking at the door.

They left before the dinner hour with only Rebecca on hand to say good-bye. Dad was who knew where and Mom was furious with Robin for leaving. Rebecca's expression was grim; she hugged Robin tightly to her, said she would call her later. "He's a pain in the ass, I know, Robbie. But he doesn't mean to hurt you."

"Huh—that's strange, because he's an expert at it."

"Just get some space and think about it," Rebecca said, then turned a kind smile to Jake. "It was really nice to get to meet you." Robin had the distinct impression Rebecca did not think she would ever see him again. She leaned over, waved at Cole in the backseat. "Take care of yourself, Cole!"

"Say bye to Frannie for me!" he called, his young mind still on horses.

As they drove away—Jake insisted on driving, which left Robin to stare morosely out the window at the ranch house—Robin half expected, half hoped Dad would come out on the veranda and wave.

He did not.

She tried to grapple with the myriad emotions that besieged her as they sped down I-10. Anger, frustration—a hurt so deep that she felt like she was drowning in it. A sharply real, palpable fear that she would never see her father again, that he would die despising her. With her forehead against the cool glass of the window, and Jake's comforting hand on her knee, Robin tried to make sense of it all. Not that there was any hope of that, how could there be? Her father's constant criticism was so unfair—she had never, in a long and prominent line of boyfriends, had a serious, heartfelt relationship with anyone. *Never.* And now that she did (she *did*, didn't she?), it was with the wrong man? Jake's life was so far beneath the lofty Lears' as to make him untrustworthy? And why hadn't she ever noticed how harshly her father judged everyone?

Maybe because she did the same thing? God, was she *like* him? Robin stole a glance at Jake from the corner of her eye and had a startling, sickening thought—maybe she was just like her father. Maybe she couldn't separate a man's essence from his circumstance. It wasn't like she had given Jake the benefit of the doubt when she first met him. Had it not been for his good looks, she probably never would have spoken to him. She probably would not have looked at him at all until she wrote him a check, and only then to see if he was scamming her. The rest of the time she would have looked right past him, just like Mia looked right past him and Lucy and everyone else she met that did not travel in their elite social circles.

But maybe, just maybe, Robin thought hopefully, she was selling herself short. Maybe she wouldn't have gone so far as to disrespect him like Dad did. Maybe she would at least have respected him. Funny, wasn't it, that now she adored him? *Yes, but...*did she adore him enough to walk away from the Lears? Did she *love* him? Really, even the word sounded fragile. Okay, so what if she admitted that she did love him—not that she was ready to admit such a huge thing—but what if? What would happen in two, three, even ten years' time? Would she grow bored of him? Would he still love her? Or would he, like her own father, grow to despise her? And if he did, where would that leave her? Completely alone?

Like she wasn't already completely alone. Like she had some rich, full life to be envied. What a fucking joke.

Robin was really beginning to despise herself and what she had become, was really beginning to believe that what she had been searching for all this time was not a thing, but maybe something as simple as herself. It almost felt like there was a person, the real Robin, a better Robin, lying beneath a shroud of privilege and the Lear name. Still very much alive, but buried by the weight of her name.

"Hey, baby," Jake said, interrupting her thoughts with a gentle squeeze of her knee. Robin glanced up, realized they were almost to Houston. She pushed herself out of her slump, stole a glimpse over her shoulder. Cole was stretched across the backseat, asleep.

"You haven't said a word the last hundred miles," Jake said.

"Sorry," she mumbled.

Jake smiled thinly; his hand slid from her knee. "Listen. I've been thinking."

"About what?"

"About…us. And this…this *thing* between us. There's something really special between us, I think, but I'm starting to worry that the whole goddamn world is conspiring against us."

"Are you talking about my dad? Because if you are, believe me, I am—"

"No, not just your dad," he said, and reached up, rubbed his eyes. "I don't even know how to talk about all the things going around in my head right now. I just know that when I look at you, I think to myself, God, is this woman for me? Am I that lucky? I have fallen in love with you, Robin. I can't think of anything else, there is no other place I want to be, and honestly, the more I am with you, the harder it is to be apart from you."

The warmth of his sentiment, however undeserved, or frightening, seeped through to her jaded heart. "*Jake…*"

"No wait, before you say anything…" He looked at her, held her gaze for a moment, his hands gripping the steering wheel at ten and two o'clock. "I feel that way about you, but at the same time, I know that I don't have what you have—I will never have what you have."

"Please, you have no idea what you are saying. I don't have anything—"

"Looks to me like the only thing you are missing is your own country," Jake said, sighing. "I'm only saying that I understand why your dad feels like he does. I can understand why my mom believes you are just messing around with me. But I guess the question is, how do we feel? How do we know this is right and we aren't headed for a fall? How do *you* feel? I love you, Robin. But I need to hear you say it."

Damn. Damn damn damn. She could feel it coming, the crash and burn—the Inevitable Question, the defining moment in a relationship where the couple must pass on to the next level or abandon their attempts at togetherness. The strange thing was, Robin could feel her answer to the Inevitable Question in the pit of her belly, where a horde of butterflies flitted about every time she saw Jake. But she couldn't deny the fear that what he said was true—he was not accustomed to her lifestyle, and by the looks of things, he would not achieve her lifestyle anytime soon. She had heard him grouse enough about his bills to know that he lived from job to job. It wasn't that she didn't have faith in him. That wasn't it at all. If anyone would succeed, it would be Jacob Manning.

But at the moment, she had no faith in herself, no faith that she would not retreat to the cover of her shroud, no faith that she could turn her back on the Lear wealth and all its privilege and walk away.

Jake sighed. "I guess your silence is my answer, huh?"

"No," she said quickly. "I'm thinking."

"That's not good."

"Please don't misunderstand me. I think you are wonderful, Jake. But I...I'm afraid of the expectations."

He shot a quick, confused look at her. "What expectations?"

"Yours. Mine. Everyone's," she said, shrinking into her seat. "How do we live up to it all?"

"Ah," he said, nodding slowly, and frowned, his brown eyes filled with confusion. *And hurt. A lot of hurt.* "Okay, I get it—"

"No, you don't get it, you can't get it," she blathered helplessly. "I am just trying to figure out where I belong."

"I think you belong with me," he said gruffly, now staring straight ahead. "But you have to come to that conclusion yourself."

"You're angry," she sighed wearily, her inability to explain herself dragging her down. "I am just trying to be honest. I am trying to say that...that expectations are inevitable, aren't they? And we might not be able to fulfill each other's list of them. Where will that leave us?"

He didn't answer right away, just stared straight ahead. After a moment he said softly, "I don't know where anything leaves us right now."

They rode in silence the rest of the way.

An hour later, Jake pulled into her drive and roused Cole from his sleep, directing the stumbling teen to his pickup. He hoisted their bags onto one shoulder and turned to face Robin. She was standing at the passenger door of her Mercedes, silently watching him, despising herself for having hurt him. He looked at her for a long moment, his jaw working with the clench of his teeth, but then he looked away, down at the ground.

"Jake..." she said, but couldn't finish, having no idea what to say, her confusion as deep as his hurt.

"No, never mind," he said solemnly. "Don't feel like you have to say anything, because you don't. Frankly, I'm not sure I want to hear it."

"Please don't—"

"Look, I gotta go," he said, and turned abruptly, headed for his truck.

From the truck cab, Cole was watching, and as Jake pulled out of the drive, Cole turned and looked at her over his shoulder. Even though it was dark, and she could barely make out his face, Robin could have sworn that he looked as confused as she felt.

After a restless attempt at sleep, Jake passed Sunday at Hermann Park at a baseball game. He swung at the ball with fury, wrenched his back twice, but went three for four before it was all said and done. Part of him expected to hear her calling out to him to get up on his toes; another part of him hoped he never heard her voice again. The hurt or the disappointment was too much for his puny, unused heart to hold. And he resented the hell out of the fear, which, no thanks to her, had kept him awake most of the night. A dull fear he had once felt about the prospect of even falling in love was now a fear that he might not ever be in love again.

And then there was the fear that he might never touch her again...or be touched by her.

As he stood in right field, waiting for the batter to swing at something, he thought he should have seen it coming, should have known the minute he kissed her the first time that it couldn't last, that all his little fantasies were just that— fantasies. The first time he laid eyes on her, he knew—a woman like that would never settle for someone like him. How he had allowed himself to believe otherwise was a great mystery and had to be his greatest, crowning stupidity.

When the game was over, and his hope that she might come completely obliterated, he drove out to his mom's to get Cole, thinking they could go for an ice cream.

Mom was sitting on the back porch, snapping peas. "Hey, Mom," he said, leaning down to kiss her cheek.

"Jacob."

He sat down next to her, stared out over the clover-infested yard.

"You doing all right?" Mom asked, without looking up from her work.

"Yeah."

"Cole says you had a fight with the girl."

The girl. Jake sighed, unwilling to have this conversation, and looked down at his hands. "I wouldn't call it a fight."

"Well, you can't say I didn't tell you so," Mom said, shaking her head, and Jake couldn't decide if he despised his mother or loved her for her keen, unwaveringly critical insight.

"No, I can't say that," he said, and with another sigh, stood up. "I'm going to take Cole to get an ice cream."

Mom kept on snapping peas.

Jake found Cole in his room, lying on his bed and throwing a tennis ball against the wall. In usual fashion, he barely acknowledged Jake when he came in, but at the mention of ice cream, seemed to perk up a bit.

Neither of them said anything in the drive over to the TasteeFreez; Cole stared out the window. When they were seated in the orange plastic benches, and Cole was hunched over a double banana split, Jake asked, "So why are you in such a rotten mood?"

Cole shrugged, took a huge bite. "Tara," he said through a mouthful of butterscotch- and chocolate-covered ice cream.

The admission surprised Jake; he couldn't believe Cole was willing to talk about it. "What about her?"

Another shrug, another bite. "She dumped me. Sorta."

"Then she's stupid."

"No, I'm a jerk," Cole said, putting down his spoon.

"What do you mean, you're a jerk? You're not a jerk," Jake said, figuring that in truth, Cole likely was a typical, fourteen-year-old insensitive clod. What male that age wasn't? "What happened?"

"Robin said I should ask her to this dance. So I did, and she said yes. And I was gonna ride with Danny Futrell, but Grandma said no, 'cuz she doesn't like his dad, and *she* was gonna take me and all that, and that was just like really stupid. So then I started thinking about it, and I dunno…it just seemed really weird or something."

"What, the dance? When is it?"

"It was last night," Cole said, and picked up his spoon, took another bite as if that explained it all.

"Why didn't you say something? I could have got you to the dance—"

"No, I decided not to take her."

Jake groaned softly. "You called her, right? You made some excuse?"

"Yeah," he said in a less than convincing manner. "I told her I had to do something for Grandma. She said I was a jerk and now she won't talk to me. And I found out today she went to the dance with Danny Futrell."

"Well, hell, kid, don't worry about it—"

"I'm a *jerk*. No girl is ever gonna like me. Especially if Grandma has to drive me."

Jake definitely felt the kid's pain on that front and tried not to smile. He looked at Cole's young face, could see the handsome man he would become and knew that girls would be sticking to him like white on rice sooner than he knew. "Girls are gonna like you fine, Cole. But here's the thing. When you sign up for girls, you gotta expect to crash and burn now and then. Girls are strange creatures—they get upset about funny things and make us miserable. But it's worth it in the long run, and I promise, you will recover from Tara. There will be another girl."

"Except I don't want another girl," Cole said, twirling his spoon in the melted ice cream.

"So she's pretty special, huh?"

"She's got really pretty eyes."

Man, oh man, Jake thought, as he reached across and helped himself to a spoonful of melted ice cream, he and Cole were exactly alike in that regard. Who would have thunk it? The two of them, captured by a pair of pretty blue eyes, unable to look away, running headlong and fast toward a massive wipeout.

"Robin says girls like presents when it's not their birthday or anything. You think I should give Tara a present?"

Cole looked so hopeful, that Jake believed for a split second he was looking at his own reflection. He nodded, took one last bite of the banana split. "I think that's an excellent idea. Let's go over to Walmart and see what they've got."

They spent an hour at Walmart going through long aisles of girl stuff. Cole finally took Jake's advice and got a little bottle of perfume. When Jake dropped Cole off at his mom's, he went out back, found his mother on the porch drinking coffee and smoking a cigarette.

"Cole has a gift for Tara. Will you help him wrap it up nice?"

"Oh *Lord*," Mom said with a roll of her eyes. "He's just gonna get his feelings hurt, that's all."

His mother's bitterness was endless, and Jake was suddenly struck with the thought that he did not want to end up like her, bitter and angry and old. "Mom," he said evenly, "Just this once, could you not criticize?"

That startled her; she looked up at him with her watery eyes. "Well, I'm not *criticizing*—"

"Yes, you are. You always do. You're so unhappy that sometimes I think you try to make the world around you just as unhappy so you won't be alone."

Stunned, Mom blinked. She swallowed, looked as if she tried to find something to say, but when she couldn't, she looked down and methodically stubbed out her cigarette. "Well, I never meant to criticize."

Jake instantly felt contrite, and put a hand on her bony shoulder, squeezed it lightly. And she managed to startle him by reaching up and covering his hand with hers, patting woodenly. It was a rusty show of affection, but affection all the same, and it touched a rusty part of him.

"I best go find the paper," she said on a sigh as her hand slipped from his, and stood up, wrapped the ratty old sweater tightly around her and walked past Jake without looking at him.

"I'll talk to you tomorrow, Mom," he called after her and thought he heard her say good-bye in return.

The clouds were thickening as he went outside, rows and rows of big black clouds hanging low over the city. Jake drove slowly, hardly noticing the lights or pawnshops rolling by, not even noticing when yellowed lawns turned to the lush green of the Heights. His mind was too wrapped around a hodgepodge of thoughts, all of them too vague to really latch onto, the cacophony of them exhausting him.

It had begun to sprinkle lightly when he turned onto his street, and at first he didn't notice her car, parked politely at the curb in front of his house. As he turned into his drive, he saw her sitting on the top step of his porch just beneath the overhang, her arms crossed over her knees, hugging them to her.

For the first time in his life, Jake really didn't know what to do. He had never been in a situation he didn't know how to get out of, especially when it came to women, but this woman had him turned all around. Hadn't he given up on her just hours ago? Hadn't he convinced himself that he could no longer afford the personal toll of their affair, not after giving over the very best and last pieces of himself? Yet here he was, his heart leaping at the sight of her, fighting the urge to jump out of his truck and grab her in his arms. Instead, he turned off the truck and gripped the wheel in white-knuckled confusion, afraid to let go, afraid of what he might do if let go his anchor.

From the corner of his eye he saw her rise slowly and gracefully like a mist on the lake, and he suddenly let go of the steering wheel and felt himself fall. Hard.

He got out of the truck, testing his weight on each leg, oblivious to the sprinkling rain. Likewise oblivious, Robin walked around the front of the truck, her hands shoved deep in the pockets of her jeans. "I know the answer now," she said, and Jake felt his heart shift precariously in his chest. He leaned against the open door, moving with it until it closed behind him, bracing himself.

"Do you want to hear it?"

Hell no. But he had to. He nodded.

Robin blinked, bit her lip. "Okay. Well, I did a lot of thinking last night and today, and I realized something about myself," she said, taking a tentative step closer to him. "I realized that I am really nothing without you."

The disbelief knotted in his throat. "That's crazy—"

"No," she said, shaking her head so fiercely that her cork-screw curls bounced about. "It's not crazy at all. I realized today as I was walking through my empty house, that without you, there are definitely things missing from my life."

"Like what?"

"Like a life," she said softly. "Do you know how I would melt into nothing if I ever had to watch you walk out my door and know you weren't coming back? For a long time now, I've known I was looking for something, but I couldn't quite put my finger on it. Until now...and now I realize that this desperation inside me is not the fear of getting tangled up, but the fear of being untangled. And that's when I knew."

Jake risked a glance at her now saw the shock of light in her pretty blue eyes, that preternatural glimmer from some-where deep inside her. "Knew what?" he managed.

"I...I love you. I love you, too, Jake."

His heart surged—how he had wanted to hear her say that! But could he trust it? "Robin…are you sure? Are you sure this is what you want? That would make me so incredibly happy…but I can't help wonder, what about all those expectations you're so afraid of?"

The rain was coming a little harder now; Robin pushed a hand through her damp hair, looked wildly about. "I don't know, I don't *know*! I only know that I don't want to be without you, not now, not ever. I can't imagine how barren my life would be if you weren't in it, Jake. Can you just accept that for now?" she asked and flashed a rueful smile up to the leaden night. "I don't know how to explain, because I am still trying to sort everything out. I just can't seem to put it all together yet—I only know that you make me happy," she said, her eyes pleading with him.

It was enough.

Jake reached for her, pulling her possessively into his embrace. Robin turned her face up to his like a sunflower. Raw need and desire was flooding him now, swept along by the rain. He devoured her lips as he pushed her back, and when she stumbled, he picked her up, holding her against the full length of him until he reached the garage, where he put her down only long enough to push the small side door open.

Just as he pushed her through the door, the skies opened above them.

Robin was reaching for him inside the dark cavern of his garage, and he pushed her up against his Harley, buried his face in her neck. Her arms tightened around him and they clung to one another, Jake nuzzling her neck, Robin stroking his damp hair.

"How did you do it?" she murmured helplessly in his ear. "How did you manage to crawl under this shroud with me? I've never let anyone in, no one, yet there you were, lying next to me, forcing me to breathe—"

Jake cut off her examination of a thing too precious and fragile with his kiss. "*Hush*," he whispered, caressing her face, and kissed her more fully, tasting her sweet breath, dipping into the soft recesses of her mouth. Robin's hands slid down his back, to his waist, circling him, pulling him into her body and pressing against his hardening cock. He ground his hips against hers, acutely aware that she felt so right in his arms, fit so perfectly, and wondered madly how he ever thought to give her up.

His hands slipped beneath her blouse, covering her ribcage, and moving slowly up, until his fingers brushed against the hardened nubs of her breasts beneath her camisole. Robin arched her back, so that her breasts filled his hand within the confines of her shirt. Eager and tantalized, Jake slipped one hand out and roughly handled the little buttons up the front of her shirt until it fell open, then pushed the garment from her shoulders.

Robin stepped out of his embrace, leaned against his bike, holding on to the handlebar. A soft smile spread across her lips as he gazed down at the lush fullness of her breasts beneath a thin camisole. Slowly, carefully, he lifted his hand, let his palm graze her breast on a whisper. Robin moaned, unthinkingly lifted her breasts, seeking his palm, and Jake obliged her, his fingers closing around the pliable mound, his thumb brushing across the turgid nipple. Robin's eyes fluttered shut; her head lolled back as he moved his hand over and around her breast.

Her breath was coming quicker now and his cock was throbbing against the prison of his jeans. Yet as much as he wanted her, as much as he wanted to be deep inside her, he wanted to prolong the moment for as long as he could, to admire, with all due reverence, the beautiful woman who had come to say she loved him. His hand drifted over the camisole again. "Take it off," he whispered gruffly.

Robin reached for the hem, slowly lifted it over her head, revealing two perfect globes as she settled back on the seat of his bike. Jake stood motionless, marveling at his sheer dumb luck. With a dip of her head and a wicked smile that would have sent lesser men to their knees, Robin propped one leg on the gas tank, the other against the floor as her fingers fluttered over her breast, against the dark, almond nipples. One hand drifted down her bare belly, to the top of her jeans, which she easily unsnapped.

Jake's heart was pounding like a drum now

She quickly undid the rest as Jake removed his shirt, her eyes never leaving his, her hand never leaving its careless play with her breast. And when she slipped her hand inside her jeans and moaned softly, Jake thought he might come before he ever even touched her.

"Do you know how hot you make me?" she whispered. "When I look at you, I get so *wet*—"

He was groping for her now, managing to encircle her in his arms as his mouth landed on her breast, suckling it, nibbling it, desperate to consume it. Robin withdrew her hand from her jeans and placed her damp fingers against his mouth. Every fiber of him filled with her scent; his lips tasted the fragrance, and his groin somersaulted in one giant, sensuous leap. He grabbed her hips, lifted her with one hand as he pulled at her jeans with the other. Robin was laughing deep in her throat, helping him to rid her of the denims until she was sitting on his bike, completely naked, her skin made milky blue by the thin light of a streetlamp.

"I love you, Jake," she whispered. "I love the way you make me feel."

Oh God, dear God. The rain was beating a steady rhythm to the passion mounting in him; coarse desire mixed with tender feelings of devotion, the likes of which he had never felt in all his life. The tumult of emotions within him drove him to his knees, between her legs sprawled across the bike, and enticed by her scent, he buried his face between her legs. *Ah yes...*hot, wet.

Robin moaned above him as he began to delve between the delicate folds of her flesh, reaching deeper, lapping her up. Her hands fluttered about his head, pushing at him, but not hard enough to dislodge him, while she struggled to lift her hips to his seeking mouth. The smoky scent of her, the lush taste was driving him mad, tantalizing him beyond reason, making him want more. Suddenly Robin cried out, her voice lost against the sound of rain on the metal roof above them, her body shuddering against his mouth as her hips lifted one last time and her thighs closed tightly around his head. And then her hands were grasping at his head and shoulders, lifting him up.

Completely unconscious of how he managed to discard his jeans, Jake was only aware that he was suddenly thrusting deep in her liquid heat, feeling her warmth close tightly around him. He straddled the bike, held himself above her, and Robin propped her legs against the handlebars, her hips rocking back and forth to meet each powerful surge.

She moved like silk over his body, over every inch of his flesh, urging him to feel every inch of her.

Swept away into his own private oblivion, Jake's heart and body responded, harder and deeper, to the need to possess her, until he cried out, erupting deep inside her with pent-up longing. Pure bliss rained down on him, covered them both in the dark garage, and gasping for air, Jake lowered his forehead to hers, held on to the moment of ecstasy for as long as he could. Her breathing was ragged; she softly caressed him, murmured his name.

When at last they dislodged themselves from the bike and found their clothing scattered about the oil-stained garage, Robin slipped her hand around his waist and leaned into him. "This is what it is to feel love."

If only she knew. If only she knew how this moment would bear down so deeply in his conscience that it would create a scar, beyond which there would be no room for the past. Only the future.

CHAPTER TWENTY-NINE

In the days that followed that rainy evening, Jake and Robin fell into a comfortable, unspoken truce. Jake didn't press Robin for more than she had given him. He was content for a time that she had declared her feelings for him, at least until the doubts began to creep in and he realized he was working very hard to convince himself that her declaration of love was the big bang he had been waiting for.

But it wasn't.

As the next few weeks went by, Jake realized that the uneasy fit of his skin was not a disease but simply the physiological effects of being crazy in love with Robin. He had it so bad he rarely knew which end was up. He thought about her in the morning and at night, and all the hours in between. The workday went by too slowly where it had once zipped along. He was happiest just hanging out with her, watching baseball, laughing together at Elmer Stanton's latest repair scheme, taking Cole out for a burger. They were relaxed in one another's company, as comfortable as an old pair of shoes. And although Robin seemed to love him, too, maybe just as crazily at times, there was one thing lurking on the fringe of his consciousness.

That *thing* finally hit him like a bolt of lightning that knocked him square on his ass one night over dinner at another zealously priced restaurant, courtesy Planet Robin. It happened as Jake was relating his conversation with Cole's court-appointed counselor. In truth, Cole had been doing pretty well the last few weeks. It helped that Tara seemed to like her perfume and had selected Cole as her favorite for the time being. But Jake couldn't help worry that perhaps Cole was doing *too* well. His highs were off the charts as were his lows—there was absolutely no middle ground with the kid. And while Jake could appreciate part of that came with the teenage territory, he wondered what would happen when Tara decided she wanted a new boyfriend. Cole's counselor had confirmed his fears.

"She says Cole does pretty well, but that he can't handle any sort of rejection, especially from a female," he said to Robin over a plate of prime rib that cost right around what he figured a whole prize steer would bring. "Sort of a throwback to his missing mother, I guess. Anyway, the counselor says I need to work with him on that."

"On what?" Robin asked.

"Rejection. Because he doesn't handle it very well."

Robin snorted. "Who does?"

"Well, Cole does tend to overreact. And girls can be brutal."

"Girls can be brutal? What about boys?"

"What about them?"

Robin lowered her fork, glared at him from across the table. "Boys are mean. Boys will use girls just to get what they want. Sex, money, you name it. A few sweet nothings, then *bam*, he gets what he wants and he's outta there."

"Wow. That's pretty harsh."

"You don't know harsh," she muttered irritably, retrieving her fork. "I know harsh."

Jake watched her take a bite of lamb, debated asking her to explain, then thought the better of it. "Okay, kids can be cruel, male or female. But as far as Cole goes, his counselor says that he really needs special attention on this subject. She thinks I should give it to him. It sort of supports my theory that he should come and live with me."

Robin glanced up at him. "What about your mom? What would she say?"

His mother would have a lot to say, and none of it good, but what else was new? "I don't know. But Cole needs a strong hand right now, and she doesn't really have that with him. Now me, that's a whole other ball game." Sort of. He really felt pretty clueless, had no idea why the counselor thought he was the right man for the job.

Robin chewed thoughtfully, nodding after a moment. "You're right. He does need a strong hand. I am sure you two can work it out. You've got enough room in your house, don't you? You guys will be okay, I think."

That was when it hit Jake smack between the eyes. Her statement was really very innocuous, but it struck him that it was the same thing she said every time the subject of a future cropped up. It was suddenly very clear—she didn't see herself as part of his future. She said she loved him; okay, he believed that she did—but she hadn't taken that extra step toward a long-term commitment. It was that simple. It was that disturbing.

Why it had taken him so long to figure out the root of his vague discomfort he couldn't begin to guess, but at that moment, sitting in that stuffy, overpriced, overly-pleased-with-themselves restaurant, he could see it as clearly as the nose on his face.

"What?" she said, curious as to why he was staring at her.

"I was sort of thinking *all* of us would be okay. You. Me. Cole."

Her cheeks darkened; she glanced at her plate with a slight frown. "I was just talking about the long run."

"Yeah. So was I."

Robin didn't say anything. She avoided his gaze, attacked her lamb, and remarked that the wine seemed a little flat.

And Jake was too stung to press it any further right then—after all, there was the inevitable arguing over the check, which he won (but not without some polite scuffling and an instant coronary upon seeing the total). And there was the ride home, and the inevitable question of whose house they would go to.

Nor did Jake press the issue over the next several days as he tried to balance the end of the semester finals, Cole's counseling sessions, and finishing up the work at Robin's house. The problem was too big, too fundamental to be handled casually, and though he tried to push it down, the damn thing wiggled its way back up until it was playing major head games with him, finally weighing him down like some friggin' mental boulder.

It was *not* an issue he wanted to face. But he was once again conscious that he and Robin had, in his humble opinion, crossed over that line where the relationship demanded an explanation of intent, at least a road map. Anything to indicate where they were going.

Except that he wasn't sure he could handle the answer.

And oh, the irony of his anxiety was not lost on him, not by a long shot. *He* was the one who had never been able to maintain a relationship more than a while, and Lord knew the only thing *he* had ever committed to was his Visa bill. Yet here he sat, floundering about like a fish on a hook, so lousy at the relationship thing that he really didn't know how to go about the next step.

Worse, he wasn't certain Robin even knew there *was* a next step.

And there to help him through the minefield was the ever-helpful, ever-present Evan Iverson. If there was one person who personified the differences that loomed so huge between Jake and Robin, it was him—capital A, capital Hole. God knew there were enough reminders without Evan. For starters, Aaron Lear, who hadn't called his daughter since Robin had decided to choose the course of her own life. Norma Manning, who lectured Jake about the perils and pitfalls of loving a woman with more money than God. Mia and Michael, permanent and empty fixtures in Robin's living room, perpetual sneers on their surgically enhanced faces. Lucy and Zaney, smart people that they were, who came from the same place as Jake, but were not, as far as he could see, stupid enough to aspire to Robin's world like him.

But among all of those contenders, it was Evan who magnified their differences and held them up for inspection. Evan, who could, just by walking in the room, spotlight all of Jake's glaring inadequacies. And as Evan and Robin happily plotted the last stages of her grand acquisition, the man came to embody for Jake all the reasons why Robin would never—*should* never—commit to him.

It was not any single thing Evan did, but every thing he did. From the little gifts he foisted on Robin, to his ability to sound so damned smart about this acquisition thing. It was the way he dressed in clothes that cost more than a house, or the fact that he did not appear to have even an ounce of fat on him. It was the way he looked at Jake with complete contempt, as if he was a mass murderer pretending to be a choirboy.

His little gifts came under the guise of congratulating Robin on her work, or thanking her for some silly thing. Gifts like tropical flowers, imported candy, and trinkets in silk-covered boxes that came waltzing in, just so Robin could ignore them or eye them dispassionately. Gifts that *bored* her, gifts that Jake couldn't contemplate affording on his annual income, much less on a whim.

He tried to take solace in the fact that he wasn't the only one to be disgusted. On the days Lucy came to the house, she, too, seemed pretty put off by the whole gift scene. "What a waste of money," she said one day as she looked in a blue Tiffany box that had arrived the day before.

"I know," Robin muttered absently.

Lucy pulled a little porcelain something or other out of the box; it looked too small to be anything practical. "You know," Lucy remarked, "for what he probably paid for this, you could buy Z a new brain or something." She was, of course, referring to Zaney, now known as simply "Z" within the bounds of their improbable friendship. Lucy was always one to call them as she saw them, and on this point, Jake couldn't have agreed with her more.

And Jake hated the way Robin and Evan would pore over work papers, their heads so close to one another as they punched numbers into a calculator. He hated the way Robin would look at Evan at times when he explained things, hated it so much that he could not wait to finish the job, get out of her house, and onto something where he could feel himself again.

Right. And when exactly did he expect to feel himself again? There would still be the issue of money between them. Not his lack of it, precisely, but Material Girl's irreverence of it. She bought whatever, whenever, whether she needed it or not, and every time she came home with a handful of brightly colored bags, that old Madonna song would jingle in his head. All right, he knew she had a lot of dough, an amount he was pretty sure was too huge for his brain to even conceive. Every time she paid according to their contract, she rounded up to the nearest thousand. *The nearest thousand.* "You never know what might crop up," she said airily when he protested. Any other job, he would have been stunned and relieved. But on this job, it made him feel like a charity case.

Yep, the money thing was really beginning to grate.

Robin never seemed to think of it all, just acted as if it would always be there, and in mass quantities. The weekend Robin called her sister Rachel on a whim and suggested they meet in Chicago for a "jazz thingie" alarmed him. The week she and Mia took off for Paris (not Paris, Texas—Paris, *France*) for a little shopping astounded him. "We'll be back before you know it," she had said, kissing him as she flew out the door.

And if that wasn't enough, it bothered him greatly that her money bothered him at all. Jake really, *honestly*, didn't begrudge her a dime of what she had—he just wished she would appreciate it. Even her father's threat of cutting her off had not seemed to make an impression—she continued to spend freely.

And just what was he going to do about the money thing? He could hardly ask her to denounce it all and live in true Manning fashion, contract to contract, month to month. But on the other hand, he could not seem to get used to the idea of her having so much more resource than him. Between Evan, her endless stream of money, and her questionable commitment to them—to Robin and Jake, The Couple—Jake was starting to wonder all over again if he was living in a dream—fantasy or nightmare.

He would have been very surprised to know he wasn't alone in his bewilderment.

Robin was also figuring she had somehow managed to get herself locked in some parallel universe where she had actually fallen in love, money *was* an object, and she was struggling to understand a business she had once thought was hers by birthright alone. This was definitely not the world as she knew it.

First and foremost was this business of having gone off and fallen in love, the one thing she had always believed would never happen to someone who was alternately known as The Man-Eater. But the night they had come back from the ranch and Jake had left her looking hurt and angry and really, plain disappointed, had undone her, affecting her in one of those buried places within her. She couldn't sleep that night and spent the next day wandering irritably from room to room (as she was prone to do when he wasn't around), pretty much hating her big empty house. Pretty much being mad at him. She thought he was a baby. She thought he was asking too much of her. How hard would it have been to let it go, to let her nurse the wounds her father had inflicted?

It was the tiny initials, the *LH and DD Forevermore*, carved so carefully in the wood trim of the master bedroom that had finally cracked her hard veneer. She imagined that the tiny little inscription, but monstrously huge sentiment (if Jake's theory was correct) was all that was left of two people's lives, not this house, or the many things *LH and DD* might have had. Lockstep into eternity. How wonderful to be so completely devoted to someone that you would wish forevermore. And gazing at it, Robin had sunk down onto the window seat, had felt her hard heart shatter, brick by brick, until there was nothing left but the raw pink thing underneath, eager for someone to hold it. Not just anyone. Jacob Manning. Forevermore.

It was, as they say, an epiphanous moment. So epiphanous and gushing that Robin had sat on his front porch for almost two hours, waiting to say she loved him, that she needed him and his strength, his comfort, his affection. Worried that he might have dumped her and called Lindy in a fit of frustration. Fearing that she would have to retreat from this feeling and from his porch when the clouds started rolling in, but unwilling to give in, she had waited until the last possible moment.

When at last he had turned into the drive, she had silently cheered herself. Her perseverance had paid off! It was a sign from the Relationship Gods that she had finally done something right, that she *did* have it in her! But then Jake had gotten out of his truck, and she had seen the look on his face and felt that horrible rush of fear and regret all over again. But it was also the moment she knew that she really loved him, without reservation, loved him so much that it was reverberating throughout her entire body.

And she still felt that way, the feeling growing stronger each day.

Unfortunately, she had also discovered that opening the door to her heart did not make everything right with the world like it did in the movies.

First, there was the money thing. Or her sudden and serious lack of it to be exact, along with the new and intimidating sensation of getting an overdraft statement from the bank. Robin Lear, negative fund balance. Yikes.

All her life, she had never wanted for money. If she ran out (which she did on a pretty regular basis), she simply dipped into the account her dad had set up. But after the horrible showdown at Blue Cross Ranch, she wouldn't touch a dime of Lear money that she hadn't earned. Her new and fervent determination never to accept another dime from Dad had left her to her own devices. Only, she had no devices. And she didn't earn nearly enough to support the lifestyle she had created. Jesus, but this house, the renovations, her extensive wardrobe cost a *lot* to maintain. Not to mention the cost of shoes and handbags and food. There ought to be a law for what food cost.

Actually, it was much worse than that—she didn't know how to stop spending. When her paycheck from LTI was deposited in two-week intervals, she resumed her lifestyle, certain that she would do better. And then she would proceed to her usual rounds of fine dining, lots of good wine, an occasional long-distance outing. By the end of the said two-week interval, she found herself staring at a long line of zeroes and minus signs in her checkbook. Her hopeless money management was made worse by the fact that all those little sayings Grandma and Grandpa had said throughout the years were beginning to make sense. Just to name a few: *Money doesn't grow on trees, young lady! Do you think it rains pennies? You're just throwing good money after bad!* Frightening how accurate they were.

Of course, this was not something she could confide in Jake, seeing as how he was so sensitive about money to begin with. And while he could be really irritating with his remarks about her spending (*Don't you think if you are going to shell out a couple of grand, you might want to know more than it's a jazz thingie?*), she had to hand it to him—he did seem to keep a pretty firm rein on his spending. Like down to the penny.

Mia was no help, and in fact, she was really pretty dangerous. Mia Carpenter lived off her family's oil money and had never worked a day in her life—unless one counted that three-month stint at Tina's boutique. If she wasn't shopping, she was sleeping, and up until this year, Robin had been her staunchest supporter. But the week they flew to Paris to look at wedding gowns, Robin began to see a side of Mia she didn't particularly like.

The problem was, with all those minuses in her checkbook, Robin could not live up to her share of the shopping and was forced to watch Mia spend without thought. Okay, she was ready to handle that—it wasn't like dropping a couple of grand here or there was new to Robin. But what she wasn't prepared for was the horrible discovery that without a lot of things to seek out and buy, she and Mia had precious little in common. In fact, she didn't particularly *like* Mia. All the woman could talk about was what a bastard Michael was while she looked for a wedding gown. When

Robin tried to engage her in conversation that was a little more meaningful, Mia acted bored and quickly changed the subject. Remarkable—after twenty years of friendship, Robin discovered Mia had the personal depth of a tea saucer.

Just one more thing Grandma was right about. God, was there no end?

Honestly, Robin couldn't get back to Houston fast enough.

To Houston, where Evan was there waiting for her. Evan, brilliant Evan, who knew every aspect of the freight business. He grasped everything so quickly, immediately placed it in a proper context and explained it to her, taught her so much about the business. He showed her how Lou Harvey was manipulating his books so his operation would look more profitable than it was. He taught her how to age the equipment in Girt's operation so they could offer a fair price for it. He showed her a neat little trick for figuring out profits-to-earning margins. And he managed to keep tabs on what American Motorfreight was doing so he would not be out maneuvered. How could she not admire that?

But while Evan was very good at what he did, he could also be terribly condescending. He spoke to her as if she were stupid, performed the same analysis she did without even looking at what she had done, and sent her expensive gifts for things so trivial as to be laughable (*Good job with Lou on the phone yesterday!*). Robin was beginning to realize that Evan didn't believe anyone was as smart as he was, with the possible exception of her father, and even that was debatable. It was bad enough she was struggling to understand the business, but Evan's constant disregard of her abilities was confusingly hurtful. There were times Robin was convinced she was an idiot, incapable of carrying the mantle of the family business. Still other times she mentally kicked herself for letting Evan's arrogance derail her—she *could* do this!

And to confuse matters, he kept bringing up the new vice presidency in Dallas. "Sort of a super VP, in charge of acquisitions nationwide."

Of course she was interested, notwithstanding her desire to be some place other than where Evan was. But still, the job sounded perfect on those days she wasn't assailed with doubts of her abilities. At the very heart of all her doubts was the increasing and monstrous desire to finish the acquisition, to hold that single accomplishment up to everyone around her and dare them to discount her now, to call her window dressing. In fact, it was so important to her that Jake's annoyance with the whole Evan thing was taking a toll on the extraordinary affection and love she felt for him. No matter how she tried to convince him that Evan wasn't interested in her, but rather, the deal, Jake would not believe it.

To be fair, in spite of the friction about her job, everything else about Jake was wonderful. Robin loved his company, thought him terribly sexy and handsome. He was a good man, an exciting lover. Still, Dad's ridiculous and unfair objections to Jake weighed heavily on Robin, and she remained cut off from her father because of it, waiting for Dad to make the first move toward an apology.

By the looks of things, that wasn't going to happen anytime soon.

Mom had gone back to California, leaving the old man at Blue Cross. Even Rebecca had bailed after a week. When she called Robin to see if she was "still seeing Jake," she said that Dad had become even harder to be around after Robin and Jake had left. "I just couldn't take it anymore. He had to go back to New York, anyway," she reasoned, more for her own benefit than Robin's.

"He is going to die all alone, you know it?" Robin had said, tears welling. "But that's the way he wants it."

"Don't say that, Robbie!" Rebecca had said angrily, and their frustration with one another and the way they each viewed their father hung between them, finally forcing them off the phone. That was the way with Dad. Every conversation with him or about him ended in hurt.

Well, for her part, Robin was prepared to show Dad he was so wrong about her. She'd never take a dime of his money again, would show him that she was capable and worth a whole lot more than he ever gave her credit for. Hello.

And she was working so hard toward that end that she was taken a little off guard the morning Jake said he was through with her house, with the exception of the cleanup.

She had just hung up with Girt—things were looking really good for their purchase of Wirt, which made the old girl very happy, particularly since American Motorfreight had lowballed their offer. "Those assholes are trying to take advantage of David's situation," she complained. Robin's thoughts were on that when Jake made his announcement. It startled her because she really hadn't thought of anything but this acquisition, and especially and very specifically had not thought about life after Jake and the work on the house. She instantly had a hard time imagining working each day without seeing Jake and Zaney. Worse, she really didn't have the money to furnish it. What was she to do with this huge house? What was she to do with Jake, not to mention herself?

That night, they went to Jake's to grill steaks and share a bottle of wine, although neither of them was very talkative. Robin felt almost disembodied. It was as if some monumental milestone had been reached, but instead of celebrating, they were having a wake. She didn't care for the feeling at all and attempted to make small talk to avoid the tension as she made a salad.

"What are you going to do next?" she asked Jake.

He crunched a piece of celery. "I have two jobs lined up. One is a garage apartment redo a couple of blocks over from your house. The other is adding on to servant's quarters in River Oaks."

"Not Mia's, I hope," Robin joked.

Jake couldn't muster more than a smile and merely shook his head. "What are you going to do next?"

"Me? Finish this acquisition," Robin said and tossed a handful of chopped radishes into the bowl.

"Then what?"

Then what? Robin couldn't look at him, pretended to be chopping more radishes. "I guess you mean after the acquisition."

"Well, you have to be finishing that soon, right? What will you do then?"

Wholly unprepared to answer, Robin forced a laugh. "Just keep working, I guess."

"Where? In your house, or a new office?"

Jeez, what was this, twenty questions? She did not want to have this conversation right now. "I guess a new office is possible." She tossed some dill weed in the bowl and steeled herself. "Maybe Dallas."

Expressionless, Jake looked at her. It was almost as if he expected it. He put down his wineglass. "I better check on the steaks," he said and walked outside.

Okay, so now she felt like the Wicked Witch of the West. What was she supposed to do? Ignore all offers of gainful employment? Give up her career? Live on her good looks and charm?

She testily continued with the salad, tossing huge chunks of Raymond's killer tomatoes in the bowl. She heard Jake's cell phone ring, heard him talking. In a moment, he came back with the steaks and put them on the counter. "That was Cole. Tara broke up with him."

"Oh no!" Robin momentarily forgot her anger. "Why? Did she say why?"

"No. Just said she didn't want to go steady anymore. Who knows? Probably a bigger and better deal came along." He turned away from Robin, rummaged through the pantry.

"Maybe it just wasn't working out," she offered.

"And maybe she was just too wrapped up in herself."

Robin stopped chopping, looked at Jake's back. "What's that supposed to mean?"

He shrugged.

"Am I imagining things? For some reason, I have the distinct impression you aren't talking about Tara."

Jake slowly turned, tossed a package of buns onto the counter. "You're right. I'm not talking about Tara."

"Are you talking about me?"

He clenched his jaw and nodded.

"Well, isn't that rich!" she said sharply, tossing down the knife. "Suddenly I am too wrapped up in myself?"

He picked up his wineglass, took a swig. "Well, now that you mention it—there doesn't seem to be any us with you. *Dallas*, Robin? Since when?"

"I don't know!" she exclaimed hotly. "Evan keeps telling me about a new vice presidency—"

"Yeah, I knew he figured in there somehow."

"Just stop it, Jake! This insane jealousy—"

"Not jealousy, baby. I despise him."

"Well, stop despising him. You really have no reason—"

"Like hell I don't. But that's not important. What's important is that we have to figure out where we are going, Robin. What are we doing? Anything? Or am I the only one in this? Why the hell are you thinking of going to Dallas?"

"Please don't start this now," she said wearily, turning back to the salad.

"Not now? Then when? When do we decide what we are doing?"

"Why do we have to decide anything?" she cried to the ceiling.

"Because I love you and you are talking about moving to fucking Dallas!" he shouted. "We have been dancing around this ring of fire since we left your father's ranch!"

"Don't push me, Jake," she warned.

"I don't *push* you, Robin, I never push you," he said hotly. "Maybe *that's* what I'm doing wrong!"

She turned so quickly to dispute that ludicrous statement that she knocked the salad bowl to the linoleum. "Dammit," she muttered and went down on her knees.

Jake joined her, helping to pick up the lettuce and radish. They cleaned it up in cold silence; when Robin stood again, Jake caught her by the wrist. "Look," he said, his voice much softer, "I love you. And I can't help that I want more."

Robin bit her lip, looked down at the bowl of spoiled salad.

"I have an idea," Jake was saying, brushing a tress of hair from her temple. "Let's take Cole and go down the coast for a couple of days. Maybe do some fishing. But let's just get out of Houston and decide what we're doing. We owe that to ourselves at least, right?"

Yes, they owed it to each other. Jake's question was legitimate—it wasn't his fault that that she didn't know the answer. "Where?" she sniffed.

"I know where there are some nice fishing cabins down around Port A. We'll just go down there, turn off the phones, and talk about what we want to do."

"Okay," she murmured, nodding. "Okay. When?"

He shrugged. "Tomorrow afternoon? We can make a long weekend of it. I can finish up what I have left to do at your house in the morning, and then we'll go, okay?" he asked, gathering her in his arms, holding her tightly to him.

"Yeah," she sighed and buried her face in his shoulder. "That would be great."

The next day, as planned, Jake finished up the work on her house while Robin packed for the long weekend and made a call to Lucy, to tell her she'd be out of town for a few days.

"Oh yeah? Where to this time? London? Madrid?"

Robin laughed. "Port Aransas. I'm going fishing."

"Fishing!" Lucy exclaimed. "You don't fish! You never fish!"

She never did anything before Jake came along. "I'm going to learn."

Robin and Jake said good-bye to Zaney when he left early that afternoon, his destination, "to see a dude about a band, man." Then Robin reviewed the alarm instructions with Grandpa for the hundredth time since buying the place, in case he felt the need to come over and check on things. Which he often did. But for what, exactly, he couldn't say. And finally, she paid Raymond, who gave her a dozen gargantuan tomatoes to take along to the coast.

They had just finished packing her car (the tomatoes posing a bit of a problem) when the phone rang. "Thank heavens, I'm glad I caught you," Evan said breathlessly when Robin answered. "What is this about you going fishing?"

"I'm just getting away for a couple of days," Robin said as Jake walked in the front door. Self-consciously, she pushed her hair behind her ear and turned away from him.

"Well, you need to postpone your little outing. We have to get to Minot right away."

"Minot? Why?"

"Lou Harvey has a new twist we need to consider, one that may make this look a lot better than we originally thought. But American Motorfreight has already offered for Girt's outfit, so we need to wrap this up before she accepts."

Robin laughed. "Girt's not going to accept their offer—they low-balled her."

"Well, that's not what she told me this morning. Look, Robbie, I'm sorry to ruin your plans, but it is only Thursday, and most people work the whole week…"

"All right," she said, sighing. "When do we leave?"

"First thing in the morning. Tell what's his name that we'll have you back in a couple of days, and he can bait your hook then."

"Shut up, Evan," she said.

"I'll pick you up at seven in the morning." He hung up.

Robin clicked the phone off. She was aware of Jake standing somewhere behind her, could feel his gaze boring through her.

Slowly, she turned around.

With his arms crossed over his chest and his weight on one cocked hip, he stared at her, waiting.

Robin could feel his displeasure emanating across the room. "Umm...that was Evan. We have to go to Minot."

"When?"

"Tomorrow."

A muscle in his jaw jumped. "It can't wait?"

"No."

"You're certain."

It was a statement, not a question, and it was clear that even if Robin wasn't certain, he sure was. She sighed wearily. "Jake...it's my job. I have to go."

He clenched his jaw tighter, looked at the floor. "No, Robin, it's not your job. It's Evan. He doesn't want you to be with me." He lifted his gaze. "Don't go. Call him back and tell him it will have to wait."

She gave a little groan of indignant surprise. "You can't be serious. This is my job, and this little trip of ours was a last-minute thing. Surely you can understand—"

"This little trip," he repeated, rubbing the back of his neck. "I thought this little trip was important to us. I guess

446

I really was the only one to understand that. But you know what? I'm tired of trying to understand. I'm done. We're done."

"What?" she said, her heart starting to race.

He dropped his hand from his neck. "It's obvious to me that you are not going to commit to us and in fact, you're going to work real hard to avoid it. Hey, no problem—I was the one who jumped off the high dive into this thing, not you. Oh well. Can't win 'em all." He turned on his heel, started walking away.

"Wait, *wait*!" she cried. "What are you doing? Where are you going?"

"I told you, Peanut—I'm done. You are now free to move about the country."

Panic. Sharp, choking panic. Jake really meant it—he really was going to walk out her door, for good. "Is that it?" she shouted angrily. "You come into my house and make love to me, and now you are leaving? Just like that?"

He stopped at the door, studied it for a moment. "No, not just like that."

Hope trembled in her knees.

"There is one last thing—I wish you well."

"You *what*?" she asked, confused.

He turned to her once more, his gaze desolate. "I wish you well. I can't offer you anything else, baby, so I wish you well. Don't you get it? I wish you big soft beds with clean sheets. I wish you warm fires on cold blustery nights and hammocks for spring days. I wish you Christmas trees and homemade cookies and fat puppies and sweet-smelling babies to make you smile. I wish you ice cream and thick green grass beneath your bare feet. I wish you butterflies when you jog and moonbeams at night and dreams that reach the stars and…and I wish you peace."

Riveted by his wish, Robin was unable to speak, unable to move; her hand fluttered helplessly to her throat.

Jake smiled sadly, shook his head. "I wish you well." He turned and walked out of her door without looking back.

CHAPTER THIRTY

Jake spent that night on the inside of several beer cans, making a pile at the foot of his armchair of all those not hurled against the wall. He tried, he really tried to figure out why he had, after thirty-eight years, fallen so hard and so deep for a man-eating woman. He had known it the minute he had clapped eyes on her that she would never settle for the likes of him. Just as he had known that he couldn't go up against her without coming away scarred.

But he hadn't realized that Cole would come away scarred, too. "We're not going fishing," he said when Cole came bounding down the steps of his mom's house.

Cole had stopped almost midstride. "Why?" he asked.

"Robin and I...it's over, Cole."

"Over?" the kid had scoffed. "Why? What did you do? Why did you make her leave?"

"I didn't make her leave—look, it's too complicated for you to understand—"

"Can't you buy her a present or something?" he had demanded. "Can't you fix it?"

"Look, Cole, I'm sorry, but we're not going fishing."

"Well, how come we have to go with her? Why can't we just go?"

Jake had thought about that, but the truth was, he didn't have the heart for it. "We just can't. Maybe some other time."

Cole's face had turned red with fury—he had thrown down his overnight bag and turned his rage on Jake. "Good! I don't want to go with you! You keep trying to be my dad or something, but you're *not*! You're nobody!" he had shouted at him, then run inside before Jake could say another word.

Man, Jake thought, this sucked. And it hurt like hell.

In his maudlin state of inebriation, Jake barely heard the phone ring. He heard it ring several times before he could actually focus on it, stumbling across the room to get it, stubbing his bare toe in the process. "Yeah!" he barked, holding his toe, hopping precariously on one foot.

"Jacob? What in the Sam Hill is the matter with you?"

Great. Mom. "Nothing." He put his foot down. "What's up? Is Cole still moping about the trip?"

"How would I know?" she said sharply. "He ain't here to tell me."

Jake jabbed a finger in his eye, tried to clear his murky thoughts. "What do you mean, he's not there?"

"I mean, after you left, he didn't come down when I called him. He's run off again."

Shit. "All right, all right," Jake said, grimacing at the weight of his head. "I'll be over soon." He hung up before his mom could say anything like, *I told you so,* and headed for the shower to sober up.

When Evan arrived to pick Robin up the next morning, she was wearing her darkest Ray-Bans. As the driver took her bag, he peered at her. "Are you all right?"

She nodded, walked past him to where the driver was holding the door open for her. The truth was she wasn't all right at all, and in fact, was suffering from a killer hangover. Not the alcohol kind, more the pity—but the dream kind.

That was because what little fits of sleep she had been able to get had been tortured by dreams of Jake, dreams of Jake leaving, of Jake hating her, of Jake running from her. All of them too vague to be remembered with any clarity, but brutal just the same. Robin had sobbed in her sleep, had wept huge, invisible tears until she could barely open her eyes this morning.

And then, because she didn't feel sufficiently tortured, she debated calling him, had picked up the phone twice, only to put it down again. After all, what could she say? He was right, of course—she was afraid of commitment, afraid of failing, afraid of losing. Afraid to feel. Jesus, Dr. Phil would think he had died and gone to heaven with a head case like her. Maybe that wasn't such a bad idea because Robin sure as hell couldn't figure herself out. The only thing she knew with any certainty was that she was sick with grief.

With Evan sitting uncomfortably close, the limo pulled out onto the boulevard and headed west. Evan put his hand on her knee. "What's wrong, Robbie? Don't you feel well?"

"I'm okay." *Liar. Not okay, not even close to okay—too screwed up to ever be okay.*

"You look pale."

Robin looked away from Evan, stared out the window, blind to the mansions, the greenbelt, the tennis courts rolling past, blind to everything but her stupid mistake. "I'm okay. Just tired," she lied again. God, she really had screwed this up, hadn't she? That thing she had been searching for had been found, right there in Jake, and she had acted like it didn't matter, wasn't important. *I wish you soft beds with clean sheets...*

Robin closed her eyes, squeezed back the burn in her eyes. Those heartfelt words, so simple, worth so much more than anything she could ever own. It was like opening a door to the morning sun, a sensation so beautiful that it was almost blinding at times.

"I spoke to Michael last night. He just got back from Toronto and said there was a great little Italian restaurant there with the best food he's had in a long time. We were talking about flying up in a couple of weeks."

Whatever.

"Think you could make it?"

God, was he insane? No, actually, he was just like she was a scant five million years ago. Robin glanced at Evan from the corner of her eye. "No. I can't."

Evan shrugged. "Just thought I'd ask. But I think I'll wait until you've had a cup of coffee before I ask anything else."

If he thought she would object, he was wrong. They rode in silence until they turned onto a major thoroughfare that led to Hobby Airport. "Almost there," Evan said and patted her knee, and Robin suddenly felt like a child. He really had a knack for making her feel that way, didn't he?

The limo came to a stop at the terminal; the driver opened Robin's door and she made herself get out. Evan grabbed her bag before she could reach it, but Robin stubbornly took it from him. "I can do it," she said icily and hoisted it over her shoulder. Small victories with Evan were everything.

"I know, I know," Evan said with a smirk and a roll of his eyes, and with his hand riding possessively on the small of her back, he began to navigate their way through the crowded terminal, dodging children and grandparents and business passengers who weren't lucky enough to have their own plane.

"They ought to have another entrance or something," Evan groused impatiently.

Oh right, that's what the two of them needed—yet another cutoff from the world at large, another secret entrance into their special little universe. When Robin didn't readily agree, Evan sighed loudly. "Look, Robin, you really don't have to go if you are that miserable. I can wrap the deal up with Lou."

Oh, hell no—he wasn't going to take that away from her. She would have her acquisition if it killed her, would prove once—

Wait.

Robin stopped, midstride. Evan stopped, too, looked down at her with one brow cocked in question. "Wrap the deal up?" she repeated.

"Watch out," Evan said, nodding at an approaching, full courtesy cart. "Come on—"

"No." Robin instinctively slapped at his hand as he tried to take her arm. "Why did you say 'wrap the deal up with Lou'?"

"Because, sweetheart," he said, furtively glancing around, "that is what we are doing—wrapping the deal up with Lou. I told you."

"You said he had a new twist we needed to consider. You did *not* say 'wrap the deal up with Lou.'"

"Well, then you misunderstood me," he said, grabbing her elbow and pulling her aside. "Why do you have to be so difficult?"

"I didn't misunderstand, Evan," she interrupted him. "Tell me what you mean by that."

"Oh for God's sake!" he exploded. "Let me spell it out for you—for all intents and purposes, I have made an offer to Lou, contingent upon this last bit of information."

Somewhere, a plane took off; the floor beneath Robin shifted as it lumbered skyward. She stared at Evan, trying to comprehend. "You made an offer?" she asked weakly, her mind slowly coming to grips with the truth.

"Yes, a very good one, too. If he can show me the numbers I want on the hazmat containers, we've got a deal."

It was all beginning to make sense. All crystal clear now. His phone calls to Girt, to Lou…the papers in the file duplicating everything she had done. Evan had cut this deal behind her back. He'd been negotiating all the while and humoring her attempts to do what he had already done. Robin felt suddenly and ridiculously small and inconsequential. And stupid. Naive. "You cut a deal," she echoed incredulously, the betrayal sinking even deeper. "What about Girt?"

Evan smiled in that condescending way of his that twisted Robin's gut. "Girt got an offer from American Motorfreight, remember?"

She jerked her arm up and away, out of Evan's grip. "Yes, I remember. They *lowballed* her, Evan. It's not enough for what she needs to care for David—"

"Robin, don't be absurd!" he said hotly. "We don't do business on the basis of who needs day care. Christ, you can be such a child!"

In that moment, Robin had never despised anyone as much as she did Evan. She thought of Girt, of David. Thought of Jake, his distrust of this bastard before her, his warnings that she had refused to hear or heed. He had known Evan was a snake, had tried to tell her, but she had to be bit to believe it. Robin felt her heart constrict in her chest and stepped back, away from Evan, disgusted. "Is that all you care about, Evan? The best deal? We could have offered Girt what she needed and *still* made a very good deal. And I suppose it was okay to cut Lou Harvey's offer to the bone, too, because he needs the cash, right? Whatever works for you, it doesn't matter if it's fair or decent or—"

"Spare me your bourgeoisie working-man crap," Evan hotly interjected. "You lost your mind the moment you ever took up with the handyman." He reached for her arm again, but Robin stepped back, out of his reach, shaking her head.

"You asshole," she breathed. "What about me?"

Evan's face colored; he glared at her, now oblivious to the milling crowd and the few heads turned in their direction. "What about you? Aaron is right about you, you know that? You don't know what you are doing—you're a spoiled little girl playing at grown-up games. Well, go back to your Ken, Barbie doll. I don't need the aggravation and neither does LTI."

"I get it," she said in wonderment. "I finally get it." It was a clarion moment in which everything suddenly fell into place. She took another step back, oblivious to the people stepping around her. "Guess what, Evan? You can have LTI! I don't want it—I quit."

Evan rolled his eyes. "Stop pouting—"

"Oh no, I'm not pouting!" She laughed. "For once, I know what I am doing!" She laughed again, turned around, and started walking.

"Robin!" Evan called after her. "Stop acting so childish! We have a plane to catch!"

She paused, looked back at Evan, and shook her head. "Uh-uh, not me! I don't want anything to do with a company that will undercut small businesses just to make a buck. You and Dad can have it, Evan. It's all yours!"

Evan's facade slipped; he stared at her as if she finally had gone completely bonkers, right there in Houston-Hobby Airport. But Robin had never felt freer in her life. With a smile, she gave him a cheerful little wave, and began striding down the corridor, her mind suddenly full of Jake, only Jake, and the need to see him, touch him, tell him he was right. *I wish you dreams that reach the stars and I wish you peace...*

And then she was running, pushing through, darting in and around the crowd, pausing only to take her shoes from her feet, then running again, bursting through the glass doors outside to the taxi stand.

At home, she quickly changed into Levi's and a T-shirt, sat cross-legged in the middle of her bedroom floor, and went through the acquisition file to assure herself she wasn't wrong. She wasn't. And now, looking at it with different eyes, it amazed her how clear it was—the time Evan had spent with her was really just about his pursuit of her. And it wasn't because he adored her—she was sure what feelings he'd had for her ended the night she'd told him she'd slept with him by mistake. After that, he'd played the game, because she was the better deal. He stood to gain everything her father had worked for if he married her. This was all about LTI, not her.

Robin closed the file, bit her lip as she stared at the phone, finally picking it up to call Girt. It was the hardest thing she had ever done—telling Girt that she had no out for her and David, and in fact, apparently never did. Girt took it like a champ, though. Robin apologized profusely, told her she would help her in any way possible.

"I'll figure it out," Girt said, upbeat.

"I'll help you."

"You know what, you could help me figure out what I need to say to American Motorfreight. Think I can get them to come up on their offer?"

"We can try," Robin said hopefully.

"Ain't got nothing to lose, I suppose," she said and paused to exhale smoke from her lungs. "You know, the truth is, I should have trusted my instincts. I never liked his skinny ass to begin with."

"Me, either," Robin said softly, knowing she should have trusted her instincts, too, way back when. She promised Girt to come first thing Monday to see if they could salvage anything with American Motorfreight, apologized again, and hung up. Then, wondering what in God's name she would say, she dialed Jake.

No answer.

She tried his cell phone, too, but got nothing there, either.

Throughout the day she tried several times more, but to no avail. She reasoned he had gone to the coast with Cole without her, and even thought about driving down to look for him, but had no idea where they might be staying. By Friday evening, Robin was resigned to waiting until Sunday.

She spent a miserable evening in her empty, finished house. Everywhere she looked, she was reminded of Jake. She tried to read, but her thoughts were too full of Jake, of pink flamingos, motorcycles, and wildflowers...

When Mia called Saturday morning, Robin let the answering machine take it. Saturday afternoon, she was so stir-crazy that she drove across town to Grandma and Grandpa's. Grandma almost fell over in a cold faint when she answered the door and saw Robin standing there. Little wonder—Robin never came to see them, content to let them come to her. "What a wonderful surprise!" Grandma exclaimed after her initial shock, opening her arms and smothering Robin in a tight embrace.

She finally let go, bustled on to find Grandpa, who, as it turned out, was in the backyard with his garden. He came shuffling inside in bright, new, mighty-white Easy Spirits, holding a couple of tomatoes for her inspection. "Robbie-girl, what a surprise! Say, what do you think ol' Jake will say to *these?*" he asked, obviously pleased with the size of his tomatoes. "He thinks an awful lot of Raymond's tomatoes, you know. So does Raymond, for that matter."

"Jake will be very impressed and Raymond will be jealous," she proclaimed honestly.

"Oh, you think so? Then wait 'til they see this squash I got out back," he said, hurrying off to find one to show her.

Robin wandered into the kitchen where Grandma was already busily mixing flour and butter. "I'm making chocolate chip cookies," she announced before Robin could ask. "Remember when you girls were little how I'd make these when you were sick? Then when you got older, I'd make 'em when you were feeling down? You're feeling a little down now, aren't you, honey?"

Reluctantly, Robin nodded and glanced down so Grandma wouldn't see the tears welling in her eyes.

But the old gal was far too perceptive for that ruse. "Hand me that bag of chocolate chips," she instructed, and as she began to mix the cookie dough, she said, "Your grandpa, I'll swear. He's eat up with this tomato business, just has to grow one bigger than Raymond so Jake will be impressed. He's really taken with that young man."

"Yeah, I know," Robin sniffed.

"That's because your grandpa knows a good man when he sees one, and Jake, he's a good man. What he doesn't have in wealth, he makes up for in integrity. Hard to find a man like that these days."

Boy, that was the understatement of the year. Robin sniffed again, dipped her finger into the cookie dough, swiped a huge dab.

"And if you *do* find a man like that, you better hang on to him, 'cuz you won't find better," Grandma added as she began to mold the cookies.

Robin knew that, too. She just hoped it wasn't too late.

Grandma bent to put the cookies in the oven then turned and smiled brightly at Robin. "I've learned in my seventy some-odd years that you won't ever know true happiness without a little hurt, but if it's meant to be, it will be."

"*Lil!*" Grandpa shouted from outside. "Lil, come out here and see this squash! I'll be jiggered, that is the biggest darn crookneck squash you've ever seen in your life!"

Grandma laughed warmly, patted Robin's hand again. "It'll be okay, sweetcakes. That man loves you as much as you love him," she said and walked outside to see Grandpa's squash before Robin could argue.

Robin stayed until Sunday afternoon. Thankfully, neither of her grandparents remarked how odd that was, or pushed her for why. Grandma just fed her cookies and chicken spaghetti and more cookies, and by the time Robin waddled out to her car Sunday afternoon, she was feeling more hopeful about Jake and life in general.

But in the evening hours, when she still couldn't reach Jake on any phone, she began to panic, and looked up Norma Manning in the phone book.

Her fingers trembling a little, she punched the numbers into the phone. It rang several times—Robin was about to hang up but a woman answered breathlessly, "*Hello?*"

"Uh...I, ah, I was trying to reach Norma Manning, please?"

"She ain't here. She's at the hospital. Who's calling?"

Robin's heart seized. *Hospital.* Oh God, oh God, if anything had happened to Jake—

"Hello?"

"Uh...Robin Lear—"

"Robin! It's Vickie!"

Robin jumped to her feet. "Vickie! What happened? An accident? Who—"

"Yeah, he had a pretty bad accident, but he's holding on," Vickie said, and Robin couldn't breathe, couldn't move, could only stand rooted to the floor, staring straight ahead at the freshly painted walls around her. "I came by to get some of her clothes. Norma's been there all day and night, and she's just about worn out," Vickie was saying.

Breathe. Breathe, breathe. Robin tried, but caught a sob in her throat.

"She ain't leaving his side, I'll tell you that right now. Can't say as I blame her, I mean, just last night we thought we was gonna lose him. But he's better today and they upgraded him to stable, thank God. Not that he's out of the woods yet, but that's a whole lot better than what we was dealing with yesterday."

Robin felt sick. The guilt was already choking her. If only they had gone to the coast like they had planned, if only she hadn't been so damn selfish, so intent on that goddamned acquisition. "What happened?" she forced herself to ask. "When?"

"Thursday night. He snuck out, got caught up with that little Frankie shit, and before Norma knew he was gone—"

"Frankie?" Robin closed her eyes. "Did you say Frankie?"

"Yeah, you know, that little juvenile delinquent?"

A wave of unconscionable relief swept through her. *Not Jake. Not Jake*—Oh God. Robin opened her eyes, felt cold fear wrap around her heart and squeeze tightly again. Not Jake…Cole. *It was Cole!* "Where is he?"

"Ben Taub."

"Thank you, Vickie! Thank you!" she cried and hung up, already running for her shoes.

The family was gathered in the intensive care waiting room of Houston's Ben Taub Trauma Center. All of the family except Jake, that was. Nevertheless, Robin clenched her fists to stop her hands from shaking and walked in.

Norma was the first to see her; her icy gaze passed over Robin as she folded her arms defensively across her middle. The woman was even more drawn than usual, Robin noticed; her jaw set in a smokeless clench, her lips all but disappeared.

Vickie and Wanda were there, as was Derek, and a few others Robin didn't know who seemed to be with the group. And Zaney, thank God, Zaney.

He got up when Robin stepped across the threshold, met her at the door. "Hey," he said flatly, the buoyancy gone from his voice.

"How...how's Cole?" she whispered.

Zaney frowned, shook his head. "Things ain't lookin' too good for the Colester."

"Where's Jake?"

"He's down there where's he's been the whole time, just standing outside the little dude's door," Zaney said. "But he ain't in a talkin' kinda mood."

She ignored that piece of advice and pointed to her left. "Down there?"

Zaney nodded.

She smiled thinly, patted his arm, and walked to where the family was sitting. Vickie and Wanda looked up, smiled uncertainly. Norma wouldn't look at her, even though she stood directly in front of her. "Mrs. Manning, I am so...so sorry," she said sincerely.

Now Norma lifted her gaze to Robin, piercing her with it. "That's real nice of you. But right now, we're a family trying to cope with a tragedy. It'd be best if you came another time."

That took Robin aback—okay, maybe she deserved it; she wasn't sure. She wasn't sure of anything anymore. She simply nodded, turned on her heel, and walked out of the waiting room and in the direction Zaney had indicated.

She found Jake in the second hallway, staring intently through a bank of windows across from the wall that seemed to be holding him up. She approached cautiously, not quite sure what to expect. God, he looked awful, like he hadn't slept in days. The stubble of a beard shadowed his face; his cheeks looked almost sunken.

Jake saw her from the corner of his eye; he seemed surprised, stiffened straight, and shoved a hand through his uncombed hair as if he didn't quite know what to do.

Robin walked to where he was standing, followed his gaze to the bank of windows...and saw Cole. Oh Jesus, there were tubes hooked up in his arms and nose, bandages covering what she could see of him. Stunned, Robin moved toward the window, put her hand against the glass and gaped at him, trying to absorb the extent of his injuries. He wasn't moving at all; a nurse changing one of his IV drips smiled sadly at Robin. She turned around, saw the tears glistening in Jake's eyes as he looked at his nephew.

"It's my fault," he said hoarsely. "If I had taken him to the coast like I said...but I didn't, and he went out with Frankie—"

A stab of guilt knifed right through her. "Where is Frankie?" she managed to ask. "Is he okay?"

Jake snorted ruefully. "Minor scratches, that's all, can you believe it? Cole has two broken legs, internal injuries... they don't even know about his head yet. And that little shit Frankie walked away from it."

He shifted his gaze to Cole again. He looked terribly lost. Robin instinctively reached for his hand, but Jake shoved it in his pocket.

That stung. She clasped her hands together and looked everywhere but at Jake. "Do you know what happened?"

"He snuck out with Frankie. They went down the levee, smoked a couple of joints, apparently. Then Frankie got the bright idea to go for a ride in his brother's car. He was speeding down one of those little two-lane roads that go down to the bayou. They went off the road where there wasn't any shoulder, and they rolled."

"Was there anyone else in the car?"

"No, thank God," Jake said wearily. "Just Frankie and Cole." He sighed heavily, pushed away from the wall and went to the window, pressed up against it to look at Cole. After a long moment, he shifted his gaze to Robin. His eyes were swimming in grief; he shook his head. "Thanks for coming by, but...I wish you hadn't."

Those words were a painful blow.

"I just can't do this right now, Robin. You and me—it's obvious we're just not meant to be. And right now, I need to think about Cole. He needs me," he said and looked through the window again. "So like I said...thanks for coming." He turned fully toward the window, gazing down at his motionless nephew.

Dumbfounded, Robin stood rooted to her spot, unable to take her eyes from Jake's back. She could understand, really, she could, on some level. She thought it only fair to walk away and leave him to his grief. Except there was one little problem. "I need you, too, Jake," she said to his back.

His shoulders tensed. "No, you don't. You just think you do, and you feel sorry—"

"I feel sorry, all right," she interrupted him with a strangled laugh. "Sorry for all the things I should have said and didn't. Sorry that I didn't listen, sorry that I didn't understand, sorry for Cole, for you, for your family. But I...I *need* you. And damn it, Jake, you need me."

He bowed his head for a moment, then glanced at her over his shoulder. "You don't need me, Robin. You need Minot and—"

"I didn't go." That clearly surprised him; Robin seized the opportunity and took a careful step forward. "You were right. About everything. I realized it when we got to the airport. And then...then I just ran. I ran as fast as I could to find you. But you didn't answer your phone, so I thought you had gone to the coast and I waited. Only then I couldn't wait anymore, and I found your mom's number, and when I got Vickie on the phone, I thought it was *you...*" A sob lodged in her throat; she looked up at the ceiling tiles, blinking through hot tears. "I thought it was you," she said slowly, "and it literally sucked the life right out of me."

"I wish it had been me," he muttered, looking at Cole again. "But I was wasting that night away, pining for you. Pining for something that was beyond my reach to begin with." He swung his gaze to Robin, his jaw firmly set. "I appreciate your concern, I really do, but I just can't afford this anymore, Robin. Look, I gave it my all and it didn't work out. I've accepted that and I'm ready to move on. I have to think of Cole. You need to move on, too, baby. Don't...don't drag this out and make it harder for us both."

Man, that sounded like something she would say. Maybe *had* said at some point. And she stood there, searching his face, but his expression was stony, the set of his jaw unyielding—he honestly looked as if he never wanted to lay eyes on her again. "Please just go."

God, she *had* screwed it all up.

She nodded; she let her gaze fall to the blue-and-white linoleum tiles. "Okay. Just one last thing. The thing is, I have already moved on. I already moved out from beneath my shroud, and without that shadow hanging over me, I can see very clearly now that I love you, and I need you, and I want to be with you, however that has to be."

Jake didn't respond; she couldn't bear to look at him, afraid she would beg like a little girl when it was really too late, just as she had feared. "Okay, I'll go," she said hoarsely and turned, took a step away from him. But her body stopped, her heart unwilling to give up just yet. "Okay, I'm going," she said again, trying to will herself to do just that, tears blurring her sight as a curious nurse walked past them. "I'm gonna go, but you know what, Jake? I wish you well, too."

"Robin—"

"I wish you fields of gold and wildflowers, and clear summer days for baseball. I wish you sweet dreams when you lay your head on your pillow and infinite hope when you wake up. I wish you homemade quilts to lay on when you stargaze, lights in the windows when you come home after a hard day's work, easy fly balls, and good friends to laugh with." She heard a rustling behind her, imagined he was walking away again, and closed her eyes. "But most of all I wish you peace, and I wish you love, and I wish that whoever it comes from loves you even a tenth as much I love you, because—"

He startled her by pulling her into his embrace and burying his face in her hair. "*Don't*," he said low. "Don't do this unless you intend to stay, because I can't let you go, do you understand?"

"Yes, yes, *yes*," she whispered, twisting in his arms, bringing her hand to his face. "I understand."

"God, Robin, I do need you. Cole and I both need you, but we...we can't bear to lose any more."

"I *know*. I know. Neither can I, Jake."

"Then promise me," he said and leaned back to look down at her. "Promise me forever."

She looked up at the brown eyes shining down at her, eyes filled with tears of grief and hope, and could not imagine even a single day without him. What the hell had taken her so long? She smiled, brushed her thumb beneath his eye. "I promise. *Forevermore.*"

EPILOGUE

Upon the conclusion of Jake's college graduation ceremony, and the reception immediately following, Robin, Jake, and Cole piled into the Chevy Suburban Robin had bought when she sold her Mercedes and drove to the old Victorian house in the Heights that now, they all called home.

As they motored along, Robin singing the wrong lyrics to an upbeat little tune on the radio, they turned onto North Boulevard, and laughed when they drove past the house Robin had sold last fall. The new owners apparently liked her pink flamingos so much they had put several in the front flower beds. The rest were around the pool they had installed in the back, in the exact spot Robin had thought a pool should go. This, Jake and Robin knew from having peeked over the fence one night.

In the backseat, Cole was twirling the tassel from Jake's cap around his finger, talking excitedly about where he would go to college one day. After months and months of physical and emotional therapy (and, fortunately, no Frankie, due in large part to Cole's coming to live with Jake and Robin), Cole had hope for the first time in his life. Just as Jake had once dreamed, he was a flourishing sixteen-year-old with a girlfriend that both Jake and Robin liked. Cole had a long way to go—because of his injuries, he'd never be a baseball player—but he didn't mope anymore and now had friends and a purpose in life. He was going to be an astronaut if he had his way, and Robin and Jake were prepared to move mountains to make it happen.

Cole's recovery was just one of many milestones they had passed since Robin had run out of Hobby Airport. She had moved in with Jake shortly after leaving LTI. When she left the house on North Boulevard, she left her old life behind, including Mia and Michael (who separated shortly after their wedding), and LTI, where Lucy said Evan was now the COO in place of Dad. Robin didn't really know what was going on with that, because Dad had managed to alienate himself from the family again. But curiously, she didn't care about LTI and didn't miss the work. She had become Jake's bookkeeper and office manager, bringing a level of organization to him that enabled him to take on more work. He needed her, was constantly telling her he couldn't do without her. She liked that. She liked what she was doing, so much so that she had become Girt's book-keeper, too. They had determined, after American Motor-freight wouldn't up their offer, that the thing to do was to make Girt the new Queen of Styrofoam Containers—not to be confused with Robin, otherwise known as Peanut, the retiring Queen.

Even Zaney was doing well. He had finally formed that band he had always wanted, and the band had, at long last, performed at their first real live paying gig. Jake, Robin, and Lucy had gone to cheer the band on, and actually had been blown away. Who knew?

The surprise party they were about to reach was another accomplishment, although Jake didn't know it yet. For the first time ever, the Mannings and the Lears would join together to celebrate (music provided courtesy of the Zany Zaneys). Rebecca and Grayson, Grandma and Grandpa, Mom, even Rachel would all be in attendance, as would Norma (who was starting to come around to actually tolerating Robin), her sister Wanda, and Vickie and her crew, of course.

They turned onto Montrose. Jake was beaming ear to ear, telling Cole what to expect in college. They had become very close in the course of Cole's recovery, much to their mutual surprise—but Jake stopped midsentence when they turned onto his street and he saw all the cars outside the house. "What the—"

"Surprise!" Cole yelled as Robin turned into the drive.

Before Jake could respond, they all came rushing out beneath the homemade banner someone had hung across the porch (*Congratulations Jake!*) clapping and shouting for the graduate to join them.

Cole was the first out, hobbling on one crutch into their midst with Jake's tassel now hanging from his pants.

Slack-jawed, Jake turned and looked at Robin. "I can't believe you did this."

"You deserve it," she said happily.

He laughed, shook his head. "No, I don't deserve a damn thing. But I thank God every day that I have all this." He reached across the truck, slipped his hand behind her neck, and pulled her close to kiss her. "I thank God I have you," he said, and kissed her again until someone pounded on the window. Laughing against her mouth, he let go, got out, and was instantly overtaken by a swarm of buoyant, beer-drinking well-wishers.

Proud of him, and pleased with pulling off the party, Robin got out, too. As she walked around the front of the truck, she caught sight of a lone figure up on the porch, a little stooped, but still… Her heart stopped; she shaded her eyes with her hand and peered up to make sure she wasn't seeing things.

Nope. She'd know Dad anywhere. He was looking at her, his jaw clenched tight, and slowly, uncertainly, he lifted his hand and waved.

And Robin waved back.

ABOUT THE AUTHOR

Julia London is the *New York Times*, *USA Today*, and *Publishers Weekly* bestselling author of more than twenty romantic fiction novels. She is the author of the popular Desperate Debutantes, Scandalous, and The Secrets of Hadley Green historical romance series. She is also the author of several contemporary women's fiction novels with strong romantic elements, including the upcoming Homecoming Ranch trilogy, *Summer of Two Wishes, One Season of Sunshine,* and *Light at Winter's End.*

Julia is the recipient of the RT Bookclub Award for Best Historical Romance and a four-time finalist for the prestigious RITA Award for excellence in romantic fiction. She lives in Austin, Texas.